The Labrador Resonse

Melissa Crickard

ISBN: 9781732680807
ISBN 13: 9780999205921
Library of Congress Control Number: 2017910814
LCCN Imprint Name: **City and State (If applicable)**

Any society that would give up a little liberty to gain a little security will deserve neither and lose both.

-Benjamin Franklin

-1-

Dr. Sara Sullivan
September 20th, 2014

Dr. Sara Sullivan lived where she was from—Washington D.C. But she also lived to travel. Paris. Vegas. Malingu Pambu, Peru. Whenever she had a full week off of work, she was gone. A woman on the move. The wilder the adventure, the better: the medical mission to Haiti, backpacking through Switzerland, and her favorite, the one her fiancé, Marty Thompson, had tried the longest to talk her out of—a month long expedition to Antarctica. Sara's favorite place was anywhere she'd never been.

Until things started to change around the District.

She laid her three-month old daughter, Elyse, down in her crib and kissed her and remembered how Marty had tried to settle her ambitions. Rein her in. Bring out her maternal instinct, somewhat unsuccessfully. She'd agreed to marry him when she'd found out she was expecting, but she'd joked that he'd replaced her birth control pills with Tic Tacs, even called Elyse her little Tic Tac. She'd been born a month early and was still a peanut-like seven pounds. Nothing kept her in one place for long, not even Elyse. Now she just brought her along whenever, wherever she could.

But this week she'd barely left the house.

"Stop toting that poor baby around with you like your purse and stay *home*, Sara," her mother, Charlotte Sullivan, kept telling her.

It wasn't her mother's advice keeping her home, though.

She closed the nursery door quietly and she peeked into the bedroom. It was barely dusk, but Marty was waiting in bed. Their time alone was rare now since Elyse had been born. Tonight, the evening was sticky, humid with the heavy smell of pollution outside. She closed the hall window, cranked up the air conditioning.

A viral illness was sweeping the capital. The mortality was high. In African-Americans, the survival statistics were even more ominous—moribund, to better put it. Not just the way hypertension was twice as likely to affect a black patient as it was a white man or woman. And not even like when she gave a sign out report in the E.R. to the next doctor coming on, telling him she had a known drug abuser who'd suffered a stroke following cocaine use, and he gave her that flat affect stare, followed by the, *'I got it, is there anything in the nurses' break room worth nibbling on?'* look, like he wasn't even paying attention.

The virus was claiming the lives of over 90 percent of the African-Americans it infected.

Ninety percent.

It was almost as if it were designed to do just that.

Sara stared at herself in the bathroom mirror.

She was half black—from her father's side. And half white—from her mother. But sometimes she was all one. Or neither. Or both, and truly biracial. Her identity was complex and malleable and dependent on her mood. The company she was in. The weather, the time zone. She wasn't confused. She knew exactly who she was. But as a woman, she maintained the right to change her mind, even about how she felt about herself.

Lately though, the only thing she felt was scared.

"Sara?" Marty called.

"I'll be right there."

In the bathroom, she stood before the mirror and picked up a hand held mirror and examined the small American flag tattoo on the back of her neck and sighed.

Yep, it was still there.

Maybe she'd been a little too impulsive after the eighth round of tequila shots at the karaoke bar on her birthday. Maybe she should've opted for a less conspicuous place for her first tattoo, not to mention a karaoke song much better suited to her low and divinely hoarse and sexy voice, than the octaves in the Whitney Houston song—what was it again?

Now she sighed at the *Aha moment* she was having just then, realizing why the drink that had pushed her over the edge of her rational decision making cliff was called a *Mind Eraser.* Maybe that *flag* could've found its place on her body where only Marty could see it, or at least someplace on her body that didn't raise so many eyebrows with her patients and her physician colleagues. She wondered if it was the tattoo itself, or that it was a flag, a presumed badge of right wing solidarity, that had the *tsk-tsk* choir at work singing in national anthem decibels.

Too late now.

She examined her hazel eyes and splashed some water on her face. She couldn't change her DNA. Her blood line. And she didn't want to. She was proud of who she was.

Sometimes she was more black. Other times, more white — Marty was as white as they came. Pick-up truck. Shot gun. Country Music.

Loud country music.

He had a tough exterior, got a little bossy sometimes, downright rowdy when they drank, but she still considered him a *nice* guy — not the kind of nice white guy who a girl would walk all over and spit out like a strawberry seed between her first and second molars, but he was good enough to her.

Or maybe love was just blind.

Now that the murderous virus had reached George Washington University, where she practiced medicine, she wondered if she still wanted to be a doctor.

Today, she'd seen three patients suspected of being infected with the mysterious virus. The only thing more lethal known to man was the Ebola virus *Zaire* strain. But this was right here in the nation's capital, where outside the cherry trees vomited a pink carpet of blossoms, a hot confetti mess of cheer that people came from all over to see, blocking up traffic all over the Beltway, and where inside the hospital, patients were now vomiting their blood and brains out. When her shift in the emergency room had ended, she'd raced home and showered and thrown her work clothes into the washing machine on a hot, extra rinse, max extract cycle with color-safe bleach just for good measure, before she even touched Elyse. Now she undressed and she climbed into bed with Marty under the covers where she felt safe, protected.

"Everything okay?" he asked.

"Yeah." She tried to put away the day's events in her mind. Closed the desktop window. Told herself not to double click on that icon until her alarm went off tomorrow morning.

She found herself in the middle of making love with Marty, with the windows open and the scent of jasmine blossoms floating into the bedroom of their Georgetown home, when she heard the neighbor scream for help. A flock of bleating sheep would've sounded harmonious next to whoever was shrieking. At first, she ignored it, and kissed Marty harder on his neck, climbed on top of him.

"Deputy Thompson," she heard Mary Jenkins call.

Marty picked her up at the waist and moved her off him just as she was nearing orgasm.

The sex with him was great as usual, and she'd been only vaguely aware of the scuffle outside between the neighbors' kids—two gangly teenage boys trash-talking each other and throwing cuss words around, trying to own those words that had no business coming out of their prepubescent mouths. Now she heard the Jenkins' boy use the word 'cracker.' The other threw out the N-word. The racial tension across the capital had been mounting every day for the last month and now, it seemed, it had trickled down from parents to children. The virus behind the epidemic was a racial profiler. On the streets, it led to suspicion.

Racism.

Violence.

Marty was a D.C. deputy with nearly fifteen years on the force. He'd been working overtime nearly every night since the epidemic began.

"Shit," said Marty.

Sara sank her head into the pillow in frustration.

"Do you have to get involved?"

Mary Jenkins was always overreacting about something. This was probably no different than the time she thought the Junior Girl Scouts were racketeering, collecting imaginary cookie money for imaginary Thin Mints and Tagalogs and Samoas, in exchange for protection against their teenage mischief. The situation diffused itself when Mary pointed out to everyone in the neighborhood, including her, the one with the street rep as the biracial wild child that it was no longer politically correct to call them Samoas or Tagalogs, redirecting Mary's attention instead to her next project, a short lived block-wide *Identification with Compassion* initiative.

"Yeah, I have to get involved."

Daddy issues.

That's what he would say she had if she begged him not to go, begged him to stay with her in bed, safe from everything going on out there.

She rose from the bed and she covered her shoulders with her white blouse and she watched. With his pants half buckled and his uniform shirt still draped across the back of a chair, Marty ran across the street like the house was on fire, straightening his holster across his bare chest. The shouting match escalated quickly into a fistfight. The first punch to Ty Jenkins' jaw made a hollow sound. The Caucasian boy, Danny Moore, cried out when Ty returned the blow.

"Break it up." Marty threw himself between the two boys, pushing them apart.

She watched from the breezy window, not sure if she should dress or just lie naked and wait for the conflict to play out. She knew the two neighborhood boys, and she didn't expect either to have a weapon.

The Jenkins' boy pulled a knife from his pants pocket.

She saw Marty switch to autopilot. He grabbed Ty's wrist, bending it backward to make the flexor tendons of his hand actively insufficient. The boy's fingers loosened their grip on the weapon enough for Marty to pry it away.

"Stop it!" screamed Mary Jenkins, dropped her iced tea.

They looked solemn now, and they stared down at their dirty sneakers and their torn jeans and their bloody knuckles. The private school kids were getting off the late bus at the end of the street, dressed in crisp collared shirts and plaid skirts and patent leather shoes.

She watched Marty send Danny Moore in with his old auntie, a fate that cast an instant pallor across the boy's face. Marty pulled the older boy aside and removed his field interview notebook from his pocket. She pulled her shirt over her shoulders and listened to his deep voice, a deluge of authority that sent the private school kids rushing into their homes from the spot where they'd gathered at the bus stop, gawking. Now they scattered from the sunlight like little roaches.

She was glad they'd had a girl, and she didn't want any more.

One and done.

She buttoned her blouse as Marty took the boy's name, address and telephone number. The child trembled fearful, meek, with darting eyes, as Marty finally let him go and turned toward the house.

Washington, D.C.
Edward Marburg

Edward Marburg pushed past a group of reporters outside the Capitol building. The Democratic Congressman from Virginia kept his head down and avoided eye contact, carried his brief case close to his body. The president had called an emergency session to brief the legislators on the flu-like illness devastating Washington, D.C. He left feeling uneasy.

Sweat covered his palms.

His neck was breaking out in a blotchy collar of wheals and hives.

If there was anything that scared him more than psychotic gun violence, the threat of nuclear war, or the IRS—it was infectious disease. The thought of a global pandemic of fatal germs made him crawl in his own skin, like the time he'd flown coach to Dubai and the airline had lost his luggage and he'd had to wear the same pair of underwear for three days straight.

Unsanitary, and demoralizing.

He loosened his tie.

"What is the death toll, Senator Marburg?" the female reporter pressed.

"Were you aware Senator Marseille was ill before she passed away last night?" asked another.

Marburg pushed the phallic microphone out of his face, ducked under a cameraman's equipment. These weren't green twenty-something reporters in short skirts and hooker boots that the camera cut off. He recognized their faces from the major networks, and he apologized to the petite Asian reporter, Angela D'souza, who he'd shoved off the curb.

"I'm sorry. We're shaken by Nancy's sudden death." He crossed the stone foundation at a brisk pace and walked over the lawn toward the taxi stand on Independence Avenue. A security guard held back the reporters. While there were over thirteen-thousand lobbyists in D.C., only the big players were out today—the ones with deep pockets trying to tip the tables in their favor for precious government resources. Who got what, and when they got it, was Ed Marburg's job to decide. Power suited him, and he knew how to dole it out without going too far. He was in no mood for bullshit this morning. Virginia State Senator Nancy Marseille had succumbed to the viral infection that was spreading across the District. There were fifty deaths in D.C. that week alone, and there was talk on Capitol Hill of closing the northern border at the recommendation from the Center for Disease Control and the Surgeon General.

Twenty-two cases were confirmed in Toronto, fourteen in Atlanta, twelve in Miami and over two-hundred in the District. Many of the cases had a travel history of being in the U.S. capital in the previous week, leading the epidemiologists at CDC to conclude that the infection had spread from an index case here. It wasn't contained, and if it was anything like the avian flu outbreak of 2003, it had the potential to devastate and overwhelm the capabilities of the healthcare system. The House was proselytizing about patients on ventilators, dialysis machines, negative pressure isolation rooms, the costs of intensive care units and the lack of access to them, mass casualties, all gloom and doom. He'd be the first to admit that using fear to control populations wasn't exactly an *ineffective* method, but he'd had to breathe into a paper bag when the Speaker of the House had taken the floor. Bioterrorism hadn't been ruled out, but no one wanted to admit that possibility.

Not yet.

"Constitution," he told the driver. "At the other end of the mall near the Lincoln Memorial."

Marburg's muscular chauffeur ushered the reporters away from the black car without comment, and he sat down in the driver's seat and he tipped his cap at him in the mirror and he made a turn, heading northwest to the destination.

He loosened his collar more and he opened the air conditioning vents. He was sweating around his hairline like he always did under pressure, and the humidity didn't help. He dialed the number of his girlfriend, Sofia, on his cell phone.

"It's me. Going to be a little late. See you around seven." He disconnected the call without waiting for her response, put the phone back in his suit pocket.

The car pulled up to the curb on Constitution.

"Here's fine," he said to his chauffeur. "This shouldn't be long. Then there are arrangements at Arlington."

"Sure," said the driver, as he stepped outside and closed his car door.

"And Kenny?"

"Yes sir?"

He searched the area for suspicious activity, but there was nothing unusual. Tourists snapping pictures of the Lincoln Memorial. Students loitering on the grass. Businessman in suits—nondescript look-alikes, none of any special importance—breezed by at a type-A personality pace. Not stopping. A wind tunnel breeze howled around them, scattering cherry blossoms from the cherry trees which, like many of his politician colleagues, looked better than they came off smelling.

But not him, of course.

"Phone Jo and tell her I'll get to the hospital as soon as I can. Order some flowers for her."

The driver nodded, looked around.

He approached the park bench where a sixty-something man was waiting. The man, Wes Lindstrom, lobbyist for Phaedrex, the mammoth pharmaceutical company, rose and shook his hand. Lindstrom offered him a cigarette, lit one for himself.

"No thanks. I quit cold when Joanne was diagnosed. Haven't touched one since." He hoped Joanne's surgery had gone well, but it was one more ulcer-causing thing to deal with right now. Everything seemed to be going to shit all at once.

"Smart man." Lindstrom took off his sunglasses. "How's she doing?"

He ignored Lindstrom's small talk. His neck made a Parkinsonian jerk the side. Joanne hated when he did that, hated his mannerisms, his walk, the way he chewed his food. In fact, when he recalled the look of disdain he saw on her pale face every day now, he could say that she pretty much hated everything about him. As much as he tried, it seemed that more and more, their relationship was just for show.

"Look, I'm not sure I can help you out here." Of course he could. For the right amount, it was always about the right amount. Everyone in Washington could be bought like a boutique handbag. They couldn't be referred to as purses when you paid that much to own them, they were *handbags*. Every politician he knew was somebody's old bag, or new bag, depending on the how far back the connections went, which is why not only did Joanne, his old bag, hate him, but why he also pretty much hated himself at this point in life.

He tasted Lindstrom's cigarette smoke as it blew back in his direction. Lawyer's bait and switch. He'd graduated top of his class, just ahead of Lindstrom at Harvard Law School. It seemed like ages ago.

"We have a big problem—you and Bergsma," Lindstrom said, referring to David Bergsma, who Marburg hoped would be his running mate in the next presidential election. He was certain he could win the Democratic nomination.

"Our drugs can't stop this thing, Ed."

He narrowed his blue eyes and he looked directly back at Lindstrom, unflinching. If he could say he had a friend, it would be Wes Lindstrom. But even their friendship had its price. He kept his face empty, emotionless, unimpressed by Lindstrom's fear mongering. It was typical of big pharma and the insurance companies.

He waited to hear more.

"Neither Phaedrex nor any of the other pharmaceutical giants has anything in the works. We had a prototype chemical, something we thought could hold off the infection in those afflicted, but it's had an unusual outcome. The infection isn't behaving like anything Phaedrex has dealt with in our animal studies, and we've been unable to reach Claus since we made the deal."

He was skeptical. "You must have something in your back pockets. Something due for release—maybe a phase one clinical trial wrapping up that we can help you push through to resolve the epidemic? You always do, Wes."

"No, Ed, we don't." Lindstrom looked over his shoulder— joggers, slackers, self-entitled Millennials littered the mall. "Not this time. We've got nothing promising in the works until December, and by then it may be too late to make a difference in your election. But more importantly, Ed..." Lindstrom leaned in close to him, face to face. "It may be too late for thousands of Americans, maybe millions—real Americans like you and me, Ed."

Lindstrom loved to mock the press, but he knew it was exactly how the story would go. Negative advertising. Smear campaigns. Gallop polls. They all terrified him, not like the coral snakes that swam in the backwoods lakes where he grew up, or the severely turbulent flight that he and Lindstrom had taken in law school from Grand Cayman when, for exactly seven minutes and fifty-seven seconds of his life, he'd become a born again Christian, but the press kept him up at night, caused him cold sweats and tremors that terrified.

He swallowed, wiping his forehead, as Lindstrom leaned in closer, just licking his chops.

"You need FDA approval to push through something experimental." He was guessing. There was always a motive. It was up to him to decide if the ends were worth the means in terms of time and money. What was in it for him? He gave the lobbyists for the big interest groups a little power from his right hand, and they washed the other. And he didn't waste his time with the small ones. There were only a dozen or so interest groups he catered to—he just didn't have the heart and soul to deal with the petitions to save libraries, soccer fields, petting zoos. It wasn't that he didn't like prairie dogs and Billie goats and polychrome hogs, it was that his own kind—the Siberian tigers and poison dart frogs and apex predators—naturally, came first.

Lindstrom shook his head. "No, Ed. That's what I'm telling you. We've got nothing. Everything's in chemo drugs now."

He was confused. If Wes Lindstrom didn't have a drug in the works, ready for release at his stroke of a pen that would skyrocket Phaedrex's stock as it saved thousands of Americans from infectious peril, why the hell was he here? If he didn't need a clinical trial approved or a medication pushed through the FDA to market in time to conveniently coincide with the predicted epidemic, what did he want from him? Why had he contacted him today? It seemed he had nothing to offer. No inside information. No campaign contribution for the upcoming election year as he'd hoped. Was he trying to bribe him to fund a larger scale study? That wasn't how this game worked. It left him feeling unnerved. They'd had a deal. He'd always had a good relationship with Wes, and they played by the rules of the game.

"The infection is worse than we thought." Lindstrom took a long drag from his cigarette and placed his hat over the widow's peak of his forehead, smoothing it backward, but the wind blew it across the sidewalk into the path of a female jogger. He smiled as she stopped to pick up the hat. The woman gave it back to him. Lindstrom crushed his cigarette under the heel of his leather shoe and he placed the hat back on his head with both hands. "Much worse."

"This virus out there—*Labrador,* is out of control. Claus has the magic bullet for it. He developed a vaccine at Newfoundvax, but Phaedrex doesn't have it in our hands like he promised, Ed—he's missing. This healthcare overhaul has left the system without the capacity or any hope of dealing with what comes next. There'll be major access problems, rationing of care, death panels, street riots to get to nurses, doctors, hospitals, if we don't get this under control."

"What do you mean?" He rose from the bench and he eyed his driver, who was waiting at the curb. "This was supposed to be a run of the mill flu season—that's what you told me when you convinced me that a little fire wasn't a bad thing. You lobbied for the release of that antiretroviral—what the hell was it called?"

"I don't remember."

"You had pie charts and graphs and a million reasons why it needed to be pushed through and we did it. I did it for you, Wes."

"Listen to me, Ed." Lindstrom pulled a piece of paper from his coat pocket. "When you see what this thing can do, it'll have every pussy-whipped Democrat whistling Dixie. No offense." Lindstrom straightened his collar and he put on his sunglasses and he handed him the piece of paper with the contact information for Dr. Graham LeTorneau at the National Institute of Health. "And I'm telling you that as a friend, Senator."

Lindstrom reached out and straightened his coat collar, where the howling wind had whipped it up and out of place.

"Get me out of this, Wes." He leaned in closer beneath the tree, but it was so windy that if anyone nearby was listening, they'd never hear a thing. "If this isn't handled, it won't bode well for my election. This isn't just about the cost of drugs anymore?"

Wes shook his head, smirked. "Our industry only charges what the market can bear."

He let out a cynical chuckle. "And not a penny less."

Lindstrom pointed to the name on the paper. "This guy at NIH—Professor LeTorneau—he understands the implications of this thing better than I ever could. He's had connections with Claus Recart in the past. He's developing a cure in concert with Recart's vaccine."

"Is he expecting my call?" He backed away, looked toward the driver. "I've got to run—the arrangements for Marseille. Burial is later in the week. Can you attend?"

"Yeah," Lindstrom replied. "We're in over our heads, Senator. But I'm working on it." The lobbyist lit another cigarette, started northeast from the mall.

As Marburg approached the car, flames rose from the hood. The driver dove out from behind the wheel, just as the fire and gasoline burst into a ball that billowed up and outward exponentially. Debris shattered in all directions from the black Lincoln. The politicians guarded their faces, turned from the orange and yellow glow of the blast.

Then, the engine ignited into an explosive burst.

Dr. Graham LeTorneau

McGarrity's wasn't the kind of bar that Graham LeTorneau frequented, which was why he'd chosen the off-the-beaten path college dive. The bar rags left sopping wet on the scratched mahogany counter, the spilled drinks from every drunk Georgetown freshman who bumped into him as they leaned over to order a drink, and the dusky lighting around the billiard tables ensured that he wouldn't run into any of his white-collar colleagues from the National Institutes of Health in Bethesda. They'd be out in suits and drinking eighteen-dollar cosmopolitans in the upscale hotel bars of D.C.

"Hi there," a woman said. Years of smoking had etched lines on her face and stained her teeth a pale yellow. A distant remnant of a simple sort of pretty flashed in her eyes, hanging on with bloody fingernails and too much rouge.

Graham couldn't get over those teeth though, and he managed a polite smile and he looked away. She leaned in closer and she sipped her beer from the bottle. He summoned the bartender for another round and he craned his neck and he pretended he was looking for something in the opposite direction. He knew he should be rehearsing his presentation, preparing for the controversial speech tomorrow at the Omni, but the letter he'd received at the hotel room had shaken him. Ordinarily before this sort of thing, he'd practice his speech over and over in front of the mirror until he could do it without breaking into a cold sweat.

Then he'd order a burger from room service.

Jerk off.

Fall asleep before ten.

Lately, though, he'd found alcohol a relaxing alternative.

Why hadn't he done more drinking in college? His graduate students seemed to know how to find a work-life balance, even tried to get him out once in a while, which he resisted. He never felt like he fit into a social scene, never had anyone to drink with, for one. No girlfriend, not even a wingman. And now he only had his lab.

But he had *Labrador*, which wasn't an amiable yellow dog that was good with children, whose tail wagged in affectionate loops each time he came in the door.

Labrador was the most lethal, biohazardous virus known to mankind.

And it was his baby.

What he'd spent years of his life researching.

A toxic strand of miniscule RNA coiled and hooked and single stranded on scanning electron micrographs.

He grabbed a handful of cashews off a wet napkin and he ate them and he washed them down with the last sip of his beer. The rough-looking woman next to him with the rhinestone-studded jeans wasn't going anywhere.

"Are you a Georgetown student?" the woman asked. "I know a lot of them."

"I used to be." It was getting late. He pushed his chair back, scraping it against the soggy floor.

"So what did you study?"

Now she was chewing gum, which plunged her IQ down even further, in his opinion. A member of Mensa, he'd graduated Georgetown only fifteen years ago, but it seemed like so much longer. He looked at her worn face again and he sighed and he checked his watch. The empty hotel room wouldn't offer much solace for his nerves. What harm would another cold one do? The bartender twisted the top off of a Heineken, smirked at him. The professor threw down a few dollars and nodded awkwardly and feigned a look like McGarrity's was his kind of place.

"I'm an evolutionary biologist." He imagined himself at the podium, blocking out his fears, consciously trying to bring down his rapid heartbeat. He wiped his sweaty palms on his jeans.

This woman didn't belong here anymore than he did. The bar was full of eighteen-year- olds drinking on fake ID's. She looked a tired sort of forty-five. Or maybe she was thirty-five and she looked forty-five. Was she a prostitute? They were both surrounded by fraternity and sorority students, kids who saw getting up in the morning as an option, not a responsibility, and the bar was getting louder.

"I'm presenting a controversial theory of evolution and how it's married to everything we know about climate change."

The woman took a gulp of her beer and she offered a confused but sober stare, giving thought to his words. Then her face looked like she understood him, like it had all clicked, and she shook her finger.

"Everybody knows about global warming already, hon." She snapped her gum and she rubbed her finger against the top of his wrist. "But are you tellin' me that you're one of the lucky scientists that get to swim with the dolphins?"

She flashed her crooked smile again and he cringed, returned a fake smile.

You can't fix stupid.

And Stupid was a bull in a china shop tonight, crashing and breaking every dish and Waterford goblet in sight. It was no use describing his dissertation on the Red Queen theory of evolution. It would be lost on her, although he needed practice articulating it. He was already mortified at the thought of his own colleagues accusing him of racism.

Social engineering.

Eugenics even. He hadn't slept well in weeks. But it was all just data he'd spent years compiling and analyzing and trying to make sense of—not a personal opinion.

Not his own beliefs. How could he put it? How could he convince his colleagues of the imminent dangers that faced the human race? The migration and expansion of races, whose skin contained the most melanin, away from the Equator, as the entire planet warmed.

The lower birth rates in those who were less apt to thrive in a warmer climate.

PowerPoint slides and statistics flashed before him. His right hand started to tremble. His mother always warned him about the chemicals he worked with in the lab. Maybe he was turning into a hypochondriac like she was.

Was the air conditioning working? His sweat beaded, his heart skipped into nervous palpitations. *You're too young to be having a heart attack*, he told himself.

He chewed a baby aspirin, said, "Let's just say the planet is getting warmer and certain, uh, *folks* are better equipped to handle it than others."

Her short hair was dull and split in every direction, forming a rough blonde mane that clung to her jaw. Her Southern drawl wasn't slurred, just slow, when she said, "I know. They say Sasquatch is just a legend—folklore or just made-up nonsense by folks tryin' to get attention. But I tell you what—I don't care. I believe in it. Believe he can survive here."

He had to smirk at the way she'd convinced herself of this, or maybe she was just trying to get him to warm up to her, making conversation the best she could. He unbuttoned his white collar. The redneck lioness was amusing him if nothing else.

Anything was better than being alone in the hotel room. His third beer was starting to hit him. The lines on her face looked softer, and he pitied her, and he wondered if she'd been abused. The college girls paid him no attention, which was fine. He'd come there to take his mind off of the threatening registered letter he'd received, and his anxiety over being the keynote speaker tomorrow for the NIH conference on health and climate change. His unpopular theories were supported by hardcore facts, and the data spoke for itself. Still, he feared that the public wasn't ready to hear it. Even most of his research partners preferred to drink away their mid-life angst, smile at each other, drink some more, and repeat this ritual on subsequent evenings.

He pushed back the bar stool. It stuck on the filthy floor as he caught his balance and stood up. Then he tossed another five-dollar bill on the bar.

"You need some company tonight?"

Slowly, he turned to look at her. "I shouldn't." He apologized, started toward the door. Then he recalled the red letters before his eyes from the note:

WE WILL KILL YOU RACIST MOTHERFUCKER

The hotel was three blocks away.

Three long, stumbling blocks.

Now she was rubbing the small of his back. The stale scent of cigarette smoke was strong on her unwashed clothes. She pulled him in and she kissed him hard on the lips, and he complied, oddly complacent.

"Okay," he said, removing her hands from his body and returning them to her sides. His eyes avoided hers. "What's your name?"

"Jessie. Let's get a cab." Her Southern accent seemed to thicken and to slow even more. Had she put something in his drink? His vision clouded into a wiry palette of blurred waves.

He blinked several times, refocusing his gaze.

She pulled him by the hand, led him to the nearest corner, where a man sat in an idling black pickup truck. The man got out and he opened the door for him, but as he did, the man hit him over the head, and he shoved him into the back of the truck.

His left foot was in the door when the blonde slammed it and hopped in the front seat. It throbbed with an unremitting pain, but he quickly realized this wasn't his biggest threat. The blonde directed the driver to an address he recognized as the 14th Street area, a red-light district of bars and low rent housing and massage parlors even seedier than McGarrity's. As fast as he could protest, a man's rough hands grabbed him around the neck from the cargo space, choked him with metal cord. As he kicked his feet hard against the front seat and grabbed at his neck, unable to gasp a breath as he tried to pry his fingers beneath the wire, the blonde twisted his ankle and took hold of his feet, binding them where a bruised welt was forming from the door injury.

They rounded a corner with squealing tires.

He heard the lock of the door button between his strangled screams. Hungered gasps of air sucked against his obstructed throat. He inhaled the rank smell of old cigarette smoke and alcohol that pervaded the interior of the vehicle. The man pulled tighter, starving him of oxygen with what felt like piano wire.

The metal chafed against his neck as his attacker pulled it against him from behind, cutting at his skin as it obstructed his airway. He thought that if he wasn't choked to death first, he'd surely have his head sliced from his shoulders. Severed and exposing every hacked vessel pulsing beneath his skin.

Then the blonde pulled something from her purse, a syringe—the stainless steel kind with a long needle that his dentist used to anesthetize patients' teeth. The assailant relaxed his grip as the woman plunged the needle into his thigh. He swore and he planted mad bull kicks into her left arm, bucking himself by contorting his back where he could muster the greatest force, bouncing her back off the front seat.

"Fuck," she swore. "You wanna watch it around the corners, Sal?"

"Yeah, sorry," the driver muttered. "I thought we had a tail there for a minute. Where is the place?"

"I almost stuck myself with the needle. I don't know this guy's clean. He could have anything."

His vision hazed to cotton wool as he watched her lower the window and toss the syringe out onto the street. Indistinct silhouettes moved before him, their forms softened by the streetlamps.

He pulled harder against the wire on his neck.

The faceless man from behind was loosening his grip, but he felt his own grasp loosening, too, and his vision clouding, blurring to a twisted picture of the two abductors in the front seat.

"Let go," he gasped, but the man in the back had already released the wire as Graham slumped over on his side.

The last words he remembered were the blonde's, as she gave the address: 101 Legion Drive.

The driver swerved around another corner.

101 Legion Drive.

Phaedrex Clinical Trials Lab
Bethesda, Maryland
Veronica Laughlin

Veronica Laughlin placed her last Marisa snail carefully on the Petri dish containing the highest concentration of platinum. Frowning skeptically, she observed the other four colonies of snails. The escalating concentrations had been proven to result in the surviving snails developing without shells, a huge change in their structure that made them behave similarly to having a genetic mutation. Her team was determined to find ways in which major leaps in evolution happened suddenly in nature, changing the whole course of a species' existence. The snails were behaving exactly as expected, making it a perfect experiment—one that could be repeated with the same result, and not some contrived notion with data and statistics that had been manipulated and contorted to fit the needs and desired outcome of the researchers' personal agendas. There were plenty of dishonest scientists out there, and she refused to succumb to the pressures of corporate science.

Veronica was regarded as the math wizard among the four graduate students who'd been assigned to Dr. LeTorneau's lab. She'd completed her Master's in chemical engineering at Georgia Tech, and after working for a pharmaceutical company for a year, she'd decided to pursue research full-time. She'd witnessed the greed and competition among the chemists at Phaedrex, the backstabbing and sabotage to get their own drugs out first, and the ass-kissing to win grants and woo politicians in order to channel drugs through the FDA's obtuse, slow-moving and poorly understood committees. It had soured her impression of private industry, and she'd returned to academics where she best fit in. She'd have the opportunity to teach students about the dangers of unethical science, and more importantly, how legitimate experiments were run.

"Do you think human beings will ever see a change of this magnitude? Something so simple, yet causing such a large scale change?" Hans Raedl, her research partner, asked.

Hans was big and barrel chested and German and married.

She had a thing for his accent, his ropy, thick hands, the way he could solve differential equations like cereal box Sudoku. She was self-admittedly a bit of a geek, but she embraced her faults like a homeless puppy, and so did he. They'd been stuck with each other in a cold lab, surrounded by snails and beakers and countless horizontal surfaces, for almost sixty hours a week, for the last five years, so naturally things between them started to heat up like a row of Bunsen burners. Hans struggled with English and parking his car and finding pants that were long enough for his 6 foot seven height.

She didn't care though.

He was an outsider.

She was, too.

A kaleidoscope always churned in palettes, prismatic, dynamic, images, before her eyes, of how they'd work out perfectly, together.

Just as soon as he left his wife.

And though of course she'd deny it to anyone who suggested she had even a remote thing for Hans, she secretly, someday, wanted to have a million of his babies.

"You mean the way the snails just lose their shells like a mutation, and evolve into slugs instantly?" She was thoughtful. She smirked and she sucked up the snails' food into a glass pipette and placed a drop on each of the Petri dishes. "Maybe in men."

"The more evolved species, you mean?" Hans couldn't match her wit, but he tried.

She shrugged, said, "It's happened countless times in nature—squid, clams, oysters, gastropods, mollusks. There are so many examples of major structural and functional changes in the species. Not always gain-of-function mutations. I think we're foolish to think it couldn't happen to humans—and my graphs on survival prove that the extinction rate for every species to ever inhabit the earth has remained relatively constant over time, and has nothing to do with how long the species has lived on earth. So it could happen to humans. Absolutely." She peered into the side of the Petri dishes, flicking one's side to settle the snail's food closer to its subject. Looking through the glass, she flashed Hans a coy smile. She wore a faux diamond nose ring, and her Rock and Republic T-shirt, ripped at the sleeves, stuck out from her jeans, which her thick belt barely held up over her skinny frame. Despite her appearance, she maintained the confidence of any debutante, and could never stand to play the part of a whiny, helpless female. She took off her dark rimmed glasses. "If we could only get around sex."

"Oh, yes—the Queen," Hans said.

"The *Red* Queen," she corrected him. "We're very close to proving in another way, how sexual selection is the reason for our diversity, and the basis for our evolution."

"It scares me, Vera." Hans laughed. His huge upper body towered over her, but he always told her that he was more intimidated by her self-assurance than she'd ever be by his physique. "If what the theory and your figures suggest are true, then one million sexually reproducing individuals of a species could be replaced in only a handful of generations by a single asexually reproducing female."

She moved in closer, hugging him, but he backed away. "And yet they say women are the weaker sex? We all know that theory is true—we've seen it our snails. Maybe interspecies competition is the real reason why men are so aggressive, start all the wars in the world, and have kept women at bay all these years throughout history, evolving as the stronger sex physically." She scratched down some notes on her clipboard next to her measurements on her snail colonies, mused over her novel hypothesis. "You guys know women could rapidly wipe out all the males." She smiled and she scratched him playfully on the shoulder, looking down at his wedding ring.

"You're smart. Scary smart." They locked eyes. After a moment, Hans broke away and he picked up the flasks they'd used to prepare the platinum mediums for the snails. He grabbed a bristle brush and he washed the flasks at the sink, sighed. "At home I'm made to feel completely useless 90 percent of the time, so that's no surprise."

Hans had flipped into his mopey, woe-is-me Eeyore persona again, and she rolled her eyes. She found this so unattractive about men, the way they played the victim—as if everything negative that ever happened to them was the fault of women. His wife isn't into him?

Clearly, she must be a frigid bitch.

She kept her sarcastic comments to herself, and she merely looked at him, raising her eyebrows. He'd been depressed at his research proposal being rejected by the NIH and the Internal Review Board of John's Hopkins, and he somehow always blamed his wife.

Pick up the pieces of your ego and get your shit together.

For a big guy, he was actually a huge baby, she'd decided. She could've dressed him in green and gold and shoved him in a King Cake just then. But like all men in her field, she thought, he figured he was God. She wanted to say it, but Hans was sensitive. He had layers like a big, round onion. If he was so unhappy with his wife, why did he stay with her? She turned on her heel and leaned down on the black marble lab bench, examining the Petri dishes again.

She couldn't let it go.

"Wah-Wah," she mocked. "Of course we need sex, and therefore males, as hard as it is for me to admit it. Besides, you men provide the genetic variability unseen in an asexual population. It confers safety from parasites and disease—the asexually reproducing colonies of snails are wiped out by parasites much faster than those reproducing sexually. Sex and sexual reproduction preserves genetic variants that might prevent extinction in the case of a massive parasitic infestation, one that could doom an entire species."

The snails were behaving just as she'd predicted.

Orderly, methodically, repeating the previous results just as good subjects in a well- designed experiment should.

There was nothing suspicious about the data at all.

She touched the inside of Hans' wrist. "Don't you see how important sex is, Hans?"

Hans was sipping his coffee from his favorite mug, and he coughed on it then. "Saving the entire female species from widespread disease—big shoes to fill." He shook his head, taking another sip as he stepped back, moved the tray of glass dishes off the bench and placed them under the fluorescent lights in the corner of the room.

She followed behind him. "Hans, you know what they say about men with big shoes."

"You kill me, Laughlin." He was trying to change the subject, so she gave up. He never took her seriously when she flirted. "And here I thought sex was an earth-moving act I do to rock my woman's world and make me feel like a Roman god."

She shot him a look of *'as if.'* "Get over yourselves— you and every other man really think that way, don't you?" She offered a flirtatious smile, and hopped up on the lab bench where she sat face to face with him.

"Do you always have to think so methodically? Maybe there doesn't have to be a scientific reason behind everything we do, Laughlin. That's what sets us apart from the animals."

"Yes, I do. And it *is* all about science—it's the only way to explain our repetitive patterns of behavior. We *are* animals, Raedl. And if you believe in the Red Queen theory, then you know that the majority of our behavior is motivated by sexual selection. Our intelligence is way beyond what we need for mere survival of the fittest—it's *reproduction* of the fittest that drives the diversity that allows us to survive in subsequent generations. Without diversity, a parasite too small to see with the naked eye could come along and wipe us all off the map." She made big, passionate gestures with her arms as if there was a cataclysmic explosion about to happen. An antediluvian catastrophe of Biblical proportions. It was obvious now that he found her simply amusing, and couldn't resist teasing her about her steadfast belief in the scientific theory.

"Do you wish you were a snail," said Hans, "able to reproduce sexually or asexually with or without men—take them or leave them?"

"Maybe," she giggled, pointing her finger at him and cocking her neck to one side as if daring him to keep going.

"So it all comes back to sex and science with you, Vera?" Hans mussed up her already spiky hair with his right hand and let his left arm fall beside her thigh. He stepped in closer, stood between her legs. "On the other hand, there's what we *feel*."

He leaned in and he kissed her hard, on the lips, and she was pleased that he'd regained his confidence and that he was behaving more like the intelligent PhD candidate she'd known since they'd started their research together years ago. It was a nice kiss—just right, not too stiff or sloppy or weak—yet it felt mechanical to her, forced on her part, not his. She broke away and she smiled and she wiped her lip.

"On the other hand…" She took his left hand and wriggled his ring finger on which he wore his gold wedding band.

There was a rattling of a key in the copper lock of the wood and glass lab door.

She hopped down from the bench as Jorge Bourdain, their research partner, came in, carrying a box of pizza atop a bag with one of the preserved research primates. Kayla Reeves followed behind him.

"I didn't know you two were here," Jorge said, as he carried the animal and the box with his left hand like a waiter. "Care for a slice of pizza?"

As a teenager, Jorge's right hand had been injured in a crush injury under the wheel of car. Kayla frequently offered to assist him when he worked with the lab equipment, but Jorge was proud and always declined. The hand had sustained nerve damage, never regaining full use. The muscles were shrunken and it had failed to grow to the same size as his left, and sometimes it hung at his side in a flaccid, atrophied pendulum of flesh.

Jorge entered the lab, carrying his crippled arm scrunched like a bony checkmark, close to his chest. As he tried to set the pizza and the primate down now, steadying them with his weak hand, he dropped both of them. The primate slid out of the bag and the cheese pizza landed face down on the floor of the laboratory.

"Five second rule?" teased Hans.

Kayla rushed to help clean up the spill. But Jorge turned away, looking mortified. Lately, there seemed to be something distracting him, more than his obvious crush on Kayla, which he always denied. He seemed nervous about LeTorneau's research, as if there were something more behind it that he wasn't sharing with them. Veronica brushed it off, just thankful for now that the two of them hadn't noticed her indiscretion with Hans.

-2-

Sara Sullivan

Sara ran her hand down the banister as she descended the oak stairs in her half-buttoned blouse and panties. She stopped to stare out across the street at the red brick house with black shudders where all the commotion had taken place. The bushes made a full border around the house, and just outside them the cobblestone street was now empty. The crescendo of a police car siren roared and passed, and the street was calm again with only bicycle horns and teenage boys and a few hours of daylight remaining in the evening.

"Sara," Marty called.

She was right there. Why did he need to shout? His voice was always louder than it needed to be.

The front door slammed shut.

He smiled and scooped her up as he reached the fourth step where she stood—the one that creaked when he came in late at night and invariably woke her. The children had gone inside, but Marty's pager for the police department was beeping a cacophony of unanswered messages.

"I saw the whole thing," she said, as he kissed her neck and carried her back up to the bedroom. "Wait," she protested, but he kept going.

"It's over honey. It was just a couple of kids." Marty set her down on the bed and closed the door behind them.

She sat up on the edge of the bed. She wanted to know more about the incident.

"But the boy—he had a knife. I saw it." She ran her hand through her short hair and the blouse fell from her light brown shoulders. Marty pulled off her white panties. She appeased him by returning his kisses. Over the last month she'd become worried about the neighborhood. She'd heard gunshots more than once, and vandals had scrolled racist graffiti on the garage of the home three doors down. Even the teenagers put her on edge. Marty reminded her that although they'd bought the home in the wealthy Georgetown area, it was still D.C.

That didn't help to reassure her.

Not with the viral epidemic spreading throughout the capital.

A police officer had been killed only a block from their home. His skull blown apart through his face, shattering his bone structure that defined his image and leaving him unrecognizable, precluding a dignified open casket wake. Fragments of gray matter still spattered the pavement. Marty had described it to her in grotesque detail. Showed her the crime scene photos, graphic and bloody, as if she didn't see enough trauma in the E.R. The tension in the capital was escalating, and she'd had to turn off the news more than once in the past week. She couldn't watch the officers trying to contain a crowd while being pelted with glass bottles and rocks. What if it had been Marty?

"Let it go," Marty said.

"What business does that boy have with a weapon? He's barely a teenager."

Marty's voice grew assertive. "Don't worry about the boys. I took care of it."

She forced a smile. Marty always seemed insulted when she questioned him.

He reminded her that she had nothing to worry about with a policeman in the house. He pulled the headband out of her hair. "That's better."

She frowned. She wasn't convinced, and Marty's schedule with the force was getting more unpredictable every week. Her schedule was getting busier, too, it seemed. With the epidemic spreading, she might be mandated to work overtime.

Weekends.

Additional shifts.

On most Saturdays, Marty went hunting at a cabin in Charlottesville, over an hour from their home. She wished he were home more often, to cook his famous bacon cheeseburgers on the grill, topped with a sloppy heap of avocado and tomato that she loved, to show her his goofy rock collection from the Blue Ridge Mountains that he'd taken out and shown her for the fiftieth time last night, to rake the leaves into a multicolored mound of molded foliage that she loved to push him into when he turned his back and for a second, let down his cop guard, and, as much as she hated to admit it, to just *be* there.

With the rioting plaguing the capital, every branch that scraped the windows at night terrified her. Every raccoon in Mary Jenkins uncovered garbage cans, every bunchy rabbit gnawing their daffodils beneath their bedroom window. And there was so much to do—the old home needed renovations and was bought on foreclosure. It was the best they could afford in the expensive neighborhood with her large student loan debt.

"Did you think about what we discussed at dinner last night?" Marty asked.

She swallowed, stared into Marty's blue eyes. They held hers in a serious, almost sullen gaze. She and Marty had been engaged only a week when he'd brought up his unique ideas on how their marriage should work.

She remembered: They'd gone to the French restaurant, Allons, on M Street. The candlelit wooden booths and the brocade wallpaper and chandeliers created a romantic atmosphere. She had snails and Merlot and champagne to toast their engagement and steak *au poivre*. For dessert there was a soufflé that took a half hour to bake, and as she sipped her champagne, alternating it with her coffee, waiting for the dessert to arrive, he'd brought up the suggestion.

"I'd like us to try a more traditional marriage."

The water boy bustled around, topping off their glasses in the dusky restaurant.

"I'd love to stay home with Elyse full-time." Most of their beliefs seemed more in sync everyday—except when it came to her career. He always seemed to have to take the lead. She cleared her throat, said, "But I've worked my whole life to get where I am in my career, Marty."

"Good," Marty said, took her hand.

He seemed not to hear a thing she said sometimes.

"I need to be the head of our household, Sara. The one making the decisions."

He stroked the insides of her wrists as he spoke to her. The Merlot made her cheeks flush and she laughed at first, hearing this. It all sounded so old-fashioned, archaic even, like *Good Housekeeping* magazines from the 1940's that recommended putting on something pretty before your husband got home every day, taking off his shoes for him. Marty just kept staring, locking eyes with her as if she were some vulnerable prey waiting for his next move. A gazelle or a Lorie bird or something equally cute and helpless, stalked by its predator.

Sometimes, he could be downright creepy. She reminded herself that he was simply intense.

And she wondered if maybe, there was something wrong with her, because she was so intensely attracted to him.

They'd discussed how many of their friends' relationships were based on mutual acceptance of misery and tolerance, a symbiotic exploitation of one another, and they'd promised each other that they'd never live in the redundancy of an unhappy marriage. Is that what he meant?

"Have you heard of domestic discipline?" he asked her.

Now she was sure he wasn't serious.

She coughed on her wine as the waiter set down the soufflé. Then she wiped her lip and she set down her glass and she looked around, worried that others were listening to their conversation. "I'm looking to the right and to the left, because I *know* you're not talking to me."

Marty sighed, relaxing his intense stare a bit. He held both her hands. She leaned back in the booth, just wanting to reach for her fork and attack the chocolaty dessert.

"Don't worry, honey," Marty said. He winked at her. "I'm not some weirdo like in those S and M books you're reading. And you know I haven't led a tortured childhood or anything crazy. Anyway, I was just kidding, really."

"How do you know what I'm reading?" She felt herself blush and she broke her right hand away from his firm grip and she reached for her fork, plunging it into the decadent soufflé. The chocolate flowed out and it was hot on the roof of her mouth and it was sweet and it smelled slightly burnt and she forgot for a moment that Marty wasn't amused.

"It's a means of running a household where one partner voluntarily gives the other the ability to lead the family in important decisions."

"Uh-huh," she said, with a doubtful, flirtatious smile. She devoured half the tiny cake and realized she hadn't offered him any and she licked her fork, now teasing him as she brought it to his lips. Marty bit the soufflé and licked his teeth. She had to admit, she'd been turned on when she'd read mainstream stories of bondage and S&M where no one got hurt.

She figured this was his way to keep the spice in their sex life.

No marriage could sustain itself more than twenty years on straight missionary sex.

And with Elyse never sleeping, their passion seemed to have cooled off a bit.

Marty's domineering personality excited her at times—especially in the bedroom, but their day to day life was a different story. If she didn't want to do something, she didn't do it. More than once when they'd argued, she'd told him to take a flying leap over the Francis Scott Key Bridge.

Marty reached under the table and squeezed her thigh where her skirt hem fell on her stockings. "I know what's best for us."

Sara jumped in her seat, and shifted her weight on her bottom side to side, smiled. They were both on their third glass of wine, and now the champagne was enough to push her subtle buzz into a fully drunken state.

The maître d' dimmed the lights.

"Who turned out the lights?" She laughed a bit too loudly, so that the couple at the next table looked over at her. He wasn't serious. Was he?

Looking irritated, Marty brushed off the conversation, paid the bill. They headed down the cobblestone street of chic restaurants and designer clothing shops and bookstore cafes, walking home arm in arm, a little crooked. She tripped over a few of the large cobblestones in the road, laughing. Marty picked her up and took her to bed and made love to her hard. He kissed her goodnight and she fell asleep, forgetting his unusual proposal as he tucked her in, just before he left for his third nightshift that week.

Had he really gone to work?

She was suspicious of his behavior, but too exhausted, and too drunk, to investigate just then.

Now, in the bedroom, just before he left again, his pager was still sounding. She wore the balmy, humid air on her skin, heavy, glistening with it. Fully exposed before him, she swallowed, saw the same look in Marty's eyes that she'd seen in the restaurant.

"Remember what we talked about last night, Sara?" Marty asked.

She nodded.

He sat down on the bed beside her.

"I love you, Marty." She suddenly felt uncomfortable, tapped his nose playfully, and tried to anticipate his next move.

She couldn't.

Something felt out of place.

"I know you do." Marty moved closer. "When I ran down there to break up the argument, I asked you to wait for me in the bedroom. We weren't done. You put your clothes back on before I was through."

"You—"

He held his finger up to her lips.

He went to the bathroom and took out a wooden hairbrush and bent her over his knee. He paddled her across her backside with the hairbrush very hard twenty times and it hurt. It happened so fast that she had little time to protest the humiliating nature of it. The sound could have been heard outside their bedroom through the closed door, and their Amazon parrot, Jimmy, began squawking, loudly. Then Marty stopped and he picked up his pager and he dressed.

The baby was screaming down the hall.

Phaedrex Clinical Trials Lab

Laboratory of Dr. Graham LeTorneau, Chief Researcher for Phaedrex

And the National Institute of Health

Bethesda, Maryland

Jorge Bourdain

"That is some sexy writing." Jorge Bourdain handed the publication to its author, Kayla Reeves. He wasn't just saying so because he wanted to sleep with her. There was no doubt he wanted to—he thought about it a few dozen times each day, especially when they worked alone in the lab without their partners, Veronica Laughlin and Hans Raedl.

But the compliment was sincere.

Kayla was cuter than a speckled pup.

She had fair skin and blue eyes and breasts that were round and perky and natural.

Beyond that, she was *smart*.

Their paper for *Nature*, had finally been accepted for publication. Both were completing their theses on the scientific basis for evolution, examining a controversial theory known as The Red Queen, a theory based on the despotic character from Lewis Carroll's *Through the Looking-Glass*. Jorge's thesis was almost complete, and he'd promised himself that before he presented it in May, he'd get up the nerve to ask Kayla out on a date.

After Veronica and Hans had run out like they'd been caught with their hands in the cookie jar, he was alone with her.

This was his chance.

Standing six feet four, with dark hair and eyes, "Big Jorgey" as Kayla affectionately called him, knew he made a rather intimidating first impression. It wasn't uncommon for people to walk the other way when they saw him coming, and it made him feel misunderstood, always the odd man out.

He watched her moving about the lab, throwing open the windows, crinkling up her nose like she always did when she didn't like the smells from the hood. After some time, the odors of Veronica's experiment fell away from them and finally, she paused.

He summoned his courage, perspiring at his armpits.

Before he could speak, Kayla blurted out something terrible, told him that she planned to take on a full-time faculty position at the Sorbonne in Paris.

Dropped that bomb on him like the invasion of Normandy.

His heart sank, and he regretted that their time doing research together had flown by. Having come from the poorest area of Louisiana surrounding New Orleans, he still felt like an outsider in D.C., like he was never truly accepted.

But not around Kayla.

The petite 101-pound Georgia peach didn't take any disrespect, but she was reserved, polite, never needed to dole any out, either. Big city Americans, especially ones up north, were so blunt, to the point of rudeness, but not Kayla. She retained a proverbial southern clout in saying, *'Bless your heart,'* and knew how to use it as both an insult and a compliment. Like Jorge, she spoke slowly, and said, *'yes, ma'am'* and, *'no, sir.'*

Jorge wore his shirt and tie to Sunday sermon, not jeans and flip-flops, and even though he was the first in his family to attend college, he knew where he was from and he never forgot his roots. Kayla didn't fit the mold up here either. She was different than the rest of the cutthroat academics, and like him, she didn't quite belong. She stood out with such innocence about her—like a Cheerio on a church pew.

That's what he loved about her.

And she looked at him like he'd hung a harvest moon all up in a cornfield.

A year from now, she'd be sipping her coffee in some Parisian café with a Frenchman, maybe having her picture sketched by starving artists who would flatter her shamelessly, making her blush, maybe she'd be walking arm in arm down Montmartre with Frenchy or worse, some American expat hippie.

His anxiety thumped inside his chest.

He'd never see her again.

"What's wrong, Big Jorgey?"

"Nothing."

The nights their research group had spent in the Georgetown bars after they'd left the lab would be forgotten for croissants and crème brulee and frogs' legs. And buttered snails. Now he suddenly hated snails, all of them. He pushed Veronica's agar gel full of them away, filling with disdain.

He made a mean etouffee that Kayla loved, but he could never compete with Paris.

Freaking Paris?

Here they drank Bud Lights and shot pool and laughed and talked about their futures until they ran out of beer money. Mulledy's was his favorite hangout, since it was right near Kayla's apartment. She always asked him to walk her home along the rows of brownstones, up to her third floor place with the black wrought iron fire escape patio garden full of sunflowers and Gerbera daisies, and tomato plants that dangled off the porch, looking to him like beanstalks that he wanted to pull down and climb right up from the street, up to her bedroom.

"Give me a hug, you big, lovable Cajun. I'm glad you like the paper. I couldn't have done it without you. Do you think we'll get any credit for any of this, or will Graham get all the glory?" As graduate research students, they worked under their faculty mentor, Dr. LeTorneau, a pioneer in the field of evolutionary biology.

"I don't know," He took a pair of tweezers and gently placed one of the moths, their research subjects, back near its cocoon. "I'm just having nightmares over the dissertation. It's all I can think about."

"You know this stuff cold. It's just the faculty you're talking to—it's not like we have to present to thousands of speakers like *Graham*. Now that's nerve-wracking."

She didn't have to accentuate his name the way she did.

Graham was a goddamned genius—everybody knew that. He'd come up with theories that sounded downright mad to those outside the scientific community. But he could also be kind of a prick the way he used his grad students to do all the work while he took all the credit for the Royal College of Evolutionary Biologists grant. He'd received hundreds of thousands of dollars from NIH in funding, and countless key note speaker awards, and he reveled in the attention. Kayla looked up to him as a mentor, though, and Jorge never bad mouthed him in front of her.

"Are you going to the lecture at the Omni tomorrow?" He loved the way the fluorescent lights from the botany students' experiments gave her skin and blue eyes a magnificent glow, like some kind of sylph-like mystical creature. A delicate winged sprite or a water nymph perched at the water's edge of the Potomac. They'd kayaked there last spring, almost been alone long enough for him to tell Kayla how he felt, until Veronica's loud mouth, trumpeting all the way from the shore, had spoiled the moment, and he'd fallen out of the kayak clumsy and sack-like, into the river. "LeTorneau wanted us to bring some of his back up audiovisual equipment by, but I don't think he'll need it in a place like that."

"I wouldn't miss it for anything. Aren't you going, Big Jorgey?" Kayla smiled and gave his abdomen a playful rub.

He could never accept that Kayla was flirting with him, despite all the mixed signals she sent him. Coming from any other daft, uneducated woman, he'd know they meant she liked him.

The way she always found a way to touch him.

The way she called right back whenever he called her.

The way she asked his opinion on everything, hung on his words.

The naive thing about Kayla, though, was that while she understood science, she didn't understand the depth of

LeTorneau's research like he did—he'd spent sleepless hours online reading up about the significance of it. Blogging about it in all sorts of groups and chat rooms. Its sociocultural ramifications. The magnitude of its ultimate outcome. Maybe if he could share the deeper meaning of it all—teach her about what LeTorneau was really trying to convey to others—he might be able to keep her here after graduation. He smiled at her weakly now, imagining what the lab would be like without her there.

He decided then that he had to find a way to make her stay, whatever the cost.

If anyone was going to eat croissants in a Parisian café with her, it was going to be him.

Africa
January 14, 2014

Dr. Claus Recart examined the diverse plant species of the African rift valley through his binoculars, pointed to a plateau where the Bell 407 turbine helicopter could land. The helicopter whizzed over the hillside near Mount Morungole, Uganda, circling the green mountains where they aspired to reach the cloudless sky. Mvule trees and umbrella thorn acacias loomed high in the forest as the chopper whistled by them, blowing the elephant grass sideways. Below, Recart sighted a lone African girl dressed in a bright orange sarong tied beneath one arm and up and around her other shoulder. The wind from the aircraft blew her clothing in all directions. She looked up and then dropped her belongings and took off running in the direction of the tribal village, the dwelling place of the ten thousand or so members that had migrated from Ethiopia and settled in the mountains near the Kenyan border.

"She saw us," said Recart. His French accent was thick. He rubbed at the grey hair in his neatly trimmed goatee. The heat was unbearable. He sipped water from his canteen.

The man behind him was dressed in a suit, and he now grabbed the binoculars and glassed the region—dozens of thatch huts and wooden shanties built on a flat plain of thirsty ground in the hard to reach mountain region near the Kidepo Valley Park area. Open fires and stone cook stoves burned. Villagers gathered on the parched clay plateau high in the hills. The man in the suit, Edward Marburg, focused the binoculars on the ground where the emaciated girl had dropped her things: She'd left behind a water pitcher and a small animal on a stone slab.

"It's alright," said Recart. He was dressed in khaki shorts and a white linen shirt and a safari hat. The clove smell of his cologne and the other men's sweat filled the cabin of the aircraft. "Land here."

The pilot raised the collective lever on the chopper and increased the engine speed and pulled up and circled again, blowing the elephant grass in wild gusts. The young girl stopped and looked back, held down her sarong in the wind, before she disappeared out of their sight. They descended near the home of one of the most remote tribes in East Africa, the Ik people.

Recart stepped down and visualized the mountains beyond the landing place. It was too far to see the village now through the indigenous flora, but from the air they'd seen it clearly to the east. There were no other signs of a village or animal life, and no other passages in or out of the Ik village that he could discern. He ordered the pilot to help him, and the two of them lifted the canvas duffel and the tent and the foodstuffs out of the cabin. Then they pitched the tent to make camp a few hundred yards away from the chopper, kept watch with the binoculars. Marburg smoked.

On the second day of the expedition there was a brisk wind that carried the smell of a fire and mouth-watering aromas from the village.

"What is that delicious smell?" asked Marburg. "I'm starving."

"Matoke, a starchy type of banana picked green and steamed in a cooking pot. A traditional tribal dish," said Recart.

"And what have we got?"

Recart tossed him a granola bar.

An afternoon rain shower caused the visitors' own emblazoned pile of sticks to smoke and crackle. Recart scathed a trail, cutting down grass and brush, and walked along the path to the village where the tribe was gathered in their huts. He examined the shelters from a distance and he returned to the camp and he removed the cooler from the cabin of the helicopter. Then he took out a metal trap with the macaque they'd transported from his own lab.

He slaughtered the animal so that it bled all over the stone slab like some funereal and atavistic ritual, so that the smell of its blood would travel in the wind toward the Ik village. He spread figs and bananas on the stone near the spitting fire where the girl had left her own fruit bat, a treasured delicacy for which she'd surely return. And when the sun set, he walked with his flashlight toward the Ik huts. There was dancing in the central village, where the villagers played drums made of animal hide and lyre instruments and the *omubanda* reed instruments of Uganda.

He hid in the brush, on the outskirts of the community *okoks*, or neighborhoods—walled off sections of the village—until he saw the young girl. She didn't appear to belong to any of the *asaks*, the partitioned houses with small front yards. Nor did she fit into the bands of cunning teenagers who roamed in search of food. He strode around to the stone wall of the village, observing her through his field glasses from a distance. She stole a few vegetables from an open stone fire before she was chased away with sticks, and she almost managed to steal a few more from another neighbor. She looked aware that she was being watched by the old women inside the granaries, and she squatted beside one of the huts and waited, where there was no one nearby to pursue her.

Later, she was lying alone on the wet dirt near an open fire, witness to a tribal ceremony. She talked to no one as the elders danced about and no one paid her any attention. Finally, he caught her eye and he smiled at her, a child of about twelve or fourteen. She looked back at him in the light of the fire, hiding, and she looked away and then back at him, hidden in the shadows. She rose from the mud and she hurried inside one of the huts, and then she pulled back the animal skin curtain from the doorway and she peered out again at him.

He motioned to her with his head.

He motioned again to follow, and then, with his hands, he motioned her to come and eat. Thunder cracked, loud, in the distance. The temperature had cooled considerably since the afternoon, and the ground smelled of wet arthropods.

A flash of lightning and the splitting thunder shook the plateau.

The villagers kept dancing, their feet pounding like war drums.

The girl offered a timid smile, stepped forward, but then a name was called, which sounded like "Acanit." One of the elders stood at the doorway and shouted and chased her out. The woman pulled the animal skin curtain closed, disappeared into the thatch hut.

The next day, the ground was still wet from the rain.

"Here," he said, to the man in the suit. He handed Marburg the last of their foodstuffs. A white container marked: BIOHAZARD was secured in the back of the chopper. "I let out the rest of the animals over there."

"Ain't no safari coming through here, Claus," the pilot said, kept looking over his shoulder. He tapped his leg and complained that he was down to his last cigarette. "What the fuck are you doing here?"

"Just shut up. We need a few more hours."

The scientist lifted a pipette into the biohazard unit and deposited a clear liquid from it onto the fruit on the stone slab. Viscous fluid seeped between the stone cracks.

"Don't know if we've got enough gas to make it back to Kampala," the pilot said. "We circled around more than expected."

Recart was dressed in the white hazmat suit now, with no skin exposed and a respirator mask tightly adhered around his mouth and nose. He breathed in and out in shallow gasps, and this claustrophobic exchange of air made a raspy sound as he hovered over the stone hearth and drew back the pipette and injected a multitudinous load of the *Labrador* virus into the body of the wet fruit bat. He'd named the virus for the province of Labrador and Newfoundland, where he'd cloned the virus and discovered its vaccine.

"I hope you know what you're doing." The pilot lit his last smoke.

"Absolutely." He looked on with sagacity, self-acknowledged arrogance, twisted the lid back onto the container with what little dexterity his bulky gloves offered, and placed it back into the containment unit. It was no bigger than an oversized picnic cooler, but it contained a specialized airtight negative pressure system and a refrigeration unit. A backup generator protruded from the side of the unit in case of initial power failure.

"What are you studying?" The pilot stood on the plateau where they'd landed, looking out onto the rim of tropical mountains, beholding the vast expanse of the rift valley. The edge of the cliff glistened wet beneath his boots, where it was still slippery from the rain.

A small waterfall off of a tributary sustained the village, where birds gathered along the entrance to a cave.

It had been a tough landing, and with the crosswinds coming in over the leeward side of the mountain, it would be tough getting them out of there. The elevation was only around three thousand feet, but the pilot looked short of breath, standing there at the edge. He'd been paid well for the expedition. He counted the money now that Claus had given him. The wind blew his hair and clothing back toward his face. He shoved the money in his pocket and he took a drag of the cigarette. The rest of the money was due at the conclusion of the charter.

Recart ignored his question.

Marburg, still dressed in a suit, disappeared down the path. A few moments later, he came running up the trail toward the stone pedestal. The rain had turned to a finer mist that carried heavy with each humid breath the scent of the massive banana palms. The sharp chirping of the birds and croaking frogs and laughing capuchins in the Fauvist paradise gave it the illusion of Dionysian overabundance, but famine and drought and its geographic isolation made it a competitive landscape for self-preservation.

"She's coming," Marburg said. "The girl is coming. The one we saw from the chopper."

"*Pourquoi est-elle seule?*" Recart asked. Much of his research had been top secret in his eastern Canadian lab. He articulated his thoughts out loud in French frequently, as if the others weren't even there.

"Fucking speak English, man," said the pilot. He crushed his cigarette. "That shit's getting annoying."

"Why is she alone?" Recart demanded.

Marburg was at once attentive, said, "The anthropologists will tell you it's a classic example of individualism, even in a civilized society." He kept his binoculars pointed toward the path. "When they're starving, the basic need to survive trumps all else. Children of the Ik are expelled from households as early as age four, left to fend for themselves. Sometimes they're raised by other children—called age bands."

"Extreme famine and deprivation," said Recart. He peered through the plastic visor of the suit, then at Marburg. "It brings out the worst in mankind."

"It just means that we're all bloody animals, Claus." Marburg began to pack up the hazardous material in haste. The green lights were still flashing on the containment unit, indicating that it was open to the atmosphere. As the girl approached, Recart ushered him behind the foliage. He removed his biohazard gear, starting first with his gloves. Then he peeled the suit away from his chest. The pilot was waiting beside their manufactured feast. "If the vaccine you gave me works, why are you still dressed in protective equipment?"

"To put it simply, my motto has always been, 'trust no one'," he said. "My research has always been top secret. I don't care for an audience either, no matter how small."

The girl appeared along the temperate forest path, ambling slowly toward the fire, where the pilot began handling the bats, cooking them over the fire.

Blood oozed from the rare meat of their bodies.

The smell of their burned flesh drifted ripe on the wind.

"*Zut alors!* Why is he touching those?" the scientist demanded. He cursed loudly in French. "He hasn't been vaccinated."

The girl appeared to be enjoying the misty rain beneath the treetop brise-soleil. She made no attempt to take shelter or keep dry. When she saw Recart, she stopped in the grass, but he smiled and motioned for her to come. He mimicked eating one of the animals, raising his hands to his lips. Surely, a starving child would never refuse such a delicacy. The Ik sustained themselves on stone-ground grains and vegetables and avoided keeping animals altogether, for fear of having them stolen, their village raided.

"Here," Recart said to the girl. He took the bush meat from the fire and he held it out, and she slowly smiled and she took it off the spear.

She understood.

She bit it and she chewed at it and she took another bite. Then she looked back at the path and she stopped chewing and she grimaced after she'd swallowed a few bites. Gratitude spread across her face, and soon she'd devoured every bite of the winged mammal.

"There you go—eat more," said Marburg.

Recart moved to the pilot's seat of the chopper. The pilot was looking over the ravine now. He walked over to the makeshift barbeque again and he shrugged and he tore a piece off the bat. He smelled it and he chewed at it and he bit off another piece.

"We have to go," said Recart. The blades began to rotate, slowly at first and then faster, the helicopter whipping the foliage and violating the paradisiacal calm through the acres of surrounding jungle. "I can drive."

"Stop," shouted the pilot.

"We can't leave him here," said Marburg. He waved the pilot toward the chopper, calling out to him through the open cockpit door.

"No, we're going without him," Recart said coldly. He put his hand over Marburg's wrist as he leaned out the door of the aircraft. Then he pushed him backwards and he yanked the door shut.

The blades of the helicopter spun faster.

The wind was picking up.

An age band of children were running out of the muddy forest, the mist kissing their bald, glistening scalps as they chased after the girl, toward the smell of the meat. The blades chopped stringy and metallic, humming like the plates of a clavichord at first, but the sound picked up intense and brutal and before long, it was hard to hear over the chopper, the wind. The children approached the helicopter with sticks, throwing them at the cabin. Held back by the whirring blades, they picked up stones and pelted them at the chopper. The sound of stone on metal resonated inside the cabin as a large rock hit, dented, the hull.

"They'll kill him," yelled Marburg.

Recart grabbed him by the collar now as the stones assaulted the windows.

"Those savages have just contaminated him with a virus like you've never seen." He looked down at the pilot in disgust. "A virus so hellish that it makes a man lose all human function, vomiting and leaking fluid and bleeding from the eyes and ears and every orifice of his body."

He relaxed his grip and he opened the cockpit door and he fired a warning shot with his .22 pistol at the children. They scattered, grabbing the onions and plantains and root vegetables and what was left of the bush animals, and running toward the fifty-foot high canopy of hanging trees. The pilot had gathered the containment unit and some of the supplies and was now running toward the chopper, carrying them in both arms, leaving much of the material behind him as he escaped the youths.

Marburg's face paled. Lips thin and quivering. "Are you saying we're at risk?"

"I'm saying this is nothing like you've ever seen. It's darker than the deepest pits of hell—something horrific enough to bring down the whole lot of mankind."

"What the fuck did you and Lindstrom get me into?" Marburg cursed. The rain was pouring down on the aircraft now. One of the windshield wipers waved askew, damaged by the youths. "You told me this was some sort of routine science experiment—and a safari expedition was coming through. A few cases of the flu."

Recart removed a stack of bills from the deepest pocket of his khakis. He angrily stuffed it in the pilot's canvas jacket and he threw it from the chopper and he locked the cockpit door. The pilot removed the stack and he gauged the amount of hundreds in the billfold and he shook his head. He threw the bills up into the air at the chopper. Recart raised the collective lever mounted on the cabin floor to the left of his seat, twisted the throttle.

"What'll happen to him?" Marburg asked.

"The virus will weaken him within hours," he said, matter-of-factly. "Bring him to his knees. It will kill him within days. And if we don't get out of here, those savages will kill us."

He secured the locks on his door as the pilot kicked and punched at the thick glass window. He had dropped the biohazard unit: The alarm was screaming and its red lights flashed urgently on the outside of the box. With the rain beating down on the windshield and the engine going full throttle, he couldn't hear the man. "Now go, dammit."

"I'm not an expert helicopter pilot, you know."

"We'll figure it out. Go!"

Marburg looked away from the pilot, stranded, still shouting and screaming as the helicopter rose above the mud into to the southern mountains of Uganda near the Kenyan border. Recart turned the rudder using the floor pedals against the windward rain, raising the rotorcraft further into the air and leaving behind the pilot on the boggy jungle plateau. He was still wildly protesting as they flew out of his sight and into the soaring canopy of the Ugandan rainforest.

Sara Sullivan

Ordinarily Sara limited herself to one glass of wine when she and Marty were out for a late dinner—any more than that made her too tired for sex, which led to poorly feigned excuses and more arguments and ultimately, more wine. But tonight, she ordered a third glass as she waited for Marty to show up at Raugh's restaurant, filling up on the bread and olive oil with cracked pepper and rosemary.

He was late again.

What else was new?

She was starting to think he was up to something more than just work.

"Can I get you an appetizer while you wait for your…?" The waiter shot an impatient glance at the empty seat. He seemed annoyed that she was camping out at the hottest table in town on a Friday night.

"Fiancé. He should be here any minute." She wanted to go home. Put on her pajamas. Order a pizza. Marty had insisted they get out of the house, and she'd given in again.

"Maybe you would like to wait at the bar?" With an arrogant nod, he turned on his heel and made a comment to the maître d' about not seating people until all members of a party were present, which she heard clearly. She put her headphones on and tuned into the local newscast on her smartphone.

The reporter was stationed outside George Washington University Hospital, where Sara worked as an emergency room physician. The mysterious illness that was spreading across the nation had hit their ER.

The snarky waiter returned with her Shiraz.

"I'll try the pumpkin squash gnocchi and he'll have a Stella." She managed a weak smile.

"Of course. Right away, madam." The waiter snapped his neck sideways, placed her napkin on her lap.

She sank down in the red velvet chair, felt her cheeks flush from the wine. She turned up the volume on the newscast and she looked around again for Marty and then back at her phone.

"This is Deborah Brussel, live outside George Washington University Hospital. The teaching hospital has not been able to avoid the virus that has spread nationally. Today, fourteen new infections were confirmed in the nation's capital, and half of those were diagnosed at George Washington."

Horrific images of dehydrated patients in Third World clinics bleeding from their eyes and covered in their own vomit flashed across the screen. Workers covered from head to toe in white hazmat suits and yellow gloves and blue shoe covers.

Sara swallowed.

They seemed distant, far removed from the U.S. But now the camera panned toward the entrance of the emergency department where ambulances were lined up around the circular drive. The reporter pointed the microphone toward Dr. Richard Ambrose, her colleague and Chief of the Department of Emergency Medicine. "Dr. Ambrose, do we know what's causing the rise in the number of infections?"

Another reporter interrupted, pushing her microphone at Ambrose. "What is George Washington doing to protect the healthcare workers here on staff?"

"It's proving very difficult to contain, Deborah." Ambrose scratched his bald head the way he always did, which made her relax as she took another sip of the Spanish wine. She watched her colleague under fire, glad it wasn't her.

She looked around again.

Where was Marty?

Was Elyse okay at home?

The lights dimmed.

Her spine curled where she sat anxious and impatient, slouching in the dark, nibbling an appetizer plate of cave-ripened cheese like some aging troglodyte, and feeling exhausted, like she and the cheese were past their prime.

Sara watched as Ambrose answered another question. "When we know one our doctors or nurses have been directly exposed, we're forced to place them under a two-week quarantine, during which time we monitor all of their personal contacts. We take their temperature daily for any signs of developing illness."

The questions kept coming at him.

"Do you see any resolution to the epidemic that's now killed more than half of those infected?

"How do you think this epidemic began in the District?"

Dr. Ambrose paused, as though he was choosing his words carefully. "Anytime healthcare professionals are the ones getting seriously ill from an infectious disease, it's extremely troubling, and right now, we're searching for answers and trying to bring this outbreak under control."

Ambrose scratched his head again and straightened his white coat.

Things were getting much worse.

She surfed to the webcast on the opposite station.

Channel Seven News was reporting from Howard University Hospital, which had staggering mortality statistics. Channel Two News was there, too. At the door now, Marty was taking off his jacket as the maître d' snapped his fingers. The waiter directed him to the table. He sat down across from her as she placed the phone in her purse, accepted a bouquet of supermarket flowers from him. Withered half-off daisies dyed indigo and lemon yellow, and baby's breath. Lots of it. She smelled the bouquet and she smiled, thanked him.

What had he done wrong? Or worse, what concessions did he want from her?

"Sorry I was held up again." Marty opened the menu and looked for the waiter. "I'm starving. How did it go today?" He poured his Stella Artois into a pilsner glass.

"Four more rejections, and one partial request," she said. After her 27th publication in a medical journal, she'd grown weary of research, and even her occupation at times. She enjoyed practicing medicine, but she craved novelty and sought out the next exultation of her spirit. As if working in an emergency room didn't provide enough adrenaline—she needed adventures. Obstacles even. To take her *joie de vivre* and *carpe diem*. Expand on her *Weltanschauung*. She'd written a screenplay and two novels to keep herself challenged.

The waiter placed the steaming gnocchi before them. She stabbed her fork into the soft pillows of pasta and she blew on them and she swallowed them whole.

"I meant at the hospital, sweetie." Marty perused the menu. Pointing to the entrees, he said to the waiter, "We'll have the *chateaubriand*."

"I don't want steak, Marty."

"Sara."

He was so bossy sometimes. Medical school had taught her how to choose her battles, but ordering her meal for her?

"Fine," she conceded. She wanted the hovering waiter to leave them alone. "*Chateaubriand*."

"Do you mind if we switch seats?" Marty asked.

She was comfortable. She enjoyed the view of the restaurant, people watching. She had just started to relax. But she sighed and said, "Fine," again. They traded seats. Officer Marty always had to sit with his back to the wall, his eyes scanning the room nonstop for signs of trouble. Bad guys. Suspicious characters.

After fifteen years on the force, it had become instinctual. Almost part of his DNA.

Like susceptibility to a lethal infection was part of her DNA.

She changed the subject from her mother and Elyse when the entrée came. Her mother didn't approve of them having Elyse out of wedlock. She didn't approve of their upcoming marriage. And of course, she never liked Marty in the first place. It was a relief to hear about Marty's workday: a drug bust, an arrest for grand theft of an automobile, a handful of garden variety misdemeanors. So far, he'd managed to stay out of the racial violence and rioting surrounding the epidemic.

Yet she couldn't get it off her mind.

"George Washington diagnosed fourteen infections." She scooped up two more gnocchi and finished her second glass of wine. Then, as she looked around again for the waiter to ask him for a glass of water, she spotted a well-dressed couple near a table for two against the exposed brick wall of the French restaurant. Their corner of the restaurant was candlelight dim, surrounded by dark Gothic paintings of gargoyles and angels and Notre Dame with all its flying buttresses, but the woman's face was unmistakable. She grabbed Marty's wrist. "Honey, that's *Jane*."

"Why are you whispering?" Marty asked. The strolling string quartet and clanking of the dishes and orders being called out from the kitchen staff near their own glad-to-be-there table made it impossible for anyone to overhear their conversation. The open grill sizzled. "And who's Jane?"

"The editor." She smoothed her hair and she sat up straighter and she turned her chair a little toward the brunette in the Chanel suit. The man's suit was Armani, perfectly fitted. "From Jaguar Publishing?" She gave him the, *'please tell me you know what I'm talking about,'* look, but he shook his head.

"I don't follow."

Marty's suit was a little too short at the sleeves, and he threw his beer back a little too far onto his palate for a Michelin star-awarded French restaurant. She rolled her eyes.

"You know I don't like it when you do that. It's disrespectful."

"Listen, you remember when I pitched my novel about access problems in the healthcare system and a wicked plot to release a virus that could wipe out mankind, all for the profit of the evil drug companies?"

Marty laughed, fed her the last gnocchi. "Yes, sweetie, I do."

"Well that's *her*." Sweat was forming on the bridge of her nose. She stole another glance at the Editor in Chief of Jaguar Publishing. Then she looked back at Marty who was now cutting into his steak. "The editor I pitched the story to when I attended the writer's conference a few years ago."

"Delicious." Marty chewed at the perfect medium rare, ordered another beer. "Are you still hung up on writing a book? I thought you'd moved on to screenplays."

She hadn't touched her meal, and the wine had made her lightheaded.

She placed her hand on his forearm. "If I don't publish a bestseller by the time I'm forty, I'll consider myself a complete failure."

He put down his fork and knife. "Baby, we talked about this. I'm not even thrilled with you working the hours you do at the hospital. In fact, with this virus going around, I'm not even sure I want you going in on Monday. What if Elyse gets sick? They said on TV that healthcare workers and their families are the ones most at risk."

"Well I suppose *the news reporters* know everything." The wine made her feisty, and she couldn't resist arguing. She picked up the glass to sip it, but it was empty and she set it down a bit too hard. "I can't just take days off like you. I'm a doctor."

"Do you want another?"

"No, thank you." She was curt, added, "The media calls everyone *healthcare worker*. As if doctors and nurses have no greater role in all this than the men servicing the elevators and the little old ladies in the gift shop."

"Have you ever even been in the hospital's gift shop, sweetie?"

Damn. He knew her so well. She snapped back, "Every hospital has little old ladies working in the gift shop. And yes, I resorted to buying your mother's Christmas present there once, when I had no time to shop."

Marty laughed. "I'd trust those little Dollies to do a better job protecting us from this disease than our politicians—with guys like *that* greasing their palms." He nodded at the man in the Armani suit seated next to Jane Morgan. The couple had paid the bill and was getting up to leave. "Her husband is Wes Lindstrom?"

"Who's that?" She'd never heard the name, but apparently, Marty recognized Jane Morgan's husband.

"Wes Lindstrom, the wealthiest investment banker in the country and well-known—some would say infamous—lobbyist for the pharmaceutical giants. He works for an investment firm that lobbied over six billion last year for the drug companies. He raised over 300 million dollars for a few of the government's favorite ones to come up with a cure for this virus in 2010." Marty polished off his baked potato and was cutting her steak for her. "It was all over the news, sweetie."

"I'm going to take it to go." She stabbed the meat with her fork before he could lift it off her plate. "But we'd never heard of the virus before the outbreak."

"*He* had, apparently." Marty motioned for the waiter. "Ask me how I know that."

"How, baby?" She was too silly from the wine to say hello, and certain the woman wouldn't remember her, but she regarded her with wide-eyed admiration as the couple approached.

"He's been investigated for corporate fraud on multiple occasions. Always manages to come out with an alibi, though. I was interviewed by the Feds during an investigation—thought he had some ties to organized crime in the city. Shady guy. He must have an 'in' with someone in Washington."

"Is there anyone in this city who doesn't?"

"Good evening, Doctor," Jane Morgan said, as she touched Sara on the shoulder.

"Hello, Ms. Morgan." Sara rose, shook the woman's hand. "I'm so flattered that you remembered me."

"Of course." Jane Morgan shook Marty's hand. "Wes, this is the young lady who pitched that fascinating premise I told you about a few years back—about an intentional viral outbreak."

"Pleasure to meet you," Wes Lindstrom said.

He had wolf-like features with high arched brows and a cunning smile and a deep, sexy voice. The kind of confidence that made her think he knew what she was thinking before she thought it. She blushed and hoped it wasn't too obvious to him or to Marty that she found him attractive.

"Honey, I'm going to get the car from the valet." Wes Lindstrom kissed his wife on the cheek, excused himself.

Marty was paying the bill and finishing off her last pieces of steak. She hadn't touched her meal.

"How is your writing coming?" Jane Morgan asked.

"Pretty good." Jane Morgan's sheath dress was pressed and showed only toned arms. Sara, in contrast, knew she was showing too much cleavage, and her wrinkled blouse had a few drops of peppered olive oil on it.

"Yes, I remember your manuscript well. Fascinating premise. I recall it got right to the heart of what truly frightens me. I'm not quite sure if people would want to read it right now, though, with the viral outbreak that's crippling the nation." She stoked her chin. "The narrative would have to be flawless."

"Jane the car's ready," called Wes Lindstrom from the maître d' stand.

"Send it to me when it's complete and I'll take another look." Jane Morgan was sincere. "And keep up with your writers' group."

She nodded in awe as Jane Morgan left to join her husband. She sat back down next to Marty. He was filling in the tip amount on the credit card receipt.

"Pretty good?" Marty teased her. "You couldn't put together a better English sentence for a big-time editor than a clichéd 'pretty good'?"

"Don't pick on me." She pinched his arm. Hard.

"Ow!" He rubbed his arm near the triceps muscle where a fleshy lump was forming.

"I told you this was the best idea I've had for a thriller thus far. I could kick myself for not polishing it. This would be perfect timing." They headed toward their cars. "She liked it. I knew she liked it."

Marty opened her car door for her and took her hand. "Sara, I need you to focus on our family. You can't spend all your free time writing stories. And I'm concerned about you getting sick at the hospital."

"I need to stop there on my way home," she said, as she sat down in her BMW and started the engine. "There's too much going on that doesn't make sense." She couldn't help feeling she'd missed something in the patients she'd seen earlier that week.

"This was supposed to be our night out. Your mother has Elyse. We have the house to ourselves."

Marty looked handsome in his suit and tie. She was used to seeing him in his police uniform, or in jeans, sweats, without a shave. He pulled the flamboyant bouquet from behind his back that she'd left behind on the table.

"I have you to myself." Marty smiled.

"Do those flowers have an *'off'* switch?" She winked, definitely knew how to pick her battles. And this was one that he was going to lose. She smiled back and she kissed him and she closed the sedan door. "This won't take long. I promise."

-3-

George Washington University Hospital
Washington, D.C.
Sara Sullivan

Sara's tires squealed as she pulled into the ramp, parked crooked. The George Washington emergency room was a crime scene of police cars and officers with German shepherds and POLICE LINE DO NOT CROSS tape leading up to the sliding glass doors. Without an escort, it prevented her from getting access to the building.

Protesters gathered behind the lines.

They screamed and shouted at the officers and news vans that were reporting on the scene. As she pushed her way through the crowd, they shouted about the lack of national response to the deadly infection. It was taking the lives of many of the best doctors and nurses in the District. An officer held a hand up, stopped her as she ducked under the yellow tape.

"Where are you going this evening, ma'am?"

"I work here. I'm Doctor Sullivan." She clutched her purse tightly on her shoulder.

She looked up. A Caucasian student wearing jeans and a Duke ball cap in the crowd was gesturing at her. He had buck teeth and braces and orangutan arms flailing in all directions.

"Go back to Africa where this disease came from," shouted a man from the crowd.

"This isn't Howard University," yelled another voice, referencing the historically black college.

"I'll need to see some ID," said the officer.

She fumbled with her keys and her credit cards as she fished through her purse and located her hospital badge with the picture of her with longer hair. He looked at it and looked at her and looked at the badge again.

"I'm talking to you, brown sugar," the college student shouted again.

What was this all about?

Suddenly, she just wanted to be back home with Marty.

Maybe he was right.

Another officer escorted the student back from the police line and eyed him up and down for a weapon. The other protesters egged him on.

The officer jabbed his finger in the young man's chest and warned him: "The employees here need to be able to get to work safely. One more outburst and I'll have you in handcuffs."

"And the cop's sweatin' like a nigger tryin' to read." The protester quickly ducked into the crowd after his comment, but the officer grabbed the back of his shirt and pulled him back over the police line. The crowd's derogatory shouting intensified into a vehement uproar of cuss words and shoving and fist fights.

Picketing signs poked up through the hostile congregation.

White knuckled fists clenched, punched in unison with staccato chants of *"Lab-ra-dor!"*

"What's going on?" She cowered from the mob.

The officer's partner ushered her toward the entrance. "We've had a large increase in racial tensions since the outbreak began. The crowd is suggesting the virus originated in Africa. Authorities are calling for travel bans. The media's hounding us. Nothing's gone right tonight and patients can't even get access to the hospital."

She'd never been the target of such emphatic racism. She looked over her shoulder as she rushed behind the closed doors of the emergency ward.

She thought back to her childhood, growing up in the city, when she was teased for her biracial background. She'd been on the swings of the school playground swinging alone. The white girls taunted her, and called her names, made her feel like she didn't know where she fit it. Until then, she'd never given her skin color much thought. Her best friend, Katie, had been white. Her mother was white. She was white—partly. And until that day when the mean girls had brought up the color of her skin, pushed her off the swings into the mud, calling her *Darkie*, she'd never seen herself as different. Her mother had always told her she was extra *special* because she was both black and white, though.

Sara Sullivan you're special.

Over the years, she'd grown complacent to the occasional clutched purse as she passed on the street, and the locking car doors, as she pulled up next to another car, as if she had the ability to steal something while driving, herself. Complacent to the closer scrutiny of her shopping cart, the suspicious looks that weren't directed toward white women.

She ran up the back stairs to her office now, peered out the window. The police had the young man who had bellowed the racial slurs at her in handcuffs, but the scene still made her uneasy. There were several kids rubbing their eyes—the cops had resorted to using pepper spray. She turned away from the window and she opened her laptop and she searched, "Wesley Lindstrom," in the web browser.

The search immediately returned thousands of results: Wes Lindstrom was a top investment banker at Gnash Financial. He was a graduate of Harvard University and Marty was right—he had raised billions in capital lobbying for the drug companies. Why had she never heard of the guy? She clicked on the full-page article that had appeared on the front page of the *New York Times* back in 2009 when she'd first met with Lindstrom's wife, Jane Morgan. The blue blooded couple had been married the previous year and there was a three-page photo spread of their nuptials in the Hamptons in *Town and Country*.

She had to admit, she was envious after reading that one.

She continued searching down the results and discovered something intriguing: Wes Lindstrom had raised over 300 million dollars in capital for two small drug companies, NewfoundVax in Labrador, Canada, and Phaedrex in Bethesda. They'd received the funds from the U.S. government in December of 2012 to develop both a cure and a vaccine for the *Labrador* virus, a deadly hemorrhagic RNA virus more contagious and virulent than any previously known in Africa, including the most deadly known to man thus far, the Ebola virus *Zaire* strain. *Labrador* contained ribonucleic acid as its genetic material.

It could mutate rapidly.

The zoonotic virus was believed to emerge from eating bush meat, including fruit bats that many Africans considered a delicacy, and it spread when the animals came into contact with humans. Only two outbreaks had been known to man, and both had killed over 70 percent of those people infected.

She swallowed, knowing a similar illness was now hitting several U.S. cities hard, including Atlanta, Baltimore, Detroit, and D.C. And from the news broadcast she'd heard earlier, she knew it might even be the same virus at her doorstep in the George Washington ER.

How did Marty know so much about Lindstrom?

And why did he think the guy was such a creep?

It sounded like Lindstrom had things under control; his group was correct to secure funds and try to work out a cure. What was the hold up? Why wasn't the medical community getting a vaccine out to people while the virus was devastating the nation? Was it even the same virus? She had so many questions now, and so few answers. She didn't even know where to look to find them.

A knock at her office door startled her, and she snapped her laptop shut.

Dr. Amy Daust opened the door. "Didn't realize you were working late, Sara."

"Come in, please," she said.

Amy Daust lingered in the doorway. Short stature and short red hair and a long white coat and ballet flats. Hands in her pockets, turned up nose, scoping out her office. "Anything important?"

The hallway was empty. The air conditioning was on too high. She was freezing.

"Just had a few odds and ends to tie up. Marty and I were out for dinner."

"I need to verify a few things about the patients you saw this week."

"Okay."

"Regarding the patients you admitted with fever, nausea, and vomiting, do you remember their duration of their symptoms?"

"Two had been symptomatic for a few days, and one had symptoms for over a week."

Daust said, "As you may know, we've had several cases at GWU that have presented with symptoms of *Labrador* virus."

"Is that all?" She wanted to do a more thorough search on Wes Lindstrom, but Daust was hovering over her desk.

"Unfortunately, no, Sara. Because you've come into direct contact with these patients, you're at risk. Healthcare providers and their families and people who care for the sick seem to be the ones at greatest risk for contracting the disease."

"And blacks."

"Yes, Sara. African-Americans."

Her stomach knotted. The lulling effects of the Shiraz hadn't quite worn off, and she thought about what Marty had said about being more committed to their family.

"You'll need to self-monitor your temperature. The incubation period for the virus can be up to two weeks." Daust stepped back. Another mean girl accusing her of carrying cooties or looking for a reason to exclude her because she was *special.*

Or was her childhood past overanalyzing Daust's behavior?

Terrified, she said, "Okay."

"If you develop any symptoms—including high fever, nausea, vomiting, headache, sore throat or fever, you'll need to quarantine yourself for fourteen days, until the deadly virus can be ruled out."

She took off her white lab coat and she put on her jacket and she grabbed her purse. "Self-quarantine? Two-week monitoring?"

"Those are direct guidelines—orders—from the Department of Health and the CDC." Nervous ballet flats shuffling, anxious to leave.

"Got it."

Daust stepped further away from her now, like she was afraid. Paranoid, even.

Sara wasn't imagining it.

"We're waiting for direct confirmation regarding the specimens we sent to CDC. I'll call you with the identity of the virus as soon as I have answers. I'm sorry, Sara. Try to get some sleep tonight. We need everyone on our team here on board and healthy," said Daust.

"Perfect," she said.

She shook her head and she closed the door behind her, locked her office. She hadn't done anything wrong. She took care of her patients with empathy. Compassion. Why did she feel like an outcast?

-4-

Sara Sullivan

The crowd had dispersed when Sara left the hospital. She drove down Independence, thinking about what Marty had said. Exposing Elyse and him to the virus was too much of a risk. She decided she'd tell Amy Daust on Monday that she was taking a leave of absence.

Marty made more than enough in overtime to support the three of them, give Elyse a good life. As much as she hated to admit it to him, maybe he was right. Maybe she couldn't have it all.

Maybe she was afraid to even try.

But she hadn't driven more than a block before she saw the police strobe lights flashing in the rearview mirror. At first she laughed at the luminous beacons, certain it was Marty, stirring the pot. The college students walking to and from the bars and cafes all turned and stared as she pulled the car to a halt on the red brick street dotted with wrought iron lampposts and hanging potted petunias.

The officer approached the car, but it wasn't Marty.

"License and registration please."

"I'm sorry officer," she said. "How fast was I going?"

"Ma'am, you were all over the road. You didn't stop at the stop sign and you were going ten *under* the posted limit. Where are we going tonight?"

She fumbled through the console and the glove compartment and her purse. She found her registration, but her license was expired. "Dinner—work—I mean, I was out to dinner with my husband—he's a cop—and then I went into work. I'm a doctor and I'm—"

"How much have you had to drink, Doctor?"

Police Headquarters, 16ᵗʰ Precinct
Washington, D.C.

Sara paced the holding cell of the 16ᵗʰ Precinct, waiting for Marty to arrive. She stared at the other woman in the cell, who'd been brought in for possession of marijuana. The evening had gone from bad to worse, and she wanted more than anything to collapse in her own bed. Slip into a sonorous dream like she always did when she was sleep deprived, even though Marty always complained that she snored like a drunken sailor.

Tonight was a nightmare.

"Did we get the right girl, Frank?" The two officers in blue sat behind the desk, sipping coffee and peering through the bars. One unwrapped a chocolate bar, offered it to the other. "She's sweating it out in there."

"Plates match the ones Marty gave us." Officer Frank Bochialo shrugged and tapped his pen on his report and took his feet down off the wooden desk. Then he walked over to Sara's cell.

"You alright in there, Doctor?" officer Killian asked.

Sara grabbed the bars as she rose from the bench, madder than a hornet, but sober, finally. She skipped the honeypot routine. Skipped any sweet talk. It was too humiliating now. "You're going to have a lot of explaining to do when my fiancé gets here. And I want to talk to my lawyer."

"Alright, Miss, just sit tight." The officer went back to his desk and he sipped his coffee and he rubbed his neck.

Her cellmate was a middle-aged woman who reeked of alcohol and urine. The woman shook her head and mumbled to herself and picked at the cuts and an abrasion on her forearm where maggots had infested it. Pearly grubs burrowed in her inflamed flesh. She circled the room.

Outside the cell, the officers shook Marty's hand as he arrived in the holding center. Marty took his jacket off and hung it on the back of a swivel chair. She cracked her knuckles as she sat on the wooden bench behind bars, trying to make out their conversation.

"What's this all about—you two have a falling out? Calling off the wedding?"

"Nothing like that. Thanks for finding her and bringing her in, Frank." Marty patted his partner on the back. "She's been drinking a lot lately. I felt we needed an intervention."

Sara heard only mumbled voices through the mirrored glass.

Marty's partner nodded, said, "She refused the Breathalyzer test and requested it be done by a physician. Whatever was in her system is gone now, but refusing to take the test is an automatic license suspension. You tell me how you want it handled."

"Perfect. She's got a lot going on at work with this virus having D.C. by the short hairs. Our daughter's so young." His partner escorted him to Sara's cell, unlocked the gate. "She can use the time off to focus on what's important."

"Easy princess," Frank said to the other inmate, who pushed past Sara to the entrance. "You'll get your turn." Bochialo held the female prisoner back and locked the gate and ushered Sara and Marty to a conference room.

"Will you please tell him I'm fine? Tell them I'm sober."

"It's okay." Marty put his arm around her. "I'm sorry this happened. I'll bail you out and we'll just follow the proper channels and get you out of here."

"How does that help me, Marty? I wasn't drunk. I had some wine but—you know what? Never mind. I'm not saying another word until I talk to my attorney." Sara pointed her finger at Marty and whispered, "Do you have any idea how damaging this could be to my career?"

Phaedrex Clinical Trials Lab
Bethesda Maryland

Ordinarily, the students and employees entered the lab from the front using their ID badges, even when working into the night. But tonight, while the lab was closed for a student holiday, the darkly clothed individual parked his car several blocks from the Natural Sciences Building on campus and knocked on the door until the nightshift janitor, who, more often than not, could be found in the back hallway break room, let him in without showing identification. The man proceeded down the hallway with the brim of his Braves ball cap pointed down and his sunglasses on, avoiding the cameras at the ends of the hall, toward Professor LeTorneau's office in the middle of the corridor. He grabbed the professor's laptop and then searched through his two desk drawers and his shelves. Then he put every USB flash drive and CD he could find into his jacket pockets, and took the elevator up to the fourth floor.

Sara Sullivan

Later that evening, Sara sat alone at her computer, searching for information, waiting for a call from her attorney, Harold Patterson. The way the illness was spreading around D.C. didn't make sense. If Lindstrom had secured so much capital for the drug companies to cure the horrible virus, why wasn't the CDC making it available? And why weren't they doing more to contain it? She'd witnessed firsthand what these tropical filoviruses could do. Ebola caused hemorrhagic shock. Internal bleeding. The recovery rate was dismal. Filoviruses were rare, but incredibly deadly.

And now one was spreading through the District with no explanation.

In her third year of medical school, she'd traveled to Sierra Leone on a medical mission. She was idealistic. Ready to save the world. Rescue poor starving children. Back then, marriage and a family was the last thing on her mind. What she'd seen in the poorly staffed hospital clinics made of rotted wood with tin roofs and dirt floors, lined with filthy mattresses instead of sterile hospital gurneys, was permanently etched in her mind. Children lying in pools of their own vomit. Orphans knocking at the doors in search of their deceased relatives. Violence in the streets, rioting victims struggling for limited access to the clinics. The horrific tropical fevers that swept the area grew to endemic proportions until the Department of Health had ordered all of the doctors to evacuate the area. The scorching African heat and hundreds of victims that were turned away now flashed in her mind.

The smell of blood and vomit.

The poverty was so unbearable to witness that she didn't fault others for turning their heads to it, when there was little they could do to help. Without the money to build sanitary hospitals and educate the people, progress was slow. It terrified her as a doctor, but so much more so now as a parent. Luckily, the outbreak had been contained, but the death toll had been in the thousands. Some had suggested that the virus remained dormant in those that survived, in the vitreous humor of the eye, immunologically sequestered and hidden, waiting to reemerge. She'd returned home healthy, and no cases had occurred outside of the isolated rural areas of Africa. *But in the United States?* How could this happen in the greatest country in the free world?

She searched the extensive database of international news websites, but she couldn't find a current African case of *Labrador*. *What was the common denominator?* The phone rang as she was dozing off at her desk now, but it wasn't her lawyer. It was the hospital.

She let the call go to voicemail.

If she was convicted of DUI, it could mean a loss of hospital privileges or worse, suspension of her medical license.

"Sara this is Amy Daust. I'm sorry to bother you. It's imperative that I speak to you regarding the patients you treated this week. We have CDC lab confirmation on the specimens you sent off. The RNA sequencing for the virus in this outbreak has been matched with the biohazardous *Labrador* virus housed at NIH. All three of your patients came back positive and have been moved to isolation. Please call me at the hospital as soon as you can. Let me give you my cell phone number as well. It's—"

She erased the message.

Labrador virus—the same microbe that Lindstrom had commissioned Phaedrex and NewfoundVax to cure and prevent. If the research started in 2009, back when she pitched the story to Jane Morgan about the biologic weapon being released, she should've heard about it. Was the FDA really that bureaucratic that they couldn't get people the help they needed when they were dying? Her eyes darted back and forth as she examined the CNN website for the latest case numbers nationwide.

The case numbers weren't just *increasing*, they were *doubling exponentially* with every incubation period.

She did the math.

With a fourteen-day incubation phase, during which time the virus could travel by airplane or cruise ship or subway, undetected—combined with the 90 percent mortality associated with it—millions of people worldwide would die if *Labrador* wasn't stopped.

Just like in her novel.

Even the most sophisticated healthcare systems in the world couldn't handle exponential numbers of critical care patients. An ICU stay could cost well over one-hundred thousand dollars. There was no way that even the United States, or other developed nations, could provide healthcare access to those numbers of patients. There weren't even enough beds.

Ventilators.

Dialysis units.

Labrador caused multi-organ system failure.

She swallowed the hard lump that had balled up in the back of her throat, shut down her computer.

Millions will die.

It's an apocalyptic certainty.

She approached Elyse's crib where she was sleeping soundly. Her delicate infant took a few sniffle-like breaths in, and a long breath out, rolled onto her left side. Elyse placed her tiny hands on her face. Her skin was even lighter brown than Sara's complexion. Her eyes were blue like Marty's, her cries angelic. She wondered how Elyse would see herself in the mess of the world around them, and if she'd live to be a mother herself. She'd blessed their lives on the Fourth of July when she came into the world. How ironic, she'd thought.

Fireworks.

Celebrations.

Now surrender your independence, mama.

She and Marty had been struggling to maintain their relationship. Now, somehow, when she looked into her eyes and saw the reflection of everything she wanted for herself and her family, it was enough to sustain her for another day.

She wound Elyse's music box, played a soft lullaby. She closed the nursery door and cuddled up next to Marty in front of the television. MSNBC was broadcasting another riot, sparked by the suspicions brought on by the epidemic. Apparently the survival rate in the white population was much higher than in blacks, which spurred accusations of racism. Some claimed Caucasians received better medical treatment. The overall mistrust incited brutal outbursts of violence and conspiracy theories of all kinds that she watched now from their living room sofa. She could still smell the scent of Elyse's baby powder on her hands.

"Maybe *you* should be the one staying home from work." She kissed him on the cheek.

Marty chuckled, stiffened his frame. "I think I can handle it."

"Oh, you're such a tough guy," she mocked.

"Two officers shot in Detroit during a riot that started in an ambulance. They were just trying to do their job." Marty shook his head. "We can't control the crowds these days without this fucker showing up and playing the race card." He poked an angry finger toward the activist for the NAACP who was being interviewed about the unfolding conflict.

"When I went into the hospital tonight," she started. "There was protesting—kids throwing racial slurs at me. *Me, Marty!* I was just trying to get to work. It's not always blacks not cooperating with authority." She and Marty had had so many interests in common and such an intense attraction to one another, that she sometimes forgot that they were a biracial couple.

But tonight, he seemed different.

"Sara, I'm sorry." Marty stood and put his arms around her and pulled her close and turned his baseball cap around, but she pulled back. "I never assume that. I don't see you the way I see everybody else."

"I never used to think you did." She turned away and she opened the fridge and she poured a glass of milk.

"I mean it, Sara." Marty followed her into the kitchen. "I hope in that huge heart of yours I love, that you can understand why I did what I did tonight."

"What?"

She was still holding the milk carton. It was as if she was watching her own life from a distance then, in slow motion, as she slammed it on the granite countertop. It splashed on the floor. The events made sense now.

He'd set her up.

Her partner was supposed to make life *easier*. Not orchestrate a plan to sabotage her career. He touched her forearm, but she demanded the truth. "Did your buddy, Frank, *know* I was leaving the hospital?"

"Sara, I care too much about you and Elyse to let you risk your life at that hospital. This is what we needed—a break from it all. Trust me." His voice was gentle, pleading, but to her it all sounded patronizing.

She backed away from him, pointing her finger at him. "*You* did this to me? Marty this is my career we're talking about. I waited an hour for you and had one extra glass of wine just so you could set me up like a common criminal. How could you betray me like this?"

"Sara, I love you. You're just so stubborn."

She overturned the flowers he'd presented her at dinner, spilling the water and shattering the glass vase all over the floor. Then she removed her engagement ring and she held it up and she tossed it at him and he caught it.

"Leave me alone, Marty," she insisted, as he held her wrist. There was no arguing with her. She pulled away and she grabbed her purse and his keys and the paper on which she'd written the address of the Bethesda lab.

"Sara, you can't. Your license—"

From the second floor of the brownstone, she heard Elyse begin to stir. Her gentle crying quickly progressed to loud wailing, but Sara headed for the door.

"I'm warning you, Marty." And she left and she slammed the door behind her.

Miami Beach

2009

Edward Marburg

Wes Lindstrom lit a cigar. He sat poolside in his trunks and hotel robe at the Four Seasons Miami. "Can we count on the NIH funding for these companies, Ed?"

Edward Marburg considered the request, applied sunscreen to his light-skinned nose and cheeks. Without it, his fair complexion burned like a biscuit. Lindstrom offered him a Cuban.

"Thank you, no." It was amazing what details the paparazzi could zero in on if they wanted to launch a smear campaign, and midterm elections were close. He had recently created a public initiative on smoking cessation, focusing on public places. No sense in destroying that goodwill now.

"This heat excites my sex drive." Lindstrom tasted the cigar and slid his beige 70's style sunglasses up on his forehead. "I'll have another Scotch. Thank you, dear," Lindstrom said to the poolside waitress, uniformed in sneakers and a visor and a short tennis skirt.

She smiled, hurried off with her notepad. The Florida palms shaded their table, and a breeze off the briny Atlantic made the humidity a bit more tolerable. Beautiful Latina models and their wealthy companions were lunching at the poolside grille nearby. Bronzed bodies passed their cabana, leaving a trail of expensive perfume in their wake. But Miami wasn't his scene. Lindstrom, on the other hand, looked at ease with the barefoot-couture culture. Guests drunk by noon and rubbing elbows over blueberry mojitos. Mango chutney chicken salads coasting by atop white linen serving platters.

"Wes," he began, "you know I'm your biggest voice when there's a profit to be made. It's just that these rare diseases don't usually pay off. And you're asking for over three-hundred million in capital for these companies? It simply wouldn't be profitable."

"FDA is focusing on neglected diseases, Ed. They're offering incentives to push companies' newest products through faster, if they can develop cures for rare ailments and curb the cost."

Marburg winked at the waitress. She set down his drink, smiled at Lindstrom.

Lindstrom continued, "There's no future in chemo drugs anymore. The insurance companies are figuring out fast that they've always got another one in the pipeline that's basically the same as the last. They cook up a research paper that claims the drugs prolong survival a few more months. Turn a cis-Platinum into a trans-Platinum, throw on an alcohol group, cook up a few changes in the old medicinal chemistry lab. Nobody wants to reimburse them. And if the privates won't pay, then neither will Medicare, and without government purchasing blocks, the stocks will tank."

"I hear what you're saying, Wes. But the costs are astronomical. There's never been a case of *Labrador* virus in the U.S." He took a cigar now and he lit it and he tasted it and he ordered what Lindstrom was having. Fuck the paparazzi and public opinion. Florida was like a different country altogether. "There is just no pay off. It's like all these rare genetic diseases. They only occur one in hundreds of thousands. The treatment costs a cock and a leg and the patients have no money to pay for them."

He looked toward the ocean. The breakers were high and the resort had posted a red flag warning against surfing. The current was strong. Jellyfish littered the beach.

"Ed."

"Drug companies aren't into doing charity work, Wes."

Lindstrom's voice was cocky and his wide grin impossible to refuse. "What if I could guarantee a profit? I'm not talking a Google here, but at least twenty million in a year or two once we get it to market—enough to make an easy couple million on the stock without any Feds questioning you." Lindstrom leaned back and put his feet up on the teakwood lounge chair. An attendant offered him a lemon-scented moist wash cloth with stainless steel tongs from her tray. Lindstrom took it and wiped his face and tasted the cigar and adjusted his glasses.

"How?" He loosened his blue silk tie and removed his jacket. "We're not into sending money to help the plight of the poor and sick and famished unless it aligns with our own finances, Wes. You know that as well as I do."

"That's why it's a guarantee." Lindstrom leaned in closer now. "I'm talking about starting a little *fire*, Ed."

"Nothing short of an outbreak on our own soil would make treating *Labrador* profitable."

"*Exactamundo*. Nothing we can't handle, of course. Why, we've got the finest healthcare system in the world. These Third World countries have no chance against these tropical fevers, but in *America*, land of the free..." Lindstrom held the cigar and his arms toward the sky. His arched brows rose and he smiled his wide, sexy smile. Then he put down the cigar and he took his feet down and he crossed his arms. "A few cases here wouldn't hurt a thing. In fact, it would show the world what we're made of."

"We're not talking about a cold and flu here. You do realize that, don't you? Even the influenza vaccine has its roadblocks with these anti-immunization nut jobs running off at the mouth on social media. They're a menace to public health."

Lindstrom rose from the teakwood chair now, and his back looked stiff as he walked. "Senator, I'm in bed with these drug companies. It's an impossible undertaking sometimes. Take pity on me—but it's what these guys do. You have to trust me."

Lindstrom held the cigar up in the air now as he spoke and he rubbed his temple where his aviator shades rested. He walked to the glass water pitcher filled with cucumbers and hibiscus and he poured himself a glass and he sat back down with his elbows on his knees.

"*Labrador* is designated as Biohazard level 4, Wes. Except for a few outbreaks, it's only been kept in a high security NIH lab in Wisconsin. Fucking Wisconsin, Wes." He tasted his own drink again, imagining an isolated lab in a frozen tundra speckled with moose and lumberjacks and wood chippers. "You're suggesting it would be okay for it to float rampantly through Manhattan? Miami? *The capital?*"

That was Wes Lindstrom's special, and what had made him a multimillionaire—turning adversity into opportunity. He'd known him for years. One man's loss was another man's gain. Wes pooh-poohed his concern and waved it off with the cigar.

"That's *exactly* why we need to treat and cure *Labrador*, Ed. Especially for the military. Did you know they're predicting an 80 percent chance of a biohazardous act of terrorism within the next few years?"

"*They* certainly have a lot of predictions, don't they?"

"Ed."

A Latina model swam up to the edge of the pool. Long stem legs. Grapefruit breasts. He sipped his Scotch and he saw her smile at Lindstrom, a man at least thirty years her senior. Lindstrom estimated a few calculations on a napkin of what it would take for an investment of three million to pay off in terms of drugs and vaccines, passed it to him.

"Well that is something I can take to Congress," he said. "You're talking about a few serious cases? Enough to get everyone at FDA onboard and America demanding a vaccine?"

Lindstrom nodded. "One that's ready to go. That's all I'm talking about."

He rose from his lounge and shook Lindstrom's hand and the investor flashed his inarguably sexy smile. It was going to be a good day.

Sara Sullivan

Sara fled down the steps of the N Street brownstone, across a cobblestone path to the garage. She started the ignition, and although she'd only driven a standard transmission a handful of times, she raced down the Beltway in Marty's truck, around the curves, and out onto Highway 66, heading to the southwest quadrant of the District. The late summer foliage, beneath the lights, was full of Chardonnay and pumpkin and mocha hues now, and the smell of the leaves and the midnight air was crisp and cleansing. She put both windows down.

The road seemed synonymous with her life—an endless ribbon of changing responsibilities, and everyone thinking they had it all figured out for her and that's all there was until she rounded a corner and there was another one-way street pointing her which way to go. Marty had decided they should get married. Her family didn't openly discourage her writing screenplays and novels, but they didn't exactly take it seriously either, and they all kept telling her to focus on Elyse. Even her boss at the hospital seemed to have an opinion on right where she needed to be professionally, and the hospital protocols seemed to dictate her every medical decision. She didn't necessarily disagree with any of them—well, maybe Marty sometimes, but it was this quest for control over her decisions that she resisted, so much so that she sabotaged her own endeavors at times just to defy all of them.

She checked the rearview, and after she'd driven a few minutes, she slowed the truck and turned down the music, aware that she was driving with a suspended license. She didn't exactly have a plan for where she was going, but she'd just needed to get out of the house.

12:23 a.m. She pulled over and called her mother.

"Hi, Mom," she said. "I was wondering if I could swing by? And I forgot to ask if you could take care of the bird while we're out of town next weekend."

"That Amazon is a filthy animal," said her mother, Charlotte Sullivan, referring to Sara and Marty's Amazon McCaw parrot, Jimmy. "Why do you allow it in the house? I never kept animals in the house when you were growing up."

"Jimmy's not going anywhere. I didn't like it when Marty suggested getting a bird that lives longer than some people do, but I've gotten used to him."

"There's no telling what that Amazon will do. I won't have any part of it."

"It's not going away, Mom."

"No good can come of that beast. It will bite the baby's fingers off and eat them like tater tots," her mother predicted, in her syrupy drawl. She told Sara that she'd been out late and was in bed for the night, and that she'd call her in the morning, refusing to admit that her male companion was spending the night.

"Alright, Mom." She was close to tears now.

12:30 a.m.

She continued down Michigan Avenue, past the college bars. She entered the parking garage of the Westin Hotel and she checked into a single room and she told the desk not to allow any calls.

An hour later, she lay awake in bed. Marty had called her cell phone seven times now. She answered on his eighth attempt.

"What?"

"Are you okay?"

"I'm fine, Marty. How could you do that to me?"

"How's the room? Is it on your credit card or mine?"

"How do you even know where I am?"

"Vehicle recovery, sweetie. It's on my truck."

"Christ."

"Sara, please just come back. The attorney called. This will all be fine. I promise. I'm sorry for what I did."

"Marty, I don't want to see you now. I want to be with Elyse and you. But I need to be the one running my life, not letting it—or you—run me." She turned on the light and the laptop computer on the desk and connected to the hotel's Wi-Fi network. "I'll be home in the morning." Her little Tic Tac was still screaming in the background, but Marty was a big boy. He could handle it.

She hung up the cell phone.

She logged into her email and read a few pages of the story she'd sent Jane Morgan. There were so many similarities to the crisis unfolding before her eyes. She flicked the hotel TV on and tuned to CNN, which was broadcasting another riot. This time it was in Detroit. The virus was killing African-Americans in staggering numbers, but infected Caucasians had a more optimistic prognosis. Meanwhile, some people directed blame to Africa, insisting that the virus had somehow spread from the jungle, yet no index cases had confirmed that. She shuddered as the reporter spoke. Behind him, a body was carried away by men in hazmat suits.

Protesters screamed.

A building burned in the background.

The footage cut to the station.

No wonder everyone was falling apart. What was more alarming to her was the number of healthcare workers becoming infected. Each patient seemed to infect two to three healthcare employees, yet the press was mitigating the scenario, and reporting that everything was under control—indoctrinating the masses.

No need to panic.

Run of the mill Biohazard level 4 virus.

She felt alone now and she thought of Elyse, and she wished she were home. She typed Wesley Lindstrom's name into the search engine again, tried a different approach.

Everything in D.C. was political.

She searched his campaign contributions and found that Wes Lindstrom's investment firm had contributed over two million dollars to elect Senator Edward Marburg by way of a 527 political organization, a tax-exempt group created to influence the appointment of a candidate, with no upper limits on campaign contributions. Marburg was a powerful advocate for the drug companies, objecting to Medicare's negotiating with the drug companies. This kept their rates based on supply and demand, and the profits high for the big pharmaceutical giants.

When she finally felt her eyes start to close, she turned off the laptop and crawled beneath the tightly tucked sheets. The cell phone rang again but this time, it wasn't Marty.

-5-

George Washington Hospital
Sara Sullivan

When Sara came to work the next day, the protesters and the police had reconvened in an even larger and more raucous crowd outside the emergency room entrance. The group seemed to have doubled in size, and the police were using wooden sawhorses to contain them to a well- defined area. Signs that read: STOP THE SPREAD in big red and black letters were hoisted in the air. George Washington had reached the maximum number of patients with the deadly virus they could accept. Caring for infected patients required a specialized negative pressure room ventilation system, and the critical care staff was simply overwhelmed. The officer informed her that currently, all patients were being diverted to Howard University Hospital.

Around her, the sky grayed to an electric pallor. Thunder cracked. Her hair bristled as she hurried toward the doors, past a sick man, a homeless black man, convulsing on a bench beside a huge dumpster. His back rose off the splintered wood in violent contortions and he coughed, choking on his own vomit, perspiring in a drenching sweat. The blood of his excrements streaked his torn clothing. Healthcare workers in white suits and blue gloves swarmed the crowd. She covered her mouth and she gagged on the odor of urine and vomitus and she paused at the scene and her face hollowed, observing the impecunious man, ravaged by fever.

Behind her, she felt a hand reach across her back.

She spun around, startled.

"You belong in the slave pen, Kizzie," One of the protesters, a college kid, shouted at her, referring to the old slave markets or so-called pens that once stood outside Wisconsin and M Streets, where taverns and upscale designer clothing stores now flourished. The officer on duty held her back as she lunged toward the young man, who continued to laugh and taunt her. With pagan eyes and alabaster skin, his simian dance mocked her.

"A pen is for a pig and I'm looking at one," she shouted back. She felt a ferocity in her eyes until finally, they glazed with tears.

She was broken.

The officer restrained her from going any further.

"Dr. Sullivan is importing disease from Africa," someone called.

"Naw, she should go *back* to Africa," another protester yelled, "with the rest of the monkeys." The man punctuated his remark with a crude imitation of a monkey scratching its ribs.

"How do they know my name?" She turned to the officer, who quickly released his hold on her.

"Easy, Doctor," the officer said as she faced the crowd's racist remarks. He eased her back onto the sidewalk. A security guard stepped in to push the protesters further back off hospital property. "You are Dr. Sullivan, then?"

"Yeah, that's me." She was furious at the demonstration, felt her adrenaline surging as she looked into the sea of faces. Malevolent, racist faces looking back at her, smoldering an eruption of hate. She rushed toward the sliding glass doors, under the red neon emergency room sign.

"I'll need you to follow me." She was puzzled, but she obliged. "This way, Doctor."

The security guard led her to the conference room and asked if she wanted some coffee or water or soda to drink. She waited in the sterile room, a black hole with décor bereft of human warmth, as though all the so-called empathy of the medical profession had been sucked from it by some massive celestial vacuum. She sat down at the granite table, waiting for the chief of the department, and she cracked her knuckles as she thought about the verbal assaults, anxious to hear what the administration planned to do to stop them. Presently, Dr. Daust entered the room and sat down.

"Sara, we have laboratory identification from the patients you admitted. The CDC has finally matched them, along with the majority of the unrecognized viruses that have surfaced in major cities over the last few days, to a very rare strain of virus." Dressed in her usual white lab coat and well-tailored suit, Dr. Daust eyed her critically, and then smiled. "I'm glad to see you're feeling well. I tried to call you last night."

"Except for the way I've been treated coming into work, I'm fine. I'm tired, Amy. I went to sleep last night after the first time you called." She stole a glance at the paper in her superior's folder as Amy Daust flipped though her pages. "Do you have any idea of the racism I've seen lately? I didn't believe it when

I saw it on TV, but I've experienced it right here this afternoon and last night."

Suddenly, Daust was no longer smiling. "Dr. Sullivan, my sincerest apologizes. We're actively working to maintain our employees' safety."

Even Jimmy sounded more intelligent when he parroted the lines of others. And he was a real parrot. Daust sounded like she had memorized the entire *Labrador* public relations manual—if there was one.

"I don't feel safe coming into work and being called a monkey. And a nigger," she said, rising from the table.

Daust remained cool. "I understand you performed the blood draws yourself and labeled the specimens for the lab. Is that correct?"

"That's right." She sat back down. "The nurse was having trouble getting blood, so I helped her draw the sample and I labeled it for the technician. The patient had been vomiting profusely for two days and was very dehydrated." She prided herself on being very skilled at difficult IV access. She was the one they always called on when they couldn't get a blood draw from a patient, or an IV on a patient with poor venous access. It sometimes made more work for her, but she was always happy to help.

"Did you come into contact with any of the patient's bodily fluids?"

"No. I mean—I don't think so. I'm always very careful and wear gloves."

"What about a mask?"

She shook her head. "I don't remember, why?"

"The virus the CDC has identified is called *Labrador* virus, Sara. It has only been identified in one previous outbreak in Africa. The only other virus specimens are housed at top security NIH labs."

She knew all this already.

"How are the patients doing?"

"Two of them are doing fine." Amy Daust shifted her papers nervously and took a sip of her tea, cleared her throat. "One of them has rapidly deteriorated and has been placed on a ventilator. She'll need dialysis."

"Which patient? I saw three." She already had an idea.

"Lydia Monroe."

"The black woman?"

"Yes, Sara. She's not progressing well. She's quickly entered the most serious phase of the illness and her body is mounting very prominent inflammatory and immune responses to the organism. We're not really sure why some individuals react so strongly."

"You mean black people."

"Yes, Doctor. Different races are behaving with various presentations with regard to the illness." Daust slid the folder across the table now to her along with a pen. "I'd like you to take a look at this form, please, Dr. Sullivan."

She opened the folder and her eyes darted back and forth as she read the disclosure marked: VOLUNTARY QUARANTINE.

"What is this about?" She closed the folder and slid it back to Daust.

"Sara, this virus was previously only housed for study and is communicable and known to the government as a potential biologic weapon. Anyone who comes into contact with it infects an average of two additional people. Those people infect two more people, and so on…I'm sure you can appreciate the implications."

"How did this outbreak get started?"

"Sara, did you travel to Africa in the past?"

"Yes, but I never got sick, and—"

"Sara, we're both doctors. But naturally there are a lot of things we don't know. We have no experience with it. We have to trust that the government knows more than we do. They've been studying it for years."

She looked at the form again. "You want me to stay home and not report to work?" *Marty will love that.* Everyone had it all figured out for her, but she was starting to think he was right.

"Actually, Sara, the people at most risk of infection are healthcare workers and their families."

"Is that what we are now—healthcare workers? So you and I are the same as Ms. Principal serving wheat cakes in the cafeteria? Is she going to save the patients from *Labrador* then?" She looked away and then back at Daust. "I'm a doctor, Amy. I thought about taking a leave of absence, but—I can't stay home. I want to help people."

"We take your health very seriously and we want to keep you and your family free from this infection, Sara."

"Why aren't they protecting us from this virus?"

"*They,* Sara?"

"Yeah, *they*. The CDC. The FDA. The United States government." She stood up now, but the security guard held the door closed. "Why is *Labrador* only devastating the African-American population?"

"Sara, please sit down," said Amy Daust.

She turned and ran her hand through her short brown hair and then returned to her seat. "I'm not going anywhere."

"We're trying to protect *everyone*. That's why we're most concerned for our staff and their families. I trust you don't want your newborn daughter to get sick?"

"Of course not," she said, opening the form again.

"She's beautiful, by the way. I saw her picture on your desk. What's her name?"

"Thank you." She smiled, but it was forced. When had Amy Daust been in her office? The other night, she seemed afraid to come into contact with her. Didn't even cross the threshold. "Elyse. Elyse is her name."

"We're asking that you sign the voluntary fourteen-day order of self-quarantine. That's the longest known incubation period during which symptoms can occur."

"And not come to work?" She rubbed her temple as she read the form, feeling defeated, exhausted.

"Actually, we'll need you to remain in quarantine at the hospital. We've arranged for you to use one of the on call rooms with a kitchen, and access to your chart work, the Internet, the—"

"You want me to stay *here?* For fourteen days? But I don't even have symptoms of illness. I've researched *Labrador* virus myself and it isn't contagious until symptoms appear."

Another doctor in a long white coat and a tall blond-haired man in a poorly fitting suit entered the room now, blocking the door behind her. She immediately recognized both. The physician was one of the hospital psychiatrists and he served on the administrative board. The other was the CEO of the hospital, Benjamin Lawrence. Lawrence was a stout man who spent more time in the cafeteria than he did seeing patients.

"Sara, the consequences of spreading the infection in exposed individuals is something the CDC is weighing very carefully," said Daust. "They've successfully handled outbreaks such as this in the past by contact tracing and isolation."

"And if I don't sign the voluntary quarantine?"

"We are under direct orders by the Department of Health to use the two physician consent rule whereby two physicians' signatures can mandate a treatment or medical intervention."

She turned around to face the door to the conference room, where Benjamin Lawrence and the psychiatrist, Dr. Tomassi, were standing with their pens in hand.

-6-

Sara Sullivan

The hospital room assigned to Sara was nothing short of depressing, devoid of windows and everything but the most fundamental amenities: a toilet and a porcelain sink and an open shower without a curtain. A small desk and a computer were positioned beside the bed, and a television was mounted in a corner of the room. The kitchen they had promised was in fact, a microwave and a compact refrigerator. Dietary came by at mealtime with a tray of food. She was isolated from patient and staff contact at the end of an unused corridor where construction had begun on a new unit. Exposed electrical wires and patches of broken drywall and garbage littered the hallway. Trays and rollers were left behind where an army brown paint job had been left unfinished. The pungent smell of VOCs still saturated the air.

She found it hard to breathe, covered her mouth.

A doctor who was fully gowned and gloved and wearing a respirator mask came by periodically to observe her, peering in the window. Twice a day, he took her temperature and reported back to administration and Dr. Daust.

Her colleagues no doubt appreciated her equanimity under the trying circumstances, but her mind found no repose. Why had she agreed to this? She remembered angrily, she'd had no choice in the matter. Explaining the quarantine to Marty was a dubious task all its own, and he had of course, accused her of her usual recalcitrance and asked her over and over why she'd been so stubborn and not listened to him in the first place, even joked about spanking her again, which was the last thing she was in the mood for now, but would've chosen over her current lot, given the options. Two days passed, and she demonstrated no symptoms consistent with infection. She remained afebrile.

98.6 degrees. Another week and a half to go.

She looked at the pictures of her baby, Elyse, on her cell phone, and she missed her terribly and she felt a simmering anger and a hunger now, longing to see her chubby, luscious little legs and cheeks and experience her baby smell all diapered and soft and downy. Elyse's tiny hand wrapped around her finger.

It was two weeks she'd never get back.

On the third day, a physician entered the room to draw blood from her to test for the presence of the toxic organism. He was dressed in a white sterile suit, impervious to fluid and hiding every inch of skin from exposure. Thick yellow goggles covered his eyes. Blue plastic booties over his shoes. His face was hidden by an n95 respirator mask, worn tightly over his nose and mouth.

"If this second set of lab tests come back negative from CDC, you can almost guarantee you're out of the woods, Doctor. But we still have to follow protocol." The man's voice echoed through the insectine mask. He moved awkwardly, wobbling around the room. The love child of the Creature from the Black Lagoon and the StayPuft Marshmallow Man.

"I didn't know there was one."

"Your husband dropped off some more clothes and some personal belongings." The man tossed her Marty's old duffel bag. Then he scanned the electronic temperature probe across her forehead. "Are your family members exhibiting any signs of illness?"

"No, but neither am I," she snapped.

"Just checking."

Although her body was toned and muscular, she felt diminutive with the man in the white hazmat suit hovering over her bed, looking rather curious. A magnanimous praying mantis.

"Should I be worried?"

"Virus transmission requires close contact. Did you have sexual intercourse, or did any of your secondary contacts come into contact with your blood or bodily fluids?"

She thought now of the quirky sex that she and Marty shared, often.

"My fiancé and I had sex—we do that a lot. Or I should say we did. Before he set me up, and before you all locked me up in here." The quarantine and isolation and personal questions about her family left her feeling violated, but she thought back to that evening, with their safety in mind. "And I breastfed my daughter. As if it's any of anyone's business here."

"Any signs of illness or fever in the child?"

Her brown eyes flashed to him, stormy with resentment now. "Now how would I know that when I'm holed up in here?"

"Sorry, Doctor, just doing my job." The physician was covered from head to toe in personal protective equipment, allowing no exposure, but the goggles gave her a glimpse of his empathetic look.

"It's okay," she said, staring out the window. She looked down at the cars passing on the street. The windows were sealed shut, without even an emergency exit. She changed the subject and she sat on the bed and she regarded the infectious disease specialist. "The baby is doing fine. She's laughing and playing and doing everything I should be doing with her."

"Then there's probably not much to worry about, Doctor. We're not mandated to isolate secondary contacts at this time. But there's the chance that she could develop signs and symptoms before you do—*if* you are *infected*. Infants and children have variable presentations. We'll contact your husband."

She wiped a tear from her eyes, looked away. "How are my patients doing?"

"I'm not allowed to discuss that with you. You're no longer their doctor."

She rose from the bed. The doctor in the protective gown backed away, and she noticed how the stigma of the illness had affected even the most knowledgeable of her colleagues.

The doctor was breathing heavily.

Panicking.

It's not affecting Caucasians the way it's affecting people with color though, is it? She thought for a moment, regarding him patiently, but she wanted to scream and let go of all the repressed anger up inside her that *Labrador* and Marty had created.

Instead, she asked if he needed help.

Slowly, he regained his composure.

Why did the virus have this effect? It seemed to her that *Labrador* virus was an internecine savage, not only attacking people of color, but pitting races against one another, destroying entire families in the process. Was the virus alone an unrelenting murderous killer, or was there something more behind the near state of martial law in the District?

The man breathed heavier now, sinking to the ground in the white suit.

-7-

Sara Sullivan

September 28th, 2014

Almost a week later, Sara sat in the quarantine room, searching the Internet. Its speed seemed stagnant at best, but she had an interminable, discriminatory, unreasonable, five days longer. And what if she went back to work and she was exposed again? The more she researched *Labrador* online, the more fearful she was about even being in the hospital. Yet the media seemed to downplay the calamitous potential of the virus. The American Medical Association was already publishing articles online about how to care for patients with *Labrador*, but doctors and nurses were the ones dying everywhere the virus popped up, and every doctor knew that the AMA was a largely politically-motivated interest group.

Why weren't they doing more to stop the spread?

The press claimed that doctors and nurses were being trained to prevent infection.

Lie.

That hospitals were prepared for *Labrador*.

Lie.

And the biggest lie—that they had *Labrador* under control.

Why hadn't an index case from Africa been identified yet? If no security breach had occurred from the high security labs, then the patient zero for the outbreak must have occurred outside of the United States. Animals were the natural habitat for the organism. All of the other hemorrhagic viruses had a suspected natural reservoir in African mammals including fruit bats, primates and rodents.

But the natural source of infection had never been confirmed.

Anywhere.

She Googled the number to the NIH lab for special emerging diseases and had the hospital operator connect her to their top security lab in Wisconsin. The teleprompts directed callers to press '1' if they were a physician. Then she waited for the next choice; then the next, until she finally reached the lab.

"Hello?"

"This is Dr. Sara Sullivan. I'm calling from D.C., where we're experiencing a large number of cases of *Labrador* virus, as you've probably seen on the news."

"I'm very familiar with the media attention the virus is receiving."

"Who am I speaking with?"

"This is Dr. Simon Oliver. I'm head of the zoonotic lab, and the lead researcher on hemorrhagic viruses, including *Labrador*. If you're calling to report an exposure, I'd be happy to give you the number to the CDC." Oliver's voice was high and light and grating.

"That won't be necessary." She toyed with the pen on the desk and surfed to the medical record system for the hospital. She logged in and she pulled up the information and online records of the patients she'd admitted and diagnosed with the aggressive virus, wrote down some notes. "I have a few questions about some research that may have been commissioned a few years back before the outbreaks occurred. Research on vaccines and treatments for the disease."

"Yes, Doctor?"

The phone went dead.

She rose from the desk and she checked the connection of the landline phone to the wall, and she pressed the receiver several times. The call hadn't disconnected—she'd lost service. There was no dial tone now. She redialed the number from her cell phone, but Marty was calling.

She transferred to his call.

His voice sounded reassuring, even after the stunt he'd pulled, and part of her wanted to tell him that he was right all along. He cut in when she said, "Hi, honey—"

"Sara—Elyse is running a high fever. She's not acting like herself—vomiting, diarrhea, not eating a thing. I'm bringing her into the hospital. I'm driving, so I can't talk. But I'll call you as soon as I get there."

"Marty, wait—they won't let me see her. I'm quarantined for a few more days, but—"

Marty had already disconnected. She was frantic as she called back, but he didn't answer.

Pick up. Pick up.

Elyse was symptomatic. Elyse, her little Tic Tac, who shared her biracial heritage. The same blood that was susceptible to *Labrador*. Sara had almost another week to face in the depressive isolation room. Lydia Monroe had succumbed to the virus in a matter of days. Gone, never to see her family again. She was certain now that there was something more behind the *Labrador* epidemic. And somewhere out there *someone,* had a cure for it. She wasn't sure if they were in D.C. or Bethesda or Wisconsin. If she had to go to Africa to find it—she was going to make *damn sure* her daughter got treatment—and fast.

She rifled wildly through the duffel that Marty had dropped off. Inside was a change of clothes.

A toothbrush.

Toothpaste.

A box of Tic Tacs.

She paused and she smiled and she put them in her pocket. Then she examined the doors and she searched the drawer beside the bed.

Empty.

She picked up the phone and she dialed the extension for dietary on her cell phone.

"Can I get a lunch tray, please?" She ordered pizza and a fruit cup and carrot sticks and a Coke—something quick.

"Yes, Doctor. I'll send an orderly up right away."

The aproned attendant knocked at her door twenty minutes later, wearing a hairnet and latex gloves and black sneakers. Sara had the duffel bag over her left shoulder as she peered out of the leaded glass window. The young woman opened the door with her key and placed the food at the doorstep.

"Good evening, Doctor Sullivan," the attendant said.

Sara smiled, picked up the tray.

Now was her chance.

She quickly placed her foot ajar in the doorway and spilled the tray of fruits and vegetables and pizza onto the attendant as the woman fumbled with her key ring. The attendant stumbled backwards, dropped the key ring. Sara snatched it off the ground, shoved the attendant and spun her around, grabbed her badge lanyard. She pulled it tightly against her throat as the woman clawed at it and struggled against her grip. Then she untied the woman's apron and she removed her hairnet and she twisted her arms behind her back. She'd seen Marty do it plenty of times. He'd shown her the way in which he secured a prisoner's wrists, by placing the muscles of the forearms in a position where they couldn't generate enough leverage or force. The maneuver was effective now, and with her own badge lanyard, she tied the woman's hands behind her back as best she could, and she shoved her forward onto her knees, locked her in the room. The attendant screamed and kicked at the door as she grappled behind her to loosen her wrists.

Sara put the hairnet over her head and tied the apron around her waist. She kept her head down as she approached the elevator. She swiped the attendant's badge in the access control reader and pressed the down button. The reader beeped and flashed a red message across the digital screen: ACCESS DENIED. Had someone seen the incident? She looked up to the far corner of the corridor. A video monitor was blinking green. It pivoted left and right as it scanned the otherwise dilapidated unit.

She ripped the wire from the camera and wrenched it from the wall, ran to the other end of the corridor. She climbed the ladder to the next level, parting the exposed electrical wires that hung from the level above. She navigated her way across a steel beam and she pulled herself up onto a wooden platform on the eleventh level where the floor was littered with construction equipment: two by fours and large sheets of chip board, dry wall and diamond saw blades. Painting supplies and work buckets and brooms and power tools were scattered about the floor and counters.

The hospital foundation was building a new vascular unit, but it had been delayed due to the exorbitant costs that the hospital anticipated in caring for patients in isolation with the spreading epidemic.

It was expected to get worse.

Much worse.

She knew there was a back stairwell exit to the 23d Street lot, but where was it? She ran her hands along the trim and tapped on the walls, listening for a hollow point. Then she picked up a sledgehammer and slammed it against the fresh drywall, exposing plumbing. Dust and debris scattered around her. A large chunk of ceiling tile fell down and the wooden beam came with it, narrowly missing her head. Then she wielded the hammer a second time with all her strength and she smashed the wall, which now exposed the back corridor to the old skilled nursing unit. She found the back stairwell to the parking exit, but the steel lock was clamped shut. With the sledgehammer, she hit it four times with all her might, broke the lock.

From the floor below, the elevator bell rang now.

The attendant was still shouting and kicking at the locked door, but Sara still had the key.

She ran down the stairs and out onto the 23d Street parking lot. She was fortunate to hail a cab headed northwest, but military trucks and armed soldiers in green camouflage prevented her from getting far. Riots prevented traffic from moving along the Beltway, and check points now obstructed the movement of automobiles around the D.C. metro area.

"Where to ma'am?" asked the Latino driver in a thick accent.

She didn't hear him at first.

She picked up her phone, distraught over the possibility of Elyse now falling ill with *Labrador* virus.

She tried Marty again.

No answer.

She listened to a message that Marty had left while she was in quarantine: "Sara, I'm trying to get to the hospital, but the streets are barricaded in all directions. They're checking temperatures and ID's, and there are soldiers and tanks everywhere." Why had she missed the call? The GPS location icon flashed on her phone.

Strange.

She never allowed location services on the device. She quickly pulled the battery from the device, placed it in her duffel.

"Lady, I ain't got all freakin' day," said the cabbie. "Where ya headed?"

"Sorry." She gave the driver the address of the Phaedrex Clinical Trials Lab in Bethesda, Maryland, the office of Dr. Graham LeTorneau.

They inched forward through traffic, slowly, but as the cabbie turned right into Washington Circle, there was a hostile knock on the window by an armed soldier.

-8-

Sara Sullivan

Sara was certain she'd be taken back to the hospital. The soldier banged on the window of the cab again. She sank down in the back seat of the vehicle.

"Where are you headed?" the National Guardsman demanded, as they approached the Francis Scott Key Bridge. Traffic was gridlocked. The man motioned for the cab driver to lower the window.

The cabbie took his time, scratched his clean shaven chin, gave the guard the convenient, *'I don't speak English,'* look, shook a coiffed curl off his pockmarked brow, and looked back at Sara. She repeated the address.

"Center Drive, Bethesda, Maryland," he said to the Guardsman.

She fidgeted with her belongings as the Guardsman walked around the vehicle, looking in the windows. She turned her head away from him and looked to the colonial row houses and red brick roadway across the bridge, keeping her eyes down.

"That's a long ride. Open the trunk."

The driver muttered under his breath. He put the vehicle in park and got out. His jeans and T-shirt were tight and neatly tucked, like a bullfighter. A middle-aged Pedro Romero. The Lexus behind his cab honked its horn. The other cars behind him followed suit. She didn't dare turn around. Soon, the driver returned to his seat.

"Let's see your ID."

He cussed in Spanish and pulled his badge from the ripped plastic casing and held it up.

"What about you?" the Guardsman asked her.

"Sir, I lost my driver's license," she lied. She held up the dietary services badge, covering the picture. He wasn't looking at it anyway. He blew his whistle and motioned to his partner on the bridge.

"Go ahead."

The Metropolitan Matador charged ahead, then slammed abruptly on his brakes. Her head and neck whipped back. She sighed and craned her neck outside the cab as they made a slow crawl onto the bridge now. There were men in yellow hazmat suits near the bank of the Potomac beside some of the old stone hearths that remained in various spots along the majestic river where it picked up its pace before entering Chesapeake Bay. The hearths were scattered about the canal, remnants of what folks cooked on after losing their homes in the Great Depression. They remained a conversation piece for tourists on the river-guided trips.

Suddenly, she knew exactly how the homeless families must have felt.

Uprooted.

Rueful.

Lost.

It wasn't out of the ordinary for environmentalists to sample and study the river. Its condition was once putrid and disgusting as a consequence of pollution, but when the Clean Water Act of 1972 had been enacted, it had improved somewhat over the years. Now, the men in hazmat suits were drawing samples, and there was a white truck marked with a red biohazard symbol parked on the bank. Two more National Guard tanks were moving into the area. There were barricades to the south, heading toward George Washington Island, and it looked as though some sort of contamination had occurred. Dusk was imminent, and the spotlights on the monuments were coming on, giving the water a crystalline glow. Pedro was circling around unnecessarily, but she was too deep in thought to object.

She chided herself for stereotyping.

Where the hell was he going?

She glanced at the Lincoln Memorial, where dozens of tourists were crowded around, many wearing surgical masks, still snapping group pictures and selfies in front of the capital's iconic monuments, despite the threat to public health. She had a tortuous ride to Bethesda, and she prayed Marty would be able to get Elyse to the hospital through all the military roadblocks.

The driver rolled his window down, lit a cigarette. She slid the filthy Plexiglas divider window up and removed her credit card from her wallet. She swiped it in the reader, picked up the cab's phone. The second number on her list was Devin Finnegan, a fifty-three year-old Caucasian woman who'd come in shortly after Lydia Monroe. Finnegan's husband answered the call.

"Hello, sir. This is Dr. Sullivan. I'm the physician who admitted your wife a few nights ago. I understand her condition is stable, but there are a few important questions we have regarding her illness."

"I have a few questions of my own."

"I understand."

"Like what's with the military vehicle parked outside my house 24-7?" The man's voice was gruff, impatient. "I told 'em we weren't goin' nowhere until we're sure we're healthy. And they're still camped out in front."

"I see."

She swallowed.

She realized she wouldn't be able to return to her home after she visited the lab. The same military surveillance would soon be monitoring Marty and Elyse for quarantine compliance. How long did they plan to isolate people—whole families—this way?

"Then we got people coming to check our temperature, and now they've started going door to door, askin' the neighbors questions, when it ain't none of their damn business."

"What kind of questions?"

"Like what race am I," the man said. "I knew I shouldn't have filled out the census."

"I assure you, Mr. Finnegan, I'm not part of the public health measures to contain the viral outbreak. I was quarantined myself after exposure. I can certainly understand your concern, your distrust." She waited for his response and she played with the necklace Marty had given her when she'd delivered their daughter, rolling it between her thumb and fingers. Devin Finnegan didn't object, so she continued. "I'd like to ask you a few questions about your wife's history."

"If you're a doctor and you're taking care of her, why don't you just ask her? I'm not allowed to see her, and they've isolated my family from all contact for two weeks."

"I'm no longer in the hospital, sir."

"Are you infected?"

She glanced up in the rearview at the driver, but his eyes were firmly on the road, and the radio was blaring. The cab smelled of his sweat. She cracked the window. She thought her eyes looked red. Conjunctival injection—or bloodshot eyes—was one of the symptoms of *Labrador,* but she was also exhausted.

"I don't believe so. All of my lab work has been negative, and I haven't spiked a fever." She hoped he would assist her. Elyse's life might depend on it. There had to be something more behind the epidemic.

An explanation for an index case—a location.

Somewhere.

And she knew that's where she'd find the cure for *Labrador.*

"Go ahead then," he said.

"Thank you. Did either you or your wife travel outside the country before she became ill?"

"Not at all." He coughed—a loud smoker's hack. "We haven't left Maryland since our honeymoon back in '75, Doc."

"What about children? Do you have any young children?" She thought of all she knew about viral hemorrhagic fevers and how outbreaks started and ended.

"Do I have any young children or did my children travel outside the country?"

"The first question."

"No, ma'am. But we sure had fun tryin'," he said, lapsing into another coughing spell.

"Do you mind if I ask your wife's place of employment?"

"It's the same as mine. We own a funeral home. Family business."

"Anyone you know work in a lab? In Bethesda or any of the research institutes in D.C.?"

"No, ma'am." Impatience festered in his voice now. She thought it best not to press too hard.

"Thank you," she said, hung up.

No travel history.

No children.

No reason for contact with the virulent *Labrador*, housed in top security at the NIH and the CDC. What about the other patient, Raymond Barry? She swiped the credit card and dialed his home number.

His wife didn't speak English well. She was distraught, barely able to hold the conversation. If she'd seen the woman in the E.R., she would've given her an intramuscular injection of Ativan. After her hysteria subsided, the woman explained that she and her husband had just buried their teenage daughter, whose last wish had been to take a safari before she passed away from cancer.

"My husband. My husband! Is he alright? They won't let me see him. They take him!"

She'd taken medical Spanish, but her speech was far from fluent. She offered her condolences, tried to assure her that Mr. Barry was doing as well as could be expected, but the woman was hysterical again.

"Ma'am, please." Sara's voice was calm, but it trembled for Elyse. Letting go of a child seemed unimaginable. "What kind of cancer did your daughter die of?"

"The cancer, the cancer!" the woman cried out.

She held the phone away from her ear, said, "I understand." She apologized for rattling the woman, disconnected the call. She stared out the window at another group of protestors. She wanted instead to look at her pictures of Elyse on her smartphone, but she didn't dare turn on the device now.

Her location could be traced.

Her calls could be monitored.

It aggravated her when Marty followed up on her whereabouts, but the government quarantines and contact tracing made her downright paranoid.

What critical info about *Labrador* was she missing? None of the cases at George Washington had any travel history to endemic areas, and neither seemed to have any association to the labs in Atlanta or D.C. that had classified information. The driver circled the clinical trials lab at Cloister Court where she hoped to find Dr. LeTorneau, the world-renowned researcher who'd been commissioned to discover a treatment for the swiftly killing super-virus.

It was her only lead.

33d Meeting for the Society of Evolutionary Biology
The Washburn Mansion
Washington, D.C.
Kayla Reeves

Kayla Reeves looked around the Lafayette Room of the Washburn Mansion for her mentor, Dr. Graham LeTorneau. After the tuxedoed butlers had made their third round with bacon-wrapped scallops and grape tomato *a la mozzarella caprese* and *beef tartare*, the bartender signaled the last call for open drinks before the dinner with the keynote speaker. The room was the finest in the historical building, adorned with early eighteenth century crown molding and craftsmanship found nowhere in the modern concrete skyscrapers of Manhattan or Miami. The Washburn mansion had character. It was one of the District's many architectural jewels, and the decision to move the Society of Evolutionary Biologists annual meeting from the obstructed District venue at the Omni had been a last minute decision.

None of the society members had questioned it.

The event was arranged swiftly for the well-respected group of members, mostly well published PhDs and physician researchers affiliated with Harvard, Georgetown, Brown, all the Ivy Leagues. Well-heeled spouses and valeted luxury cars filled the grounds now, but the keynote speaker was absent. The ornate grandfather clock chimed a quarter past the hour.

7:15p.m.

The butler rang the bell for the guests to be seated.

Kayla, Hans and Veronica were dressed for the black tie event and seated, at the insistence of their mentor, not at a token table in a corner, but adjacent to the mahogany podium. Jorge had regretfully been unable to make the event and had informed them of his sabbatical. He had insisted the trio celebrate without him in honor of Dr. LeTorneau's accomplishment and all of their years of tedious graduate lab work. Dr. Peter Farkash, one of the international committee members, was seated across from them in the front row, with his much younger wife.

There had been mention of LeTorneau getting a nomination for a Nobel Prize in Science.

The president of the association, Dr. Jack Klosterman, appeared apprehensive as he approached the students' table. Klosterman faltered and knocked the wine glass across the pristine tablecloth, spilling Chianti on Kayla.

"My sincerest apology, Miss," Klosterman said, offering her a napkin. "We need to start the presentation, and I have no word from Dr. LeTorneau. Will he be arriving shortly?"

Kayla wetted the napkin in her water goblet and she dabbed at her strapless cocktail dress and she looked around. "We're not sure where he is. I've texted him several times, but he hasn't responded."

The three students exchanged worried looks. Then Veronica and Hans smiled at Kayla.

"What?" she asked. "Why are you two looking at me like that?"

"Kayla, you have to do the honors," Hans said. "You prepared the slides for Graham."

"You know the material better than any of us," Veronica insisted. "Kayla, you've got this."

The waiter made his way around the table and filled each of their glasses with wine. She dipped her baguette in olive oil and she shoved the large piece in her mouth. Then she took a large gulp of Chianti, then another gulp of ice water.

"Guys, I couldn't. I'm just a grad student. I—"

Hans got up, excused himself. She watched with interest as he conferred briefly with Klosterman.

A moment later, Hans returned to his seat.

The president tapped his wine glass with a fork.

The crowd grew silent.

"What was that all about?" she asked.

"*Shh*. You'll do fine," said Hans.

"Ladies and gentlemen of our fine society, a toast," said Klosterman, after grabbing the microphone from the podium. "To the work from the laboratory of Dr. Graham LeTorneau, Nobel Prize nominee." He held his glass high. The crowd responded in kind.

"Hans," She scolded him in a whisper. She looked up at the president, who was holding his glass high up for the members of the society.

"Unfortunately, Dr. LeTorneau is delayed this evening. However, I present to you…Ms. Kayla Reeves."

The crowd clapped. She felt her eyes grow to the size of her china saucer. A lump formed in her throat, and she instantly wished Jorge were there. "Hans, what did you do?"

"Veronica and I nominated you to speak," Hans said. He shrugged and bit his dinner roll.

"Payback is going to be a bitch," Veronica whispered to him.

"Nah, she'll get over it," Hans said, stuffing the rest of the roll in his mouth.

"No, I won't," she muttered. "I *will* get you two geeks back for this."

The crowd turned to her.

Her face turned a crimson that matched her dress.

She meant what she said.

She would get them back.

George Washington Hospital

Dr. Amy Daust and Dr. Benjamin Lawrence, raced into the elevator. Daust swiped her badge on the card reader. The physician who'd been monitoring Sara Sullivan's temperature, Dr. Robert Pierce, followed. The LED lights flashed green, allowing the doctors' access to the isolation wing where Sara had been quarantined. They got off the elevator on the fifth floor with the security guard, ran down the hall to the room. They peered through the leaded glass on the metal door where the dietary employee, Susan Gavin, was sitting on the bed.

Gavin rose, pounded on the window with her bound wrists.

The doctors whispered amongst themselves as they examined the room through the glass. Before entering, they donned their hazmat suits and personal protective goggles and blue gloves. Gavin was irate, screaming. The woman tore at Dr. Lawrence's white protective clothing until the other two physicians restrained her.

"Did you come into contact with Dr. Sullivan, Miss?" asked Daust. She kept her distance from the woman as the others lingered in the doorway.

"She threw the tray at me. Then she tied my wrists and took off—trapped me in here. Is this place contaminated?"

Dr. Lawrence removed the badge lanyard from the woman's wrists, where a knot had been tied with adept surgical precision. Lawrence glanced at Sara's ID photo, barked at Daust: "Get me the CDC. She's broken quarantine. She may be infecting hundreds of others. Have the police search her home."

"Do we have a second set of lab work on her?" asked Daust.

"No, sir," said Dr. Pierce. "I drew the second set, but the sample clotted. The first set of labs was negative."

"She may be asymptomatic, but we can't risk it. *Labrador* is costing the hospital millions of dollars already. Another handful of cases here will bankrupt us. I want the names of every man, woman and dog she comes into contact with."

"Yes, sir."

"The District is one step away from being declared a disaster area."

"Sir?" asked Daust. "We have information from inside sources that Dr. Sullivan's daughter may be experiencing signs of illness."

Lawrence clenched his teeth, looked around the room, behind the bathroom door, and then up the ladder where Sara had escaped.

"Find her," he said.

Center for Disease Control
Atlanta, Georgia

Pleistocene desktop computers lined the floor of the CDC office. Ancillary cubicles equipped with laptops and wireless phone headsets surrounded the periphery. A disaster management center had been erected adjacent to the main building to oversee the infectious disease response to the *Labrador* virus. It was 95 degrees and sunny in Atlanta. Sunlight streamed into the glass atrium filled with flourishing banana trees and red ginger and diverse birds of paradise plants, but with the air conditioning broken, the temperature felt more like 110 degrees. Twenty-seven interns manned the phones of the contract tracing unit for the *Labrador* response team, complaining about the heat, listening to rap music, twerking about each other's cubicles and eating their lunches, waiting for the phones to ring. They turned down the iPod speaker as a call came in, ringing every one of their phones and ending their faux mating ritual. The first to answer was Alex Hammond, an intern from the University of Georgia, who wore his Dawgs hat sideways.

"Hello CDC? I have a new secondary contact exposure to report and a woman who's broken quarantine in the D.C. area," the man said. "This is Dr. Benjamin Lawrence."

"Is the exposed patient symptomatic?" asked the intern, with rote intonation.

"No, but she came into contact with the woman who fled quarantine. The initial contact was also asymptomatic on day nine of isolation and she has one set of negative labs. She admitted several patients who tested positive for a highly virulent strain of *Labrador*—she's a doctor."

"Thank you. The first negative blood test indicates she probably presents a low risk of infection and little risk of spreading the virus to others," Alex Hammond paused, as he read the boilerplate language from the laminated information card on the stainless steel ring on his desk, "but CDC officials are taking public health precautions seriously."

The other interns went back to chatting as he placed his headset over his ears. Alex Hammond took the name of the dietary employee, her name, address and phone number, and opened a link in his browser to assist him with tracing her secondary contacts.

Hammond continued reading, "*Labrador* virus is often lethal, but it is not contagious until a patient demonstrates symptoms." He flipped the ring of cards to the next page of information.

"Goddamn it, you sound like every television and radio station out there. Who the fuck is running the show there?"

The student flipped back a page on the ringed information packet, read dispassionately: "Senator Edward Marburg is head of the *Labrador* response. He is committed to stopping the spread of the illness."

"Jesus. What am I supposed to do with the secondary contact? And what about the first one who escaped quarantine?"

"What measures have been taken to locate the exposed contact?"

"The police have been notified."

"I will inform Senator Marburg. He's been appointed by the president to oversee the *Labrador* response. And as a presidential hopeful in the upcoming election, he is committed to stopping the outbreak. Thank you for the call, sir slash ma'am—I mean sir."

Alex Hammond pulled up the name Sara Sullivan and entered her information into the system, including the details about her escape from monitored isolation. The computer flashed: HIGH RISK, and immediately linked to an NSA watch page reserved for suspicious activity in citizens exposed or suspected to be ill with communicable diseases.

Hammond scrolled past a list of inmates who had been arrested for recklessly and knowingly exposing others to the AIDS virus. He clicked on Dr. Sara Sullivan under the *Labrador* and viral hemorrhagic fevers tab. He typed her information and logged off his workstation computer. He walked beside the window in the large greenhouse-like atrium and he wiped the sweat from his brow and he dialed the direct number of Senator Edward Marburg.

Four Seasons Hotel
Washington, D.C.
Edward Marburg

Marburg sat on the edge of the hotel bed and answered his cell phone. He pulled his pants up and he gave the woman on the hotel room bed a kiss on the cheek and he fastened his belt. She rolled over, tousled her dark hair. He pulled his undershirt onto his torso, tossed her a stack of bills, put his wallet in his back pocket. Then she pulled the sheets up and over her naked body, and kissed his neck as he listened. He brushed her off and he pointed to the phone and she pouted a little and he lit a cigarette.

He walked to the window, his shoulders tense, looking out at the tanks and the National Guard moving up Pennsylvania Avenue. A helicopter circled overhead, rather close to the mall. He gave the pilot the middle finger, drew the long curtain closed.

"I told you not to smoke in here." He waved off the fumes. "I just quit."

The woman set down the cigarette, sat up and fastened her bra. "If you're too busy, I can leave."

Her Latina accent was always saturated with drama, but he tolerated it because she had great lips, the kind of lips that could only make him think of blow jobs when she spoke and nothing else.

"Alright. Don't bunch your panties."

She blew smoke in his face. "Do you mean, *don't get your panties in a bunch?*"

Lindstrom was so much better with women.

He wished they were back in law school.

He gave her another kiss and he handled her ass. "This will only take a minute. Call room service and have them send up some of those white peaches you like. I like them, too." He winked at her.

"I don't want any." She seemed satisfied with this, and she pulled her knees to her chest and she pointed the remote and she turned on the news.

Channel Two was broadcasting another violent police standoff.

"Well where did she go?" He jarred open the night stand drawer and he looked for the little notepad that every hotel room had. There was none, so he tore the first page out of the Holy Bible and he wrote on it: Dr. Sara Sullivan

DOB: 1.14.76

Officer Martin Thompson

DOB: 2.17.74

Daughter: Elyse Thompson

DOB: 7.4.14

"How many new cases?" He nodded and he put on his shoes and he opened his briefcase. On his iPad, he connected to the CDC contact database tracing system, and he pulled up the picture of Dr. Sara Sullivan with the words: HIGH RISK CONTACT, flashing across the entry. "Thank you. Get me the NSA and the plates of their vehicles, home address, their cell phone numbers. Arrange for contact tracing, temperature monitoring, home surveillance."

Anywhere else but D.C. Not before my election.

He'd arranged for the CDC to connect his system instantly to NSA. District employees were deployed to monitor and trace all exposures and contacts of the *Labrador* virus, to report to him.

"Yes, Senator," said Alex Hammond, the CDC intern. "The National Security Agency is monitoring her calls, sir. She contacted the National Institutes of Health facility in Madison, Wisconsin, where *Labrador* is housed in the level 4 research unit."

"Really." He paused and he scrolled through the information and he repeated Sara's name. "Dr. Sara Sullivan."

What is this minx after? What does she know?

"Confiscate any pistol or weapons registered to her name," he ordered.

"Her fiancée is a police officer, sir. He carries a Glock. He also has a Smith and Wesson and several other firearms registered to his name."

"*Was* an officer. Not while he's on leave under quarantine."

"I'll inform the NSA, Senator," said Hammond. "We'll get a handle on the epidemic, sir. Strict contact tracing and isolation has averted public spread of these highly virulent diseases in the past."

"I already fucking know that," he said. "Find Sullivan. She's dangerous."

"Understood, sir. Fortunately, she has a set of negative lab work and has shown no signs of illness that we know of, sir."

He rubbed his hand on his downy chin, devoid of stubble. His baby fine hair stirred like a windblown dandelion as he shook his head. He looked in the mirror and he smoothed it down across the top of his head. "Never mind—she's broken quarantine and she'll face imprisonment when she's found." There was an incongruous silence on the line from the intern. Marburg sensed the young man's discomfort, and he changed his tone, added, "We have to protect the American people."

"Of course," said Hammond. "We're on top of it."

"Get dressed," he told the woman. He disconnected the call and tossed her dress across the room from the brocade chaise lounge that he'd screwed her on, just before the call.

The Washburn Mansion

Washington, D.C.

Kayla Reeves

Kayla stood at the podium in the ornate Lafayette room, giving Veronica and Hans a deliberate glare for volunteering her as orator understudy for the evening. Veronica, in the middle of a gluttonous indulgence of filet mignon and lobster tail and crab-filled button cap mushrooms, looked unconcerned. Hans was similarly enjoying a bite off of his plate, chased with his Chianti. He raised his glass to her in a gesture of solidarity that said: *you can do this.*

In an informal setting, she could speak off the cuff on the subject of evolution, fascinating everyone with her substantial knowledge, and suitably impressing them with her passion for her work. But suddenly, she became conscious of her speech, reminded herself that Graham was nominated for a Nobel Prize. She stammered as she regarded the slides, starting with the picture of the Red Queen, a character from Lewis Carroll's

Through the Looking Glass. The Red Queen character was the basis for the popularly accepted theory of co-evolution on which their research had focused. She looked the part in her red satin evening gown, and the voices diminished to a hush in the room adorned with trefoils and quatrefoils and Tudor revival arched doorways.

According to the character, in Wonderland, it "took all the running one could do just to stay in the same place." Kayla explained how species were always at odds with one another—trying to gain an evolutionary advantage. In doing so, one step forward for one species, meant a step back for another, so that all creatures—or viruses or parasites—seemed to evolve together without one gaining any tremendous advantage over another.

In effect, they stayed in the same place.

An evolutionary treadmill.

"In an arms race," she began, "one side builds up enough weaponry to survive a first hit and keep running, keep surviving." She flashed the photos from the Cold War and Graham's pictures of Soviet and American flags and nuclear weapons. "But it isn't sufficient for us to remain alive. It is the ability to reproduce that is most critical."

Now she was stiff, frozen.

She couldn't remember what came next.

Shit.

She was the one who'd prepared the slides.

Veronica held her fork and stopped chewing, extended a conciliatory smile. Dishes clanked as the guests set down their silverware, looked around.

"We're certainly seeing a lot of competitive behavior for resources today, aren't we?" the moderator prompted.

Dead silence.

In desperation, Hans gave her two thumbs up, which just made it worse. Sweat formed on her palms. She coughed. Then she continued.

She nervously advanced to the slide of the bacteria and species of moths and Marisa snails that she and Jorge had been studying. If Jorge were there to get her through the presentation, he'd know exactly what to say. They were both from the South and he *got* her like no one else did. "The treadmill effect keeps us running in the same place in a symmetrical arms race, if you will, but turning up the speed faster than one contestant can run, can result in annihilation of the other." She flipped to more chilling social parallels of nuclear arms races, then to her biologic correlate to the lecture, her moths and snails. "If a bacteria or parasite can evolve rapidly and gain an advantage sufficient to take out a large portion of a population, it could have devastating consequences, even resulting in extinction, if not for—what?" She now engaged the audience as Graham always did, and their smiles warmed.

Veronica was finished with her filet mignon and was all but jumping out of her seat with her usual, *'I know! I know!'* look. Kayla turned over the microphone to her.

"Sexual reproduction—It provides the genetic variability, selecting for those organisms that are better able to maintain their own fitness against a particular predator or threat, like infectious disease," Veronica chimed in. "And according to the Red Queen theory, it makes them better able to survive to reproduce, bringing forth more, and more importantly, heartier offspring."

"Exactly," she said. She was quite comfortable giving the lecture now. She grabbed the microphone back from Veronica. "A large portion of Dr. LeTorneau's work has examined which populations of humans are evolving the fastest. While the human race is one of the few that hasn't given rise to any daughter species, our genes are constantly evolving. We don't always appreciate this because it happens on a scale of millions of years, but we see that people with higher melanin levels in their skin are reproducing at faster rates. Why is that?"

The topic of evolution of various races was always a touchy subject, but Graham approached it fearlessly. There was a scientific reason for everything. It had nothing to do with personal prejudices or social correctness—and if those things were involved, then there were scientific reasons for them, too. No one had an answer for her question, so she continued. She advanced to the slides on the projections on global warming and the exponentially increasing temperatures. There were images of helpless polar bears confined to miniscule ice floes, and acres of wilderness once covered in ice and frozen tundra, now bursting forth with vibrant green plant life.

"Dr. LeTorneau would reason that people of color with more melanin are more suited to a warmer climate, and with the earth's average temperature warming drastically, we have a migration away from the equatorial and tropical regions, and a decline in birth rates for Northern Europeans as well," Kayla said. She spoke with the most engaging speaking voice she could muster, and the audience was rapt. "The question is whether we can adapt quickly enough, or will the warmer temperatures allow for the proliferation of viruses and parasites that emerge faster than we can outrun them, like the rabbit can outrun the fox. Earth has flourished for hundreds of millions of years. It will sustain our every assault."

This was the part of the lecture that always pissed off the climate change experts, because they always put the earth before mankind, but she dismissed the viewpoint for the time being, and she smiled and she paused for questions. There were none, so she continued. "Take the sickle cell gene, for example. Up to ten percent of blacks carry the sickle cell gene. Two copies confer sickle cell disease, resulting in anemia and painful crises involving bone ischemia, pulmonary chest crises, and decreased oxygen delivery to tissues, but surprisingly, the gene has survived, because a single copy offers resistance to malaria in warm, tropical climates where mosquitoes are abundant and mosquito-borne diseases are endemic. Dr. LeTorneau has sequenced several genes that we've found to be adaptive in a warmer climate. These have been evolving in individuals of these populations for some time now."

"But hasn't the rate of species extinction always remained constant?" asked one of the younger members in the back. "How could we possibly evolve quickly enough with the changing environment on Earth?"

"That is an excellent question that begs further research." She pulled up a slide relevant to the discussion. "Here we demonstrate that it doesn't matter how long a species has been on earth. The rate of extinction of any species has been constant in history. It suggests that the evolutionary race ramps up in a predator-prey relationship quickly, so that one organism cannot keep up, ending the race, or some random event occurs."

"Like a meteor killing off the dinosaurs?"

"Yes, something catastrophic to the species."

"What about the emerging virus we are battling now? The *Labrador* virus begs for an evolutionary leap in mankind, young lady," said Dr. Klosterman, the society president, rising from his seat.

"We've been working on that as well, sir," she said. "In the case of the infectious and lethal, *Labrador* virus, we've demonstrated natural immunity in 20 to 25 percent of the Caucasian population in Nova Scotia, and there are many more genetic variations in immune regulation genes—mostly encoding proteins—that allow certain individuals to better combat the infection than others. But you're absolutely correct. It doesn't matter how long a species has been on earth—some random event comes along every time as species co-evolve. If we don't get ahead of it, *Labrador,* and the social conflict it's causing—a state verging on all-out martial law—could be that event."

"So at the same time interspecies competition is selecting for genes better suited to a warmer planet," Klosterman ventured, "this deadly virus is emerging in the same warm climates within its hosts—human beings."

"Socially it may not be correct to say so, but it is supported by the research," she replied. "An adaptation in one species may change the selection pressure on a population in another species. But *Labrador* is running faster than humans can." She put up the picture with the electron micrograph of the infectious organism. "It's a little piece of RNA that doesn't stop for bureaucracy. It knows no borders." She clicked on another picture of the filovirus' effects on the bloodstream, and the graphs on its current mortality in black Americans.

Klosterman looked perturbed. Instead of the society president's face, she imagined she was talking to Jorge, and she pictured his goofy grin without his bridge in place—missing one of the incisors on the top of his mouth.

She relaxed, smiled.

Klosterman said, "There are complimentary arms races within our own species as well as competitive evolutionary pressure from parasites to evolve to survive their ill effects. This is a well-accepted fact. What is new about LeTorneau's discovery that's so deserving of a Nobel Prize? And where is he?" demanded the president.

The other members murmured in agreement.

"Right now the viral disease is causing some degree of racial tension—interspecies competition," she agreed. "It's the genes within organisms that are selfish, and that determine every roll of the dice, begging for survival, pressing onward." She forwarded to the slide of the NPC1 gene, which encoded a protein that made Caucasians better able to fight the *Labrador* virus. "Viruses like these haven't yet had a chance to evolve to be as lethal as they have in blacks, but that shouldn't make any of us rest easily."

One of the eldest members of the society stood up. The man took a few unsteady steps forward with his cane, and he scratched his white beard and he cleared his throat before he spoke. "*Labrador* is certainly pitting races against races. There's rioting, public quarantines, misinformation being disseminated by the media. Don't you think we should be sure of all of this research before everyone gets up in arms even further?"

The voices in the Tudor-style room rose, and she looked to Hans and Veronica for support. They were busy stuffing their faces.

No help to her.

She pictured Jorge again.

This time she imagined him in his backwoods overalls, his oversized flannel shirt.

Her parents loved him, and now, she could finally admit it—she did, too.

He'd gotten a tattoo recently, but had refused to show her, said he was waiting for the "right time." She thought of what that meant—the right time. She thought of being intimate with him, his shirt off, his large chest, and she got lost in her own daydream.

Veronica cleared her throat loudly.

Her attention returned to the lecture.

She scowled at Veronica, reluctantly continued.

"In its arms race, *Labrador* has been able to evolve from its natural origins in the temperate regions of Africa in those most susceptible to infection—African-Americans," she said. "The virus can mutate faster than a human being can evolve to survive it. It can mutate over several generations like lightning, with selective pressure, to survive and replicate—copying itself like computer code. It takes us nine months in the womb to do that."

The voices in the crowd grew even louder, in unanimous disagreement until, in Kayla's defense, Veronica stood up.

"*Labrador* has a lethal predilection for people of color, but it has the ability to mutate and evolve much faster than humans with a nine-month reproduction cycle could hope to match at present," Veronica said. "The running speed—or mutation rate—of *Labrador* in the evolutionary arms race is so swift, that it could quickly consume *all* races if we don't act quickly."

Veronica turned the microphone over to Hans.

Hans stood up and added, "The emerging hemorrhagic viruses are fine tuning their fitness at their place of origin—in Africa—but it has nothing to do with racism. That's why the treatment Dr. LeTorneau has developed is as important as a vaccine—because the virus can mutate faster than a common cold. Our reproductive systems can't keep up with that enough to put any amount of evolutionary pressure on the bugger. It's a swift and effective killer."

"But there hasn't been an outbreak in Africa," Klosterman pointed out. The room grew silent. "And Dr. LeTorneau was granted one-hundred fifty million dollars to develop the cure before this need arose? To quote from Lewis Carroll: curiouser and curiouser."

Kayla stepped in. "I can assure you, Dr. LeTorneau's work is ethical. That is entirely coincidental."

Klosterman crossed his arms.

Skepticism fell over his face.

Kayla was still full of optimism, enthusiasm. She knew Hans had more experience with the pitfalls of science, the pressures on drug makers to be the first to market, the manipulation of data that occurred to fatten up the significance of the results. The importance of the *bottom line*. She turned to him now.

He took the microphone.

"We are so far behind in this arms race against the virus, that getting the drug through the FDA is paramount." Hans' voice was deep and forceful and passionate. "It's always the primary obstacle, but this time, our survival as a species depends on it."

A loud rumble of assent swept through the audience, but Klosterman was not swayed.

No wonder Graham lost sleep over these presentations.

He was probably miles from there.

Sparks on his shoes.

She wiped the sweat from her palms.

"I find the lack of an index case in Africa most vexing, young lady," said the president.

"We're all concerned, but Dr. LeTorneau's work is honest, sir," she said.

"You're certain?"

Kayla nodded. "*Labrador* could be the random event that produces a rapid species extinction. It has the potential, in the wrong hands, to quickly evolve faster than all of the strains of influenza, killing swiftly before humans can adapt and survive and reproduce. There is the potential in impoverished areas for it to spread out of control." She paused and she swallowed and she took a sip of water. "Or the potential for genocide as a biologic weapon."

"But if species evolve side by side, where does the sudden urgency come in? Why now?" asked Klosterman.

Her voice was impassioned. "We have a life-dinner principle here. The rabbit has to run twice as fast to outrun the fox, because the fox is only running for its dinner, sir."

Klosterman pondered this, said, "You're saying *Labrador* could create an asymmetrical arms race against the human race?"

"I'm saying the weapon, *sir*, is the running speed."

Klosterman's face grew sullen.

He turned, addressed his colleagues.

His jaw was limp as he removed his bowtie and tossed it on the table and pulled at the loose skin around his neck. His face grew stark white and his expression, flat, as he addressed the society. "I know Professor LeTorneau to be an honest man as well. My regret for mankind is that unfortunately, manufactured causes are more common than coincidences."

The three students stood at the baroque podium. Hans took the microphone again. She was relieved to be near the end of the talk, where she presented the cure that Dr. LeTorneau had developed over several years with their assistance—an antibody to the virus capable of neutralizing the infection.

An antibody to conquer the disease.

"If we don't get the treatment that Dr. LeTorneau has developed through the FDA immediately," she said, "*Labrador* will cause millions of deaths. It is mathematically impossible to think otherwise."

-9-

Edward Marburg

Lindstrom pulled his BMW up to the north wing of the Capitol. Edward Marburg was waiting curbside. He got in and he slammed the door and he lit a cigarette.

"Tell me some good news, Senator." His irresistible grin was hopeful, but Marburg only swore under his breath. He folded his sunglasses neatly and he placed them in his jacket pocket. Then he opened his briefcase and he tossed the paperwork containing the 412-page bill on the console. They drove down Independence Avenue and exited at the east end of the National Mall.

The proposed legislation aimed to allow Medicare the same ability to negotiate with the big pharmaceutical giants that Lindstrom represented. That was bad for the companies.

And it was bad for Lindstrom.

A professional lobbyist, Lindstrom made sure the corporations could collect the payments they demanded so that enough money flowed into research and development, marketing and of course, profit.

Medicaid could negotiate the prices down.

The Veterans hospitals could do it.

But Medicare, the largest government payer, was prohibited from doing so by the hard deals and slick pocketbooks of guys like him. The large purchasing blocks of funds the companies got from the Medicare system—without the Fed's ability to negotiate down their costs—kept drug costs high, pharmaceutical profits high, and congressmen's palms greased to keep that status quo. Most of the near billions spent lobbying to keep it that way went to Republicans, but Marburg was the odd man out, the Democrat who played on big pharma's team. Their friendship went back to their days at Harvard law school, despite their age difference. Lindstrom's lap dog, as the other Democrats called him.

Fuck them, he thought.

"Without more money, Wes, you're going to lose the provision that prevents Medicare from negotiating with big pharma," he said. "There are even a few Republicans on the fence who want the law dissolved. This *Labrador* epidemic has everybody in a state of panic. Especially with Senator Marseille's death."

"We can handle it." Lindstrom waved his hand airily.

"Do you think you could be a little smugger?" he groused. "We've got big problems, like you said. People can't get to the hospital. They're worried that if the case numbers rise any higher, there won't be enough ICU beds, ventilators, dialysis units. The people need a vaccine and a cure for this virus and fast, and they're afraid most Americans won't have access to it."

"How much are we talking?" Lindstrom handed him a wrapped drive-through cheeseburger and took a bite of his own veggie burger. "Here—I guarantee your sandwich has more pork than this bill."

"Just the way I like it. I love bacon." He unwrapped the burger and he took a large bite of it and he sipped his Coke and he wiped his upper lip.

"So a couple hundred thousand?"

"Millions, Wes—at least a few." He fastened his seatbelt and adjusted it at the shoulder and he looked behind them to see if anyone was following: just construction vehicles and taxis, and a black pickup truck. "This virus is worse than we imagined. You told me it was just a little fire. Well it's burning down the whole city, Wes. It's breeding distrust—and that's not good for my election chances."

"We can do a few million. That's no problem. Give me the names of the Republican Representatives that need more *reassurance*." Lindstrom's pointy brows rose and his voice exuded confidence. His suit was pressed and his head, although balding, was perfectly coiffed at the sides where it receded away from his widow's peak. His cologne was strong and sexual and he always wore enough for both of them to get lucky with the kind of women they got lucky with.

"That's just to keep them at bay a few more weeks," he said. "Congress proposed legislation today to abolish the law that Medicare can't negotiate with pharmaceuticals. After blowing a 300-million-dollar load on these companies to develop a cure, they want results, Wes. You promised me results, and a fast payout."

"How much did you put into the market on Phaedrex and NewfoundVax?" Lindstrom turned left at the light as he checked the rearview. The pickup truck was still behind them. "The parent company, Origen, is always a safe bet."

"I put two million in each, Wes. Was this a bad tip you gave me? I'm expecting these stocks to hit—at least twenty million." He shook his head and he looked out the window and Lindstrom made a screeching turn off Independence.

"No, No—they'll hit. Don't *worry*." Lindstrom pulled the steering wheel and made a few turns, losing the truck, and got on the Beltway. "I didn't like that truck behind us."

"Where the hell are you going now?"

"I'm taking you where I always take you when you need to unload."

"This is no time for a Thai hooker, Wes. We've got real problems. Where's Recart? And you said the CEO at the clinical trials lab in Bethesda said he had the cure ready to go into an FDA fast track phase 3."

"I'll be the first to admit, Recart's a bit of prick," said Lindstrom.

"I found that out when he flew me out to east Africa and left the helicopter pilot for dead." He rubbed his brow, shaking his head. "I couldn't reach him at all."

"*Senator*," Lindstrom said. "Have patience."

Lindstrom drove over the Key Bridge and out onto I-66 through Virginia and got off and put the BMW in park at the NRA shooting range. Looking at him, Lindstrom raised his brows and put on his tan sunglasses. "I'll get in touch with LeTorneau and Claus. We'll fast track the treatment—it's ready—and we'll clean up this mess. The stock will peak and you and I will be sipping Cruzan Rum with *ten* Thai hookers in the Caymans by February recess." Lindstrom silenced the ringer on his phone and gave his friend his iconic, *'trust me'* look. "You just keep those two Dems on our side happy and veto the bill. The Republicans are easier. I'll handle them the old-fashioned way." Lindstrom got out of the car and came around and opened his door. The ground was muddy and he cursed as he stepped in a puddle, soiling his Italian leather shoes.

"How's that?"

"The same way I handle you, dear friend—with obscene amounts of money and distastefully cheap women."

"Why are we here, Wes?" he asked, getting out. "You know if anyone sees me here it's bad PR, Wes."

Lindstrom lit a cigarette and slammed the door. "Because the only thing that gets me harder than a Thai hooker, Senator, is watching a Democrat unload a 9mm Uzi the way you can." Lindstrom put a baseball cap on him and they walked through the entrance of the NRA headquarters shooting range.

The Washburn Mansion
Veronica Laughlin

Veronica Laughlin lit a smoke and she hurried out of the Washburn Mansion as the formal presentation concluded. The entire society was still unsure why Graham had requested the change in venue, and why he never showed up to present his research, the Nobel Prize-worthy findings linking his work on evolutionary biology to a cure for one of the deadliest diseases to imperil the human race, and one that had mysteriously popped up in the District.

Now, as the graduate students left the grand building, with its baroque stone columns supporting the elegant bay windows, Hans took her hand. The sun was setting, making the wrought iron ornamental gates look silver. She removed her high heels and walked barefoot. Her strong, bare shoulders exposed all her tattoos of moons and owls and a snow leopard and of course her favorite one, the Red Queen character.

Hans' large frame towered over her with his broad shoulders and legs that were too long for his body. Even in formal attire, his muscles bulged. As she looked down, stepping carefully over the large cobblestones in her bare feet and her cocktail dress, Hans suddenly pulled her back from the street. A black truck peeled out, narrowly missing her, as the crowd left the building. The commotion sent a flock of pigeons straight up into the pink and orange sky.

"Did you see that guy? What an asshole!" She looked up, grasping her chest.

"Are you okay?" asked Hans.

The driver sped off too fast to catch the license plate.

"Still alive. Hey, where's Kayla?"

"I think she's coming. Some of the members of the society had questions for her." They both stepped back on the curb, waiting for their classmate.

"She's going to kill us, you know."

"Nah, she'll be fine. She was incredible."

"Yeah, wasn't she though?" she agreed. "But they think Graham is a racist and a eugenicist. They didn't like his theory that African-Americans are genetically better suited to climate change. The fact that he's black doesn't help."

"Yes, but the man developed a cure for a virus that's taking the lives of thousands of black Americans. They're only playing devil's advocate, Veronica." Hans spun her around and tried to kiss her hard on the lips, but she backed away.

"Lucky bastard. And they gave him money to do it before he had any idea what an impact this would have. No one had ever heard of *Labrador* when we started working on these antibodies." She looked out onto the canal. The humidity made her thick hair even more unruly. She smoothed it down, pressed her lips together. "Don't you find that odd?"

Hans shrugged. "You can't argue with science. He's going to make millions on the cure and save American lives."

"Tell that to the rioters. Or the police that are trying to keep them from killing one another." She pointed across the canal, where a Coast Guard ship was stationed. A National Guardsman stood watch. He was armed with an automatic, patrolling the cars that passed near the D.C. Bridge and George Washington Island. She allowed Hans to pull her closer now. "I can't argue with Chemistry."

The military presence made her edgy, nervous.

Everyone's guard was up.

Soldiers were stationed on every corner.

But her defenses melted as Hans' strong arm encircled her waist. Her frame softened, giving into his pull. His hand rubbed the small of her back. "*That's* science."

"Go for a river boat ride with me?" Hans asked, spinning her toward him, smoothing her spunky hair behind her ear. "It's the perfect night for it. Be romantic. Spontaneous."

And it was the perfect night. The Georgetown-Alexandria river taxi was parked alongside the shore, transporting tourists and sweethearts and business people across the Potomac, glassed and shining. The water reflected the brightly-lit memorials as the sun set, illuminating them as tourists floated by on the boats. Nearby the canal, a colossal American flag cast a rippling shadow across them. A huge smile spread across Hans' face. She knew he loved America and all she stood for. He had shared with her his intent to make a life for himself here, and she knew he didn't want to leave and return with his wife to Germany. In America, he could be a self-made man, becoming everything he had the potential to be. His intentions weren't that innocent with her, however—he'd been married over ten years and he had a young daughter, Ruth. But his ear-to-ear grin was like a child's. She couldn't resist it, not his big, wide eyes that twinkled when he looked up at the flag and down at her.

She finally gave in and kissed Hans harder. It was a long, lingering kiss—much more than the usual peck on the cheek and cordial hug she gave him when they parted ways. She'd never made any apologies about being a flirt, but tonight was different. They were officially up to something. Finally, she broke away, wiped her lip.

They were interrupted when her cell phone went off with multiple alerts at once. The smart phone screen revealed seven messages, all from different numbers, but bearing the same message: GET OUT NOW.

They looked back at the mansion.

Kayla and the remaining guests were running from the building.

The wait staff and society members were following fast, herded by firemen and police. As they bolted out the door, black smoke mushroomed from the eastern most window of the mansion, and soon after, the building erupted into a ball of fire.

Beams and glass flew in all directions from the explosion.

The explosion demolished the east side of the building, set fire to the remaining structure with rapidly expanding tides of flames ballooning out of the windows. The guests screamed and dashed for safety, some throwing themselves to the ground with their heads in their hands. The roar of the blast peaked and then subsided into the squelching sound of fire. The survivors ran from the massive heat as the once proud Washburn mansion burned brightly in crackling flames.

-10-

Police Headquarters, 16ᵗʰ Precinct
Washington, D.C.

The precinct was crowded with atypical arrests—ordinary citizens ordered to be brought in by the National Guard for breaking quarantine orders, isolated in cellblocks and portable trailers outside the station by Executive Order Number 101,593 of the president of the United States. Tents were going up for the overflow patients and inmates. Until the military doctor could evaluate them for signs of *Labrador* virus, trace their history—a list of everyone they'd been in direct contact with in the past two weeks—and connect them with the NSA for security surveillance, they remained alienated from their families with the bare minimum in food, water, shelter. The tan trailers adorned with the Red Cross emblem and the American flag surrounded the holding center. Guards stood watch around them, and with every hour, it seemed, more army reservists were rounding up citizens believed to be infected, bringing them in for evaluation and arraignment.

In the street just outside, a male victim lay bleeding from his mouth, pallid, his face vacuous and hollowed. It was impossible to tell from the window if he was dead, or still clinging to his last breaths.

The detainees awaited release or transfer to the area hospitals, but access was limited; medical resources and ambulances and paramedic transfers were carefully rationed to the patients at greatest risk of infecting others, or to the ones exhibiting serious signs of illness.

None of the officers had signed up for infectious disease work. With no medical training, it made them punchy and short-fused, which only served to compound the rioting, the distrust of the government handling of the public health crisis.

Inside the precinct building were suspects brought in for the usual offenses—drugs, murder, rape, domestic violence—that the officers seemed far more at ease handling. But this evening, the routine was anything but normal. As an officer opened the door of the cell to secure a newly booked Hispanic prisoner, a rough-looking Caucasian inmate inside the cell lunged forward. He knocked the officer backwards. The Hispanic prisoner laced the fingers of his cuffed hands into a ball and smashed the officer's face with a vicious pile driver punch, drawing blood from his nose and mouth.

"Racist fuckers," the Hispanic man screamed. Spit sprayed from his mouth. His eyes were bloodshot, enraged. The cell was hot and stuffy and the prisoners were greased with their own sweat.

The Caucasian prisoner pinned the officer's arms against the bars, the Hispanic man fumbled for the officer's gun. Yelling and foot stomping from the other inmates echoed throughout the cell block. Two more officers rushed to the cell and beat the prisoners with their clubs. The three policemen secured them both behind the cellblock bars and slammed the gate.

"Try it again, you fucking animals," he screamed, touching his nose. The officer who'd been attacked spit on the Hispanic man, who grabbed the iron bars. Then the officer pulled his club and delivered a final blow against the man's knuckles where they gripped the cell gate.

The Hispanic man let out an agonizing scream.

"I'm just getting warmed up tonight." The officer twirled the club, showboating, and secured it against its holder in his belt.

"I'll bust your head open like a goddamn watermelon, pig," shouted the prisoner.

The outer door to the cell block slammed shut with a reverberating clang, and the officers returned to the interrogation room. Kayla, Hans and Veronica had witnessed the event from behind a two-way mirrored window. Hans put his arm around Kayla, trying to settle her nerves, and Veronica paced the room where the three students had been brought in for questioning regarding the explosion at the Washburn Mansion.

Kayla was the main suspect.

Virginia
NRA Shooting Range
Edward Marburg

Wes Lindstrom's cell phone rang. He held the phone to his right ear while he covered the other with his hand in the basement of the NRA range. The 15-position range had been cleared out for Senator Marburg. Marburg had the bump stock of an AR-15 semiautomatic rifle pressed tightly against his shoulder. He stuck his thumb in the trigger guard again with his knuckles pointing down the range, and he placed his other hand on the barrel of the gun. Using the weapon's recoil and maintaining forward pressure at the barrel, he fired the weapon like a full-speed automatic. Shells flew to his right. He hit the practice targets on the range with remarkable precision. He shook his hand to cool it off from the heat of the barrel, admired his marksmanship.

Lindstrom gave a whistle of approval. "I've never seen anyone bump fire a rifle with that level of accuracy, Senator."

"Don't let that get around town." He removed his ear protection and clipped in another magazine. "Try it?"

"Senator, I'm a lover of irreverent sex, I've a penchant for fine art, and I consume expensive wine in excess. But in all honesty, I wouldn't know the difference between a submachine gun and a Super-Soaker 5000." Lindstrom buttoned his jacket over his open-collared white shirt and held up his hand. He put his cell phone is his jacket pocket. "There's no answer from LeTorneau's lab."

"Come on. Give it a try." Marburg's phone rang now. He ignored it, placing his ear protection back on his head. It rang a second time.

"I'm just happy watching *you*. Excuse me." Lindstrom answered Marburg's phone, placing it on speaker.

"This is Thomas with the NSA. Edward Marburg?"

"This is his associate. I'll take a message for him. I don't like to steal the senator's bravado." Lindstrom waved his hand in the air.

"We have a location on Dr. Sara Sullivan, sir."

"Go ahead."

"We've located her at Phaedrex Clinical Trials Lab in Bethesda, Maryland. We were able to ping her cell phone and get a trace on her. She's only using the device intermittently, but we later achieved video confirmation."

"The Phaedrex lab? What the hell is she doing there?"

"Unclear, sir. They're conducting research on the *Labrador* virus here, sir."

"Yes, I know that. But why do you?"

"That's classified, sir. But we don't have satellite imagery of what goes on inside. We only got as far as the courtyard and the front door, but we're following her location now since she's considered infectious. We have communication with officers on the ground."

Marburg looked back at Lindstrom, who made a hand gesture and frowned and waved him off the range.

"Thank you. I'll inform the senator," said Lindstrom.

"Was it Joanne?" he asked. He hoped she was alright.

"No."

"Jane?" She always called him when she was looking for Wes.

"No, that nimble little MILF who broke quarantine at George Washington—the writer—the one who knows my wife—she's at the lab snooping around. But I can't reach the mole there."

"What about Claus?"

"He's got the vaccine into fast track at the FDA for a clinical trial, apparently."

"We need the treatment, though—fast. Midterms are coming up. This whole thing is turning into a big fucking mess."

He returned the weapon to the range attendant at the desk. Lindstrom handed the kid two one-hundred dollar bills.

"Thank you, Senator," said the range attendant.

"You never saw me here." He gave him an extra fifty.

The young man nodded and said, "Come back again."

"I'll try Claus again," said Lindstrom. "He's got a mole in the Bethesda lab, but neither of them is cooperating according to plan."

They walked out to the BMW.

"What does Sullivan have to do with the lab? Why is she snooping around there?"

"She knows something, Senator. She knows about our plan—our plan to release the virus and create the cure, to make a killing on the profits when the vaccine and the antibody stocks peak. The whole *plan*."

"How could she?"

Lindstrom started the car. His brows rose and he looked directly at his friend and he confessed earnestly, "Because she's the one who wrote it."

Sara Sullivan

Sara didn't have any legitimate reason for being in the Clinical Trials lab. Sure, she was a doctor. But she wasn't even wearing a white coat. She'd slid in through the front entrance as one of the other researchers had swiped her badge, and she'd easily obtained access to the locked facility. Most of the scientists had left for the evening—a few graduate students remained. A housekeeper was wheeling her cart down the hall. Sara strolled the halls, reading the bulletin boards for anything useful. She pulled down a flyer detailing the Society for Evolutionary Biology's symposium dinner which was being held at the Omni. Dr. Graham LeTorneau was being honored at the black tie gala for his controversial theory on the evolution of races and the parasites that co-evolve with them.

"Excuse me ma'am. Can I help you?" A middle-aged brunette woman stopped her in the hall as she peered into one of the labs.

The woman rummaged through her purse as she headed for the door. She rarely played the doctor card, even when she'd been stopped by the police while driving, but she couldn't think of anything better just then.

"Yes, I'm Dr. Sullivan." She fidgeted. She was a terrible liar. "I'm looking for the lab of Dr. LeTorneau. I understand he's doing some significant work on the *Labrador* virus."

"Is he expecting you?"

"I emailed him that I might stop by this evening, but I'm not sure he got the message." She scratched the top of her head as she spoke.

The woman's eyes narrowed.

"His lab is on the fourth floor, but it requires security clearance, Doctor. You'll have to obtain a pass at the front desk. But Dr. LeTorneau hasn't been in the lab for a few days."

She backed away, ascending a half flight of marble stairs. "Thank you. I'll head down to the desk."

She hid behind the sterile green walls until the brunette disappeared from sight, then she tip-toed back down the stairs and toward the elevator, but the woman was right—she needed a security code to access the elevator.

The labs she passed seemed rudimentary and interchangeable. It was impossible to discern the nature of the work without more information, but it was everything she remembered from her days in college. They were filled with black marble workbenches and microscopes and beakers. Pipettes and slide racks and centrifuges rested on the table tops of the first room she entered. The odors of the chemicals transported her back to college where, as a premed student, she'd spent diligent hours engrossed in cell biology experiments. The head of the lab had taken all the credit while the students performed the work, and she wondered if LeTorneau was the same. She'd been close to completing her own thesis and dissertation for the MD/PhD program at Georgetown when she'd reconnected with Marty. He'd convinced her that she should be more dedicated to building a family with him, and she'd blown off the remaining research requirement for her mentor, Dr. Adam Steinem. Marty had convinced her to fly to Paris for a semester. She'd fallen for his charm when he'd told her that he loved her on the left bank of the Seine, exactly 178 days into their relationship.

Elyse followed down the road, and now, Marty wanted her to quit her practice. She'd wrestled him on it, but now she felt complacent, internally defeated, and she wondered why she'd put up such a fight in the first place.

Her career was still everything her mother—and everyone's mother who never had a day of independence in the working world—told her she *should* want. But some days she wasn't sure if it was what she *did* want. The responsibility and the long hours and the constant longing to feel half-full on most days left her drained—and thinking it was all overrated.

But she'd wanted it.

Worked for it.

Earned it.

So why did she feel the contempt and guilt and envy when she apologized for not being able to attend luncheons and charity golf galas and *gift gathering* parties? Soon, she'd be catching glimpses of intergender sympathy from the other mothers—younger, prettier mothers with rich husbands—at the private school playground, when she declined afternoon play dates with a polite, '*I have to work*' response.

Her female physician colleagues had warned her it was coming.

Little Elyse was only an infant, they'd say. *Don't feel bad*. But she did. Her daughter had already spent the better part of her days with a babysitter, and now her very survival was at risk. She imagined her in the hospital, connected to tubes and lines, distressed, crying, and febrile.

She couldn't let that happen. She had to find an answer.

The biologist, Dr. Graham LeTorneau, was working on a cure, and she needed to know why black Americans were dying of *Labrador*. She certainly wasn't helping anyone locked away in quarantine, and she was convinced that the medical establishment was hiding something significant about the virus. It screamed overt racism at the worst, but at a minimum, there was something suspicious about the case distribution and the death toll in the *Labrador* epidemic, and the developing headlines had too much of an uncanny resemblance with the novel she'd sent to Wes Lindstrom's wife, Jane Morgan, to be entirely coincidental.

Marty was right, the guy seemed shady, but was he really so unethical to presume that he could manipulate the health and disease of the country for his own profit? Medical catastrophes were rarely caused by a single incident. More commonly, a series of mistakes of human judgement led to lethal medical emergencies. But Lindstrom was cunning. Smart enough.

It had to be him.

-11-

Sara Sullivan

Sara kept herself out of sight, hiding just behind the wall where the secretary couldn't see her. The red digital clock on her desk flashed: *5:48*. She figured the woman would be leaving soon for the day, but the woman sat at her desk, surfing the Internet. She studied the woman's office, assiduously, watching her from a distance: the woman's reflection of her face in her computer screen, the shrine of personal items on her desk, the photos and the memos pinned to the bulletin board next to her workstation. The red access pass hung from a metal hook on the wall, dangling behind the woman's teased up helmet of motionless auburn hair.

Suddenly, the woman turned around.

She pulled herself back further, and then she peered in again. She slipped down the hall and into the bathroom, looking for a way to distract the woman's attention long enough for her to grab the access pass.

She glanced at the ceiling clock: *5:52*. If the secretary locked her office, she'd never be able to get her hands on the card.

Ducking into one of the labs, she snatched a fire extinguisher from its wall mount, sprinted down the hall. It was heavier than she expected, almost too heavy for her to throw, but with a grunt, she propelled the canister down the marble stairwell before her, shattering the glass door to the courtyard. She did it for Elyse, who was now lying vulnerable, her naïve immune system ineffectual at battling the aggressive illness, isolated by doctors who refused to touch or comfort her for fear of contracting *Labrador*.

As she'd hoped, the secretary came running out of her office to investigate.

"Hello?" the woman called. "Who's there?" Following the direction of the clatter, the woman discovered the smashed door. Then she ran into a nearby office and grabbed the phone.

Sara darted quickly down the hall in the opposite direction and snatched the security key from the office. Then she ran around the corner to the back elevator. She swiped the pass on the card reader and she boarded when a green light blinked, opening the door. When she stepped off on the fourth floor, she was in a modern facility that made the old labs below look antiquated, like high school biology where she'd dissected frogs and blown up volcanoes with baking soda and vinegar.

LeTorneau's lab was more like Captain Kirk's Casino.

Futuristic automated equipment.

Huge metal machines with gaudy blinking lights that looked like they might vomit obscenely large amounts of cash.

No researcher got funding for such an enormous and complex facility unless a huge profit was expected, and now, more than ever, she felt she was close to finding out what the scientists behind *Labrador* were hiding.

A colony of moths, still in their cocoons, was housed in the center. Snails and Petri dishes and polymerase chain reaction agars were arranged on the counters around the lab's perimeter. One of the moths had escaped its chrysalis.

It landed on her left sleeve.

She quickly brushed it off, smearing its wing iridescent and ashen, against her skin and clothing, and she shuddered, observed the other insects hanging from the cocoons. She tore off a list from a bulletin board with the names, addresses and phone numbers of the graduate students: Veronica Laughlin, Hans Raedl, Jorge Bourdain, and Kayla Reeves.

Now, she moved to the rear of the lab where the cooler housing the primate dissections was labeled with a red biohazard symbol. Outside the room was the station for donning personal protective equipment.

She swallowed, moved closer.

Without full protective gear, she didn't dare open the massive stainless steel refrigerator door where the primates were kept cool. Icy crystals formed on the outside, resembling a meat locker. But inside, she might find the answers she was looking for. She'd already been exposed to *Labrador*, and she knew she might start to exhibit symptoms at any time.

Weakness.

Fatigue.

Nausea.

Headache.

Just thinking about it brought on a psychosomatic conglomerate of all of those symptoms. The disease rapidly progressed to vomiting.

Diarrhea.

Dehydration.

In the end-stages of the horrific disease, multi-organ system failure and bleeding from every orifice of the body occurred.

And finally, an undignified death.

Elyse could have had a narrow symptom window—a shorter incubation period, as an infant—and the disease could rapidly take a downhill course. The very thought of the virus being contained in the lab all around her sent an inimitable chill through her body. Her grueling workload over the last eight months had often left her too tired to even feed or bathe or console her daughter when she got home each night, utterly exhausted.

But she swore that would never happen again.

She had deemed herself a failure at motherhood in many ways, but now, with all her protective instinct and guilt amassed on saving Elyse, she hastily donned the hazmat suit, covering herself entirely from her throat to her feet, and she slipped on the blue latex gloves and plastic hooded helmet.

She opened the heavy cooler door and a gust of cold air permeated the suit, made her arm hair stand on end. She stepped inside and she propped the door open with a chair.

Red and yellow lights flashed: CONTAINMENT UNIT OPEN.

She crossed the threshold.

Diverse materials including recombinant DNA plating supplies and ELISA kits lined the shelves inside the frigid storage room. Beakers filled with pink and yellow reagent labeled CHEMOKINE and KINASE RECEPTORS collected a thicker liquid, dripping from two hanging buretrols. The stench of formaldehyde and agarose gels and immunochemicals wafted under her clear hood, and without thinking, she held her hand up to her nose. She chastised herself, and reminded herself never to touch her face, risking contamination, even while fully suited, but the odor of the preserved macaques and chimps was vile. Although the media had insisted the *Labrador* virus wasn't airborne, she didn't trust the information. The cooler reeked of suppurated flesh, like an infection had consumed the preserved mammals of the research facility.

But it wasn't the virus she was after.

Was the cure here?

She stepped deeper into the cooling unit now and she looked back over her shoulder. The massive door was still propped open. The stainless steel sliding racks containing primates lay beside her. The temperature grew even cooler the further in she went, and the liquid reagents dripped from the buretrols of the abstruse experiment. Carefully, she pulled back the handle on the inner door.

It led to an even smaller unit, recessed in the corner of the lab.

Deeper into the rabbit hole.

Shit.

A cloud of dry ice-like plumage fumed over her from above. The sublimated material filled the inner lab. She heard her own breathing, laborious, through the hazmat helmet now, felt the thumping of her own heart.

Had she contaminated herself? It didn't matter.

She had to keep going, for Elyse. The prognosis without treatment for blacks was so poor—her daughter's life depended on it.

She crouched down to the small door incorporated into the concealed, secure repository. She pushed open the door, screamed, as a formalin-preserved macaque fell from the ceiling behind her, dangling from a noose tied tightly around its neck. It had bled from the eyes, nose and mouth, and she gagged as its foul odor assaulted her nostrils. She coughed, and she looked all around her, feeling claustrophobic.

Get out. She told herself.

All she could see when she looked at the primate, suspended by the rope and dangling from the ceiling, was Elyse's innocent face.

Blood oozing from her blue eyes.

IVs stuck in her soft mocha skin.

Thoughts of her now, swaddled in a black shard, flashed in strobe images before her eyes. She shook off the terrifying image of her daughter as the lights flickered. She studied the monkey. It had all the signs of *Labrador* virus—hemorrhaging, dusky color with shocked out extremities, vomitus in its mouth, on its chest.

The lab was silent.

Except for the dripping liquid from the buretrol.

Then, she heard a quiet beeping noise near her feet. She kneeled down beside a white cardboard box with a U.S. Postal Service label addressed to: PHAEDREX. She dragged the heavy box out of the inner unit.

From above her, a cell phone, ringing, echoing.

It was difficult to localize the sound beneath the helmet.

She ran her hands along the highest shelf where the glass beakers with CD4 recombinant proteins and mononuclear and polyclonal antibodies were stored. Interferons and Interleukins were labeled in test tubes, but without full understanding of the experimental design, she couldn't make heads or tails as to which one might carry the cure for Labrador.

She had to get in touch with LeTorneau.

Or his graduate students.

But where were they?

She rarely left the lab when she was doing research. She climbed up on the counter and searched blindly for the phone with her gloved hand.

Finally, she found the ringing device. As she hopped down from the counter, she knocked over one of the Pyrex beakers. It shattered on the floor, releasing a sour odor that nauseated her and burned her nostrils as it mixed with the other chemicals. A large unbroken chard of the glass lay on the ground, labeled: DRINK ME.

Her heart pounded.

She answered the device, pressing it close to her mask. Maybe it was one of the researchers. Maybe they had the cure.

"Hello, Raedl."

"Who?" she asked. The man's voice was deep, foreign sounding.

"I think you know who this is."

"Who's Raedl? Where's LeTorneau?" She inched backward toward the door, but she was aware that she didn't yet have what she needed.

"You're not Hans. Well how pleasant to meet you. Let me see…Oh yes, there you are. Oh dear, your type won't fare well in here."

"Who is this? Where are you?" she demanded. The white cardboard box was beeping now, and lights were glowing from its sides.

"I can see you, but you can't see me."

She examined the shelves for a camera, turned her back to every corner of the room. "Where are you?" She slammed the inner containment unit shut, picked up the sharp spear of glass from the broken beaker. It was coated in a viscous red liquid.

"It won't do any good to close that now. Labrador is already out there." The man laughed.

She could feel his contempt as her hands trembled, holding the triangular wedge of glass before her, terrified to face a concealed enemy. Somehow, the man was observing her, but from where?

"Show yourself," she shouted.

"It seems you've broken the most important vial. That's a shame."

She stooped down on the floor, where the shattered beaker lay, broken into a blanket of fine chards. Another large piece was intact, and it read: *Labrador IgG and IgM Antibody*. The antibodies naturally produced by the human body or chemically in the lab were capable of neutralizing viruses and bacteria, allowing a person to fight off infection.

The cure is an antibody. Of course!

She got down on all fours, defeated, regarded the buretrols and reagents and the miniscule amount of liquid that lay on the floor, ran her fingers through the red syrup spread near the shattered container. The process of creating it appeared labor intensive.

Lots of reagent, very little product.

They must need virus to create antibodies.

Her thoughts raced, seeing no way out.

Furious, she smashed the remaining equipment, breaking it and spilling the liquid precursors and covering the floor in a sweet smelling coating not unlike antifreeze.

"Show yourself," she screamed again. "LeTorneau?" Panicked and gasping for breath, she ripped off the plastic hazmat helmet.

She gripped her chest.

Her heart thumped harder.

Another cloud of gas sublimated from the inner unit.

She held the cell phone tightly to her ear, enraged at the laughter of the male voice.

"I'm not LeTorneau—but he's with me. For a short while, anyway. See, he's one of only a handful who knows how to produce a cure for *Labrador*."

"What do you want? Who are you?"

"I was wondering the same thing, young lady. I think the more prudent question is, 'What don't I want?'"

She kneeled down and tore away the white cardboard packaging, revealing a titanium box with red and black wires crisscrossing all over it, connecting to bolts and screws that were intertwined with red and green buttons. A pressure gauge with a thin black needle blinked at the top of the metal unit, clicking and moving to the right as she turned it around. It was too dense for her to lift it off the ground. She shoved it out from under the lab bench, grunting as she kicked it into the center of the core. The smell of chemicals and the sublimed carbon dioxide intoxicated her lungs now, and a dewy precipitate formed across the front of the metal unit.

"Is it the cure—in this box?" She wiped the condensation from the top.

He laughed. "Not quite."

"I want the cure," she screamed into the phone.

"*Labrador* is the cure!"

Her eyes goggled as she discovered the flashing red numbers on the black panel across the side of the unit: *23:59:30*. She looked at the dial again. It wasn't a pressure gauge—it was a Geiger counter. She was staring at a radioactive bomb. She rose and she backed away and she tore off her remaining equipment, ignoring the protocol for avoiding contamination, threw the gloves and the shoe covers across the room and she ran out of the cooling unit to the main door of LeTorneau's lab. She yanked and turned the metal knob, and she pulled on it with all her might, but it was dead bolted. She saw the housekeeper's cart outside the tiny window on the door, but there was no one in sight.

"Help! Is anyone there? Let me out!" Her cries went unheeded.

The man laughed again over the line.

Panting into the phone, she demanded, "What have you done?"

"This cell phone call has armed the bomb. It's set to go off tomorrow evening—sooner if I choose."

"Who the hell are you?"

"You might be fixin' to run, but even if you escape, by the looks of you—your nice brown sugar color, that is—and what you've just contaminated yourself with, it doesn't look like I'll need to worry about you for too long. Goodbye."

"Wait," she screamed, but the caller hung up.

She lifted one of the stools from around the workbench, hurled it at the door, but it didn't even chip the leaded glass. The window was too small to climb through, anyway. She felt flushed, sweating now. The visions of Elyse and the macaque flashed before her again. Hallucinations. One of the symptoms of disease.

Was she infected, or just hysterical?

She flung open drawers, searching for something heavy, or sharp—or a key with which to escape.

Nothing but lab equipment.

She picked up the huge centrifuge from the center work bench and she hurled it at the window, smashing it and setting off the alarm system. Silver and red warning lights flashed throughout the room, and a deafening low-pitched alarm reverberated throughout the entire building, forcing her to cover her ears.

A few minutes later, people began evacuating the facility. A helicopter circled overhead, outside.

She reached out the side of the window, planting her left foot against the cement window ledge. With her back against the red brick, she grabbed the fire escape with her right arm and she swung her legs out beneath her, trying to secure her footing on its platform. She missed it by a foot and, swinging with her feet free and one arm clinging to the escape route, she pulled herself up to her chin. Then she climbed down the fire escape and unhooked the ladder on its lowest level. It slid on its track and she climbed down to the ground and she ran for her life, away from the lab.

The Red Cross helicopter circled again.

Police cars raced toward the lab.

She ran into an alley, and when she was sure she was out of sight, she powered on her cell phone and dialed Marty.

"Sara, are you okay? Where the hell are you?"

"Marty, I'm okay. I can't tell you right now. How's my baby?"

"Sara…"

Marty sounded different. It wasn't his usual, secure voice she was used to hearing on the other end of the line. Something was wrong.

Marty said, "They're talking about having to put a breathing tube in Elyse, put her on a ventilator."

"Is it *Labrador?* Is she sick with the virus?" She was already gasping for breath.

"I don't know, Sara. They sent off lab work. We're both quarantined at the hospital. I can't even go home. They're not as worried about me because I'm Caucasian, but they said I'm still at risk. Why is that?"

"We don't really know why. But I'm going to find out."

"They're looking for you, Sara. They came looking for me. They seized my badge, Sara. My badge for Chrissake."

"Marty, just stay put. I'm going to figure out what's going on."

"Where are you?"

"Never mind. I'll be okay. Listen, there is a cure for this," she said, panting. "A cure for *Labrador.* It's out there—and somebody doesn't like that."

-12-

Police Headquarters, 16ᵗʰ Precinct
Washington, D.C.
Kayla Reeves

Kayla Reeves sat in the interrogation room at the police precinct. She shivered as the air conditioning blew down on her neck, palms sweating, heart racing. She thought about the time Jorge had gone home with her for spring break to her parents' farm in Macon, Georgia: They rode horses and they swam in the Chattahoochee and they pulled leeches the size of sizzled bacon off of one another and they swung from a tube tied to a tree, just like the two country kids they were.

She had to get in touch with him, straighten everything out.

"When was the last time you spoke with Dr. LeTorneau?" The stout policeman asked. He gnawed at his pen. The cap was flattened from his gnashing molars.

Her attention snapped back to the present.

"Two days ago. The day before the lecture."

"Why was the lecture venue changed?"

"I'm not sure." She looked toward the door, wished Veronica and Hans were with her. Where had they taken them? "It was changed by Graham by email notification. I thought the mansion would be nicer than a hotel conference room to be honest—and I assumed it had something to do with not being able to get access to the Omni downtown. Traffic's been awful—you can't get anywhere with all the health checkpoints."

"You're telling the truth, young lady?"

"Absolutely," she said, without hesitation. She knew Veronica would never have been as patient as she was with his questioning. She would've snapped back with some sassy line. But the truth was, she was fearful of them. They were, after all, police officers. Good ol' boys. There to help. They were only following orders—even if they were rounding up citizens and restricting their movements for the safety of the public.

She had to trust that they knew what they were doing.

She went along with the questioning, the law, even if all the panic and fear mongering surrounding the *Labrador* epidemic seemed irrational.

Racist.

What else could she do?

"You're sure?"

"Why would I lie?"

Another officer entered the room. The back of the door slammed against the wall.

"There's been another explosion," the officer said. "The entire Omni is a ball of fire. We'll need to send all available cars over there."

The first officer swore and rose from his chair. "Everyone here is assigned. Get reinforcements from the outlying precincts. Jesus."

"Yes, sir."

"What's going on?" she asked. "Another bomb?"

She never should've agreed to study under LeTorneau. His research was too controversial.

"Young lady, if I ask your friends out there, I'll get the same story?" asked the first officer.

The man gave her the chills, hovering over her in his too tight uniform with his sly, reptilian look, probing her face, her expression, her every move, as if he distrusted her entirely. Gun on his hip. The baton. His words were guttural, militant sounding—like a different language.

"Has Dr. LeTorneau been in contact with you since the explosion?"

"We've all been trying to reach him. We're all worried about him. I have no idea why he didn't make it to the lecture."

"Answer the question."

"No," she said.

"Did you try to contact him since?"

"Of course—several times. We texted him both before and after the event to see if he was on his way. He never showed up."

"Can I see the texts, young lady?"

"Sure." She reluctantly handed over the cell phone, revealing the text messages she'd sent to Graham's phone. The officer took her device in his meaty hand and scrolled through her personal information.

"What are these?" The man showed her the texts reading: GET OUT NOW.

"I tried to tell you. Hans and I received the same texts right before the explosion. Someone doesn't like Graham's research. They think it's racist."

"Is it?"

"Not at all. There are people who don't understand it. There's a scientific basis for everything we're working on."

"I've seen a lot of racism lately, Ms. Reeves. And it's ugly." The police officer pulled down the mini blinds on the window and peered outside where the artillery tank and army envoy were stationed. The Red Cross truck was parked next to it. "Really ugly. I've been doing this long enough now where I know that everyone I pull over, everyone I charge, everyone that fits a certain stereotype, I look at like a criminal. It becomes instinctive. Split-second decisions can mean the difference between life and death on the street. But somewhere inside me, I know where to draw the line. What's going on out there right now—I've never seen anything quite like it."

"Dr. LeTorneau's not a racist. He's trying to get the cure to this epidemic out that's killing people—his own people." She motioned to the window, where angry protesters gathered in numbers behind cops and barricades. "And there's somebody trying to stop him."

"He's black?" The officer flipped through the manila file on the desk.

She couldn't see inside the folder. What information did they have on Graham? Did they have a file on *her*?

"That's right," she said. "And he's risked his own life exposing himself to the virus while developing the antibody— the cure."

"Would you say, you've ever been *envious* of his success, Ms. Reeves?"

Kayla laughed. A laugh like she could hardly believe the question. She blew her bangs upward on her forward in frustration, looked directly at him. "Of course I'm envious. His work is nominated for a Nobel Prize."

"Does it bother you that you and the other graduate students do a large part of the work and Dr. LeTorneau gets all this glory?"

"If you mean—"

"Just answer the question."

"No, I mean, kind of, but—"

"What are you an attorney or something?" Veronica slid into the room and now grabbed a seat next to her. "You don't have to answer that, Kayla. None of us are guilty of anything other than trying to find out where Graham is. We all want the same answers."

"I'll ask the questions—and I'll have you in handcuffs, honey, if you don't follow protocol in my precinct. I'll talk to you when I'm done with your friend." The officer pointed his pudgy finger at Veronica.

"There haven't been any charges filed." Veronica stood up defiantly and grabbed the offending digit. "Didn't your mama teach you it's not polite to point?"

Kayla gasped.

The officer twisted Veronica's arm full circle and turned her around, pressing her face against the wall.

"If you'd like to spend the next two weeks quarantined in the cozy tents outside, I'd be happy to charge you with endangerment to public health after exposing others to that virus you cooked up in your lab."

"You have no idea what you're talking about," said Veronica. "Dr. LeTorneau and everyone in the lab follow strict universal precautions. He has the cure for *Labrador*." The officer relaxed his grip, and Veronica shook her arm where he'd bent it tightly. "I want a missing person report filed."

"*Or*—" The officer's voice rose to a roar, and he leaned forward and put his hands on the desk, "you can cooperate and answer a few questions to help us in our investigation."

She sat down. Veronica did, too, reluctantly.

The second officer entered the room with Hans, and he pulled out a seat for him. The district attorney, a lean gentleman with a mustache, followed behind them.

"They're telling the truth," said the DA. He tugged on his suspenders with both hands and snapped them and poured himself a cup of coffee.

"Thank you." Veronica pulled up her strapless dress and leaned back comfortably in the chair, looking confident.

The DA sipped his coffee, said, "There's suspicious activity at the lab. Nothing major. A break in maybe. Earlier today. I was just on the phone with the NSA."

"What? By who?" Kayla stood up.

"Probably just kids making trouble," said the officer, with the fat fingers. "There's a lot of that going on, rioting everywhere."

"Nope, gentlemen, we're looking for a doctor. A black female, about thirty-five. Sara Sullivan's her name." The DA put his hands on the desk. "Here's what's going to happen, kids. We're going to file a missing person report on your professor. Then we're going to check out the lab, make sure everything's secure. That virus you're dealing with is no common cold. I have security clearance from the Feds to shut the whole place down if we need to—if they haven't already. *Labrador* is a potential agent of biologic warfare."

Hans placed his hand on his forehead and shook his head. "You're preaching to the choir."

"Are you familiar with the Tuskegee syphilis trials?" the DA asked Kayla.

"Of course." She was well versed on the history of experimentation and the medical ethics of it—or lack thereof. "Between 1932 and 1972 over four hundred black American males were given syphilis by the U.S. Department of Health and Human Services to study the progression of the disease. They weren't told they had syphilis, and they weren't offered penicillin, even when it became available in the 1940s."

"Do you see an ethical problem with that, Ms. Reeves?"

She gave Veronica a stern look.

"Of course I do," she said. "Any experiment involving human subjects raises ethical considerations and—"

"I'd like to think we've come a long way since then," interrupted Veronica.

"The truth is that many diseases affect races differently," said Kayla. "Hypertension and stroke occur much more frequently in African-Americans. That's part of the reason we're studying the genetics behind it—to better understand them. A doctor has to be able to discuss his patients' conditions and their risk factors with him—not feel like he's walking on glass."

The DA gave her a skeptical nod, tapping his pencil on his pad of paper. "Risk factors? Or are we talking about people who don't have access to the same treatments you do, Ms. Reeves?"

"We haven't even started a human trial yet. The FDA does everything they can to prevent any progress toward that," protested Veronica. She shook her head. "That's not fair."

"And you're out of line," he screamed, pointing at her.

Veronica took her foot down from the desk. "Neither one of you knows what finger to use either. Try this." She stuck up her middle finger.

The officer turned back to Kayla.

"According to the president, you also mentioned malaria in your talk this evening."

"Yes, what about it? The sickle cell gene is carried by 1 percent of all blacks in America. It confers a resistance to malaria in blacks. We're investigating the racial preponderance of the *Labrador* virus in our search for a cure."

"Scientists also investigated malaria in the 1940s in the Dachau concentration camp when they injected subjects with the virus in effort to study an immunization strategy in Nazi Germany."

"What makes you such an expert?" asked Veronica.

The DA chuckled. He sipped his coffee, said, "What makes me such an expert."

Kayla swallowed. His abrasive behavior was intimidating, but his concerns were valid. Nothing he said was inaccurate.

Where had Graham gone?

Had he told them the truth?

She wanted to sit with Jorge and tell him everything that had happened over a farmer's lunch of fried okra and catfish etouffee. In the oddly quaint district where he lived, the neighbors were so welcoming to her.

Here, she felt ostracized.

She regarded the police. "Officer, our research has been in moths and snails and now primates. Never yet on human beings. Our mentor, Dr. LeTorneau, received a sizeable grant from NIH to develop a cure, and that is *exactly* what we've spent the last four years of our lives doing. He also has connections with Phaedrex. That doesn't make him a criminal."

"Does *anyone* else have access to the lab besides the three of you and LeTorneau?"

"Access requires the highest level of security clearance in the building. Not even the housekeepers are allowed in without supervised surveillance. Only the three of us, LeTorneau, and Jorge have that privilege."

"Who the hell is Jorge?" The DA took another sip of his coffee and glanced at his watch and rolled up his pinstriped sleeves.

"A grad student like us—working on the antibody to *Labrador* virus. He also worked on the vaccine for it in Newfoundland," said Hans.

"Where is he?"

"He couldn't make the symposium due to a family emergency, a death. He's on sabbatical. He texted me, said he'd be in tomorrow. Look, we all share the same goal here—to cure this thing." Hans rose and pushed past the officers and opened the door. His large frame dwarfed the other three men. His accent was still thick, even after studying English for over five years. "Now unless there's anything else, we have a lot of work to do back at the facility."

George Washington University
Marty Thompson

Marty sat in the waiting room of the ICU, hoping to see Elyse. He looked around at the other parents. There was a well-dressed Caucasian man in a suit with his well-dressed wife. They looked too old to have a child.

But who knew these days.

Across from the couple was a rail-thin teenager pecking away on her cell phone with her fake nails. She looked like a kid herself. An overweight woman in a tank top with tight black pants and flabby bingo arms had tried to make conversation with him, but he hated them all at that moment, and he didn't care about any of their children.

He could only think of Elyse.

He didn't belong with them—his fiancée was a *doctor*.

Elyse might be his only daughter, he thought. And he'd prayed for a boy. How ungrateful that had been of him. What a precious gift she was.

And now Sara didn't want any more kids.

Every time the glass doors slid open, he stood up from the hard sofa. He dialed Sara's cell phone again, but with no answer. It went straight to voicemail.

Damn her. She's so stubborn.

Finally, an Asian man in a long, white coat entered, called his name. The man introduced himself as Dr. Harold Lee, and led him out of the waiting room to talk in a private area where Elyse was visible through a glass window. Her tiny body was enveloped in a plastic tent resembling a giant bubble, and she was screaming so loudly that he feared her mighty lungs would blow the clear tent out of the metal crib.

Her tufts of dark hair looked sweaty.

Her cheeks were crimson.

No one came in to comfort her.

Her monitors alarmed, a jarring tone that sounded more like his alarm clock.

Only she wasn't waking up.

And he wouldn't be going to work tomorrow.

She had a tube down one side of her nose and a bag connected to her bladder. As her screaming settled, her nostrils flared in succession with every rapid breath. He advanced toward the door of the room where she lay, agitated, alone, with medical personnel watching over her only from teleconferencing monitors. The doctor placed his pasty hand over Marty's wrist.

It was a frail touch, devoid of empathy.

"I'm sorry, Mr. Thompson, you can't go any closer." The man turned away from Marty's tearful expression. "Not until we rule out *Labrador*. Only individuals specially trained in contact precautions can enter the room. It's risky for even the most skilled professionals."

"So you're not even sure she has it?"

"No, but she has all the symptoms—high fever, vomiting, reddening of the eyes, diarrhea."

"If you're not sure she has it, why is she in the unit with all the infected patients?" He slammed his hand against the thick observation window.

Elyse was screaming even louder now.

"There's no way to tell, sir. But the likelihood is very high. We can't risk contamination to the other units." Harold Lee's voice was matter of fact, cold, emotionless. "And we'll need you to remain isolated until we can examine you further. You can stay in here." Dr. Lee pointed to the couch in the corner of the observation room.

"But that's my daughter. I was holding her just before I brought her in. She's crying."

"I'm sorry, sir."

"What happened here to make Sara run?"

The doctor's brows rose. "Do you know of Dr. Sullivan's whereabouts, Mr. Thompson?" The doctor flipped the page on his clipboard, clicked open his pen. "Contact tracing is critical in containing outbreaks of this nature."

"I'm not leaving here without my daughter," he shouted.

"We recommend that you stay—as a precautionary measure. If you've been exposed, it would be unwise to risk spreading it to others."

"I can't stand here and watch my daughter die of this disease. You're telling me there's *nothing* I can do?"

"There's nothing *any* of us can do, Mr. Thompson." Dr. Lee's voice was robotic, rehearsed. The doctor put on his glasses and observed the baby's monitors, alarming without resolve, wrote down Elyse's vital signs on his clipboard. "The doctors and nurses are risking their lives treating infected patients, and we only ask that you cooperate with the CDC's recommendations to help us help you."

Dr. Lee clicked his pen closed and drew the blinds on the isolation ward.

Police Headquarters, 16th Precinct
Washington, D.C.
Kayla Reeves

Kayla Reeves called after Hans as her burly colleague stormed out of the police precinct. "Hans, where are you going?"

Veronica trailed behind, carrying her high heels and running across the street in her bare feet.

"Isn't it clear?" Hans' keys were in his hands, and his blonde bangs swished with each of his heavy steps. "The cops are right, Kayla. LeTorneau lied to us. We worked our asses off. And now there's an epidemic our there of biblical proportions."

"Hans, that's not true." She defended LeTorneau, grabbing Hans by his massive forearm, but he pulled away and headed to the parking lot. "His research has always upheld the highest ethical standards. He wouldn't do anything to jeopardize his reputation."

"Really Kayla? Look around you. *Labrador* is bringing out the worst in everyone." Hans searched for his car. "You believe what you want. I'm leaving."

"Where are you going?"

"To the lab." Hans walked toward his Volkswagen.

Veronica was running faster now, toward them, as Kayla tried to stop Hans. He flung her petite frame off of him. She landed on her bottom on the grass beside his car.

"I'm going to make sure no one else dies of *Labrador*—especially now that I see the racism and depravity it's causing," said Hans.

"Hans, please be reasonable."

Veronica finally caught up to them, pleading with Hans, but he slammed the door of the Passat and sped off.

Arlington National Cemetery
Arlington, Virginia
Edward Marburg

Edward Marburg stood beside his wife, Joanne, at Arlington National Cemetery. The ceremony honoring the late Senator Audrey Marseille was attended by the president of the United States. White steeds carried the senator's ashes down the curved path, beyond the acres of perfectly lined headstones, each with a tiny American flag placed before it, toward the columbarium. Servicemen adorned in navy with white caps and gloves led the coach containing her pewter urn, inscribed in delicate calligraphy with her name and service dates.

Senator Marseille's husband, Edwin, was terribly distraught that his wife—having served in the U.S. military in Afghanistan, and being the first black female senator elected from the state of Virginia—should not be accorded the traditional burial, but the president had declared a state of emergency and ordered all bodies infected with *Labrador* virus to be cremated. The congregation on the hallowed ground grew silent now until only the sparrows could be heard.

After a while, the funeral director approached the wooden podium. He was tall—well over six feet, and had a baritone voice that carried out across the crowd of hundreds of military and civilian mourners. His red beard and mustache were long, further hiding any trace of emotion, as he maintained a stoic reverence. Across from him Marseille's widower grieved, holding his teenage daughter around her shoulders.

A lone soldier played *"Taps"* on the bugle.

Beside the soldier, the military band and Scottish bagpiper held their instruments by their sides, listening to the eerie bugle call. There was no casket for which to cover by flag, as was typical for a proper Arlington burial, only the majestic urn. Marseille's husband gripped his teenage daughter's shoulder. A light drizzle began to fall. Soon it smelled of wet leaves and the smoke of the soldiers' rifles.

Marburg squeezed his wife's hand. She stood beside him in a simple black suit, timeless and classic, didn't speak to him. The civilians placed their hands on their hearts as the military band played *"The Star Spangled Banner."*

Rounds were fired into the air.

The rifles traumatized his mind and he shed a tear, not for Marseille, but for himself.

As much as he tried to desensitize himself to the sound of the rifles—by shooting off automatics, or once in a while, going quail or deer hunting—he could never erase the memory of killing his own father. While cleaning the barrel of his dad's rifle outside the family's hunting cabin, he'd accidentally shot his father, a Virginia orchard keeper who was only forty years old at the time. He was nine. The bullet went through his father's chest, and killed him swiftly. Now he replayed the tragic death in his mind, watching every motion, even the words mouthed by both of them about the frost on the apples and how it had ruined the whole crop.

His father had said they'd be okay.

The autumn leaves fell in slow motion in the afternoon sunshine then and now. The crunchy sound they made after his father took him down off his shoulders and walked him through the rows of Golden Delicious and Macintosh and Honey Crisp was muted today. The most vivid detail was the discharge of the rifle, the harrowing echo it made, that sound, and the smell of gun powder, he'd never forget.

The uniformed soldiers of the Old Guard mounted their horses now and the procession proceeded down Eisenhower. At the conclusion of the service, the urn was placed in its niche, covered by a marble plaque. The funeral director and his staff were kept busy managing the onlookers, prohibiting photography of the grieving family by tourists. The Secret

Service had closed a portion of the National Cemetery for the entrance and exit of the president and First Lady.

At the conclusion of the ceremony, he turned to his wife, said, "Joanne, I'm sorry I didn't get to the hospital. I can't imagine what you went through without me there. But I'm glad you got to go home the same day, and I can't thank you enough for being here today."

"You have coffee on your tie," she said, looking at him with disdain. She fixed the lipstick where it had caked at the corner of her mouth and she smiled and she walked over to greet Wes Lindstrom and his wife, Jane Morgan.

"You look lovely, Joanne. I do hope you're feeling much better than when I saw you at the hospital," said Lindstrom.

"I'm doing well, thank you," Joanne said. "I start chemo next week. All of the remaining tissue biopsies came back negative."

"That's great news," Jane Morgan said. "We're heading back to New York tomorrow night. Will you both join us for dinner?"

"That's sweet of you, Jane, but I've a bit of a headache. I think I'm going to rest."

"Always a lady," said Lindstrom. He kissed her hand, grinned. To Marburg, he said, "I'll be back on Tuesday. In the meantime, I'll be arranging a trip to the vaccine lab in Newfoundland to get some answers."

The drizzle turned to a pouring rain as they walked along the road.

The congregation dispersed to their cars, covering their heads with coats and umbrellas. He attempted to kiss Joanne on the cheek as the procession pulled away from the elegant columbarium where the remains of cremated soldiers of past wars were honored. She brushed him away, turning toward the tinted window.

He sighed.

He'd said he was sorry.

Why did she always have to hold a grudge?

As the car started to move, a black Ford pickup truck at the end of the procession was the last thing he saw in the passenger's side mirror before the columbarium burst into flames. Debris rained from the leaden sky, hitting the Cadillac. Straggling mourners dispersed wildly into the cemetery now, running for their cars, taking cover behind the headstones and huge oak trees on the sprawling cemetery grounds.

The military personnel drew their weapons at attention.

He flung open the door of the sedan and he grabbed Joanne, pitching her out of the car. With his arms around her, they rolled to the ground, out onto the lawn, only seconds before their vehicle exploded, killing his driver.

He drew his pistol.

He ordered Joanne, screaming, to stay down.

Lindstrom ran from his car up the Eisenhower path, holding his cell phone to his ear. The Secret Service car escorting the president and First Lady peeled out along the path, proceeding down Hadley and toward the exit.

-13-

Sara Sullivan

Sara walked into the newly built aquarium, trying to blend in with the tourists snapping pictures of the doting penguin mamas and papas and their adorable chicks. Laughing nervously along with their antics, she looked the part of a typical suburban soccer mom.

Dinner at 5.

Practice at 6.

That is, if Elyse lived to see the first grade.

Looking over her shoulder, she was fearful that someone was on her tail. She was running out of places to hide. She hadn't showered in days. She now had the addresses and phone numbers of the graduate students, but could she trust any of them? Someone had planted the bomb in LeTorneau's lab—for all she knew, it could've been him.

But why?

She sat down in a private corner of the cafeteria and she called the CDC hotline and she waited for a response. Three rings. Her quarantine period was coming to an end, but she was still considered a missing contact for another day. The CDC was strict in tracing all exposures for the full two-week incubation period, and anyone breaking quarantine was being actively pursued. They'd even mentioned prosecution on the news. Being in LeTorneau's lab might put her back into quarantine for another two weeks, and she was running from the law like a common criminal.

Sara Sullivan.

Mommy.

Doctor.

Fugitive.

"Hello, CDC?"

"Yes. Go ahead."

"This is Dr. Sara Sullivan. I'm calling to report a contamination—an exposure—to *Labrador* virus."

"I'll need your name and social security number, the date of the exposure, and the details surrounding the contacts, their symptoms, and your current location."

"I'm at the clinical trials lab of Dr. Graham LeTorneau in Bethesda, Maryland. There's been a security breach in the lab. Something's gone dangerously wrong."

She gave them the digits in her social security number and she waited. She heard fingers typing on the keyboard over the line. She waited some more. Was she making a mistake? She was aware that her call—and her location—could be traced from her cell phone. But this was her only hope of securing the cure for *Labrador*—and Elyse.

At the lab, the epidemiologist's screen flashed red and yellow: CONTACT IDENTIFIED. SECURITY BREACH. QUARANTINE BROKEN!

"We're aware of the break in at the lab. The police are looking into it." There was more typing over the line. "The authorities are taking all the proper precautions to contain any hazardous materials. Senator Marburg is heading the *Labrador* response."

"No—you don't understand. It's more than a break-in." She swallowed and she ran her hand through her hair and she looked at the gigantic killer whale, staring at her through the other side of the glass tank. It circled around twice with its mouth open, consuming all the fish that it could swallow. Then it swam to the surface, made a gallant leap. "There's a bomb in the lab."

"Are you currently experiencing any symptoms of headache, nausea, vomiting, diarrhea or fever?"

"No—did you hear me?" She got up from the table now and she moved toward the exit. Children were running around, screaming, playful, happy, secure, with their parents. There was static over the line. "I said there's a bomb in the lab."

The woman at the ticket counter turned and glared at her.

"Hold the line please, Doctor."

"No, wait." There was silence over the line, and the tiny GPS icon flashed in the upper right hand corner of her cell phone. *Strange,* she thought. She'd kept her location services on the network turned off. Mothers sheltered their children close now, backed away from her, as she yelled, "I'm telling the truth!"

She was certain now that they had her location.

She had to run.

Virginia
Edward Marburg

In his Virginia home, Edward Marburg accepted another large delivery of flowers: gladiolas and lilies and roses in an array of warm colors. Joanne was doing better. She'd pull through this, and be by his side for the upcoming election. Marburg was confident of it. And he needed her there. It was nice that she had so many friends in her support group to get her through this. It really took the pressure off him. His cell phone had been ringing non-stop. It rang now as he set down the bouquet.

"Joanne!"

"What?"

She'd been distraught over the explosion the previous day, hadn't left their home. She remained in bed, developed a fever after the surgery, even considered returning to the hospital for evaluation, but he'd cautioned against it in light of the viral epidemic.

The phone rang again.

He answered the call. "Marburg here."

"This is Devon Hammond at the CDC, Senator."

He signed for the flowers and he closed the door and he put them in the foyer with the others.

He yelled up to Joanne again.

She didn't respond.

He watched from the bay window until the iron gates closed automatically behind the deliveryman's white van. Then he locked the massive wrought iron-adorned front door.

"I'll need to be briefed on the current case numbers. Have you located the doctor?" he asked.

"Yes, sir," the young man on the line said. "NSA registered a location in Bethesda, Maryland, and she's currently on Pennsylvania Avenue at the new District Aquarium. She's considered imminently dangerous based on her last contact."

"Has she developed symptoms?"

"Negative. She called in a bomb threat—at the Bethesda lab. The rent-a-cop there said it checked out clear. But she was nosing around the facility and got caught on their cameras. And the professor has been missing for three days."

"Rent-a-cop? LeTorneau?"

"Yes, sir."

"Are Sullivan and LeTorneau working together?"

"It doesn't appear so, but she reported him for contamination."

"She knows something alright."

He walked up the curving staircase and into the bedroom, where Joanne was sleeping in their colonial bed. He looked out the floor-to-ceiling windows and into the huge yard where his German shepherds were running around, and he drew back the satin window dressings. Then he pointed the remote and he turned off the television, where another talking head was blathering on about the latest racially motivated riots in the capital. Footage looped endlessly behind him.

"What's being done?"

"The police are investigating, sir."

"No. We're in deep shit, and I'm heading up this investigation." He removed his Walther PPK from the safe in the closet. He loaded several bullets in the weapon and he secured it in his fanny-pack holster. Lindstrom would probably refuse to be seen with him wearing it, but this wasn't a damn fashion show. He put on his jacket. "Notify the president. This is too close to home. And get security over to my house. Joanne's here alone."

"Yes, sir."

"Don't lose her this time. Stay on her. And make contact with LeTorneau. He's refused to talk with me in the past, but I need him on board with the investigation. Get a search order for his home if you have to." He turned off their bedroom light. "I'm going after her myself."

Phaedrex Clinical Trials Lab

Bethesda, Maryland

Hans Raedl

Hans Raedl swiped his employee badge. He entered the front door to the Bethesda lab. Everything looked like business as usual, but he wasn't convinced. He had to check out the lab—and maybe LeTorneau's office.

"Hi, Rayleen," Hans said to the secretary, Rayleen Banas.

The redhead was sipping coffee at her desk at the switchboard of the lab's main entrance. Her dress was too tight and the smell of her strawberry gum pervaded the hallway. There were more trinkets on her tables than a BINGO hall.

Business as usual.

"Good morning, Dr. Raedl." Rayleen Banas winked at him as he set his large hands on the counter. She drew open the glass window in front of her.

"Please, it's just Hans." He offered a modest smile. *Dr. Raedl* sounded so distinguished, though. And he was almost a PhD. He stood up a little taller.

"Going up to the fourth floor?"

"Yes ma'am. Has Dr. LeTorneau been in?"

"I haven't seen the man in over a week. Is he on sabbatical?"

"No, he's not." He was more concerned now than ever.

"Everything else okay upstairs? There were some police officers here earlier, but without a warrant I wasn't allowed to let them in—strict orders from Dr. LeTorneau."

"You did the right thing. They're not trained to access the biohazard unit."

"Said they'd be back later, though, with a search warrant. They checked out the rest of the building looking for a bomb. False alarm, though. Looks like some kids just broke a window upstairs. The lab is still locked up."

"Please make sure I'm notified if anyone else requests access."

He swiped his card at the elevator and he rode up to the fourth floor. He unlocked the door to their lab. A brisk wind was blowing through the window, and the containment unit was wide open.

A chair was overturned on the floor.

Several of Kayla's moths were fluttering around the room, out of their shelter.

The frigid air from the cooling unit gave him a chill, but it didn't cover the stench coming from the corner of the room. He held his hand to his mouth and he gagged at what he saw next.

In a puddle of blood, which she'd apparently vomited all over the marble floor, lay the housekeeper.

He didn't know her name, but he'd seen her many times. Even with dried blood caked on her eyelids and nostrils, she was easily recognizable, with signs of *Labrador* infection: vomiting, reddened eyes, and bleeding from every orifice.

He, Kayla and Veronica had been in the lab only two days ago. Had the housekeeper become infected before then? He wasn't aware that the virus could consume human life that quickly. The usual incubation phase was three to fourteen days. Their meticulous technique prevented its spread. His heart pounded against his chest now as he witnessed what infection with *Labrador* could do, fleshed out before his eyes, lying on the floor.

Was he crazy for working here?

Probably, but he realized how important, now, more than ever, LeTorneau's work was.

The containment unit had been secure until now — he was certain of that.

Who'd left the lab like this?

The housekeeper's dark skin was jaundiced and drained of its plump vigor. It hung on her face, a loose curtain of dead flesh. He was about to cover her with one of the body bags used to store the preserved primates when he stopped—she took a gasp of air.

She was still breathing, but comatose.

Her cart was overturned and all of her cleaning supplies were spilled, scattered about the floor, adding to the fetid odors burning his nostrils. Noxious ammonia. Pure bleach. Lemon Pine-Sol.

Had she tried to get help?

There were no signs on her body of a physical confrontation. Who had accessed the fourth floor? He put on a pair of gloves, being careful not to handle anything else in the lab for fear of contamination, and he checked her pulse. It was palpable but thread.

She was near death.

Maybe it wasn't LeTorneau after all. Why would he do this— more money?

It seemed there was always a race to get state-of-the art drugs to market first. Maybe another corporation had offered Graham more money.

A better lab.

A prestigious position.

Unethical behavior certainly wouldn't be the exception in his field.

He donned one of the white hazmat suits. The woman's only hope was for him to enter the cooler and administer a small amount of the remaining antidote. The chemical process to make the antibody that they'd discovered took months to produce even a miniscule amount, and he wanted to secure whatever was left—in case LeTorneau had, in fact, absconded with it. He hoped the vials were still in the biohazard storage container. He could get the proprietary data from Graham's computer to manufacture more of it. If the greedy bastard hadn't already run off with it.

As he was about to put the plastic helmet over his face and neck, his cell phone rang.

Thank God it's Jorge, he thought. Peering into the open containment unit, he saw that his fears were correct—the vials of *Labrador* had been shattered.

The viscous antidote was spilled all over the floor, frozen into a gelatinous, red mass.

He answered the call, said, "Bourdain. When are you coming back? We have big problems here."

-14-

Graham LeTorneau

Graham LeTorneau hadn't eaten anything since he'd left McGarrity's pub. By the time the man and woman returned, Graham's lips were parched, and his muscles ached, especially where they'd kicked him in his core. He now resorted to licking the stream of water leaking along the foundation of the moldy basement where they held him prisoner. His hands and wrists remained bound, and a noose had been tied loosely around his neck. He was blindfolded, but if he tilted his head back he could see under the musty-smelling rag which his captors had bound around his eyes. He sat on the creaky wooden chair, afraid to move, for fear the rope would strangle him if he shifted from the chair.

The man never spoke, except to the woman who he called Jessie. Their feet rattled the old stairs as they descended toward him, and a sliver of light shone under the blindfold from beneath the basement door. They turned on what sounded like a pull string light bulb. The man mumbled something to Jessie right before he kicked Graham.

Graham groaned.

The man delivered another blow to his ribs.

"Who is Dr. Sara Sullivan?" the woman demanded. She was chewing gum, and a whiff of strawberry-banana reached his nose as she approached his face.

He wasn't as intimidated by her breath upon him as he was terrified of the faceless man, whoever he was. The force of his blows knocked the wind right out of him.

Graham's usual gentle voice was cracked and weak, broken in pitch. "I—I don't know." He regretted his answer instantly, as he felt the man's heavy foot in his side. He leaned toward the blow, despite the excruciating pain, to maintain his balance on the rickety chair.

"She was nosing around your lab. Where did she come from? What does she know?"

"I swear to you, I don't know."

Another kick.

Sweat poured from his forehead, saturated the blindfold above his eyes.

His heart raced from fear, dehydration, but he focused on the feeling of it in his chest now, trying to block out the abductors. "I don't know a Sara Sullivan."

The man's heavy foot kicked him off the chair now, and the thick noose went taut around his neck.

He was choking, gasping for breath.

He could not pull the rope away from his airway with his hands bound.

He struggled there, starving for air, while making wild, gyrating movements with his trunk, off the chair. The man kicked his back and he fell forward. His nose began to bleed almost immediately, as it pressed against the damp concrete. He gasped, suffocating on his blood. It filled his nose, suffocated him from his mouth, too. He felt small hands, pulling the noose tighter now, against his throat from above, and he was certain he would perish as he grew unconscious, asphyxiated.

How long was he without oxygen—two minutes?

Five?

He awoke, seated on the chair again, lapping cool water as it was poured over his parched lips.

Sara Sullivan

Although Sara felt she was running on adrenaline alone—she hadn't slept well in two weeks—she ordered a drink and she plopped down in a velvet armchair in the corner of her favorite Starbucks. The baristas knew her drink before she ordered it. A Venti Vanilla latte with extra whip cream. Her body was reaching its breaking point, and she craved a shower, but she drank her favorite chemical cocktail. She had to keep going. Elyse's life—and the lives of many more, depended on her. She wanted answers, and the more she looked for them, the more questions she had.

What did the explosions and the bomb in the lab have to do with everything? Were they just part of the looting and rioting going on everywhere in the District—or was there something more? And what did Wes Lindstrom have to do with it?

It seemed hopeless. She tapped the numbers on her phone to dial Jane Morgan's number, but then she hung up. She dialed her mother instead.

"Hello?"

"Mom, I need your help. Are you home?"

"No, honey. Sue Ellen and Sadie and I are in New York. Can't believe I've never been here. This place is amazing."

There was background noise. It sounded like Times Square. Her mother was always *somewhere*. She should've known better. She was off with her friends.

"Call me when you get home, okay?"

"Of course, honey. I'll be back tomorrow. Love to Elyse."

"Mom, Elyse is—"

Her mother had already hung up. She sighed and dialed Jane Morgan's office number again. She had no concrete evidence, but something told her Wes Lindstrom was connected to the *Labrador* epidemic. Her writing seemed hopeless now—it didn't matter what Jane Morgan thought of it. She'd probably never see her name in print.

Forget movie rights.

There was no big screen in her future any time soon.

Elyse was what mattered.

She and all the other children, affected by the virus, could be crippled by its effects or orphaned by it stealing their mothers, fathers, their futures. If she could save her daughter, she promised, she'd never serve her a TV dinner or a drive-through Happy Meal. She'd make waffles and pancakes on Sunday mornings for her family and take them to church. She'd go on Elyse's field trips. She'd be a mother. A good mother. She was telling herself the honest truth, or she thought she was. But it all seemed so impossible for a doctor to set the mommy bar so high.

She sunk deeper into the armchair.

What she meant was she'd be more attentive than her own mother, who had the maternal instincts of a paramecium. Every now and then, Charlotte Sullivan brushed by, some days petting her, other days beating her down with her little cilia: *How are you honey? You're so smart. But you can do so much better than Marty. I can't babysit tonight, but maybe next Tuesday between 2 to 4 o'clock. And cover up those muscular arms, for goodness sake.* Then, she'd set off, floating away, diffusing to the other side of the Petri dish, as her love moved by bulk transport towards her offspring, from a distance.

"Hello?" Jane Morgan answered the phone.

"Hello, Ms. Morgan. This is Sara Sullivan." She fidgeted with her empty cup and the green plastic stirrer. The line was out the door now, and it was difficult to hear over the noise. She held the phone closer to her ear. "I bumped into you and your husband at the French restaurant in D.C.?"

"Yes, of course, dear. How are you?"

"Not too well, actually. My daughter is ill. I'm calling because I learned your husband is very involved with several up and coming drug companies. Perhaps he has access to some experimental treatments."

"As a matter of fact, he does."

"Would it be alright if I called him regarding a new treatment for *Labrador* virus?"

"Oh, dear." Jane Morgan's voice trailed off.

Sara's heart sunk at the emotional response.

Everyone knew *Labrador* was a horrific disease. The stigma of the illness evoked sympathy, pity and then avoidance, distrust.

She was relieved she wasn't speaking with Jane Morgan face to face. Everyone treated her like a Molokiian leper.

"Yes, let me give you his cell phone number. He'll be back in D.C. this week, working with Senator Marburg regarding the crisis. We're in New York now."

"Thank you." She wrote down Wes Lindstrom's number on a brown napkin made of recycled paper.

"I do hope your daughter is alright. How is your writing coming along?"

"I'm afraid it's taken a backseat to everything else right now."

"Yes, I can see how that would be the case. It's really a dramatic premise. It bears an uncanny similarity to the *Labrador* crisis. Wes agreed."

"He did?" asked Sara.

They talked some more and Jane Morgan asked her if she'd like to have coffee the next time she was in New York and she said that she would and then she said goodbye. She noticed the GPS location icon flashing on her phone again when she disconnected the call, even though she'd turned off the location services again at the aquarium. As she finished the last sip of her latte, she dropped the device in the trash just outside the store bathroom.

They might find her.

Arrest her.

Lock her in quarantine again.

But she wasn't going to help them.

And she wasn't going in without a fight.

Clinical Trials Lab
Bethesda, Maryland
Hans Raedl

Hans Raedl held the receiver tightly to his left ear. The lab reeked of infected flesh and chemical reagents. He looked down at the housekeeper, lying close to death near his left shoe. She was still taking short gasps for breath, but her skin was a horrid shade of blue-black.

"When are you coming back, Jorge? Is everything okay with your family now?"

"My family is fine, Hans. Who else has been in the lab?" asked Jorge.

"I was wondering the same thing. The police wanted to access it, but they were sent away. They'll be back though." He ducked down as he spoke, searching under the lab benches, lifting chairs. "But someone's been here. The place is a disaster and—"

"I know, Hans. Someone's been snooping around."

"Who?"

"Dr. Sara Sullivan is her name. She's a black woman, about thirty-five, not unattractive."

"Who is that?"

"I think you know, Hans. Why was she there? What does she know about the antibody production?"

"I don't know, Jorge. Never heard the name before. The place is ransacked and the housekeeper—what's her name?" He spoke in an urgent whisper into the phone, even though he was certain the housekeeper couldn't hear him—she was comatose and fading fast. "She's been infected. I've got to give her one of the vials with antibody and get her out of here—to a hospital or something—or heads are going to roll, Jorge. We're talking major incident reporting, breach of protocol, lack of supervision—LeTorneau's nowhere to be found."

"I can see that."

"She's dying on me here, Jorge. If you could see this place…" He stopped. Jorge's voice was distant over the line. "Wait, what did you say?"

"That's correct. I can see everything fine."

His colleague was monitoring the lab remotely.

"Jorge, where are you? I—"

"I saw Sullivan rummaging through the lab. I saw her knock over the vials of antibody. And I saw her leave the cooling unit wide open. What I'd like to know is, where she came from and who she's working for."

"Jorge, I don't know anything about a Sara Sullivan. LeTorneau, you, me, Kayla and Veronica are the only ones who know the reaction process for manufacturing the antibody to *Labrador*. Don't you remember signing LeTorneau's fifty page nondisclosure agreement? We're the only ones with access to this place besides the housekeeper and she's—"

"I'm going to make sure it stays that way, Hans."

There was a beeping sound from the cold room where the virus was kept under level four biosecurity. It was wide open now, and it beckoned him. Red and orange lights flashed, their glare calling him toward the metal door. Fluorescent reagents were spilled on the floor, radiating a dim glow. Their pungent vapors wafted in the air, burned his nostrils.

"Where the hell are you, you redneck son-of-a-bitch?"

"Walk into the cooler, Hans, and look below the bench."

"Christ, Jorge. Okay."

He looked around, certain now he wasn't alone with the housekeeper. Who was in the core? Was it Graham? The housekeeper took another gasp. Her right foot wiggled, but her color was still a ghastly blue, and the blood hemorrhaging from her nose and mouth was slowing. He put on the protective helmet, crept into the storage facility. He stepped in further and, ducking down, he found an activated explosive on the ground, its LED timer blinking. He immediately backed away, exiting the unit. Jorge was watching him remotely, but from where? He ripped off the hazmat suit and threw it on the slippery floor. Then he examined the perimeter of the room for cameras, microphones, anything that allowed access to the information transmitted from the top-secret laboratory.

He climbed on the lab bench in the center of the room and he unscrewed the incandescent light fixture. Inside he discovered a tiny camera. Across the room on the other bench, he did the same. Another camera. Where was Jorge? Could he still see him?

He raced to LeTorneau's computer in the corner of the room and opened the desktop. He searched the name "Dr. Sara Sullivan" and found an email for her faculty affiliation at George Washington University. "Jorge, what have you done with LeTorneau?"

Jorge laughed over the line. Hans' eyes darted back and forth over the contact information. *Who was she? How did she know about the antibody?* Her picture was on the University webpage. Jorge was right—she was a young professional. Dr. Sullivan was fit, of mixed racial heritage, with hazel eyes and short hair.

"You're an evolutionist, Raedl," Jorge hissed. "I'm sure it all makes sense to you. There need not be a cure for *Labrador*—*Labrador is* the cure."

There were less than twelve hours until the bomb was set to detonate. He wasn't sure how Dr. Sullivan had found the lab, or how Jorge had recognized her, but her life was in danger, and he had to notify her.

"You're not going to get away with this, Jorge. Where's LeTorneau?"

"He's with me, but now I have another one like him to hunt down."

He heard screams over the line, distant, in the background. Was it LeTorneau?

"Where is he?" he demanded again, his knuckles whitening, gripping the phone to his ear.

"Do you know what you call an African-American Nobel Prize nominee and world renowned doctor, Raedl?"

"Jorge, we were doing this to help people, to cure and prevent disease. This wasn't supposed to be—"

"You call him a nigger, just like every other nigger."

"Jorge!"

"That's right. LeTorneau isn't going to win any prizes."

He could hear LeTorneau in the background, struggling—it had to be him. He frantically dialed Veronica from the landline phone on the desk next to Graham's computer.

Pick up.

Jorge was still on the line. He had to find LeTorneau and deactivate the bomb, before all the knowledge and reagents for manufacturing the cure for *Labrador* were destroyed along with the lab. To him, the antibody was years of sleepless nights in the lab. Years he'd given up with his family. His contribution to science, and to the world. Years he'd never get back if it all went up in smoke. He held his hand over the cell phone, hoping Jorge could no longer view him remotely. Were there additional webcams?

Pick up. Pick the fuck up.

The call went to voicemail.

"Veronica, you were right—it wasn't LeTorneau. Your lives are in danger. Jorge is behind the explosion at the Washburn. He's behind LeTorneau's disappearance. And there's someone else. Her name is Dr. Sara Sullivan. You have to find her. She may know—"

Jorge Bourdain remotely detonated the bomb.

The entire wing of the building exploded, killing Hans and the housekeeper. The structure collapsed in on itself, burying the employees and students beneath them in the concrete remnants of the research facility. The alarms sounded, and the sprinklers outside of the building activated. The numerous flammable chemicals fueled the blaze, creating a huge mushroom cloud of smoke over the entire block, as the survivors evacuated the opposite wing.

It was the only remaining portion of the four-flour facility.

-15-

Dr. Graham LeTorneau

Graham LeTorneau gasped for air as he lay on the concrete of the cold cellar. Graham's wrists and ankles were tightly bound, and the dirty blindfold covered his eyes. An inch of water had risen up on the cold floor around his body, but it relieved the stinging feeling where he'd been beaten by his captors. The noose was yanked off his neck now, but his breathing remained shallow, panicked. He hyperventilated as Jorge Bourdain interrogated him. Jorge's questions mocked him, and he feared there was nothing he could do that would convince his student to spare his life.

He should've seen it coming. The long hours Jorge spent online commenting on social media. The blogs from groups with radical agendas that popped up on the computers in the lab. It had started as a superficial interest in the Internet when he'd taken on Jorge as a student, but had transformed Jorge into an obsessed fundamentalist, active with organizations that shared one common theme, racism.

"Are you familiar with the evolution of the peppered moth?"

"Of course, Jorge. We've studied hundreds of examples of evolution."

"And what happened to the peppered moth?"

"What does this have to do with anything?" He felt a boot pressing into his throat.

"What happened to the moths during the Industrial Revolution in Great Britain?"

Gasping for breath, he said, "The moths that were well hidden on pale trees became conspicuous when the trees were blackened by pollution."

"And?"

The boot pressed harder against his airway, and he turned his head, struggled to breathe.

"They were eaten by birds because they were no longer camouflaged by the trees. They stood out."

"Exactly," Jorge said.

Jorge released his foot. LeTorneau took an audible gasp of air.

Jorge said, "The light colored moths died out due to predators, didn't they? And the dark moths flourished because they could hide against the soot on the trees. All very natural — survival of the fittest."

"The experiments were flawed, Jorge. They never gave evidence for large-scale evolution happening rapidly. They only described the relative fluctuating frequencies of the moths. When the pollution decreased, the frequencies of the light colored moths returned to previous levels. The peppered moth population returned to less than 1 percent of the entire moth population."

"Aren't you smart, professor?" Jorge Bourdain placed one of the moths onto Graham's nose, with the tweezers.

He tried to blow it away, but it crawled up his forehead. "Please stop this, Jorge," he begged.

"But I think you're wrong, Doctor. We can explain how certain races come into being in the first place. These peppered moths provided the most comprehensive evidence of Darwinian evolution—until now."

"The pale and dark forms of the peppered moth belong to the same species, Jorge. They're exactly alike except for their superficial color. Only the frequencies of the species changed." A mouthful of water from the floor splashed into his mouth, and he spit it out.

"But it allowed one to survive over the other didn't it, Doctor?"

Jorge kicked him in the abdomen, and he screamed.

His rib broke with a sharp crack.

He groaned, leaning to grip the upper left side of his belly, near his spleen, but his hands were tied behind him.

"The darkening of color due to industrialization was called what, Professor?" asked Jorge.

He gagged, and he coughed up blood, squirmed about the floor.

Jorge kicked him again.

"Fuck you," he said. "You racist fuck."

"I didn't hear your answer, Doctor." Jorge pulled his head back by his hair.

"Industrial melanism," he said, gasped for breath.

"That's correct, Dr. LeTorneau. Maybe you are as smart as everyone thinks—but you won't be around to claim a Nobel Prize."

Jorge lit a candle and picked up the black moth from Graham's forehead, dropping his head abruptly on the floor of the cabin. "And I thought racist was a term to better describe *you*, Professor—going on about how Africans are better suited to global warming." Jorge flicked the moth into the flame.

"That's not what I meant. You know it. When the environmental conditions change again, so do the frequencies of the species. If you could let me explain the findings, I think you'd—"

"Shut up," Jorge said. "I know exactly what you meant. My addition to the *Labrador* virus will provide the same stunning, elegant example of Darwinian evolution."

"What do you mean, Jorge? What have you done?"

"Haven't you noticed how it affects African-Americans? There'll be no more changes in frequencies of the species, Doctor." He gave vent to laughter.

Graham swallowed and he coughed and he spit out blood. Even blindfolded, he could sense Bourdain's contemptuous smile. "That's a natural effect of where the virus evolved—on the continent of Africa. But there's a vaccine, Jorge. It can be out before more lives are lost. I've been working in concert with Claus Recart to prevent this very situation. And you have no idea how fast *Labrador* can mutate—it will affect whites, too—if we don't get it to market."

"I worked with Claus, too." Jorge laughed, saturated Graham's clothing with a burning liquid. The smell was unmistakable—gasoline. "How do you think I came to work in your lab?"

"Claus is a man of unquestionable ethics. That's impossible." Volatile fumes burned his eyes.

"He knows every one of your secrets. He sent me to work in your lab. And he paid me well."

"We had a pact," he muttered.

"I've altered the virus so that it's lethal to your race. More lethal than you can imagine."

"Claus will stop this. We had a pact. A pact. We're both aware of the unethical abuses of science—the way people exploit scientific discovery for monetary gain, or—why are you doing this?"

"You're not listening. Or maybe you're just not hearing me. Claus was making pacts of his own."

"Jorge, if you would please just—I can arrange for you to be paid whatever you're asking. Please let me go," he begged.

"This isn't about money, Doctor." Jorge removed the blindfold, and he dragged Graham up the stairs now and into the main room of the cabin. He opened the closet where a gutted deer was dressed. He pulled out a white hooded robe, tied it at the waist with a rope belt. Jorge hauled him by the wrists where they were bound by nylon cord, out to the front lawn. Jorge's right arm was weak, atrophied, and he dropped Graham three times—once, almost all the way down the flight of stairs—before they were out of the cellar. Dozens of white crosses of various heights were staked to the ground. Then Jorge doused the other crosses with gasoline and he pulled him onto a wooden palette behind the shed, and he said, "See? The others will be here soon."

Bethesda, Maryland
Dr. Sara Sullivan

A helicopter circled above Sara for the fifth time. Was it looking for her, or was she just paranoid? She had no idea how the public transportation system functioned outside of D.C., but she had to get away from the lab. She'd spent endless hours mired in the horrendous D.C. traffic, commuting from the suburbs by car, until she'd conceded to move to Georgetown with Marty. They walked everywhere after that—except for the odd night out, and when she drove to work.

Now her DUI was her other problem.

Lately though, their walks seemed less hand in hand than they used to be. Maybe Marty was really trying to save their relationship, in his own odd way. She sighed as she remembered the DUI and how Marty had betrayed her for what he'd thought was best.

Was it though?

At a minimum, they'd need to have a serious heart to heart, about where they were headed, if she were going to stay with him.

Maybe a few months in counseling.

It was all secondary to Elyse's health now, anyway.

Who was the voice on the phone in the lab? Was he connected to Wes Lindstrom? Although her quarantine from her patients had passed, she was more concerned about falling ill with the

Labrador virus now after her exposure here in Bethesda. As the U.S Army chopper flew away with its sirens blaring, and its red lights flashing, she ran in the opposite direction. There had to be a bus station nearby. It was dusk, and most of the looting and rioting was occurring after dark. Her mother had always told her that nothing good happened after dark. The last thing she wanted to do right then was admit her mother was right.

About anything.

She had only the change from the coffee she'd paid for with the twenty in her pocket, no driver's license on her. And she'd left her bag in the lab. She could've kicked herself—that was about as smart as a frog trying to cross the Capital Beltway. Organization was never her strong point, but she thought she'd done alright balancing her job and her family. Now Elyse was on death's door.

Apparently not.

The helicopter circled back. She was careful not to look up, but she looked back over her shoulder as she hurried down an alley. As she exited the narrow street, she entered a massive crowd, enraged, running in all directions.

Young men shouting.

Women crying.

A liquor store window smashed, and the property set ablaze.

Broken shards of glass everywhere in the street, and protesters banging on cars. Traffic was stopped in gridlock. The heat from the fire rushed at her as the wind fed it. She covered her mouth, coughing on carbonaceous smoke. She crossed the street as a fire truck pulled up, narrowly missing an elderly woman.

Looters ran from the store with bottles under their arms.

"Get out," the fire chief screamed, as his men turned on the hoses.

More of the rioters came running across the street toward her, an unyielding tidal wave of raw, negative emotion—hatred, fueled by bestial self-preservation.

Thicker smoke filled the street now.

She coughed, and she gasped with her arm over her mouth and she tried to blend in without being swallowed by the masses. The few policemen at the scene made an effort to push the rioters away from the burning storefront, but they were far outnumbered. Many of the men and women in the crowd appeared intoxicated, drugged.

She'd picked up Marty's nervous habit of always scanning a crowd suspiciously, looking for trouble. But now, it was everywhere. It was impossible to tell who was armed.

Her heart raced, vision tunneled.

She elbowed her way past a bloody fistfight, between two men.

She'd never lived through anything like this before—the racial tensions and the overt bigotry, the distrust of the medical system and the government. Now, more than ever, she had to find out who knew the chemical process for creating the *Labrador* antibody, and why someone was trying to stop it from getting to the people who needed it to save their lives.

"You got ID, miss?" asked the officer.

She turned. He was talking to her. She put her head down and ducked through the sea of protesters. She knocked over a woman as she tried to move away from the officer. What did he want with *her*?

"Where the hell do you think you're going?" the woman asked.

She looked up into the feral eyes of an obese, white woman with wire-rimmed glasses. Her own athletic frame moved easily through the breaks in the crowd, but this behemoth now had her hands on her.

"Let go," she said, trying to push the woman out her way.

The situation brought out the worst in her. An aggression she'd never before felt married with her blood. She drew back her fist, and with her muscles bulging where her shirt had torn, she delivered a forceful blow to the woman's jaw, knocking her to the ground.

"Get back here," the policeman shouted to her. "Identify yourself!" He spoke into his radio, and he followed her, but she was agile, and he was overweight.

The crowd attacked the cop as he raised his voice.

"Identify yourself," he shouted.

Her fist shook. She looked down at it, and at the woman, holding her mouth, and then she looked at the officer. Then she took off through the crowd, still trembling over what she'd done.

Craning her neck and standing on her toes, she spotted a bus stop about a block from the liquor store. Another mass of rioters was running toward her. She was caught between so many people that they seemed to lift her feet from the ground.

Their screams reached a high pitch crescendo now.

The police dispersed tear gas into the crowd.

From the north, a public transit bus was crawling toward the bus stop. She pushed through the crowd aggressively — she had to make the bus and get out of there and back to Elyse. She ran as fast as she could, weaving her muscular physique in and out of the thinning crowd.

She looked back. The policeman was still after her.

By the time the overweight officer broke through the mob, she'd hopped on the bus. It sputtered away. The rioters pounded their fists against the doors. Breathless, she took the only open seat toward the back, between two women, one black and the other, Asian. The black woman looked her over with thorough skepticism, frowning.

"You're sweating," she said. "You feel alright?"

"I've been running."

She shifted in her seat, and she looked out at the smoky mob, rubbing their eyes and coughing, and at last, she caught her own breath and she looked back at the woman. She couldn't afford to reveal too much about herself, but she needed help. An armed U.S. Marshall sat at the front of the bus. A man shivered beneath a blanket on the seat in front of her. He looked ill.

The situation was getting more serious every day.

She looked over her shoulder again and then out the window and back toward the front. The destination sign over the driver read: George Washington University. She figured the bus was running along the Blue Line of the subway. She could transfer at the central platform to get to the hospital, get to Elyse. The older black woman was still staring at her. Patent leather bag held tightly against her chest. Wool hat pinned with a silk rose. Finally, Sara turned toward her.

"May I borrow your phone, please?" she asked.

"You actin' real funny. Are you infected?" The woman's eyes narrowed, she leaned away.

"No, ma'am—I mean, I don't think so. I'm a doctor. I need to call the hospital." She managed a weak smile.

A glimpse of admiration flickered across the old woman's face, pride in her own race, but Sara saw it fade to skepticism.

"Better not." The woman turned her head to the window and when the bus came to a stop, the woman hurried down the aisle.

The Asian woman next to her had her earbuds in.

"Excuse me, may I borrow your phone, please?" She motioned with her hand to her ear. She wasn't sure if the Asian woman spoke English, but the woman pulled out her cell phone, handed it to Sara. Sara thanked her, dialed Marty's number.

"Where the hell are you?" Marty asked.

"I'm coming to the hospital. I have to see Elyse."

"Sara," Marty sounded worn out, defeated. "They won't even let me in to see her. She's in isolation in a cooling tent. They've got her hooked up to a breathing machine."

She was perspiring. The woman next to her was wearing too much perfume. The back of the bus was humid with the smell of body odor and exhaust. She wiped her brow, listened as Marty described their daughter's condition.

"They wanted to start her on dialysis, but they can't even get an IV into her. Her kidneys are failing." His voice broke. He was near tears, sounded sick himself.

The walls of the bus seemed to close in on her, packed in amongst strangers. Her heart pounded as she imagined Elyse, near death in the ICU. She smelled sweat and alcohol and stale cigarette smoke on the passengers around her.

"I don't think they can find anyone skilled enough to touch her. They're scared, Sara. Scared of getting sick."

"Does she have *Labrador*, Marty?"

"They screwed up her blood work, Sara. They couldn't even draw enough blood for the sample because she was so dehydrated. They came and took another sample, but it will be hours before the results come back—maybe another day."

"I'm on my way." She hung up the phone and she thanked the Asian woman and she got off at the next station to change buses. The bus line took her all the way to George Washington University Hospital, where her daughter lay in critical condition.

Edward Marburg

Edward Marburg examined the contact information that the NSA had provided. He dialed the home of Hans Raedl, the graduate student who'd been working in Dr. LeTorneau's laboratory at the time of the explosion.

"Mrs. Raedl, please accept my condolences for your loss. We're deeply saddened." He closed his laptop now and got in his car, driving onto the Beltway.

"Good for you," the woman said.

Mrs. Angel Raedl sounded angry. Not the slightest bit distressed. Her voice was tough, like the woman was made of cogs and screws and intricate mechanics rather than human flesh. But she sounded like she'd known her husband's death had been imminent.

That concerned him.

It roused suspicion.

"Be assured, Mrs. Raedl, that my people are investigating the unfortunate accident—or intentional explosion, as may be the case—with the highest level of scrutiny. We're replaying the video and looking for a runaway physician. Sara Sullivan's her name."

"Who?" Hans Raedl's wife wasn't following.

"Attractive black woman in her mid-thirties. Athletic. Short black hair. Had your husband been in communication with her?" He kept driving. Traffic was minimal tonight. People were staying home, out of fear.

"She's not the one you're looking for." Her accent was thick and German, militant. "He was messing around on me with the feisty one—Veronica's her name. *Schlampe* I call her. They all see each other more than they see their own wives there."

"Veronica," he repeated, glanced in the rearview and exited the Beltway, speeding off the ramp toward the coffee shop where NSA had located Sara Sullivan on satellite imagery and

GPS. The Pentagon hadn't ruled out bioterrorism as a cause of the *Labrador* epidemic, and he had access to all sorts of classified information, which made his work with Lindstrom even easier to cover up.

"That's right. Veronica."

"What's Veronica's last name, Mrs. Raedl? What does she look like?" All sensitivity, even feigned, was gone from his voice now. He turned down the news on his radio, which was broadcasting the latest case numbers of the infection in the District.

"She was probably upset when he broke it off with her—always does. Wouldn't be the first time." Hans Raedl's widow continued her rant regarding her husband's betrayal.

"Her last name, Mrs. Raedl. Veronica's *last name*," he repeated.

"How the hell should I know? Veronica, Kayla, Jorge—they all work with that LeTorneau guy that's reported missing on the news." She coughed, and he was envious as he heard the sound of her taking a drag on a cigarette. He wanted more than anything to smoke just then. "She's covered in tattoos and cuts her hair short like a boy. He had it coming to him. I call her *schlampe*. That's German for slut, senator. Do you know what a *slut* is?" She laughed.

"Thank you, Mrs. Raedl."

He signaled left and he cut across two lanes on the busy city street and he parked the car illegally outside the Starbucks where the NSA had located Sara Sullivan. He walked past a crowd of college students, ignoring their casual conversation, the folk music overhead, and he headed to the back near the ladies room, hand on his gun. There was no one there, but the signal from Sullivan's device was strong. He overturned the garbage can and he dumped the refuse on the tile floor and he found the cell phone powered on. He cursed and he threw the can and he dialed Wes Lindstrom with his own device.

George Washington University Hospital
Sara Sullivan

In Marty Sullivan's isolation room, CNN flashed across the television screen. The reporter stood outside a health camp, wearing a surgical mask and gown. Tents embedded with Red Cross symbols housed patients suspected of being infected with *Labrador* virus. The reporter described the advancing epidemic with his British accent. Victims sent to the health camps were held under questionable conditions.

Medical care was being tightly rationed.

Strict contact isolation and tracing were ongoing, as the virus advanced beyond the capital, and into major cities, including Los Angeles, Philadelphia, New York.

The broadcast switched back to the anchor at the studio.

"The president signed an executive order today closing our borders, as efforts continue to contain the highly virulent *Labrador* epidemic. The death toll for the deadly disease is expected to reach five thousand by the end of the month. Anyone suspected of illness must report to the designated treatment areas," the anchor reported.

"Death camps," Marty muttered under his breath. He turned down the volume with the remote, paced around the isolation room as he looked at Elyse, still comatose on the ventilator in the oxygen tent. Another baby had been brought in beside her and was screaming loudly. A knock on the glass startled him. He grabbed his chest. It was Sara, crouched down below the window and peering through the glass. He quickly opened the door, hustled her in.

"How did you get in here?" Marty held her, kissed her on the forehead. "The whole place is like Fort Knox."

She shook her head to let him know it wasn't important, and she held up her badge. "I can't stay long. If they know I've swiped my badge at the security checkpoints, they know I'm here."

"I'm so glad you're alright, Sara. I'm so sorry, I—"

"Marty, it doesn't matter." She pressed her hands up to the glass and observed Elyse, who was now awake and thrashing, fighting the ventilator. It looked like she was trying to cry, but with the tube in her throat, it was impossible. The baby next to her was screaming wildly, and a healthcare worker fully gowned in a hazmat suit and blue gloves came in to administer a medication.

The woman didn't touch Elyse, but she settled the other infant.

Sara felt her cheeks burn a furious red.

She ducked down below the glass as the worker turned toward the observation room. As the woman left the room, she dimmed the lights, and the sound of classical music piped a lullaby through the speakers overhead.

Elyse was still inconsolable.

Marty took her hand.

"I've got to help her," she said.

"Are you trying to get arrested?" Marty pulled her wrist back as she started for the door. It was locked shut.

"Oh what does it matter?" She turned, and she grabbed a hanger from the coat closet behind them. The lock on the door looked weak, easy to break.

He held her hand, but she pulled away. "What are you doing? Elyse needs to be in the hospital."

"She's not going anywhere, Marty. You said they couldn't get an IV on her for dialysis. If she goes into kidney failure, she could die."

"Well there's nothing we can do about that—they're hesitant to touch her. The virus is spread through the blood."

She looked at him squarely. He had no idea what a typical day for her consisted of, did he? "I know how to do a few things well, Marty."

"You don't have to tell me that." His eyebrows rose and he kissed her neck as she struggled with the lock.

She turned around and she rolled her eyes at him.

"Will you stop?" she whispered, pushing his arms off of her.

He retracted his hands from her waist, stepped back. The lock opened easily with the hanger, and the door to the isolation ward popped open.

She faced him. "Starting IV's is the *other* thing."

"There's nothing you can't do. I know that."

She smiled now. "I'm the one they call around here when they can't get an IV in."

She sneaked along the wall toward the cabinet in the corner of the room. It was filled with sterile gloves and intravenous fluids and medical supplies. She withdrew a blue latex tourniquet and some 22 gauge IVs and a sterile dressing. Then she crouched low as she approached Elyse's crib, careful to stay out of sight. Elyse was covered by the mist tent and connected to the pediatric ventilator.

As she approached Elyse, her eyes fluttered open.

Sara's eyes filled with tears.

She quickly wiped them away, and fought back the flood of fear in her blood, instead allowing her adrenaline to work its way through her system, allowing her to function methodically, like the skilled clinician she was. She tied the tourniquet around her daughter's chubby arm, now limp and dehydrated, and she tapped Elyse's hand to plump up her veins. Carefully, she inserted the tiny intravenous needle, but she blew the vein. A drop of blood welled at the hub of the needle, where a lump was forming in Elyse's skin.

Her hand shook.

The nurse would be back soon.

She wasn't wearing gloves as she normally would for the procedure. This was her daughter. If Elyse was going to die, she didn't care if she took her with her. She wiped the blood, held pressure on the swollen hand until the bleeding stopped, and she steadied her own hand. Then she picked up another IV and searched for another vein on Elyse's wrist.

No pressure, she told herself.

She pierced the tiny vein and she saw a flash of blood and she prayed that this time, the catheter would advance smoothly into the vessel. She pushed the plastic tip into the lumen, retracted the needle. It was secure. She connected the saline tubing and ran in a few drops, breathing a sigh of relief. Then she secured it with tape and she kissed her daughter on her forehead and she scurried back to the isolation room where Marty was watching in awe. He hugged her, kissed her cheek. She thought she might cry, but there was no time for emotion.

The healthcare worker was headed back to the isolation room.

"What were you doing in here?" the woman called after her.

To Marty, Sara said, "I've got to get out of here."

The gowned employee was headed toward them. Sara pushed the door shut and she locked it and she headed for the back exit of the isolation room.

"She can be hydrated and dialyzed now, Marty. They'll be able to place a central catheter after she gets fluid replacement. Don't let anything happen to my baby."

She swallowed, looked back at Elyse. Then she kissed Marty and she hurried out as the employee banged on the door, jolting it open just as she escaped. She looked back once more through the window at her daughter's incubator, through two layers of glass. Elyse was lethargic and pale, but her tiny hands wriggled, swatting the plastic tent.

There weren't many places to move around unnoticed on the third floor, but she was aware of one doctor's dictation room where the radiologists read films and performed interventional procedures. The darkness of the barren room made it well suited to viewing x-rays and nuclear medicine tests on the white light boards, but it was on the other side of the floor, past the operating suites and the ICU and the busiest elevators in the facility.

She had to hide.

Sara hurried down the hall, keeping her head down and avoiding eye contact with an approaching pack of residents. After she passed them, she ducked into the empty dictation room and she locked the door behind her. She slid into one of the tattered chairs and she brushed the dust off the computer. It was slow to load, and she looked over her shoulder and she gasped and she typed faster as she heard the sound of someone trying to open the door.

She waited.

The knocking stopped, the computer loaded, and she logged into the medical record system using her own credentials. She was aware that her access could be traced, but she figured she could search the database quickly, get out of the hospital. She typed in the name of the first *Labrador* patient she'd seen: DEVIN FINNEGAN. A bright red window popped up with a confidentiality warning. It read: THIS RECORD IS PROTECTED. ONLY THOSE WITH NEED FOR ACCESS

MAY VIEW THIS RECORD. UNAUTHORIZED ACCESS MAY RESULT IN TERMINATION OF EMPLOYMENT AND CRIMINAL PROSECTION. CLICK TO PROCEED.

You're no longer her doctor, she recalled the man in the hazmat suit telling her, as he took her temperature in the quarantine room. *I cannot share any medical information with you.*

Nothing to lose.

And anything and everything she valued was slipping further from her every minute.

Sara swallowed, clicked the check box, and opened the sealed record of her former patient. She scrolled to the laboratory results section of the electronic record. The woman had a confirmed diagnosis of *Labrador*. She scrolled through the progress notes and her eyes darted over the dusty screen, trying to find something that made sense about the cases. Her eyes stopped abruptly on the words, 'EXPIRED. TIME OF DEATH: 10:28.'

Her hand covered her mouth.

Nothing extraordinary stood out about the case. She surfed to the woman's demographics page. Finnegan was a middle-aged suburban woman. She and her husband owned Finnegan Funeral Home on the outskirts of the city. Her husband had told Sara earlier that neither of them had been out of the country since their honeymoon. They had private health insurance and access to medical care. At least they *did*. Now her husband was quarantined with the National Guard restricting access out of his own home.

She closed the record.

A similar warning appeared when she typed in the name of the other patient she recalled, Raymond Barry, but she ignored it and proceeded to examine the man's file. Finally, something positive. She breathed a sigh of relief. The man's latest progress note revealed that he was in stable condition and recovering. He had been discharged from the ICU after days on a ventilator and on dialysis, and he was breathing room air and ambulating about the floor. She wrote down the room number, 117, and shoved the scrap paper in her pocket. Then she logged off the computer and peered out of the door down the endless white hall. Suddenly, the smoke alarms sounded, and the tiny lights lining the walls flashed a fiery red.

The automatic doors closed at either end of the corridor.

Typical, she thought. *Probably a patient smoking in the bathroom.*

But the alarms grew louder.

Smoke wafted under the door.

She covered her mouth with her sleeve, and she coughed, and the operator's voice came over the loudspeaker. Even though the fire alarms went off frequently for false alarms and drills, the possibility of another explosion in the D.C. area was real, and by the time she'd walked half the length of the hall, her hands were perspiring, and she could feel her heart pounding beneath the skin of her left breast. This paranoia gave her tunnel vision down the now crowded hall, and she focused on the red exit sign near the stairwell, as she pushed past the people rushing from the cafeteria.

Her fear felt almost psychotic, hallucinatory, but she kept running.

"Please refrain from using the elevators. Keep all fire doors closed," the operator announced.

She needed to talk with Raymond Barry. There had to be a link to the other cases. She looked left, right, and then quickly over her shoulder.

Shit.

Amy Daust was close behind her.

Had she seen her?

She covered her face again, coughing, and she looked down.

"Sara," Daust's voice called.

She stopped abruptly amongst all the commotion, and she turned around. Why was she running from the fear mongering, the unproven prejudice? Her quarantine had expired. She'd been exposed to the deadly virus in the Bethesda lab, but so far she was asymptomatic. Everything in the medical literature suggested that only symptomatic patients could spread the illness. The more she ran, the faster she was running out of options. It seemed unlikely, but maybe Daust would help her now.

She pulled Daust aside, whispered, "Amy, I need your help."

Daust pulled Sara's arm away, stepped back. "Sara, there's a warrant out for your arrest for fleeing quarantine."

"The quarantine's expired, Amy." She looked around her. "I have no symptoms of *Labrador*. None. And my daughter is in isolation with a possible infection. I need your help to access—"

"I'm only following orders, Sara." Daust's voice was icy, steady.

She became self-conscious as Daust examined her—her wrinkled clothes, mussed up hair and dirty face. She was sweating and frantic. She knew she looked distressed. Disheveled. Maybe even ill—mentally ill. "I need help, Amy."

"Why are they after you, Sara?"

"Who?"

"The Feds."

"They're after everyone. Have you seen what *Labrador* is doing? Have you been out there?" She ran her hand through her hair. "I'm terrified. You should be, too."

"Sara, you're under direct quarantine by order of the President of the United States of America."

She swallowed. "But I—"

"What have you done, Sara?"

"I haven't done anything." Her voice cracked. She shook her head and her eyes were hazy and she backed away from Daust.

"What do you know, Sara?"

She'd made a huge mistake, approaching Daust. Her tone was determined, and she felt her eyes smolder. Hot black coals, igniting her maternal instinct. "I don't know what I don't know, Amy. But while people are in here dying, I've been running around out there searching for the answer, against the clock. And that terrifies someone."

"You're talking crazy, Sara."

Daust grabbed her wrist, but she ripped it away. "Don't give me that. You know goddamned well that *Labrador* is out of control."

"Sara!"

"They're hiding something. And I'm going to find the cure for *Labrador* before it takes Elyse." She pointed her finger at Daust as she blended into the remaining staff leaving the cafeteria.

The firemen had arrived to put out the grill fire, and were steering people in the opposite direction. Herding people like cattle. *Bzzzzt.* This way. *Bzzzt.* Get back. The whole city was under outside control. The fire didn't look like much, but it had the whole floor in an uproar. Everywhere she turned, the city was in duress. What worried her more was how everyone seemed so willing to toss away their own freedom without any clear explanation for any of it.

"Sara, this is out of your hands. Be reasonable." Daust followed her until she skipped past the firefighters, and toward the back stairwell. A fireman held Daust back with the rest of the crowd. Daust grabbed the phone on the wall, called out, "Security!"

"Ma'am, stay back, please," the officer said to Daust. "This fire is adjacent to the central supply of oxygen to the hospital. We need to get it under control before this whole building explodes into a fireball."

Sara looked back. Then she ran for the stairwell.

"Security," Daust called again. "Stop her!"

-16-

Sara Sullivan

Sara worked her way past the ICU and the coffee cart and the residents' lounge. Doctors in white coats and patients' family members dressed in street clothes and nurses wearing blue scrubs were bustling past her as they hurried out of the cafeteria, coughing. The smoke burned her lungs. She covered her mouth with her sleeve. Two firemen burst through the metal doors and knocked her off her balance. By the time she ran up the stairs to Barry's room, she was exhausted.

Maybe she was growing feverish.

Infected.

She ducked into the bathroom, and splashed some water on her face, looked at herself in the mirror.

I'm fine. I feel fine.

Raymond Barry was sleeping when she knocked on the door of his room. She'd come up the back hall, avoiding the nurses' station. She slipped inside the patient's room quietly. The knock startled the man, and he awoke coughing. Barry had salt and pepper hair, with sun-damaged skin, Puerto Rican or Mexican in appearance. His accent was strong, but he sounded at least second generation, mixed with a hint of a Southern drawl.

"I'm sorry, sir." She approached his bedside and sat down on the chair beside him.

"Who are you?"

"I'm Dr. Sullivan, sir." She smoothed her clothes and she ran her fingers through her hair and she breathed deeply, explained, "I admitted you to the hospital a while ago, sir."

"Well damn all of you," Barry said.

"It looks like you're doing quite well, sir." She forced a smile. "You're going to beat *Labrador* and make it home. Your blood has cleared the virus and you've been taken off isolation."

"I was nearly home until y'all stuck me with tubes and lines and hooked me up to machines. Wanted to see my daughter."

"I spoke with your wife."

He chuckled softly. "Well, I'd imagine you didn't get in too many words."

She took his hand. "I'm sorry about your daughter."

"Alright then."

"How long was she sick?"

"Couple years," Barry said. "She was doing better. Said her cancer was in remission 'til she came back from the Make-A-Wish trip."

"What kind of cancer?"

"She had a brain tumor." Barry looked away. "Wanted to take that safari, but I knew it was a mistake."

"Safari?"

"Oh, not too long ago." The man was getting choked up now. "She loved animals. Said on the trip she walked right up and touched 'em."

Contact with an animal host was a primary means of spreading zoonotic viruses.

Fruit bats, primates, rodents, slaughtered for survival.

Now she thought of Elyse. Raymond Barry's body looked so much stronger than hers—with sandpaper hands worn by work, and porous, browned skin—but his face was weak, expressionless. She squeezed his hand.

The room looked barren. No flowers, or cards, just sterile stainless steel equipment and bandages. The hospital bed and an end-table and a television. It was cold in temperature and feeling and it smelled of urine.

She proceeded with caution, genuine empathy, but with her own daughter's life in mind. "Where did they go?"

She swallowed, hoping it wasn't too much for him, let him remember. She felt compassion as a doctor—but there was so much more at stake for her.

His expression softened. "The African Rift Valley. I couldn't begin to describe it the way she did—all the places she traveled. It was her favorite thing—to travel. *'Para viajar es vivir, Papa,'* she would say."

"To travel is to live," she translated.

"You speak Spanish?" His smile was warm and fearless and enigmatic.

"A little. Just enough to get by in the ER. I took a medical Spanish class awhile back."

"They didn't let me say goodbye to her." Barry wiped his eye. "Just whisked her off to the funeral home. And then wouldn't let me near it. I don't understand. The whole block is cordoned off."

"Funeral home?" she repeated. "Do you mind if I ask where?"

"Finnegan Funeral Home," he said, as if it didn't matter, but she finally had a lead, and she felt her eyes brighten.

"Thank you. You must be terrified, Mr. Barry—losing your daughter and almost losing your own life. I bet you can't wait to walk out of here. I can't even get to my home, and I live two blocks from here. I'm terrified of this epidemic. It keeps me up at night, and I understand your pain. I do. I want to be home—with my daughter."

Raymond Barry put his rough hand over hers now. "I'm almost home, dear."

Barry squeezed her hand, and she worried she'd said the wrong thing, but she knew she couldn't stay much longer. She looked toward the door, and back at him.

"I'm almost home," he repeated.

"I'm sorry."

"I'm not afraid to die," he laughed softly. "Suppose I'm not afraid of anything that kills the body 'less it kills the soul, too."

He was still recovering and physically weak, and his thoughts were a little off track, Sara thought. But he was alert and appropriate and oriented. She had to believe he was giving her accurate information regarding his daughter, and her mind raced with all the facts she knew about filovirus infections— their origins, mode of transmission, the natural course of disease. She had enough evidence now to suggest that the cases had started in Africa. But she'd heard nothing at all about an index case in the media.

Could the initial infection be traced back to the Make-A-Wish safari?

Maybe Barry's daughter hadn't died of cancer.

Maybe it was *Labrador*.

A knock at the patient's door startled her. Raymond Barry was drifting off to sleep, and he stirred, but he didn't awaken. Where had the safari visited? She had a few clues, but now more questions than answers.

She whispered, "Thank you."

She ducked into the closet.

Closed the door behind her.

Peered through the crack.

Senator Edward Marburg, Amy Daust, a hospital security guard, and the unit charge nurse burst into the room. They left just as quickly. Her heart thumped as she crouched down in the large closet, listened to them outside the door.

"I thought she went this way," said the nurse. "Looked like the woman you described."

"Surround the exits," said the senator. "Don't lose her again."

"Yes, sir," said the guard.

Bethesda, Maryland
Veronica Laughlin

By the time Veronica and Kayla reached what was left of the lab, the police had completely isolated the area. Authorities searched through the rubble surrounding what remained of their wing of the building. The police scoured the debris, the dust, the still-burning fire, for casualties. They assisted limping survivors, brush burned and ashen faced, to safety. Thirty-seven deaths had been recorded in the explosion so far, and security was taking roll of all those known to be in the building at the time of the explosion, interviewing employees of the research facility.

The women sneaked past the officers and followed the foot path around the courtyard, where the entire back wall of the brick building was decimated, exposing the staircase leading to what had been Graham's lab. Glass and exploded brick and dust were piled about the ground. The area at the top of the stairs had been annihilated. Smoke and particulates lingered, the sun reddened the sky, slipping into tufts of cirrus. Veronica covered her mouth and gagged on the intense odor of smoke conjured with pungent lab reagents. It burned her lungs and eyes. She moved closer to the wreckage. An ambulance siren passed the disaster, its alarm sounding with increasing and then decreasing frequencies, as it continued on to its destination.

The bomb had ripped apart LeTorneau's hope for a Nobel Prize.

As she waded through the debris of their life's work, she single-handedly cast aside heavy planks, pieces of desk and cabinetry, and mammoth, incisorous pieces of torn metal. She ran through the rubble, cutting her leg on glass and debris. She stumbled as she sank down into the pile, wincing as her leg bled, but she didn't stop. In the dust, she found Hans' access badge. She picked it up and brushed the dust from her dear friend's picture.

She looked back at Kayla, standing at the perimeter of the destroyed structure, as she tore at the remnants. Kayla pulled away fragments of burned rubber.

"Veronica," Kayla called.

She was throwing wooden boards behind her, tossing splintered two by fours like ragdolls from one pile to the next as she dug, searching helplessly. When she saw Kayla waving, she stopped and she ran back through the pile of demolished wood and metal and stone ash.

She followed Kayla's gaze to the ground where Hans lay dead beside Kayla's feet, buried under half of the door to LeTorneau's lab. His left arm and been blown off, and his face was badly swollen, almost unrecognizable. His pants and dress shirt from the dinner were ripped, covered in dirt and dried blood.

She instantly kneeled down, broke into sobs.

She held his head with her hand and she pushed his hair away from the charred face. They hadn't been sure if he'd been in the lab when it exploded, because he'd left the police station in such haste, but his lifeless corpse removed all doubt.

"You and Hans were close," said Kayla.

"Yeah, we were close." She rose and she looked around her at the police cars, the yellow tape roping off the area, the surviving victims in the distance. Then she grabbed an unbroken beaker from a glass case and she smashed it against what was left of one of their workbenches. She seized another and she smashed it, too. "We spent almost six years here. Every day. Every hour of our fucking lives here—for what?"

Kayla stepped back, silent.

Veronica sank to the ground and she cried again near Hans' body.

"I didn't mean—" Kayla put her hand on Veronica's shoulder.

"I know you didn't, Kayla. It's just that—" She was about to explain why she and Hans had grown close—too close at times—until she spotted a tiny black-capped, glass vial in the dirt pile. "Look at this." She crawled over the heap and she reached with her shoulder outstretched, picked it up. She held it before her eyes, examining the straw colored liquid it contained—it was only about five milliliters or so.

She placed it in Kayla's palm.

Kayla looked puzzled, coughing from the soupy mix of smoke and toxic chemicals. "It's a reagent vial. So what?"

"It's mine, Kayla." Veronica rummaged through a small pile of shattered bricks from the explosion. She recognized a few untouched items from her cubicle, including one more vial of the yellow liquid. She flipped it over to reveal where she'd marked her initials, *'VL'* on the bottom. "It's antibody." She referred to the chemical they'd synthetically created to attack the *Labrador* virus and neutralize it *in vivo*.

"How do you know?"

"I saved a few unlabeled vials. It's not enough to do much, of course. The whole chemical process takes weeks just to produce a very small amount, and the entire operation is destroyed, but at least we can run mass spectroscopy on the molecules and identify their chemical structure."

"Except that we don't know how to produce them without Graham. I don't understand why he would do something like this." Kayla shook her head, kicking the stone at her feet.

They were still wearing their formal attire from the reception. It was getting dark, cool, and the police were approaching the area. More ambulances raced from the scene, alarms sounding, making it hard to hear, as they transported survivors.

"You honestly think this is Graham's doing?"

"Yeah, Veronica. I do now." Kayla looked at her, wiped her eyes. "I think Hans was right. Who else would have a reason to do something like this?"

"You might be right." She sighed, stared off into the distance, and in a flat tone, she recited an old adage by rote: "The same key that opens the gates of heaven, opens the gates of hell."

"This is hell, Veronica." Kayla stepped over a portion of concrete wall. *Labrador* is destroying humanity. When LeTorneau saw how people reacted to his vaccine—fighting over being first to market, limiting access to it with exorbitant pricing, and having to produce it secretly under confidentiality clauses when there are thousands of people out there who need it—I wouldn't be surprised if he killed himself in this lab to leave everyone to their own evolutionary defenses."

"Survival of the fittest."

"That would be the natural way of letting this evolve."

"I'm not convinced, Kayla." She stepped on something that gave way beneath her feet. Then she shrieked as they pulled back the body of the cleaning woman.

The housekeeper lay face down in the demolished ruins of their lab. They recognized her uniform, now filthy with blood and wet with chemicals and mud. Together, they shifted the lifeless body onto its back. Both women gasped, regarded her eyes, nose and mouth. She had obvious signs of infection. Kayla dropped her head reflexively and stood erect.

Covering her mouth, Kayla said, "Let's get out of here."

"We'd better." The police were speaking with survivors nearby now.

As they walked along, Kayla suddenly stopped. "Was Hans involved in this, Veronica?"

"How could you even think that?"

"Sorry," Kayla said, and she looked down, walking more carefully now over the remnants of their investments. "There's no explanation to any of it."

"I know, Kayla, but trust me. Hans didn't know any more than we do about LeTorneau's disappearance, about the explosions." She looked at her reflection in a large piece of broken glass and shook the dust from her hair. She brushed the chemicals off her leg and ran her hands through her hair, but it only messed it up more. It was jet black, but the dust from the explosion gave it an aged and grayish hue, a sharp contrast with her youthful freckles. Kayla always told her she was beautiful, but *'beauty queen'* wasn't the look she sought. Ever.

"We have to talk to the police, Veronica."

"We just talked to the police." She blew her bangs out of her eyes. "They think we're full of shit and that we're behind all of this."

"I'd like to talk to Big Jorgey. When's he back?"

"You'd know better than I would." She unzipped her knapsack. It didn't go well with her dress, but she didn't think the dress went well with her either. She craved a shower and a change of clothes.

Jeans.

Her motorcycle jacket.

A new job that paid enough to buy a motorcycle, one that didn't risk their lives any more than a motorcycle.

She placed the vial securely in the inside pocket and she pulled out her black cardigan and she covered her tattooed arms. Her skin over her tattoo of the Red Queen had been cut badly as she'd searched the remains. She dabbed the blood with her sweater now. Walking along, she twisted her ankle again and she swore, but she kept walking.

"If you meant..." Kayla said, and she walked faster. Veronica was outpacing her. "Jorge and I aren't—"

"Oh, Kayla, what does it matter? I didn't mean anything. You want to call Jorge, go ahead. He's always had a soft spot for you even though he does absolutely nothing to pull his weight around here. He missed the most important presentation of the last six years."

"Well he's no paperweight." Kayla giggled, referring to Jorge's massive frame. "He takes a lot of notes."

"True. He may have insight on how to recreate the antibodies, rather than starting from scratch." She stopped and she pulled out her cell phone and she looked at it before she handed it to Kayla. She smiled, gave a single soft chuckle, and her eyes welled again.

"What?"

"Nothing, it's just…" She scrolled through the phone log. "There's a message from Hans from earlier today, after he stormed out of the police office. Before he—before the explosion."

"So listen to it."

"I can't. What if he's still angry? Later, maybe. Not now. I can't now." She wiped her eye and handed the phone to Kayla. "You call Jorge and fill him in on everything. I think he's due back next week."

George Washington University Hospital
Sara Sullivan

When the Senator and Amy Daust and the security guard were gone, Sara slipped out of the closet. She approached Mr. Barry's bedside again. He was paler, quieter, and his lips were drained of color. She shook him gently, gasped, when his stiff body didn't rouse from his sleep.

The man had passed.

"You're home now," she said softly.

She walked to the door and peered outside. The nurses looked occupied. She unfolded a piece of crumpled scrap paper from her pocket and sat back down beside the bed and picked up the phone receiver. She dialed nine for an outside line and the number Jane Morgan had given her for her husband, Wes Lindstrom. She waited several rings before the lobbyist answered.

"Talk to me," Wes Lindstrom said.

"Hello, is this Mr. Wesley Lindstrom? This is Dr. Sara Sullivan."

"Hello, kitten," he said. "I'm here. I was just about to call you. Don't you know you should let a man make the first move?"

The man's tone changed from high-octane dealer to womanizing opportunist as she spoke. *Let's play cat and mouse, Mr. Lindstrom,* she thought. She clenched her teeth.

"If I wanted to talk to my husband I would've called him." She was fearful of being discovered, and kept a close eye on the door now. "Where are you?"

"I admire your directness, sweetheart, but there's something to be said for playing hard to get."

"You already know where I am. Stop hiding, you coward. What do you know about *Labrador*?"

"Sweetheart, I'm in New York having lunch with an advisor in my firm and admiring my waitress' posterior. Wall Street. Cipriani restaurant, the best table here." Then she heard him tell the waitress, over the line, "Take back the Caprese salad and bring me something with meat."

"Did you read the story I sent your wife?"

"What if I told you I could have your story sold in five languages with movie rights?"

"It was you all along." She rose from the bed. "You bastard."

"That's not how you make friends and influence people in politics." Then she heard him say in a hushed tone, like he was covering the receiver, "I've got to go. I'll call you later."

"You greedy son of a bitch."

"It was a cute idea, kitten. A thrilling project for me. Nothing more. And I could've come up with it myself, honestly. I make million dollar deals every single day."

She recalled the picture of him she'd pulled up online, and imagined his eyes, emblazoned with anger and greed, jutting chin, the wide lips curled in a smile. She heard the honking of the cabs from the Financial District, and she heard Wes Lindstrom say, "LaGuardia."

"This isn't about the story now. People are dying."

"People die every day." Lindstrom's tone was cutthroat.

"Not my daughter. Not on my watch." She clutched the landline phone to her ear.

She was perspiring.

Nausea swept her as she regarded her reflection in the wall mirror.

Her eyes looked red, her body ached. Had she made a mistake calling Wes Lindstrom? Now she was certain he was involved, but how? She felt light headed and the room looked like it was spinning. Was she falling ill after her exposure? She couldn't afford to be sick. She had to keep going. Elyse's life depended on it—and maybe now her own.

"Who has the cure for the virus?" she demanded, gripping the phone.

"I wish I knew, honey." Lindstrom was calm, confident.

It provoked her more.

She breathed heavier over the line.

More loud horns honking on his end.

Where was he going?

"Listen, stay put. You and the senator and I will talk when I get back into town."

"Senator," she muttered. She ran her fingers through her hair and looked down at Raymond Barry, expired, even after his body had supposedly resolved the deadly filovirus infection. *Marburg, he means.* "Like hell we will."

She slammed down the receiver and grabbed Raymond Barry's wallet and his bag with his belongings. She emptied it and filled it with a few first aid supplies—an IV start kit and some fluid for hydration. *Just in case.* Then she put on a surgical cap and gown and mask from the isolation supplies just outside his room, and she disappeared, unnoticed, down the hallway and back down the stairwell.

Bethesda, Maryland
Kayla Reeves

Kayla and Veronica finished sorting through the rubble of their once state-of-the art lab. There was nothing more they could do, and it was getting dark. Before Kayla finished dialing Jorge's cell phone number, an overwhelming feeling of nausea overcame her. She sweat and she shivered at the same time, as if she was experiencing an intense heat and a paralyzing cold, together at once. She was faint, weak, and she needed to sit down right away. The magnitude at which these symptoms overtook her petite frame terrified her. She dropped the phone and gazed at Veronica, whose silhouette seemed to drift in and out of focus. Then she looked around for anywhere she could find to sit down, staggered to the nearest park bench.

Before Veronica could ask what was wrong, she threw up a massive amount of blood.

"Kayla," Veronica called, and sat beside her friend. "You look like shit. What happened? You were fine a minute ago."

"Thanks, for the compliment." She moaned, holding her abdomen. "All of this is just so overwhelming."

"You've never been queasy at the site of blood. You're always the first one injecting the mouse and the primate subjects." Veronica laughed, but it masked her worried expression. "Are you okay?"

"I'm not sure," she said, slumping forward and putting her head in her hands. A wonderful gust of wind cooled her skin. The feverish feeling dissipated. "I think so. Seeing Hans like that—I think it was too much for me."

"I know," Veronica looked over the side of the railing where she'd thrown up. "Kayla, you're bleeding. You threw up blood."

"I think it's just nerves."

Nearby, a National Guardsman was patrolling the scene. Another two soldiers struggled to carry a body by the arms and feet, out through the uneven terrain of the disaster area. Victims surrounded them, covered in blood, unrecognizable. Veronica put her arm around Kayla's hunched shoulders, met the gaze of the larger man in the distance. When the Guardsman set down the mutilated body, one of them started toward them.

Veronica waved him off and shouted, "We're fine!"

Kayla smiled, looking worried that he might come closer. Veronica sat her up straighter, but she was heaving again as the Guardsman stopped at a huge pile of concrete rubble and splintered wood. He turned on his heels and signaled another soldier near their camouflage tent with the Red Cross symbol on the tarp. Behind the first aid tent, a tank was moving into the area, escorting a line of scientists in hazmat suits, accompanied by members of the U.S. Army.

"Kayla, how long have you been feeling sick?"

"Veronica, I swear—the feeling just came on. This place has the stench of death, and the chemicals from the explosion are burning my lungs."

"What about last week, when we were working in the lab— before LeTorneau went missing? Were there any breaks in your technique handling the virus? You and Jorge all but ate your pizza on top of one of the macaques."

"No, of course not. We all have meticulous technique. We could be exposed now, but—" She swallowed.

"It would be too soon to exhibit symptoms. The incubation period for *Labrador* is one to two weeks."

"Right."

"Are you strong enough to run?"

"I don't think I can stand." She laid her head in Veronica's lap, but her friend gave her a gentle shake.

"Come on. You've got to. If those soldiers come back and see you vomiting blood, you'll be quarantined with *Labrador* patients—black or white—it won't matter. You'll be infected even if you're healthy. And it won't help us to find LeTorneau if you're stuck in the hospital."

"I'll try." She eyed the police and the National Guardsmen. "I don't trust them."

"Me neither," Veronica said.

In the distance, one of the men was talking with his superior. The man pointed in their direction.

Veronica was the physically stronger of the two, and years of kickboxing had made her body compact and muscular. Thoroughbred arms, equine thighs, six-pack abs. "I've thought about joining the military, but this isn't my idea of boot camp, Reeves. I'll do what I can here. Help me out and we'll get to my car together."

Veronica slung Kayla's arm around her shoulders and stood up, lifting her effortlessly, but her legs buckled underneath her. Veronica pulled her up again, locking her knee into a standing position with her own leg.

As she regained her balance and hobbled along, she felt dehydrated, like she could faint at any moment, but she kept going. When Veronica picked up the pace and crossed the untouched Lutheran Church courtyard adjacent to the facility, she glanced back. Two Guardsmen were running in their direction, trampling shrubs of rhododendron, an herb garden of lavender and sage, a carpet of petunias.

The men were armed.

One of them drew his weapon and shouted, but she couldn't hear him.

It was another block to Veronica's car.

The second guard was on his radio phone.

"Stop now by order of the United States National Guard," one man shouted.

They were closer now, and she could hear their deep voices and even the sound of their boots pounding against the exploded remnants of their lab. Her adrenaline seemed to kick in at the sight of the two men chasing them, and she ran as fast as she could with Veronica still supporting much of her weight.

She rushed to open Veronica's car door and got in, slammed it shut.

She slumped down in the front seat, exhausted and panting for breath, as Veronica started the Subaru.

"You did great, Reeves."

"I can't catch my breath. I'm so tired." She wiped the beads of sweat from her brow and opened the vents to cool her face.

Veronica threw the stick shift into first and punched the gas pedal. The old Subaru peeled out, its tires squawking. A hail of bullets from their AK-47's whizzed around the car. One found its mark, shattering the left taillight. Ahead was a roadblock, and at the nearest intersection to her right, traffic was at a standstill.

Another *Labrador* checkpoint.

When did the National Guard get the authority to shoot mercilessly with automatics? The freedom to move about the city was diminishing more each day. Civil liberties gone. A state of martial law and disintegration of social order. It scared her to death—not only for her life, but her way of life as she knew it.

"Shit. Hold on to your ass, Reeves." Veronica swore and cranked the steering wheel to the left and shifted to third gear, grinding her clutch as she barreled across the lawn of a public park.

The right side of the rust-colored sedan scraped against a statue of Thomas Jefferson. Kayla screamed, ducked down below the dash board.

"Damn it." She cringed. The stone on metal sound raked down the driver's side of the car, making a welder's array of sparks that sprayed the concrete. Another round of fire hit the back bumper, knocking it off the vehicle. "Why is this whole state so obsessed with Jefferson?"

"Hang on," Veronica pulled a sharp left.

She flew across the front seat, fought the urge to throw up again. "Veronica, maybe we should go back. We're resisting arrest. And you're driving like Cruella de Vil."

"Damn right we are." Veronica adjusted her rearview mirror and clutched her fur covered steering wheel.

The Guardsmen fired again, but the Subaru was moving out of range now. "Think they got your license plate?"

"Not the way I was hauling ass." Veronica checked the rearview again. "Looks like we lost them."

Veronica bounded off the sidewalk and back onto the road, cutting off a Tahoe behind them. Kayla glanced at the passenger mirror—the SUV behind them swerved into a parking meter. Veronica gave a one-finger salute to the chorus of honking horns, pulled another sharp left, and blended into traffic. Then she circled around the block and headed south in the opposite direction toward Kayla's apartment building.

Veronica helped her up the stairs. She tripped twice, but she changed into her pajamas and she got into bed without vomiting again.

Her bedroom was nothing like Veronica's. Her bed had a ruffled duvet, and it was filled with pictures of her parents and siblings back home in Macon, Georgia, and the smell of her geraniums on the fire escape. Their odor seemed to calm her as it wafted in from the open window. The breeze from the open window blew the linen curtains onto her wooden dresser. This was the most time the two of them had spent together outside the lab, but Kayla appreciated it. She'd been to Veronica's once—she was always throwing theme parties and inviting the students and even the faculty over—they were her only family. But Veronica's studio apartment looked more like a special ops training facility. Punching bags and ropes. A weight bench. Posters of tactical guns and ammo covering the walls. Cabinets stacked with organic sundries. She wondered now what Veronica thought of her place.

"Are you sure you're going to be alright by yourself?" Veronica asked.

"I'm fine. I just need some sleep."

"I'm not so sure, Reeves." Veronica flipped on the bedroom television.

"Good evening. This is Diane Sawyer, live from our nation's capital," the anchor was saying, "where the president has issued executive orders for the third week in a row restricting access to transportation and healthcare. Mandatory checkpoints, quarantines and forced treatment within ramshackle tents have people wondering what good the recently passed healthcare expansion laws are if people can't get access to healthcare. To make matters worse, facility raids, bribes and private facilities for those who can afford better care continue to cause tension across the District."

"So basically nothing's new, Diane," said Veronica. "Thanks for that. Rich people still have better access to healthcare."

"Oh, God. Please don't get political on me," she said, pressing her head face down into her pillow.

"Reporting live from D.C. is Candace Simmons. Candace, do people feel that services are being rationed under the new law, and what's the cause of the hysteria sweeping the District?" asked Diane Sawyers.

The reporter on the scene said, "Thank you, Diane. There's definitely an air of government distrust, an intense fear of healthcare rationing, and a sense of an overall inability to get safe treatment at hospitals and doctors' offices. It started here in D.C. and continues to grow worse every day with rioting, and actual, physical blockades limiting travel around the capital, all due to the outbreak of the deadly *Labrador* virus."

"How many people have been affected? How did the outbreak begin?"

"We're not certain, Diane, but the case numbers are approaching one thousand in African-Americans. One of the reasons doctors believe *Labrador* is the cause for the rationing in care is because it is such a deadly virus, requiring incredibly costly care—often tens of thousands of dollars for treatment in intensive care and isolation. Many victims simply cannot be saved."

Veronica flipped off the television. Kayla had vaguely heard the news, but she was drifting off to sleep.

"Alright, I'll take your word and let you rest, Reeves. You have to *promise* me you'll call me if you get sick again. I mean it. It's like the seventh hour out there."

"John 4:52—when the fever left him," she muttered.

"You read the Bible, Reeves? It's just an expression. And I'm sure I screwed it up."

"You did. I'm a Southern Baptist. I didn't have much choice growing up." She rolled over and opened her eyes.

"No wonder you and Backwoods Bourdain get along so well."

"Why hasn't he called me?"

Veronica leaned on the windowsill, adjacent to a wall painting of a peacock full breasted and proud and vibrant, rolled one of the petals of Kayla's red geraniums between her thumb and index finger, crushing it. "I thought we were the ones who understood the virus. But I don't. LeTorneau's the only one who does." Veronica sighed, added, "Promise to call me?"

"I promise."

"Goodnight, Reeves." Veronica flipped off the light. Before she closed Kayla's bedroom door, she said, "I'll check on you first thing tomorrow morning."

But Kayla didn't hear her leave.

-17-

George Washington University Hospital
Sara Sullivan

Sara was back in the isolation unit now, and Marty had never looked happier to see her. She gazed at Elyse again through the fingerprinted glass. Their daughter was now hooked up to the dialysis machine, and an oscillating ventilator that shook her tiny limbs and chest with every breath. The tubes and lines coming from all over her body had Marty perspiring, his voice cracking, and even Sara, who normally wasn't shaken by the invasiveness of intensive care treatments, was terrified seeing them attached to their baby girl.

"I'm so glad you came back," said Marty.

"I can't stay long."

Marty held her tightly around the waist and brushed a chunk of her now unruly hair away from her ear like he would a child's. She sensed this need of his to protect her, and though she wanted to sigh and tell him she didn't need him to, she allowed it this once.

"Who are these people looking for you, Sara?"

"I have no idea, but I haven't done anything wrong."

"I didn't say you did."

"Who's looking for me now?"

"Senator Marburg? They questioned me like a criminal, Sara. Is there something you're not telling me?"

"I suspect he's involved with Wes Lindstrom—the one I introduced you to in the French restaurant."

"I forgot to pay attention there, Sara." Marty looked her over, then at Elyse, with an impotent gaze. "I was trying not to look like an oaf in that restaurant. I thought you'd like it and I suggested those sexual things to keep us alive. You know me—I'm happy with a hot dog and a beer. The remote control."

"You always have to be in control of the remote."

"Sara, I just—"

She smiled and she shushed him with a finger to his lips, kissed him. Even when she was furious with him, he still had an effect on her. A lasting effect. She couldn't stay angry. And she'd have killed for a hot dog just then, too, but she reached behind him and she pulled the keys to his truck from his back pocket.

Then she pulled out his phone.

Marty grabbed at his pocket.

"Is that why you came back here? Sara, you can't—" Marty protested, but she kissed him harder, gave him a wary look that reminded him of how he'd gotten her into legal trouble, intentionally.

She kissed him again, and when she pulled away, they both faced each other, holding hands. "Your controlling little mind game got me into trouble. I have to figure this out, Marty." She glanced toward the unit. "It's her only hope. And not just for Elyse. There are so many people out there affected by *Labrador*. *My* people."

He nodded. "Remember the street we grew up on?"

She recalled the old row of cookie-cutter homes on Marsh Street in Baltimore, built so close together that you could reach out and touch the neighbors' windows, the little grandmothers tending their gardens—their slice of Americana, and her own mother calling her home to suppers of beef stew and chicken and dumplings. She could've spent an hour imagining it.

"Yes, of course. We were just kids, but—"

"I made up any reason I could to see you, Sara."

"You did?" She thought back. Her mother had moved away from that little neighborhood when she was eight, and her father had left them. He'd gone out for bread and never came back—that's how it happened back then. He'd left her mother unable to afford a mortgage, even in their small home. She and Marty didn't reconnect again until after she began college at Georgetown when he'd pulled her over for speeding. "That was so long ago, I—I barely remember you then."

"I remember you." Marty looked at her again with that look that let her know what a challenge she was. Incorrigible, at times. "I came up with any excuse to see you. I made Sammy Lewandowski throw the football so far I'd have to run down the road to chase it on your front lawn."

"My mother didn't like you trampling over her flowers to get it."

"I didn't care."

"No one liked me there, Marty. I was the only colored girl. No one liked my dad, either—probably why he left."

"I did. I loved you the minute I saw you throw a softball better than the boys. And I had no idea that I could love you more than when we were eight years old and playing tag."

"I wanted to play *baseball*." She laughed, looked toward the door. Marburg and Amy Daust would be searching for her. "I felt that way about you, too, when we met in our twenties, Marty. My mom still wasn't too fond of you then." She touched his nose.

"Of course not. Look at you. You're a doctor for Chrissakes. And you're beautiful. She knew I didn't deserve you."

"Don't be ridiculous."

"When you and your mother moved away, I thought I'd lost you, Sara. I was ten." He hugged her. "I can't let that happen again. Stay here with me and Elyse. They're doing all they can," he begged her, held her arm.

"I can't. Please trust me. *They're* not." She wriggled away from his now uncomfortably strong grip, and she put on his ball cap, his sunglasses.

"Please—at least let me help you."

"I have to do this on my own, Marty. I think you've helped me enough already."

"At least promise me you'll come to *me* if you get into more trouble."

"You got me into a real situation, too, though."

"I know, Sara. I was wrong. I was trying to hold on too tight. It's just sometimes getting married to you makes me feel so powerless—especially in this place."

At once, she became aware of the cold tile covering the walls, the overwhelming antiseptic smell, and the sound of the alarming monitors from Elyse's bedside—the things she never noticed at work, but things that probably made Marty cringe. "You're not powerless. Look that doesn't even matter." She checked the door. "I love you like crazy, Marty. I still can't believe you did that to me."

"I'm sorry."

Sara remembered her mom telling her over and over—after her mother had finally accepted their wedding plans—to make Marty, *'feel like a man,'* as her mother always put it, but she'd never had any idea of what that meant. He was a cop with a gun, a pickup truck. He hunted animals. He wore jeans and a baseball cap when he was off duty—not like the doctors she worked with that dressed better than she did and got their chests waxed or even had a pedicure now and then.

They didn't come any more masculine than Marty.

"Okay, I'll call you if I need something." She squeezed his hand and stole down the corridor and out the back exit to the visitors' parking lot. It was dark now. She found his Ford F150 and she turned onto Grant Street and she got on the Beltway, headed to her mother's house for the night.

No one that knew anything about her would ever look for her there.

Georgetown

Washington, D.C.

Kayla Reeves

It was only six a.m. when Kayla awoke with violent shivers. She couldn't get warm, but her temperature was 103.5 on the digital thermometer. She vomited for the third time that morning. Then she faced herself in the mirror where a dark greenish hue was circling both her eyes like the sky before a Georgia twister. Her cheeks hung limp in sunken pockets of grey pallor that made her cringe. Her usually shiny blonde hair looked like the dull matte of a Palomino horsetail. She tightened the knob on the leaky porcelain faucet that had been dripping all night. Her eyes were reddened with bloodshot whorls of veins, and the basin where she'd thrown up was tinged with streaks of her blood. She gagged at the sight, the smell of it, and she turned on the faucet and she rinsed it clean.

In her bedroom, she pulled back the duvet and opened the browser on her tablet. The *Democrat and Chronicle* webpage reported nine new cases of *Labrador*. She sipped the stale water on her nightstand and rubbed her neck over the lymph node glands.

As she read further, her hands trembled. She grabbed her cordless phone and dialed Jorge. The lab was gone, and with it nearly every vial of antibody to *Labrador* that the students and professor LeTorneau had spent years developing. She shook her head, biting her nails as tears welled up, and she breathed faster, heavily, as she waited for an answer.

"Kayla," Jorge said. "How are you? I'm so glad you're safe. I've been trying to call you."

"You have?" She pulled the covers around her more tightly, shivered.

"I was worried you were hurt in the explosions."

"I guess the news reached you then."

"Yeah."

"When are you coming back?"

Jorge coughed, didn't speak.

"I'm not well, Jorgey." Her voice quivered, and she paused, before she told him, "I think I've come down with it." She started to cry, held her lip. She bit her nail so that he might not hear her.

"Labrador?" He was loud and gruff on the line, not like the subdued graduate student she knew from the lab. Maybe the weeks on sabbatical had restored something lost in their tiresome, mundane hours of research, the only fruits of which had been annihilated. "Kayla, that's not funny."

"Jorgey, I'm scared. I've been throwing up all night. I have all the symptoms: fever, vomiting blood, diarrhea, and a wicked sore throat."

"Are your eyes bloodshot?"

"Yeah."

"Were you exposed in the lab?" Jorge sounded frantic now, but the connection was distant and crackly, like the call might drop at any second.

"I don't think so. We were meticulous about technique. We all know the stakes." She ran to the bathroom again, gagging over the toilet, a desperate sound that she was sure could be heard over the line.

"Kayla," Jorge shouted.

She picked up the phone again, said, "Veronica and I went to the site of the explosion. We saw Hans' dead body and, and — there's hazardous material showered everywhere. That was yesterday — it would be too soon for me to show symptoms, right?" She was speaking in a flight of ideas, stressed. She wiped her lip and she pulled her hair back into a rubber band and she opened the bathroom door. She returned to the bedroom with the phone to her ear.

"Not necessarily," Jorge said. "There are new strains."

"New strains?" She sniffed and scrolled down the online news articles again. There was nothing in the report about the virus mutating or causing an accelerated onset of the clinical symptoms. "Jorge, all of the antibody we created is gone. Destroyed. I'm scared. Without it, there's no cure. What if I—" She cried now, thinking of the worst—of death.

"Never mind that." A car engine hummed over the line, and the crackling of the poor connection made it difficult to hear. He sounded so tender when he said, "I'd never let that happen to you, Kayla."

"I know you wouldn't, Jorgey."

"Where are you?"

"I'm home, Jorgey. I've been sick in bed since last night when Veronica dropped me off. She's coming back this morning. I'm going to have her take me to the hospital, but there are roadblocks and military personnel everywhere. If I don't have *Labrador*, I'll be quarantined with everyone who does, and I'll be infected."

"Don't go anywhere with Veronica."

"But I could die without treatment, Jorge. I wish I knew what to do."

She slowly rose and she walked to the window and she pulled back the sheer white curtain. Peering out over the fire escape, she saw more rioting, about a block away. An African-American boy was being pushed up against a car, placed in handcuffs, the police were using pepper spray to control the crowd. Civilians rubbed their eyes as police pushed them back behind white wooden barricades. There was shouting and police sirens and protestors with signs that she couldn't read from her room. She closed the window and yanked the curtain shut and sank to the ground.

"Stay put," Jorge said. "I'll be right there."

A car radio was audible now over the line, playing a news program, but she could barely make out his voice.

"Jorgey, can you help me get the antidote? There has to be more antibody," she said, but the call disconnected.

Sara Sullivan

Sara yanked the Hank Williams CD out and she tossed it on the front seat and she flipped on the radio. It was too country for her. She couldn't listen to another government broadcast on the radio, either. She changed the channel, but the lyrics on the station were about some guy blowing it in some bitch's face. Now that she had a daughter, those songs just didn't do it for her, no matter how good the beat was. She secretly liked Blake Shelton, although she'd never admit that to Marty, and she put his C.D. in the disc changer, but even singing along to *Sangria* couldn't distract her from the horrific reality that her daughter might die. She'd need more than a few pitchers of the fruity drink to do that, given her current level of anxiety.

What kind of mother was she?

Elyse's picture was dangling from Marty's rearview mirror. She didn't even carry a picture most of the time, except on her cell phone. The first few months of her baby's life had slipped by so quickly, and now Elyse lay in a chemically induced coma, unable to recognize her own parents. She pulled the picture down from the mirror and she kissed it and she put it in her pocket as she drove.

Marty's truck was huge, and it took all her senses to steer that boat. As her focus shifted from the picture and her thoughts of Elyse, to the roadblock ahead of her, she slammed on the brakes, nearly hitting the Chevrolet in front of her.

"Shit," she muttered, as her momentum carried her neck and shoulders forward.

As if it didn't take long enough to get around D.C. on an average day, authorities were checking identification and temperatures with a skin probe ahead of her.

Traffic on the Beltway had come to an abrupt halt.

Army guards with guns held across their chests redirected a woman in a Mercedes, three cars ahead of her, to pull off the highway. The isolation and quarantine measures seemed so extreme, and caused a pervasive distrust that made her and every other citizen in the capital nearly come unhinged.

She knew she'd have to pull away, but doing it in the truck wouldn't be easy. She'd think nothing of pulling a U-turn in the middle of a six-lane highway with her BMW, and her flirtatious wit would ordinarily get her out of anything, well—just about anything. She recalled how Marty had set her up only a few days earlier. She was still seething, but she couldn't help thinking it was her fault for exposing her daughter to *Labrador* through her contact with the sick.

No, it was still Marty's fault.

She craned her neck partly out of the window. Ahead of her there was a *No U-turn* sign and a paved area where she could turn around—if she could get over in time. She signaled and she smiled and she tried to catch the attention of the driver to her left.

No one was letting her in.

"Come on, come on," she whispered, and she checked the rearview.

Finally, she cut in and she gassed the pedal at the slightest break in traffic, cutting across two lanes. Horns blew. The guard ahead of her turned toward the commotion, blew his whistle.

Quickly, she made a U-turn, floored the pedal, accelerated into traffic into the opposite direction. In the rearview, she saw a fading image of the camouflaged guard, arms flailing, running after her with the whistle still in his mouth.

She took the first exit off the Beltway, pulled a sharp right turn at the end of the ramp. She made several rapid turns in quick succession, looking ahead for another checkpoint and checking her mirrors for anyone on her tail. When she was confident she wasn't being followed, she drove back a few blocks to her mother's brownstone, and she pulled into the driveway.

"Sara," Charlotte Sullivan said, startled, as Sara opened the door with the key on Marty's chain. Her mother was standing at the sink, pouring tea, and she grasped her chest as Sara entered and closed the large wooden door behind her.

"Mom, I need to stay here tonight," she said, taking off her shoes. She was panting. Sweating. Her cheeks were flushed.

They were going through one of their less than close periods, and she preferred not to have to do it, but she had no other options. Her mother frowned as she looked at her, shook her head.

No kiss on the cheek.

No hug.

Just that *look* from her.

"Well come on in." Her mother's accent was slow and Southern and thick, her smile warmed. "Is it that husband of yours?"

Her mother ushered her into the kitchen and she pushed her white hair behind her ear and she fluffed the back of it and she smoothed her skirt.

"Sort of." She looked around nervously. She felt she should feel more at home in her mother's place, especially since they lived so close, but there was more than a geographical distance between them. She parted the dangling strings of seashells that hung from the doorway, creating a whimsical sound.

"I'll make you some coffee."

She sank into the kitchen chair. The cups and saucers clattered loudly as her mother shifted around the creamer and the sugar bowl.

"Mom?"

Her mother was stirring in the natural sugar cubes—two of them—just like she liked. Then her mother turned and sat down on the cushioned wooden chair and stirred the coffee some more and warmed her hands around her own cup of tea.

"Did you ever feel uncomfortable dating Dad because he was black?"

"What, dear?" Her mother coughed and straightened up her posture and pulled her sweater tighter around her shoulders. Charlotte Sullivan looked like she was choosing her words, but Sara saw through her hesitation and she raised her brows, staring into her mother's blue eyes.

"Well—"

"Be honest, Mom." She'd had a few heart to heart talks with her mother over the years, but mostly their conversations involved a lot of advice from her mother. A thorough assessment of everything she'd never done right in her life. How Charlotte Sullivan, *Super Mom,* would've done it differently.

"Sara, of course." Her mother put her frail hand on Sara's and sipped her tea. "It never made life easy for any of us. There were looks, whispers. I can't say it didn't affect me."

"You never told me that."

"And I never would have either if you hadn't asked. But now that you're with Marty, I'm sure you know how I felt. I always held my head high and never let you feel disadvantaged—not once."

"You did just now, though, Mom."

"Sara, I'm being honest. I didn't say I would ever change a thing—I wouldn't. I have no regrets. But I wanted to make sure you really loved Marty before you got into an interracial relationship like I was. That's why I fought you so much when you told me you were pregnant with Elyse. I knew this road isn't an easy one. And you know I never liked him much." Her mother pointed her finger and shook her head again and took a larger gulp of tea.

"He's not that bad, Mom." At once she wondered why she was defending Marty, when she was still furious with him herself.

"I remember going to the market once with Susan Peterson and her daughter—remember the little Oriental girl she adopted? And someone stopped her and asked where she *got* her. She said it happened all the time and it didn't much bother her." Her mother stirred Sara's coffee again and then she stopped, stared out the window. "No one ever asked *me* that when I dressed you up all pretty and took you out." Her mother rose and stood at the sink.

"It's different now, Mom, or at least I thought it was."

"I know, but back then—"

"You were embarrassed of what people thought of you being with a black man, Mom."

"No, Sara—"

"You just said it yourself. It bothered you that they didn't consider that a black girl might be adopted?" She was ready to get up and run, take her chances with the authorities over the strained relationship with her mother. She sighed, and she asked, "Mom, did you make Dad leave?"

"Sara, listen." Her mother finished her tea, held her hand. "I loved your father, Sara. I wanted him, desired him—from the beginning. I—I can't explain it. They say opposites attract." She blushed and wiped her lip with the linen napkin from the old tea set. "I'd even go so far as to say I wanted to have a child with him the first day we met. I just *knew*, Sara. I wanted *you*. Never told nobody that, you know. I didn't care about what people'd say. I know that sounds like crazy talk coming from a Christian woman."

"I know. I felt that for Marty—whether you like him or not. There's something to that—opposites attract." Her mother's candor made her a bit uncomfortable, and she grabbed one of the biscuits and she broke it in half and she spread a large dollop of honey all over it. She probably would've gotten up and left on any other day. She bit her biscuit and thought about the research she'd read about that the missing Nobel Prize nominee, Dr. Graham LeTorneau, had published. "We're wired to be attracted to people most genetically unlike us—it prevents disease and improves our survival, our fitness. It's not crazy talk at all, Mom. Just wish the rest of the world saw it that way, 'stead of letting prejudices and hatred get in the way." She finished the biscuit and broke another one in half.

"I don't much understand all that doctor talk, but you sure grew up to be one smart woman, Sara—went farther than I ever did, or dreamed you ever could, coming from this house." Her mother's expression grew contemplative again, like she needed to get something off her chest, but she shook her head and picked up the dishes. They clanked together in their usual symphony of maternal anxiety. Her mother turned to her again, and said, "I stopped seeing the world like I wished it was, Sara. If you see things like they really are, you'll be less disappointed."

"I'll try to remember that, Mom." Why couldn't their talks be more encouraging? "It's not easy. I did just bring a baby into the world, you know."

"Those rose-colored glasses'll only make your tears look pink."

She sighed, changed the subject. "Elyse is pretty sick, Mom."

"She's a strong, feisty little girl just like you were. She'll be alright. She'll pull through. You always did."

"I need to stay here tonight. I can't go back home."

"Stay as long as you like. I don't need to know the details."

That was just like her mom, she thought. *Labrador* was all over the news, and she didn't even conjecture that her only granddaughter—or her daughter, for that matter—might be afflicted. Hell, maybe she hadn't even turned on the television in weeks. If she had, she probably thought the news on the capital was one big, silly conspiracy theory, and just carried on with her life: Grocery shopping. Prayer group. Bingo. Nothing stood in the way of Bingo. *Don't listen to anything on the news. It's all nonsense.* Sara thought about her mother's ways and for once, she envied her ignorance.

Her mother was back to washing the dishes now, scrubbing them much harder than they needed to be cleaned after being used for only tea and biscuits. She sighed as she watched her thrive on the redundancy of her daily life. Why couldn't she be more laid back like her mother? Her mind and legs were heavy, but she was so exhausted that when she went upstairs to her old bedroom and lay down, she fell asleep in minutes and slept until morning.

The rumbling sound of the National Guard truck coming up the street awakened her at 6 a.m.

-18-

Sara Sullivan

Sara gunned the F150 down I-95, dressed in her mother's black jeans and Lycra tank top and Marty's Braves cap. It killed her to wear it—she was a die-hard Orioles fan, but she was aiming for inconspicuous. The borrowed clothing had replaced her ready-to-wear fitted suits and elegant shoes that defined her professional image. She was certain Marty wouldn't even recognize her in all her rage. She felt incapable of anything but worry on that morning, and a primal desire for genetic perseverance, if not through herself, then through her daughter, Elyse.

She was going to save her or die trying.

Her muscles seemed to define themselves more with each pulse of adrenaline, a venom racing through her blood. The hostility she'd seen in the District since the *Labrador* epidemic started was caustic, like it could tear apart all of mankind. And she felt she could, too, at that point, as her vehicle accelerated down I-95, searching for an unknown conspirator. The specter of Elyse's motionless body haunted her.

She had driven this road hundreds of times—once all the way from Maine to Florida with Marty when they'd first dated. Now it seemed tunnel-like, and she was unable to see laterally outside the immediate horizon where the heat mirage smeared the appearance of the pavement and the sky in front of her.

The ruse twisted the image into waves, like a Van Gogh. And the ghostlike figure from the post-Impressionist painting she recalled now screamed with hands upon its cheeks inside her mind, a foreboding image. The southwesterly wind whipped down the asphalt, blowing the parched, yellowed grasses along the roadside. She gave in to this momentous directive because she didn't think she could wield to it even if she willed it.

This drive along the seemingly endless stretch of highway affected her deeply and moved her with such a terrible fear of what was to come as she drove on. She passed an overheated car with the engine in flames and the passengers milling about roadside. The entire city resonated distress. The traffic slowed and passersby stared and kept on. And Sara kept on, thinking only of her daughter, her own years passed and how miserably she had failed so far as a mother and a daughter. The ambivalence she'd shown Elyse when she came home from work. How she'd let her cry to satisfy her own fatigue with sleep. And the defensive, failed conversations she'd had with her own mother, and everything she'd meant to say but didn't. *Couldn't.*

Visions of the car on flames recycled in her mind as she drove on, an evocation of something she had seen somewhere else, but she couldn't remember where—her worry for Elyse consumed her. She kept driving 95, the spine of the east that on this day, anyway, was vivace of car horns and humming eighteen wheelers and rap music blasting from the convertible next to her, so loudly that she could hear it through her own closed truck windows. She was now playing *Home* by Dierks Bentley in her truck.

She flipped the public radio broadcast back on.

A dragonfly impacted the windshield and splattered its mustard entrails against the glass. The windshield wiper cleared the insect. It turned her concentration from Elyse to the news, and she turned down the whistling air conditioner to hear the public service announcement, pulled off I-95.

-19-

Georgetown
Washington, D.C.
Kayla Reeves

When Jorge reached Kayla's apartment it was only nine a.m., and it seemed like she'd gotten off the phone with him only minutes before, but she'd fallen back asleep, into a tumultuous dream that she couldn't remember, and she awoke with his grizzly frame hovering over her bed. The smell of his flannel shirt and jeans was an outdoorsy marriage of bonfire smoke and bourbon. Had he been drinking? She breathed in his scent and offered a comforted smile.

"How did you get in?" Her eyes fluttered open and then closed again.

"The door was unlocked." Jorge scratched his chin where his stubble had prickled yellowish red hairs over it with about a week's worth of growth. It wasn't the usual clean kept appearance he embodied in the lab. "Wide open, actually."

"Veronica," she said.

"Girl's always in a rush to get somewhere. Then when she gets there, got to get somewhere else. I was raised in a two-room cabin'n Lake Pontchartrain'n even I remember to shut the front door." Jorge grunted, clearing his throat. Then he reached into his jeans and unwrapped a piece of cinnamon gum and put it in his mouth.

"Veronica'll be back to check on me any minute. She went home for the night, but she'll be excited to see you, Jorgey."

"What's LeTorneau got to say 'bout all the attention? Bet he likes it." Jorge scratched his facial hair again, a little harder, and brushed her hair from her eyes where it fell over to one side. Holding out his hand, he said, "Mademoiselle?" and helped her sit up in bed.

"I don't know what to think about it all, Jorgey. Graham's missing. Do you think he's behind the destruction of the lab?" She rose to her feet, but faltered. Jorge placed his arm around her waist and helped her to the bathroom. "Maybe he cracked under all the pressure of being first to market. Maybe he couldn't stand to see people dying while the drug companies drive up demand. He always said he hated that."

"It bothers me, too." Jorge looked at her, said, "Everything will become clear. The virus's spread. The lab's gone. Now it's left to natural selection to see what it will do. It's in the hospitals. The schools. On public buses. Can't walk around in hazmat suits forever before normalization of variance sets in. You know what that is in math'matics."

"Of course I do," she said. "But do you mean normalization of deviance, Jorge?"

"Yep. That's what I mean. Brought down the space shuttle when I was a boy. Done a lot of research online about it, too. You can read my blog sometime."

"Okay." She sighed. "You mean when people become used to a deviant behavior, socially or a lab result, like us, they don't consider it deviant anymore. To people on the outside, the abnormality jumps out at them. But the people who grow used to the abnormality don't recognize the deviance."

"Yep, the government agency, NASA, botched the Challenger, and the CDC will botch this outbreak, too. That's exactly what I mean, Kayla." Jorge hugged her. "You know me so well."

"Okay." She looked around the room. He seemed flustered, anxious. "You alright yourself, Jorgey?"

"Course I am. And you understand me?"

"Sure."

"Then nothing LeTorneau has done will matter."

"Now what do you mean by that, Jorgey? I can't sit here and accept that all of our work—*years'* worth—was for nothing." Her voice rose, but she was too weak to mount much of an angry response. "No, I refuse to believe that."

"Our work wasn't for nothing. Far from nothing." Jorge smiled, confident and self-assured, and she relaxed. "I mean Labrador's going to affect who it's going to affect. We're all going to see what happens next."

She glanced into the mirror. She looked fragile, her complexion a withering lily-white from dehydration. But she looked up, challenging his comment. She felt a flash of fear, of broken trust. He smiled warmly, revealing his poor dentition, and she brushed off her concern. "I think I'm going to be sick again. Excuse me, Jorgey."

"Of course, my dear. Will you be alright in there?" Jorge asked. She nodded and he closed the bathroom door and stood outside. "I'll be right here if you need me."

She stood over the toilet, weakened, and wretched, a toxic heave from the pit of her stomach. Then she faced herself in the mirror and she picked up the glass of water near the sink and she drank some water. She took another sip and it stayed down and she picked up her cell phone and she texted Veronica: *'Are you coming over?'*

Veronica texted back right away: *'I'm omw.'*

She didn't throw up anymore, but she felt light-headed, and she splashed some water on her face and she took her temperature: 102.5. She tried to brush her teeth and she gagged on the toothbrush, but nothing came up. More dry heaves over the toilet. Then she washed her hands and dried them on the yellow towel with little daises and walked back to the bedroom. It still smelled of flowers and pear-scented body lotion. Jorge looked very comfortable sitting at the foot of the bed.

"I don't think you have *Labrador*, Kayla," Jorge said.

"Why not? I have all the symptoms."

"Just don't think so. Impossible."

"And aren't you afraid of catching it from me?"

"Nope."

"Why not?"

"Just not." Jorge was stoic now, deep in thought, and his gaze was distant, somewhere other than their conversation.

Jorge walked to the window and drew back the curtain, looking out onto the street. She craned her neck to see what he was staring at. Parking meters and a delivery truck backing up, beeping, tail lights blinking. And Veronica trying to parallel park her compact car in an awkward back and forth series of maneuvers.

Jorge picked off one of her geraniums and hurried back over to the bedside with a smile. "I want to make sure you're alright, Kayla. I'd die if anything happened to you." He gave her the flower.

"Jorgey," she said.

Jorge scooped her up off the bed, still in her pajamas. She didn't protest. He walked over to the big open window and carried her out onto the fire escape.

"What in the world are you doing, Jorgey?"

Jorge brushed her blonde hair out of her eyes again and kissed her forehead and looked at her with an unbroken stare. "Rescuing you. Come on."

With her still in his arms, he started down the fire escape. Below, Veronica got out of the car and, without looking up, headed straight for the front door of the brownstone.

"So help me Jesus," Jorge said, "I'm going to make sure that nothing happens to you."

The door slammed downstairs, echoed toward the apartment. Jorge raced faster down the fire escape stairs now. She looked back, and she thought she'd seen Veronica. It was only morning, but the temperature was already scorching. She was weak. Near delusional, she thought. Maybe she was just imagining that Veronica was there. She conceded as Jorge carried her.

"But, Veronica—she's on her way."

"Kayla, that woman—downstairs. The one who lives below you. Mrs.—?"

"Quartermain?"

"Yes, that's the one. She was asking questions about you. Had an officer here when I came in."

"She did?" She was confused, but Jorge would never lie to her. Still, it didn't sound like Mrs. Quartermain at all.

"Best not to trust her. Or anybody, for that matter. But me. You can always trust me, Kayla."

She was confused, but at the same time, comforted by his dark eyes. She searched his face. There was no way she could doubt him as he cradled her tenderly, like a baby, all the way down the fire escape stairs, to the bottom platform, toward the street. He placed her on the ground and hopped down himself and helped her into the front seat of his truck where his marmalade cat, Felicity, hopped onto her lap.

"Hi there, girl." She scratched the animal's ears and it purred and Jorge closed the door.

He started the Ford, said, "We'll call Veronica straight away. Pick her up. But we've got to go. Get you safe to a doctor."

"Okay, Jorgey." She rested her head on the window. The air conditioning was broken but the breeze blew her hair back, away from her feverish face, and with the cat settled on her lap, she closed her eyes.

They'd driven at least an hour outside of D.C. when her cell phone rang. The busy interchanges became rare and the traffic, once saturated with cars and semis, dropped off as they headed west onto 66. No roadblocks or police. She searched her pajama pocket for the device and she answered it. Jorge turned down the radio broadcast.

"Reeves, where are you?" It was Veronica. "I checked your place twice this morning. Where'd you go? Are you feeling better?"

"No." She rubbed her temple and she squinted her eyes and she looked around, putting the events together in her head. She stared out the window and then at Jorge, driving the black pickup truck into the country. The green and white road signs indicated they were somewhere between Fredericksburg and Alexandria, Virginia.

"Listen to me, Kayla." Her tone was anticipatory, urgent. Heavy breathing and rushed speech, higher pitched than usual.

"Who is it, Kayla?" Jorge asked.

She lowered the phone from her ear. "Veronica." The cat pushed its head under her hand.

"Can I talk to her?" Jorge held out his hand. Huge violating fingers demanding the device now. Swollen knuckles threatening her personal space. His eyes remained focused on the road.

She glanced at him and then in the passenger side mirror. Her eyes were injected and spidery red, watering, if not from her illness then from an allergy to Felicity. She sneezed and Jorge brushed the cat from her lap. The creature hissed and it hopped up again, its orange and yellow hairs bristling.

"The phone, please," said Jorge.

The cat hissed.

"Hello?" Veronica's voice was loud in the cab of the truck. "Damnit, Kayla. Talk to me."

She raised the phone to her ear.

"Sorry," she said, weakly.

"Kayla, listen to me. I listened to the message from Hans this morning. It was a cry for help before he died. It's not LeTorneau behind *Labrador*. Jorge blew up the lab. He killed Hans and maybe Graham, too. We have to go to the police."

"I'm with Jorge, Veronica." Her hand shook, tremulous and pale, veins blue-black and flat against her skin and absent of all their turgor. She shot a glance at Jorge, and he snatched the phone.

Chewing his gum, he spoke in a soft voice now, matter-of-factly, said, "Laughlin, you must be worried about Kayla."

"Why did you do this, Bourdain?" Veronica demanded.

"She's doing much better. I was worried about her, too. I'm going to get her medical attention and make sure that she's alright."

"Goddamn it, Jorge. What the hell are you doing? Why, Jorge? *Labrador* is the deadliest virus in human history. It has the potential to kill entire populations. We're on the verge of a global pandemic."

"And that's the very solution to our bigger problem, Ms. Laughlin. You fear the infection, but the truth is quite the opposite. *Labrador* will disinfect the public masses." Jorge chewed his gum some more and signaled and moved into the left lane. "And why I'm quite certain Kayla will be perfectly fine. I'll see to it myself. I'd never let anything happen to her."

"What problem? Jorge—everything we've worked for," Veronica screamed into the phone.

Kayla was leaf-like. Shaking. Her pulse bounded from her temples. She looked to Jorge. How could he betray her? Veronica had to be mixed up. Jorge continued talking to Veronica as if he were explaining things to her back in the lab, unalarmed, nonchalant—everything with a scientific reason. She felt weaker, too weak to argue, and his soft voice began to soothe her back to sleep.

She slumped toward the window.

"Shall we pick you up?"

"Where are you? I'm on my way to your place, Jorge."

"Okay, I promise I'll take care of Kayla. Natural Selection is a powerful force. You'll see. It will become evident."

"You're speaking in riddles, Jorge."

"We have to go now. It's sure been nice talking with you."

"Don't you hang up on me, Bourdain. I'll go to the police."

"Good bye, Veronica." Jorge disconnected the cell phone and tucked it in his canvas vest and continued driving into the country, off the highway now. In his often confusing Cajun Franglish grammar, he said to Kayla, "Veronica at the doctor's will catch up later with us."

But she was already unconscious.

Washington, D.C.
Sara Sullivan

Punishing hail pelted Marty's truck with the wind pushing northeast. Sara slowed the vehicle past the address she'd scribbled almost illegibly: 101 Legion Drive. The sky had opened up leaden and low with sudden urgency and poured heavy gray drops of rain now. She put the Ford in park between two compacts as she waited for the worst of it to pass. A golf ball sized piece of ice shattered a conical chunk of the passenger side windshield, as if someone had thrown it directly at the pickup.

"Shit." Marty loved his truck. The windshield wipers cleared the rain as quickly as it fell, but it was impossible to see anything beyond the swirling downpour and the metronomic swipes of the blades, presto tempo.

The block was nothing extraordinary: a tattoo parlor and a coffee shop with dirty windows, a sign that read: FRESH BEIGNETS, in chipped green and white paint. The flat-roofed brick building in the center of the low-rent block was not the stomping grounds she'd anticipated for a leader of pharmaceutical research or a pillar of academia like Dr. Graham LeTorneau.

She dug out the binoculars from Marty's camping supplies and stared up toward the building through them, but it was useless trying to see through the front windshield. Sheets of rain obscured her vision.

A sudden rap on the driver's side window took her breath.

She gripped her chest, dropped the binoculars, turned to the left: pale red bearded face up against the glass. The man was covered in a dingy white sweatshirt and pants. Drenching rain dripped from his hood, onto his facial hair, a continuous trickle running off the beard and another running down the side of his cheek and right into his mouth. The man spat and pulled the hood down, revealing the skin on his bald head. She cracked the window enough to hear him speak.

"Y'alright?" Southern accent thick as molasses.

She sighed and lowered the window a little more. The storm had brought through a cold front. The chill bit her now, the draft rushed in.

"I'm just waiting for the rain to pass."

"Don't want to wait here." The man coughed and kept his head close to the glass and pulled his hands into the wrists of his hooded sweatshirt. Was he reaching for some sort of weapon? "Block's been abandoned. Infection's took two girls. Spreadin' like it is, most everybody's left. Don't wait here."

"*Labrador* virus?" The block did look deserted. No one outside but the man.

"Yep. Guess that's the one. What do you say they call it?"

"*Labrador*. Thank you for your concern. I'll be careful."

The man lingered at the window awhile longer, peering into the truck as the window went up. Then he stepped away from her, staring, a forlorn scarecrow. But what was he trying to scare her away from? Sara shuddered, and she looked away and back again to the spot which finally, he'd left.

The rain subsided to a drizzly mist. She got out of the truck and entered the coffee shop. It smelled of shrimp gumbo and slightly burned bananas foster and chicory coffee. In the front there were three empty tables covered in white linens. Toward the back, a red velvet curtain concealed another room. Voices carried from the hidden area, but she couldn't make them out. Crisscrossing ivy decorated the checkout station where she marveled at an antique National cash register, a beautiful relic with old-timey transaction keys and ornate designs carved into its brass-plated chassis. She ran her finger along the whorls of brass, mesmerized by the seductive décor of the room.

She crept further into the restaurant.

An overweight woman in a patchwork apron tore open the red curtain, materializing out of the unseen back room. It looked like the doll was in her fifties, plucked right out of the Cabbage Patch. Chubby red cheeks, auburn hair, curled like it had been set in rollers all morning.

"Help you?" The woman was impatient, brushing flour off her hands, onto the apron. "Well I suppose I'll sit down and eat."

"Suppose you won't. We're full."

"But there's no one here." She tried to peer around the stocky woman's girth to the back room.

"That's the way we like it." The woman reached behind her kerchief as she held a bobby pin between her teeth. The she pinned her hair and the corners of her eyes narrowed. Judgmental slits with pinpoint pupils, sizing her up.

What was going on in the room behind the curtain? She wanted to know more. She noticed the embroidered nametag on the woman's stained blouse: Ruby.

"Ruby, is it?" she asked. "I always liked that name. Ruby, your kitchen sure smells good. I'm fixin' to eat. Smelled your fine cooking clear up the street."

Ruby looked like she was trying to decide if she was being mocked. "Well bless your heart. Can't help you though. Private party back there now. Then we're closing up for the afternoon. Parties here are by reservation only."

"I see." Reservations? In a coffee shop? She ran her finger along the ornate register again and popped a butter mint from the stand in her mouth.

The front door opened.

A couple entered.

The screen door slammed shut.

"Y'all are lettin' the flies in," Ruby called to them. The woman apologized. Then Ruby motioned for them to have a seat on the wooden bench beside the door, said, "Be with you folks in a minute."

She felt something more behind the woman's rebuff, or maybe it was just her own experience with prejudice lately. Maybe she was imagining that her color had something to do with it. After all, this was the twenty-first century. How could anyone be so narrow-minded? But she'd witnessed it. Even succumbed to behaving against her better judgment. She opened and closed her right hand a few times. The swelling had subsided, but it ached from having punched the woman near the bus stop.

"And who do I have to be to get a reservation?" Her tone was biting now.

"You ought to be getting on now," Ruby said. "I don't have a table for *you*."

The couple approached the hostess podium. Sara turned to leave, and then she stopped. "Ruby, do you happen to know who lives in the flat next door—101 Legion Drive?"

"I know everybody round here. We're a pretty close knit neighborhood. What do you want to know?"

"Is the owner or tenant involved in research? On the *Labrador* epidemic that's been in the news?"

"I don't know nothin' 'bout *ree*-search, but that's Jorge Bourdain's place."

"Not Dr. Graham LeTorneau?"

"That the one on TV gone missing?"

"Yes, ma'am. That's him. Tall, African-American gentleman. Glasses."

Ruby chuckled, and her laughter set off a productive cough. When the coughing spell subsided, she said, "Don't think he'd want to live on this block. Pretty old-fashioned folk here. It's still the South y'know." Ruby shrugged, jerked her melon head toward the small Confederate flag beside the cash register, winked at her and shook out her apron. "Ever'body got a right to their own ways, you know."

Was she the only one in the District not from the *Twilight Zone*? The only one not sniffing glue? The whole city had gone completely. Fucking. Crazy.

"What does Mr. Bourdain do?"

"How the hell should I know? Didn't say I go about knowin' everybody's business." Ruby suddenly grew cross, frowned, and the dimples disappeared from her chubby face.

"Ruby," a man's voice called, from the back. "The meeting's called to order."

"Meeting?" Sara asked.

Ruby drew open the curtain slightly. "Go ahead," she called, to the white couple. To Sara, she said, "Get along now. And you have a fine day, Miss—"

"Sullivan," said Sara. "*Dr.* Sara Sullivan. You do the same."

"Well lad-di da, a nigra doctor. Now get out of my shop and don't come back." Ruby waved the bottom of her apron at her for emphasis, as if she were shooing away a child.

"Don't worry, I won't. You know Ruby, I'm not from the country myself, but I sure know B.S. when I smell it. And your kitchen stinks to high heaven with it."

The wooden door slammed against its frame as she walked out onto the sidewalk. It was much cooler now, almost cold, and she shivered in her wet clothes and walked around the side of the building, between the restaurant and Jorge Bourdain's apartment at 101 Legion Drive.

The experience in the coffee shop had shaken her. She'd had no doubt Dixie was still alive in the hearts of many Southerners before the epidemic, but she'd always seen it more—from her perspective anyway—as a taut grip on a fading cultural spirit for the region itself. A resistance to change. A rather pathetic and stubborn adherence to a dying kinship of ideas that however antiquated, were once held steadfast by elders. It was of course, proper to show respect for one's elders. These traditional mores allowed old-timers to cling to so-called Southern pride, a notion like a bucolic Camelot that was no more real than the legendary kingdom. Good food, music and dance, a slow way of talking: these benign elements were harmless taken alone, even part of her mother's upbringing. But she abhorred the way folks could turn a blind eye to the years of slavery and racial discrimination that went on in parallel—now both overtly and covertly.

She cracked her neck, releasing the tension that had built up in her spine.

Maybe the epidemic had brought out deeper feelings that were present all along—a more pervasive and toxic disdain, proclaiming itself in the worst way, to the point where racist thoughts that normally went unsaid, or were conveyed in a disarmingly honeyed tone, now spewed out like snake's venom with intent to wound. Was it *Labrador* bringing out a dormant monster in everyone, or was there an inherent loathing ingrained in mankind? She'd always thought of herself as a realistic optimist, not an ideologue—medicine had ripped that right out of her—but in her eyes, most people were basically good.

Maybe she was too naïve to believe all the rote resuscitations of grade school. She repeated them now in her mind. *Everyone is treated equally under the law. The Thirteenth Amendment ended slavery. Blacks have the same rights as whites because the law says so.*

Maybe her mother was right. Maybe she was just looking at everyone with rose-colored glasses.

No, she told herself. She could not accept her mother's cynicism—not as long as she was alive and she had Elyse. She'd bring her up the way things should be, whether they were that way or not.

-20-

Louisiana, 1979

The boy peered with the flashlight at the mess of tools and junk in the back of the truck, until he found the least-bald spare tire and the rusty old jack. He laid out the tarp over the mud and he placed the jack under the truck near the right front tire. Out on the lake, the rain whipped horizontally at his face. The apple-red 1948 Chevy truck with bulbous fenders and the shifter on the steering column that was always sticking had blown a tire. They were about a mile southwest of the interstate. The water washed his mouth of the burned chicken drumsticks they'd eaten, and it ran off him in little streamlets where the peach fuzz had started to grow on his face.

His father stood on a wooden raft, left by somebody along the riverbank, or washed up from somewhere across the lake. He poked with a long stick of Cyprus he'd found drifting near the mangroves, called for the boy's cat, Betsy, that had run out of the truck and down to the bank of the Tchefuncte River where it emptied into Lake Pontchartrain. The animal was certainly gone now, and a medium-sized gator had crawled up onto the bank. The man had chased it away with his stick and taken refuge on the raft. But now the man stood floating, poking at the leathery snout when it surfaced through the green carpet of moss on the water, tempting the animal and tempting fate, as the creature's blazing red eyes lurked just above the waterline. His own eyes were petulant, enraged with moonshine, and the anger that always accompanied his drinking. The man provoked the reptile and pretended to make a half-assed effort to search for his son's pet while the boy worked on the tire. He swashed along the marshy bank, looking disorganized in thought and appearance, losing his balance several times and nearly falling off the raft.

His decline had been a slow one. Even for an old father, it had taken a good ten years before he'd lost his ability to focus on the everyday running of their shack and houseboat on the lake. He became enraged like a hive of hornets in a honeypot when he drank, and his paranoia and accusations and physical violence had finally been too much for the boy's young mother to take. One day, she'd run off and told the boy to take care of the old man and their truck and their things in the small shanty.

The boy had taught himself the entire inner workings of the truck by taking it apart and putting it back together again, because there didn't seem to be any other way to learn about such things. And every time he took the old man into Abita Springs where they traded moonshine to the Choctaws living all along the outskirts of the land, or anywhere they could settle without being run out of town, he grabbed books and magazines from the library, or anything he could find to read about—history books about anywhere other than the bayou surrounding Lake Pontchartrain. The boy gravitated toward science, and he asked his father so many questions that the old man had become obsessed with the notion that he had taken to voodoo. The old man had burned all of his books and kept him home from school for nearly a month before the child welfare protection agency had looked into it.

"Pa you'll fall. Come on offa that raft now," the boy called. He loosened the lug nuts and lifted the truck with the jack and squatted down on the muddy tarp. "Storm's comin'. Come on now. Don't mess with them gators."

"Aw, he's just a baby. You done fixin' the tire?" A sudden squall pushed the little raft toward the shore and the old man hopped clumsily off. The sky flashed purple and white and the rain poured harder now, and he tottered sideways and looked forlornly at the truck. "We're goin' to have a hard time getting back'n forth t'Abita Springs once she quits on us."

"Where's Betsy at?" The boy shined the light at his father.

The old man's eyes squinted and he stroked his white beard and kicked the flat in the mud and cussed a colorful gumbo of French and English words. He was shrunken in his old age and looked diminutive next to his son, though the boy was only fourteen.

"You worry'n bout that damn cat when she's gone clear outta this bayou. Cain't outrun it." He stepped sideways in the brackish water and soaked his leather shoe up to his ankle and he cussed a blue streak. Something snapped, and he turned and jumped and slapped the back of his neck. Mosquitoes the size of birds. He looked right and left and then watched as a water snake slithered away. A flash of lightning illuminated him for an instant, still clutching the gnarled Cyprus stick like some Biblical wanderer.

The wind bent the cattails double, blew sedge grass and moss at his face.

The storm intensified.

Spanish moss draped from the trees where they grew right up out of the water. It made a green blanket on the lake where it fell beside them on the electric water. The cat was nowhere in sight.

The boy craned his head around at the old man, asked, "Which way'd she run off to?"

"Not worry'n about a stray when we're barely eatin' ourselves. She's gone, Jorge. Run off." He looked wary of the alligator. The mangrove trees beat against one another, made it even harder for the old man to hear, so he was shouting now. "Wonder if b'fore long girls is something you'll like 'stead of chasin' animals. Then I can take you somewhere'n learn you about 'em. You like cats? You'd love a cathouse, I guar-won-tee." He chuckled, opened the door to the truck and removed a jar of moonshine. He took a swig and stumbled over the boy as he removed the flat tire and chucked it aside.

"Got one's sweet on me now, Pa."

"Don't believe it."

"I ain't lyin'. When I was takin' into foster care she was livin' in N'awlins in a foster home there herself. Went to school and she's real smart at science and better at readin' than I am. Now she lives with the Jackson's down a ways."

The old man slammed the door and stopped now and drank the rest of the moonshine from the mason jar. He spat on the ground. "Jacksons?"

The boy hoisted the spare onto the rim and then took the tire iron and began to tighten the lug nuts. His face brightened and he looked as though he'd forgot all about the cat. "We held hands and she told me she likes me and someday maybe she wants to be married. Didn't say with me but I know she means it with me."

"You talkin' about a nigga?"

"She's only half, Pa. Sweet and smart from school from the folks that take care of her all over. Said she's learned a lot bein' all over."

Now the old man grew red and hot-faced and the gobbled crepe under his neck swayed in the wind.

His jaw muscles clenched.

He threw the mason jar against the truck, shattered it.

The boy drew back in fear, but kept his focus on the tire and his arm beneath the wheel to steady it. Then his father kicked the jack and the truck lurched and the tire fell abruptly on his hand. The boy screamed and with his back turned to his father, he tried to pry it loose, but even with the wheel in the soft mud, he couldn't release it, and he cried out. The man unbuckled his leather belt and flung it off and folded it and beat him across the torso, the back.

When the boy began to sob, begging him to stop with his hand still pinned beneath the wheel, he kicked at him, whipped him harder with all the strength he could muster, and he shouted, "I'm never goin' to hear of you takin' up with a nigga, you hear me?"

The boy screamed, "Yes. Yes, Papa." He was still trying to free his hand as the belt made sharp licks against his wet skin.

"No such thing as half a nigga." When the old man tired, he stopped and jacked up the car an inch or so and pulled the boy by his shirt and threw him aside.

He was still crying loudly with his hands covering his face and his legs pulled up close to his chest. His father turned and walked out and looked at the lake. The boy sat and cried awhile as fierce strikes of lightning zigzagged around them. He shuddered with each crack until he sat up with his arms around his knees. He watched his father stumble further into the water where the gator lurked.

"Pa, we've got to get on," he called.

The storm was blowing the trees hard.

The water whipped against his face.

"Go on," said the old man.

"Pa. Come outta that water."

"Go on," he repeated. "Get on without me."

"Pa."

The boy cried, started up from the ground to run to him, but stopped. The man did not turn around, but stood, staring, unwavering, at the lake, where the lightning flickered across the sky so bright and silvery and so often that they could see out onto the bayou as clear as day. The boy waited another minute behind the man, but he didn't turn around, and the boy slowly walked toward the truck and drove it away, as he'd learned to do some time ago.

-21-

Veronica Laughlin

Veronica's hands trembled as she replayed Hans' message a fifth time. She paused the voicemail playback right before the sound of the exploding lab, slammed the phone down on the console—it always ended in the same horrific way. She reiterated the name Hans had given before he died: *Dr. Sara Sullivan*. There was no one by that name that worked in the lab. She searched the employee database from her cell phone for a third time as she sat in traffic.

Nothing.

She was on her way to Jorge's apartment. Something told her he'd never hurt Kayla, and that that part of his promise was true, and to go to the police first instead—but she couldn't be sure. Kayla needed immediate medical attention. Jorge came close to being a mathematical genius, but he was no doctor.

The driver in the car behind her was leaning on his horn.

She turned, and looked out the back window, gave the driver the finger. "Hey, fuck you!" she shouted. Jorge always criticized her potty mouth, ironically. She plopped down on the driver's seat, started moving.

At the next light, she did a web search on the name Dr. Sara Sullivan. It turned up thousands of results—one entry for a doctor who worked at George Washington University Hospital. Dr. Sullivan was a board certified emergency medicine physician. There was no connection to their research, but there was a newspaper clipping whose headline read: FEMALE PHYSICIAN ESCAPES *LABRADOR* QUARANTINE. Suspected in Bethesda explosion. Wanted by authorities. It gave a picture of the woman: tall, athletic build, African-American, with light brown skin and eyes.

Jackpot.

But why was she at the lab? She thought. Was she infected and searching it for the cure? Tied to Graham romantically somehow? Involved with Jorge? The possibilities were endless. Distracted, she veered into the left lane and then back onto the correct side. Cars honked from all directions.

She gripped the wheel of the Subaru, dialed the cell phone.

There was no answer at Sullivan's office number listed online, but she'd left a cell phone number in case of emergency.

How nice. She gives her patients her cell phone number before she blows them up. She was frantic, searching for a parking spot in Jorge's neighborhood now, the old street that looked like a step back in time. The street was reminiscent of the French Quarter of old New Orleans. Nostalgic restaurants and cafes posting their menus in both English and French. A poorly kept cemetery. Huge tombs and concrete angels projecting above the ground, referred to as 'cities of the dead.' The block had an eerie feel today. She swallowed and she parked her Subaru and she dialed the number.

Another voicemail.

She left her own name and number on the message. Then she wished she hadn't. Finally, she tried the main number of the hospital. Maybe someone—anyone—had more information about this woman. She had nothing.

"Hello?" said the operator.

"Can you tell me where I might find Dr. Sara Sullivan, please?"

"I'm sorry. Her privileges at the university are temporarily inactive," said the elderly voice. "I'm afraid that's all the information I'm allowed to give out, but if you have information about the doctor, I've been instructed to take a detailed message."

"No, thank you."

She parked the car where a man stood on the corner, smoking and drinking a steaming beverage. The man nodded at her and she ran around through the gate to the back of Jorge's apartment and up the stairs to the back porch, where he always left his door unlocked. She gasped as she stepped over the threshold.

The inside of his apartment had been ransacked.

Sara Sullivan

Sara watched a spiky-haired girl race past her, between the restaurant and Bourdain's upper apartment at 101 Legion Drive. The girl's black hair disappeared down the narrow stone path between the buildings.

Was she an employee?

Girlfriend?

She looked as though she knew exactly where she was going. There was no answer at the front door, and it was dead bolted.

She clutched Marty's Glock pistol, followed after the young woman.

An open window to the restaurant made her mouth water. The smells brought back memories, as if her mother had cooked the meal herself. Yet coming from there, she'd sooner eat sewage. Big Ruby was out of sight.

She kept her body against the chipped paint of the white wooden exterior, moved closer to the window.

There were other smells, too—she couldn't identify all of them, but the smell of the food mingled with fragrances of vanilla and cardamom and amber that smelled like church at Christmastime. She could no longer see the girl, but the back of both yards were fenced. She had to be back there. A sheer drape blew from the window, covering it only partially.

She leaned closer to the restaurant window.

It was dark inside, except for the dim illumination from a circle of votive candles. Ornamented chairs surrounded a round table, covered in white linen, with thirteen elegant place settings. Curlicues of smoke rose from incense sticks positioned around the perimeter of the room. She tugged the curtain back, peered in, but pulled it back suddenly when a loud noise startled her. She tilted her head in, and saw that the old woman had only dropped an empty pot. Had Ruby seen her?

She waited, breathing hard.

When she inclined her neck inward a moment later, she immediately yanked it back, and swallowed hard, pressing her back to the building, hyperventilating. Across from her she faced Jorge Bourdain's place, nearly an arm's length away. She gripped her chest. It felt like the walls of the two buildings in the alley were closing in on her as she gasped for breath.

The customers had assembled in a circle around the shrine of candles, in robes of white, tied at the waist with white rope, and hoods that came to a point. At once, her heart raced with images of the Ku Klux Klan lynching, and burning blacks on crosses. Was the group connected to Jorge Bourdain?

"Who the hell are you?" asked a boy.

He looked about seventeen, with curly brown hair down to his shoulders, a Washington Nationals baseball cap. He dried his hands on his dirty apron as she pulled the pistol.

"Don't make another sound," she said, eyeing him with the gun held with both hands and her arms fully extended, the way Marty had taught her. "Stay right there."

He put his hands up and shook his curly head and Sara backed down with the weapon. "I'm not one of them. I'm just a dishwasher. But if I was you, I'd run, ma'am."

She lowered the Glock a few inches, maintained her grip. "What the hell is going on in there?"

"I could get killed for talking with you. Please." He held his hands, palms open, at his sides, took a tentative step forward.

She aimed the weapon again.

"Don't think a girl like me doesn't know how to shoot. Now you tell me what that's all about."

The youth stepped back. "It's what it looks like, ma'am. Group operates under the name Louisiana Conservation Society—s'posed to be conserving the environment, animals and such. But they want to preserve white society ma'am, like the Klan. That old woman in there—she's my grandmother. Please don't hurt nobody. She's all I got left. I don't agree with none of it—just help out and wash dishes and live upstairs with her. I'm going to college in the fall. Sometimes I help her with the cooking, but I don't know nothin' more than that. I swear it."

"Why should I believe you?"

"'Cause I'm talkin' sense to you. Those men ain't foolin' around. They'll kill you first and ask questions later. You're not safe here. Trust me. Mostly they're just protecting their business, making sure the money stays where they want it— like the Mafia I s'pose—but once I saw a man shot and put in the cemetery down the street."

His eyes were honest and she lowered the pistol and she placed it on her hip. Her breathing slowed.

"What about the guy next door? Bourdain?"

"Yeah, he's one of them. He's real smart. Helped me with math in school. Haven't seen him in a week or so, though."

"Go ahead then. Get out of here. You never saw me, do you understand me?" She looked at his eyes directly, waved him off.

She had to move fast.

He was just a kid, but he might disclose her presence. Her distrust of everyone—Caucasians, law enforcement, her own family at times—was making her more cynical every day, and she detested it. She wrestled with the image of her reflection in the dusty window glass now. The boy reached his car on the street, and she backed down the alley. Would he go to the neo-Confederate society? She could still phone the police with

Marty's cell if she had to, but then again, she could be dead faster than they could arrive.

Thinking of Elyse, she ignored her instinct and climbed the stairs to the second story wooden porch. The wood was still wet from the storm, garbage was piled around the trash cans. Rats picked at the bags, and they didn't scatter as she approached. Her sneakers squeaked as she crept up to the apartment.

The back door was wide open.

Where had the spiky-haired girl gone?

She had to be one of them.

She stepped over the doorframe and into the empty kitchen, a filthy outdated room that might have been charming if it had been well kept and not rot with the smell of spoiled meat. Around her, a teal and white mosaic floor. Wooden cabinets with glass doors and star shaped silver knobs. A white 1950s Kelvinator refrigerator, left wide open.

She gagged, covered her mouth.

Flies swarmed the room.

She stepped into a cozy nook off the kitchen.

Two half-gutted, white-tailed deer hung from a nylon cord affixed to an exposed beam in the ceiling. The room was replete with threadbare furniture and a blood-spattered wood-burning stove. Whoever had been there had left amidst dressing two freshly killed doe. She'd seen Marty gut deer in the field, even tried hunting with him, but who would carry out the gruesome task like this in the middle of their own home? The animals were strung across the living space. The heads of two bucks were mounted on the walls, souvenirs from earlier kills. Whoever resided there was an expert in dressing the animals, enjoyed the task as much as the hunt.

She clutched the pistol now with both hands, holding it close to her chest, and tiptoed with her back to the wall. It felt heavier, and her hands trembled as she examined the tenant's keeping room more closely. A sharp serrated knife and nylon cord and a plastic bag with one deer's liver and heart was in plain view on a wooden table. The animals had been sliced from the breastbone to the base of the tail, around the anus to separate the viscera from the carcasses. The cuts extended upward toward the neck where the creatures' windpipes had been cut.

Heart, liver, lungs, removed.

Flies scattered from the hanging animals, a faint buzz.

Maggots were spread around the incisions.

The flies hummed, settled around the room and came back to the carcasses, resting on their own larvae. She felt a lump in her throat ball up and rise. She breathed through her mouth.

It was all she could do to keep from vomiting.

As she entered the living room, she heard a distant crackling, like a phone call with poor reception and punchy voices over white noise.

Was Bourdain there?

The place certainly looked empty. What about the dark-haired girl? Had she joined the others next door?

The air was moist, ripe with the smell of cat urine. Bright blood drops made a trail across the plush carpet to another tagged animal, a buck, hanging from a cord over the gated front door.

A huge Confederate flag draped the mantel.

She tore open the closet door with the pistol in hand: no one there, but hooded white robes hung in a neat row, pressed, clean. Black and white photos of Klan meetings were pasted on the door, boyhood photos from what looked like a riverboat on the Mississippi. A blonde woman wrapped her arms around a boy in one the photos. Another picture showed the same boy holding a fishing rod and a proud catch, a huge channel catfish. Newspaper clippings with ominous headlines announced: *Louisiana Conservation Society Suspected of Hate Crimes, Lynchings Still Plague the South, Resurgent KKK Investigated.* She vaguely recalled Marty mentioning an investigation into the so-called conservation group, but it was years ago.

Her hands cramped in a white-knuckle grip around Marty's Glock. Sweat beaded at the base of her neck.

She held her breath.

She expelled a heavy sigh as she discovered that the voices were resonating from a police scanner in the bottom corner of the closet, broadcasting intermittent commands and signals, sirens. They snapped, popped broken words like an antique Victrola. She glanced back at the pendulant animals strung across the room, and a shiver made her the hair on her arms stand on end.

The screen door in the kitchen slammed.

It was only the wind.

She was still alone.

She tried not to think about what else Bourdain used the cord for, tried not to imagine herself tied up and strangled with it, oxygen starved. She continued searching for some clue that would help save Elyse, anything to bring her closer to understanding why the vicious disease was attacking blacks, how to stop it—a formula for the cure, something to show for her reckless behavior.

As she approached the west wall, she gasped, sidestepping away from the kitchen with the pistol clutched close to her chest. A huge map of D.C. and Virginia covered a cork board with pin points making the shape of an inverted five-point star, or pentagram. Black permanent marker encircled the pins and connected the points of the star, a symbol of satanic worship and the occult.

Red pushpins marked where explosions had taken place: Arlington Cemetery where African-American senator Marseille had been laid to rest, the Omni, the Bethesda lab, and the Washburn Mansion where Graham LeTorneau had been scheduled to speak, before he went missing. All of these events had made national headlines, and yet there wasn't a clear connection to the *Labrador* epidemic.

Her eyes widened as she traced the points of the star to the last pin, The White House. She panted, trying to slow her breathing as her fingers went numb, but she could not.

This was far more than she'd expected, and how could she, one woman, prevent the collapse of national security, when so far, she couldn't even rescue her own daughter?

Was this heinous society she'd discovered tied to the epidemic? To Lindstrom? Or was she risking her own life and pulling farther away from her family, engrossed in her work as Elyse grew weaker?

She ran her finger along a stuffed opossum, eyeing her from atop the stone mantel. A cardinal and a raven looked down from the corner of the kitchen and she studied their false eyes. Inside the glassy reflection was a rogue flash of light. She stepped back, and the red in the eyes glowed, seemed to focus on her.

Cameras.

Someone out there could visualize her every move through the mounted wildlife, just like in the lab. Her heart rate accelerated. She was about to turn and run, when she saw the image of a woman, reflected in the shiny glass of the 'possum's eyes. Before she could move, she was hit across the back of the head with a forceful blow. The sound of metal smacking against her skull was deafening, her vision blurred, and she fell unconscious to the ground.

-22-

Sara Sullivan

When Sara awoke in Jorge Bourdain's apartment, her hands and wrists were bound with the nylon cord used for dragging the killed game. The cord made dragging the animals in the field easier, and several feet of it lay wound on the tattered sofa. The blood dripped down her face and onto the floor near the faux gas fireplace. She spit it away from the corners of her mouth. She recalled a vague image of a female before being hit on the head, and now as the haze lifted, the same young woman appeared before her with Marty's pistol pointed at her face.

"Where's Kayla?" the woman demanded, as Sara's eyes opened and closed.

"Kayla?" She spat the blood out of the side of her mouth, rolled to her side. The cords cut into her wrists.

The woman sat on a musty-smelling red velvet chaise, with her legs spread, and her elbows resting on her knees. The floor creaked. Sara's blood was splattered across the front of the woman's clothing. How long had she been unconscious?

"That's right. My partner from the lab. And Jorge. Where is he?"

Her head throbbed. She struggled to recreate the events, silently repeated the name *Jorge* to herself.

Lab.

Students.

How were they connected?

What did it have to do with the neo-Confederates?

The woman pulled her hair back, extending her neck.

"Where are they?" The woman held the pistol with her right hand and pressed it into her temple.

"I'm looking for Jorge Bourdain," she said.

Her captor was young, mid-twenties maybe, a tough little chick in a motorcycle jacket with silver jewelry and piercings in her nose and in her right eyebrow. Chewed fingernails painted black, raven hair short and gelled out in all funky directions. She'd seen her run down the alley. The woman held the pistol with her right hand and pressed it into her windpipe. A slow ooze of blood from her scalp had the veins in her temples pulsing. She stared at the gun.

"So am I," said the young woman. "Who are you?"

"Sara Sullivan." Her voice was hoarse.

The girl pressed the pistol against her throat harder, eyed her skeptically. "Hans warned me about you before he died. Where are Jorge and Kayla? I already know he has her, so don't bullshit me. Why were you in the lab?"

"I'm just a physician. I'm telling the truth. I promise. I'm looking for Jorge, or Dr. LeTorneau—and the cure for *Labrador*. My daughter may die from it. The cure…it's out there."

"Damn right it's out there. We developed it. Did you blow up the lab with Jorge?"

She could barely breathe with the gun pressing against her trachea. She inched further away from it with her body still contorted and restrained on the floor, and her blood still oozing from her scalp laceration, but the woman followed along, jabbing the barrel harder into her neck.

"No, I went there to find LeTorneau and the cure. But I found a bomb." She spat blood out again, mixed with the sweat from her temples. She didn't take her eyes off of the pistol. "Whoever put it there had access to the lab, and doesn't want the cure released."

"How do I know you're telling the truth?"

"In my back pocket—there's a picture of my daughter. Right now she's at George Washington University Hospital undergoing dialysis. She's on a ventilator." Sara choked on the words as much from their content as from the weapon compromising her airway.

The woman pulled the picture from Sara's back pocket and examined the wallet sized photo. She moved the gun from Sara's neck to her own side.

"You've never fired one of those before, have you?" Her throat throbbed and it hurt to talk. Maybe now wasn't the time to get smart with the spunky savant.

"How do you know? Have you?"

"My fiancé's a cop. I've done a lot of target practice. He made sure I knew how to handle a firearm."

"Is that supposed to scare me? Where's your fiancé now?" The woman's eyes narrowed.

"No, but if you could loosen this cord and get me out of here, I could show you how, before whoever lives here comes back and kills us both."

The woman looked over her shoulder and back at her. Then she knelt down beside her and patted her down, looking like she was considering things for a moment.

"Don't move a muscle." The woman transferred the pistol to her left hand and with her right, she cut the restraints around her wrists and ankles with one of Jorge Bourdain's skinning knives.

"Thank you." She expelled a heavy sigh.

"I'm Veronica Laughlin. One of the graduate students in Dr. LeTorneau's lab. Jorge and Kayla and I helped develop the antibody that cures *Labrador*, but the lab's been destroyed by Jorge. I don't understand why he did it."

She sat up, rubbing her wrists. "Me neither, but don't you find it ironic that LeTorneau and others were paid millions to develop a vaccine for a virus before anyone had ever heard of it? I wrote a novel about it that bears an uncanny resemblance to the crisis playing out on the news like a Hollywood movie. I think my story may have fallen into the wrong hands." She shook her wrists out.

"I thought you said you were a doctor."

"I'm a writer, too. Or I tried to be."

Veronica nodded and Sara stood up, stiff and wobbly in her lower joints. She stretched her neck. She ran her fingers along the satanic star Jorge had pinpointed on the map, held her hand out.

"May I, Veronica?" she asked. "Please?" Her voice was soft now. The young woman was her only lead.

Veronica placed the Glock in her palm and she demonstrated. "You have to hold it with a push-pull kind of force so it doesn't recoil against you. Otherwise you'll never hit your target." She pointed toward the push pin, placed on the White House. She watched Veronica's eyes follow her aim toward the map. Then she moved her fingers over Veronica's lips, and nodded toward the stuffed 'possum on the mantel. She placed the gun back in Veronica's hands, and whispered in her ear, "We're being watched."

The stuffed animal's glassy eyes looked diabolic, and the internal camera made a quiet ratcheting hum as it detected their movements, focused on the room. As she looked into the spying animal, Veronica's cell phone rang. Veronica pressed the speaker button.

"That's a pretty good grip Laughlin, but your stance is all wrong. Move your feet about shoulder width apart," said the voice on the other end of the call.

"Jorge," Veronica said.

The man laughed. "It's *Dr.* Bourdain now. LeTorneau signed off on my dissertation. I'll be heading the research at Phaedrex on *Labrador* when we find a new home for the lab."

"That will never happen, Jorge," Veronica said.

His laugh was vicious over the line.

Sara took the device gingerly and pointed to the mobile phone app, called Latitudes, which displayed the location of various contacts in Veronica's database. Most smart phones had it: it provided them with the precise geographic coordinates of Jorge Bourdain's location. The map indicated that he was in an area in the Blue Ridge Mountains near Charlottesville, Virginia, that she knew well. Marty hunted there frequently, but many of the roads were only dirt or gravel, with few homes or businesses between towns.

"He must've forgotten to turn the app off or to eliminate you as a contact, Veronica."

"He's a genius in some ways, but disorganized in so many others—like a high functioning schizophrenic. That's typical of Jorge."

Taking Veronica's hand, she said, "We have to go."

"Ladies, it's not polite to whisper," said Jorge Bourdain. "And I can't see you, my little raven, or your coon sidekick."

Veronica hesitated. She leveled the Glock at the stuffed raven and she stepped back into the field of view, aimed down her dominant eye, said, "Bourdain, this is for Hans." A storm of fur and sawdust filled the air. The 'possum flew off the mantel in Sara's direction.

She ducked.

"Impressive, my black-haired beauty."

"The next one will be between your eyes, Jorge. And I'll blow your brains out, across the capital and to Nevermore, if you do anything to hurt Kayla or LeTorneau, you sick fuck," said Veronica, and, handing the gun to Sara, she disconnected the call.

Edward Marburg

Marburg adjusted his collar as he listened to Randall Canin interviewing one of the survivors of the Washburn Mansion explosion on *60 Minutes*. The Society of Evolutionary Biology fellow predicted that there could be up to one thousand new cases per week if *Labrador* wasn't controlled expeditiously. The egghead further claimed that the CDC was completely mismanaging the crises, the government was failing to protect citizens, and most galling, that as head of the *Labrador* response, Marburg himself, had failed to initiate public health preparedness, availability of treatment, and any preventative measures to prevent a global pandemic. He figured the fellow was just another prick who hid behind the ivory towers of academia to cover up for his inadequate masculinity.

His small salary, his even smaller pecker.

He aimed the remote and he hit the mute button and he muttered, "Shut the fuck up."

He loosened his collar and let his German shepherds, Dwight and David, in the back door. They ran in from the rolling lawn, barking, but settled quickly. Behind them was Wes Lindstrom, wiping his sunglasses with a napkin and his feet on the back mat.

"Jesus. Don't you call anymore?"

"The press is all over your front gate. I prefer a rear entry myself."

"I'm not going to touch that," he said, shaking his head. He poured a glass of milk.

Lindstrom smiled. "How's Joanne?"

"Not good. Infection's set in. She's got around the clock nursing care. We're doing the best we can. Now this." He pointed the remote at the television mounted in the corner of the kitchen and he turned it on again and he threw down the stack of reports he'd printed from the CDC. "Have you seen the latest figures? There could be thirty thousand cases of *Labrador* by November. That would kill my shot as a presidential hopeful, Wes."

"I flew back from New York to handle this, Senator. I'll get Claus on the line now." Lindstrom held up his finger to tell him to hold on, but his calm smile only angered him.

"You said this would be a little *fire*, Wes. A few villagers in Africa. A couple random cases in the capital—enough to demand a vaccine and drive up the stock. Where's the vaccine, Wes? Where's the damn cure you promised and the quick payout?" He threw the stack of papers across the granite island and he grabbed his friend by the collar.

Lindstrom looked down through his shades, frowned, kept his composure.

"Ed," Marburg's wife called from their bedroom. "Is everything alright down there? The dogs have been barking all day, and there are reporters out by the front gates."

"Fine, Joanne. Everything's fine. Just rest. We'll handle it." He shook his head and he sighed and he listened to Lindstrom's responses with the call on speaker now.

"Good evening, Claus."

"How did you get this number?"

"The same way I'll get your address and track you down if you don't answer a few questions about the deal we have—I have *connections*." Lindstrom's voice was velvet and sardonic and savage. He frowned, remained calm.

"I lived up to my end of the deal. I even got my vaccine ready for fast track through FDA and information about the antidote—the antibody that cures *Labrador*. The vaccine is ready, but there are strains out there that are resistant to it—not the strains we worked on. I have no control over those."

"What do you mean?" Lindstrom asked.

"Something's changed. Did you contact the mole—Jorge Bourdain? I can't reach him."

"Well as you probably know, Claus, the lab's been annihilated to a pile of rubble and biohazardous debris. We can add Arlington and several other prominent landmarks to the trail of destruction. Would you like to elaborate on those?"

"Christ." Recart's gulp was audible. After a long pause, he added, "I can't reach LeTorneau either."

"Tell me about the mole you sent to LeTorneau's lab."

"His name is Jorge Bourdain. I sent him to spy on the work. He reported back to me."

"I'm not getting a good feeling about where this is going for you."

"There are new strains out there. It's almost as though someone's altered the virus itself. They're not the strains we studied in Uganda."

"How can you be sure?"

"I never released them."

"Excuse me?" Lindstrom asked, scratched his chin.

Marburg ran his fingers through his hair. They listened. The cowardly hesitation in Claus' voice. The French accent worming its way through the line from wherever he was, all the way to Virginia, like a rat-tailed apple maggot. The man's cocksure hubris made his skin crawl.

"I never released them in the capital. We had them ready to go and then I—I backed down. I couldn't do it. When I saw how quickly the filovirus wiped out the entire village in Uganda—I couldn't. The catastrophic potential was too great."

"That's a Third World country, Claus. This is the United States of America. Land of the Free." Lindstrom's arms went up, an exaggerated gesture. He wiped his sunglasses again. "We had a deal, Claus. If you never released it as you promised, then where did this goddamn epidemic come from?" His voice rose, apoplectic with anger. His stone expression moved only at the lips, thinned and determined, his eyes fixed with rage.

"I suspect Mr. Bourdain—the graduate student—the mole I sent to LeTorneau's lab. Or maybe someone brought it back from Uganda when we tested the control group—a safari group, perhaps. When Jorge contacted me and asked me to vaccinate a group of his associates against the original virus, I was suspicious, cut him off from the studies. I knew nothing of his colleagues—they sounded like radical extremists, not rational scientists like us. I contacted LeTorneau about his outside work—told him my concerns. I'm not sure what his intent was, but Bourdain grew unhinged. He kept odd hours and frequently became enraged."

"Where are you?" Lindstrom was composed again. "I was supposed to have the complete trial done by last week. This will be very disappointing to the senator."

Marburg was silent, processing his anger.

"The vaccine won't help at this point. The cases suggest it's mutating faster than a vaccine can keep up. Multiple strains. Like influenza—only virulent, deadly strains that pit black against white. Man against woman. You need the cure—antibodies created by LeTorneau—and he could be dead. If he's alive, I'm afraid he's your only hope."

"I was rather hoping to hear some more inspiring news, Claus."

Marburg's face reddened, and he grabbed the phone. "What did your mole turn up? I've got two contacts. One from LeTorneau's lab, a Veronica Laughlin. And another from NSA—Sara Sullivan—snooping around the lab, George Washington Hospital, and breaking a mandatory quarantine after exposure to the damn virus. What do you know about those two?"

"Good evening, Senator. I do hope your wife is recovering well," Claus said.

"Skip the bullshit, Claus, or I'll find you in whatever hole you're hiding in, and blow your brains out through your asshole. We're not playing rock-paper-scissors here. I want to know how to defeat this thing before it wipes out humanity."

"And your chances of reelection, Senator."

"Naturally," said Lindstrom. The phone was still on speaker. "You're familiar with politics. You got a little greedy and you thought you could cut another deal with us with the antibody by placing your mole in LeTorneau's lab. The vaccine and a few million was enough to get this deal done the last time we spoke. Suddenly, there are new strains popping up that you know nothing about. I don't buy it."

"I don't deny that. I got greedy. But you've got to find Jorge Bourdain. I suspect he has some other agenda, and his associates—let's just say these aren't educated, well-bred folks we're dealing with here."

Marburg said to Lindstrom, "You heard him. Get Bourdain. And put the other one—Veronica Laughlin, on the NSA list, too. There's enough evidence to bring her in, indict her for her involvement in the lab. She may have been directly involved with the explosion."

Lindstrom nodded. Before he disconnected the call, he said, "Don't stay in one place for too long, Claus. Because I'm coming for you next. And I'm going to kill you. That's a promise. If there are two things I don't like—besides diet soda and overweight red heads—it's being lied to, and losing money."

-23-

Virginia
Sara Sullivan

Sara drove Marty's truck out of the District and into Virginia. Veronica followed close behind her in her Subaru. They stopped for gas at a minimart at least fifty miles from D.C., where the cell phone service was patchy and the exits became farther apart. She had the coordinates of Jorge Bourdain's location entered into the truck's GPS.

She parked the truck in the dusty lot next to Veronica's car, went inside with Veronica to pay for the gas—she wasn't going to risk leaving an electronic trail by using her credit card. The front door of the store was propped wide open, the store smelled of tobacco and body odor, and it was empty, except for the attendant and a trucker obese and unshaven buying cigarettes and a push button cappuccino. Electric fan blowing, whirling humid air away from the register. The heat felt stagnant in spite, the kind of D.C. heat that made her drip sweat as soon as she stepped out into it. The woman behind the counter had brown hair frayed and tightly permed, missing teeth. Red pinnie over her black Van Halen T-shirt.

Overhead, the television displayed the news.

"A new suspect, Veronica Laughlin, was added to the list of potential involvements in the explosion of a Bethesda lab," the reporter, dressed in a sleeveless dress and showing bare, perfectly toned arms, was saying. An inset photo of Veronica appeared on the screen. The clerk looked up, kept a poker face as she punched the buttons on the register.

"Take another carton of Newports, ma'am," said the truck driver.

"Meanwhile, Dr. Sara Sullivan remains on the run after having broken quarantine." Her photo appeared.

The clerk glanced up again at the screen, then at Veronica.

Sara turned down the dried snacks aisle, peering over the tops of the potato chips and the dried beef jerky, looking up as her name and picture flashed across the snowy screen. Over the aisle, she saw Veronica waiting at the checkout, behind the trucker. Through the fingerprints on the front window, she saw Marty's truck at the pump where she'd left it running, a blue grey mist blowing from the tailpipe.

The trucker adjusted his belt buckle.

The clerk turned away from the register, held the telephone receiver to her ear.

Soon after, the clerk hung up.

"Thank you. Come back now," said the clerk.

The trucker took his change, left. Veronica set her keys down on the counter and pulled a bill from her back pocket.

"Where you headed?" asked the clerk.

"Me? Just out for a drive," Veronica said.

"Where to?" the clerk asked.

Veronica fidgeted with the earrings in her right ear, tapped her heel against the linoleum.

The woman played with the coins in the register, dropping them and retrieving them from the drawers.

Sara watched from the aisle.

"Hunting," Veronica blurted out. "My friend and I are going hunting."

"That your friend there back in aisle three?" The woman motioned toward her and looked up at the newscast again.

Outside, the truck driver opened the door of his eighteen-wheeler and stood and drank his Coke and smoked a cigarette. The trucker stared at her through the smudged window and made an obscene gesture toward his crotch and pretended to lick the glass. She looked away. She was focused on Veronica and the clerk.

"Dressed like that? Y'all don't look like you're going hunting." The woman dropped the coins in the drawers again and pulled them out along the sides of the plastic tray.

It was obvious she was wasting time.

"We are," Veronica insisted.

"That your Subaru on pump two?"

"Yeah that's me."

The clerk scanned the bar codes on Veronica's items: a pack of gum, a Diet Sprite, and a bag of Funyons, and she added her gas total. "That's ten on gas and $4.92 on snacks."

Veronica handed her a bill and helped the woman place her snacks into the plastic bag quickly.

"You're short. Need another five."

"I gave you a twenty."

"No, it was a ten, miss. See for yourself." The clerk held up a ten-dollar bill. "Got a credit card on you?"

Veronica reached for her card, handed it to the clerk. The woman ran her fingers over the raised silver letters slowly, as she looked down at the card, read the name, 'VERONICA LAUGHLIN.'

"You know, I'm certain it was a twenty," Veronica insisted. "Look, we're kind of in a hurry here. Give me my card back."

"I can replay it on the video camera if you don't believe me. It was a ten. I'm not a real smart lady, but I know what Andrew Jackson looks like."

She looked toward the upper corner of the store. Next to the old TV, the red light of a security camera flashed. Another screen hung from the ceiling near the back wall of coolers. The screen displayed the real time image at the register.

She looked opposite her toward the door again.

Two Albemarle County Sheriff's cars raced into the lot, blue lights flashing, sirens roaring, screeched to a halt, parked behind Marty's truck. Then they got out and slammed their doors and jogged towards the entrance.

She ran to the back of the store and barged through the 'EMPLOYEES ONLY' door. She raced through the break room, knocking over beverages, ran out the back of the store. She came around to the pump island and she slid into the front seat of Marty's truck and she slammed her door and she honked the horn. She called to Veronica.

"Thanks, but I've got to get going," said Veronica.

She watched as Veronica reached for her keys. The woman put her left hand over them first.

"Hold on, miss," said the clerk, as Veronica grabbed at her keys. The woman placed her other hand firmly over Veronica's. "Don't think you're the first fugitive to ever walk in here. This ain't my first rodeo."

"I'm not a fugitive," Veronica said.

The police officers approached the register. Outside, she honked again. Veronica started for the door, but the first officer held her back.

"Hold on there, little lady," the officer said. "We need to speak with you." He held Veronica by the shoulders.

The clerk retained Veronica's keys. The first deputy placed Veronica in handcuffs as the second recited her Miranda rights.

"She's the one on the TV, Russell."

"We'll take it from here, Lou Ann," the second officer said. "Thanks for the call."

She pulled the truck closer to the door now, hoping Veronica would be able to break free.

"Go," Veronica shouted out the open door, restrained by the officer. "Go!"

She punched the gas pedal.

Marty's truck squealed, sending a cloud of dust into the front of the store, peeled out of the lot, over a mat of mud and dried straw and onto the road. She'd driven halfway up a hillside when she heard the sound of sirens ahead of her in the distance. She veered off her route, made a sharp right turn onto a dirt road, crossing a shallow stream, and covering the side of Marty's truck in red Virginia mud.

-24-

Edward Marburg

Edward Marburg sat with Wes Lindstrom in the Albemarle County Sheriff's office. Veronica Laughlin sat behind bars in the jail cell, still in handcuffs.

"I'm sorry, Senator, but she cooperated with our investigation." The officer handed Marburg the stack of papers detailing their conversation. "Her answers coincide with everything the NSA turned up here, she has clean alibis for her stories, and there's not enough evidence to charge her."

"Thank you. Your job is done here," said Wes Lindstrom.

Outside, military tents housed quarantined victims suspected to be infected with *Labrador* virus. Some awaited arraignment for other crimes. Some had come into contact with sickened prisoners. Others were accused of breaking quarantines. Red Cross volunteers screened their temperature for fever, and kept watch on them for any other signs of illness. The CDC database continually updated names that appeared and were removed from their list throughout the day. Consideration for release from a camp required that a name be cleared from the list for at least eight hours earlier.

Dead bodies, crumpled in white bags, were taken from the tents every two hours.

Cremation was mandated by executive order.

"With all due respect, Mr. Lindstrom, neither one of you is qualified to deal with a potentially dangerous criminal." The officer unlocked the handcuffs from Veronica, and she spit in his face. After he wiped his eyes, he said, "As much as I'd love to keep this fireball here and teach her some manners, I have no just cause to retain her. She's free to go."

The sheriff unlocked the handcuffs.

Veronica tore her hands from the restraints.

To Marburg and Lindstrom, she said, "You heard him. Let me go."

"I think we can handle this young lady without too much trouble. Thank you, officer." Lindstrom smiled, handing the sheriff a one-hundred-dollar bill.

"I'm heading this investigation." Marburg scratched his chin. "I'm under executive order from the president to oversee the *Labrador* response. And I have a few more questions for Miss Laughlin. Mr. Lindstrom and I will see to it that she leaves here safely."

"Suit yourself, Senator." The officer rolled his eyes, left the room. He put the hundred in his pocket.

Veronica started for the door, but Lindstrom held the knob.

"You heard them—I'm free to go," Veronica protested. "I told you, I'm not the one you're looking for. Jorge Bourdain blew up the lab. He'll blow up the White House next and *Labrador* will wipe out the whole country if he isn't stopped."

He held Veronica back, as she fought like a Rottweiler on cocaine.

Lindstrom frowned, his arched brows rose. "You're just full of information, aren't you? Why would Mr. Bourdain want to do something like that?"

"I don't know. But I'm not about to sit here and watch it happen while you two try to figure it out. There's a cure out there—and I helped discover it."

"We've got to take care of this Bourdain," he said. "Claus may be right—he may know where LeTorneau is. That is, if he's still alive. Either way, the guy knows too much."

"So does Miss Laughlin," said Lindstrom. He oozed confidence from his slicked-down hair to his Rolex.

Veronica kicked at Lindstrom's right knee, but he deftly grabbed her steel-toed combat boot with both hands and twisted her leg. She fell to the floor. She got up and raced toward the door, but Marburg held her back.

Lindstrom straightened his frame, smiled. "Let's go for a little ride, shall we? Why don't we start with the GPS coordinates you put into your vehicle? Mr. Bourdain's place, in the Blue Ridge Mountains, I assume?"

She tried to scream, but Lindstrom covered her mouth and pushed her out the back door and into the back seat of Marburg's BMW.

-25-

Sara Sullivan

As Sara approached the address of Jorge Bourdain's cabin, she watched the white Tahoe creep up the mountainside, curving along the road and out of sight, into the vibrant foliage. The ground was damp and the tracks were easy to follow. She decided it was too obvious to follow any further by vehicle, and she'd noticed the driver checking his rearview mirror as she'd followed him along the gravel road, off Route 64 between Charlottesville and Leesburg.

From there, she followed the trail on foot.

She left Marty's truck beside an embankment midway from the base of the mountain near a scenic overlook of the Blue Ridge Mountains. The air was cooler here and the mist rested like a confectioner's icing over the tips of the mountains. Even her small feet sank into the muddy ground.

There were only a few hours until dusk.

She saw clearly up the side of the mountain with the binoculars as the sun shone through the covering of Appalachian flora, bright hued and diverse with yellow hemlock and coniferous spruce and oak and red maple leaves, far beyond where the truck had veered off her path at the east-facing ridge. She checked Marty's flashlight. It worked. She put it in her back pocket along with his Swiss army knife. She concealed Marty's pistol against her chest, secured it in its holster, and she threw his khaki jacket over her tank top.

She started up the mountain on foot. Her feet had always been too small for her body, and although she was skilled with her hands, she'd always been clumsy on foot. After the rain, it was impossible not to leave her tiny footprints in the mud, but she stayed a few hundred yards from the main trail, well hidden in the thick grasses and vegetation and fruit trees that marched up the side. The smell of apples was faint on the breeze. Her eyes were heavy from exhaustion. She felt she might like to lie down and sleep, right there in the meadow atop the crest.

But she kept climbing, with Elyse's cherubic face in mind.

After an hour, she approached the hunting cabin at the top of the mountain, panting and sweating from her steady progress up the slope. The majestic view overlooking the valleys left her breathless.

The feeling was short lived.

She gasped, crouched down on the ground in the orchard, where rows of apple and pear trees as far as she could see were planted with precision. The Tahoe passed again, headed down the mountainside. Inside it, a man with a red beard and a blonde-haired woman wearing sunglasses appeared to be arguing.

She hadn't eaten since she'd left her mother's house, and her stomach churned. She stood up and she picked a yellow apple from a tree and she took a bite. She ate it and she ate another and she tossed the cores as far as she could. Then she walked down the parallel rows of the orchard to the back of the cabin.

It appeared empty.

She pulled herself up onto the rotted porch, craned her neck around to see into the window. As she stretched her neck, her torso, stood on tiptoe, a dilapidated board snapped, giving way under her weight.

Heavy footsteps came quickly toward the back door then.

She ducked beneath the sagging porch.

Through the cracks in the boards and a veil of spider web, the figure of a large man appeared. The door creaked as he opened it, and a marmalade cat tore out into the orchard. Then the half-unhinged door slammed, and the figure moved away from the window.

She kept down.

The footsteps receded.

Her shallow breathing made her lightheaded as she rose, and as she stood a moment to steady herself, she gasped, covered her mouth at the sight on the leeward side of the mountain.

A hangman's noose was nailed to a wooden podium.

The body of a black man swung from a wooden cross, moving in the wind.

His lifeless body dangled, the short noose tied where the wooden beams of the cross met. Waxy skin, now thick like a pig's and dimpled like orange peel, clung loosely to his face. The thunderstorm had left his jeans, his white T-shirt, clinging soaked to his body. The body swayed a dead weight, suspended in the air, arms coiled up rigid in their final attempt to grasp at the noose around his chafed neck. Eyes popped like boiled eggs, and the mouth was set in a horrible rictus of agony. Long branches with nettles of pear tree brambles lay at his feet, and his arms were marred by them. They'd apparently been used to whip and claw at him as he struggled beneath the noose.

She'd stumbled right into the lair of Bourdain's resurgent Ku Klux Klan.

Racks of half-burned white candles in iron racks surrounded the wooden platform.

Potted white lilies were placed on the ground, surrounding the victim.

Sara stayed hidden as she stepped closer, examining the corpse. Parts of the body were burned away, bone torched to tendon and pearled ligaments, flesh pared down to yellow-red marrow in others. She looked away and then back, beyond the dead man, to the entrance of an intricate labyrinth, cut into the acres of corn. The maze stretched for miles beyond the back of the cabin.

There was no end to it in sight.

It had to be Bourdain's doing, she decided.

But was LeTorneau still alive? Here?

She swallowed.

Maybe the lynched man was Professor LeTorneau, and it was all too late. She checked the path behind her again, thinking she should turn and run back to the truck. The desolate cabin and the neo-Confederate society she'd discovered didn't appear to be connected to LeTorneau's research, and being discovered there risked her own life, even more than being infected with *Labrador.*

She imagined the man hanging, still alive, gagging with the thick rope around his neck, starved for air. Then she closed her eyes, tried to block the image from her mind. If the neo-

Confederates found her on the premises, they'd certainly do the same thing to her.

She took several timid steps into the corn maze, crunching leaves beneath her feet.

The superficial perimeter of it was bordered by orchards of fruit trees, stretching for acres, but inside was an intricate pattern of corn and stone wall and skilled masonry, surrounded by wooden doors and locked gates within the structure. Huge pits dug into the red dirt of the mountain were interspersed throughout, serving as traps. She stepped carefully around them. The walls seemed to grow taller the deeper into the maze she walked, making it impossible to see outside to the exits. Grapes crept up and down the sides of the walls, entangling their vines across arched doorways and concealed passages within the puzzle.

As she rounded a corner, a scream escaped her as she nearly ran into the decayed skull of one of Bourdain's victims, suspended from a stake, about her height. Its flesh was long since decayed, and only the fibrous connective tissue pulled taut over the bones remained, but the skull was distinctly African-American. She turned around quickly, this time going in the wrong direction, and she encountered another decayed head. Panting, she turned back the way she came now, racing out of the labyrinth, back toward the cabin.

Before that moment, she'd been willing to face the virus.

The hospital administration, the quarantines.

Even Wes Lindstrom with all his political power and influence.

Here, alone now, somewhere in the Blue Ridge Mountains at the home of a racist serial killer, she felt her life could end at any moment.

Still, she had no other choice but to investigate. If Bourdain maimed and killed her, she hoped Marty would understand exactly why she'd risked everything. If LeTorneau was alive, he was her only hope of a cure for Elyse—and the thousands of African-Americans afflicted with *Labrador* virus. She wanted terribly to put an end to the distrust, the hate crimes surrounding the epidemic, and there had to be another reason that she was being traced so closely. She felt she was close to uncovering the cure, and Wes Lindstrom and his pipeline to Washington, Senator Edward Marburg, despised that.

She approached the cabin, looking in the window for some sign of Kayla. LeTorneau. A rudimentary lab—anything, anyone, that could help her save Elyse. She heard the man's heavy footsteps on the back porch again, and she crouched under wisps of spider web, beneath the decayed wood, smelling rotted planks and leaves and wood smoke. The cat ran toward the house, but it stopped short of the first step and it hissed, clawing at her beneath the boards. It scratched at her face and chest, drawing blood, but she didn't move. She clenched her eyes tightly shut, remained motionless until the animal retracted its claws.

Beyond her, the sun was setting.

Her own blood blurred with the red sky in the west.

"Felicity," the man called.

The cat hissed again, ran around her, up the steps. Through the cracks, she saw the large man scoop up the animal. He stroked its head, scratched its ears. Then his cell phone rang, and she breathed a silent sigh. She was still crouched down in the mud on the side of the house, beneath the rickety porch.

"This is Jorge," the man said.

She crawled on her abdomen, along the side of the cabin, toward an old-fashioned storm cellar built into the hillside.

The man walked further out onto the porch.

She pressed her back toward the side of the house, lay on her left side, her heart racing. The cat hissed, peered over the man's left shoulder. There was a heavy padlock, thankfully not engaged, dangling from the hasp on the storm cellar's angled doors.

She flung the doors open.

She crept inside.

She closed the doors just as the man stepped off the porch and around the back of the cabin. She swallowed and she looked down the severe stairs, into blackness. Water dripped down the side of the stone wall, and filled the confined space with the scent of mildew and partly turned apples. Through the crack between the wooden doors, she saw Jorge Bourdain.

His boots squished as they sank down in the mud.

He was right above her, outside the underground refuge.

She had no choice now but to descend further into the cellar. With Marty's pistol clutched in her right hand, she inched down the steps, feeling her way in the darkness with the toes of each sneaker.

She didn't dare turn on the flashlight.

Over the last month, she'd witnessed overt racism and discrimination and a regression of all the values and social progress America had made over the last seventy years. Even though such behavior revolted her and was everything her teachers and her mother and society had taught her was wrong and loathsome and something to fight back against, it was there. Everywhere. It had crept back onto the streets and into America. The rioting and government mismanagement of the epidemic seemed to create instinctual, protective defenses in many people, like something inherent in her life had changed since *Labrador*.

She wasn't sure it could be returned to the way it was, even if a cure was available.

Everyone was guarded, suspicious.

Actions were governed by snap, stereotypical judgments.

Until now, she could explain part of the ignorance due to the stress reaction that accompanied falling ill with the deadly infection. It was an inexplicable, merciless killer of her own race. The way it infected blacks was incomprehensible, and people feared what they didn't understand.

But nothing justified Jorge Bourdain's barbaric demonstrations of hate.

Human nature seemed to be uncoupling itself under the *Labrador* affliction. Bourdain was a formidable monster imbued with evil. A man educated in science and reason, but bereft of even the most pathetic of alibis for his atrocities, and he seemed to kill out of unadulterated hate of those unlike him.

Now, he lurked outside the storm cellar, peering in, listening.

As she watched his boots through the cracks in the wooden slats, she too, was filled with such incarnate rage, that she bit the side of her cheek, drew her own blood. She pressed her tongue against the back of her front teeth, savored the metallic taste, and it filled her with a deluge of fear and wrath and revenge that projected onto all white people who had ever treated her terribly.

No, she told herself.

But her anger would not abate, and her heart beat stronger, faster, and she breathed in rapid gasps of musty air. He was leaning closer to the door now.

Could he see her?

Impossible.

Water trickled down the side of the cellar wall, and the smell of mildew grew stronger as she reached the bottom floor, stepping ankle deep in wet muck, and looking up toward the exit.

She heard the click of metal against metal.

Was he entering the cellar?

No, he had clamped the lock shut. She cursed to herself.

His footsteps faded away.

She was now trapped.

The cellar was devoid of light, except for the last streaks of sunlight slipping in between the cracks of the angled doors.

Then, from deep within the cellar, about a hundred yards away, she heard a weak voice.

"Help," the voice called.

She couldn't discern if it was male or female.

"Help," the voice called again, and feeling her way through the blackness, against the stone wall of the room, she moved further into the cellar.

"Who's there?" She clutched the pistol, trembling with violent movements from her wrists all the way up to her shoulders. She groped at the wall, touching it blindly, like a lost child in the dark, until she reached a corner. It was cold, flooded with a few inches of water. There, she heard the voice again.

"I'm here."

She tripped, righted her balance. The voice moaned. It was distinctly male now, but soft, humble. She knelt down, identified the feet and legs of the man, lying on the floor in the water.

"Is there another way out of here?" She was hyperventilating and sweating, despite the cold water soaking her feet. "I can't see you. Who's there?"

"My lady, we all look the same in the dark. Ah, cruel fact, there is only one way out, and I fear it's barred." He sounded delirious, with a sliver of hope in his words, after his groaning subsided.

She was far enough into the basement now to safely use the light. She pulled it from her back, but she dropped it into the water surrounding her feet. When she tried to turn it on, there was nothing. She cursed, knelt down, felt the coils of braided rope around the prisoner's wrists. She followed his arms upwards to his mouth, palpating his scalp and neck and facial features as she did her patients'. His features were distinctly African-

American, like her own. A bow tie was tied tightly around his neck, compressing his vessels and his airway, and causing him to breathe in ragged, noisy spasms, a desperate chalky sound that made her cringe. She loosened the tie, and the man sucked deep drafts of air into his lungs. His breath reeked of starvation.

"Are you—" she asked.

"Dr. Graham LeTorneau. I wanted you to tighten it. Now you've loosened it, and I'm starting over again. I'll kill myself before I'll let them kill me." LeTorneau's head shook back and forth, as if resisting torture.

She gasped, defeated, all the rage and intense fear bottled within her simmered. She quivered, but remained silent. The terror of the situation was paralyzing, and she just stood there, frozen, denying the implications of her fate. If the man who'd developed the cure for *Labrador* had been reduced to near death, was it even possible to right the situation? How could he possibly help her in his condition? And now, she was trapped, too.

When Jorge Bourdain discovered her, he would certainly kill her.

Or worse, what if he never came back, and she just wasted away without anyone ever discovering either of them? That would be an undignified fate worse than dying of *Labrador*.

No, she had to find a way out of there with LeTorneau. She vowed to get him the resources he needed to save the nation, the world, from this plague.

Blacks.

Whites.

And most of all, to save *Elyse*, whose life mattered so much more than her own now.

"I'm Dr. Sara Sullivan," she said. "I've been looking for you. Everyone's looking for you. My daughter's life—and so many others—depend on you, Doctor."

"I can't help anyone now." He sounded as though he was unaware of the magnitude of it all. "Just help let me go. Please."

She knew Bourdain was a monster, but these days, she didn't trust anyone. She wanted to believe LeTorneau was ethical, honest, but she couldn't assume it so unconditionally. She had to ask. "They say you're a racist. They say you claim that with the planet warming, blacks are more suited to climate change, have higher birth rates, and will prosper. That angers people—"

"Because they think it implicitly means that other races will not. I am not a racist. My research describes evolution as it is, not as we want it to be. Many variants occur within all species that favor their survival and reproduction over others. That is not novel to my research. What is inevitable is the nature of mankind to destroy itself."

"Did you cause the *Labrador* epidemic?"

"No." LeTorneau's voice was broken, hoarse. "Jorge, my pupil, altered the virus, making it one thousand times more virulent and destructive to the African-American races. That is the only explanation. He has told me so, and I fear it is the truth."

"But why?"

"He's become obsessed with white supremacy. It started with him reading a few blogs here and there. Then a few posts on the Internet, while working in the lab. His comments—and those of his contacts—crossed into extremism. I'm afraid he has self-radicalized into a monster."

"But the antibodies. You know how to manufacture them. You and the other students. Veronica, Kayla—they're alive. You're our only hope. Thirty thousand new cases are predicted by November."

"Then it's too late. It takes months to manufacture only a small dose of reagent. It's a costly and labor intensive procedure. The drug companies are vultures, and they are a party to this fiasco."

"We can't let either of them win." She dragged him, trying to lift him, but his dead weight collapsed beneath her, and he resisted.

"Leave me alone. I just want to die. My contribution was for naught."

"Don't say that."

"There's nothing I can do. Jorge boasted that he's destroyed the lab. He's going to release the virus throughout the country. Marburg and his investor friend wanted it released for profit. They thought they could control it, too—make millions off the cure, and the vaccine. But it fell into the wrong hands."

"Bourdain is unhinged. He blew up the lab, and he terrorized a ceremony of a black senator at Arlington. He plans to destroy the White House."

"Yes. Anywhere he can create racial unrest. He won't listen to anyone, and the virus will mutate at such an exponential rate that it may first destroy everyone of black descent as he desires, but it won't stop there." He paused. "If he isn't stopped, all races *will* succumb to *Labrador.*"

She bent down and, with all her strength, she lifted the frail man toward the door and up one, then two stairs. LeTorneau kicked against the restraints, bit at her wrists, but she heaved him further up the stairs, through the dark. She stopped, panting, and wiped the sweat from her brow as her teeth ground together, chipping at the back molars. She spit and she shook the perspiration and the blood from the cat scratches from her brow and her eyelids.

"I'm getting us out of here." Her determination would not relent, even though in their morbid plight, she thought he might be right.

"It's too late. You'd be safer hiding in this hole."

"I'm not going to die down here like a rat, Doctor, living in fear. And neither are you."

She peered out through the crack where the two wooden doors met.

No one.

She kicked at the doors so hard that her hamstring tore where it hinged at her thigh.

No luck.

Then she kicked harder, but the locked doors wouldn't budge. She whipped out the gun and she aimed a shot, shattering the lock. She threw open the double doors and her mocha-colored skin was revealed to the professor, whose own light-brown complexion was blotchy and bruised as a result of his long torture. Eyes sunken and cachectic.

A look of worry passed over his face when he saw that she shared his race.

It was a look of pity, of fear, for her.

She recognized it immediately, but she refused to acknowledge it as such.

"My lady," LeTorneau said. "Please. Save yourself—before they find us both."

"We're both getting out of here, Doctor."

LeTorneau screamed, "My leg."

The lower leg was badly wounded, with the tibia bone protruding from the skin, and a purulent yellow liquid seeped from it where infection was setting in.

She dragged his body up and out of the storm cellar and they both landed on the wet ground with a thud. She collapsed as odd, shock-like sensations ran down her leg from her buttock, but she forced herself to stand up, and she slammed the doors. She thought it impossible that Jorge Bourdain had not heard the gunshot, but as she looked toward the back of the cabin, he was assembled with an entourage of thirteen white-robed figures near the entrance of the maze.

It was dark now.

They held large candles, illuminating their hideous faces, and the light from them was so bright that it nearly extinguished the glow of the country stars. Loud music played from outdoor speakers. It was eerie, medieval sounding, with unintelligible chanting.

She grunted as she hoisted LeTorneau onto the back of Bourdain's John Deere tractor-truck with the strength of a man twice her size. It was a newer model with a cab and a truck bed and a tailgate. Marty would love it, she thought. There was no way LeTorneau could walk on his broken leg, and she couldn't carry him any further. Her back was strained badly from the move. She laid him on the bed of the truck and covered him with a green tarp. She wiped her brow and peered back at the neo-Confederates.

They hadn't seen her.

Then she whispered to LeTorneau, "Stay here."

She kept the resurgent Klan members in her sight, moved beside the murdered victims hung amongst the rows of fruit trees and mired in Bourdain's harrowed corn labyrinth. She heard horrific screams as the society enacted their pagan rituals, as if they'd risen up from the fury of hell or fallen like angels with singed wings, rejected by a wrathful and angry God with whom she'd never again make peace.

Bourdain had more victims to torture.

-26-

Sara Sullivan

Sara ran around the rear entrance of the corn maze, down the mountain, where she'd parked Marty's truck. The maze stretched for miles, and she'd lost sight of the house now. Mainly blackberry bushes grew on this side of the orchard, brambled and half eaten by deer, protected by chicken wire in some places. She cursed as she cut her leg on one of the sharp brambles, held it for a moment. The last rays of sunlight had slipped beneath the base of the mountain, and without the flashlight, she had only a pristine moon and an endless sky of stars to guide her.

When she'd walked about a quarter mile from the labyrinth, she noticed the tracks of a small car, which had made an abrupt three point turn in the mud.

She followed the tracks.

A stream trickled across the berry patches all the way to the bottom of the hill. A stone tumbled off the side, where the rock layers of the hill faulted at a steep angle. She approached the empty vehicle.

She peered through the window.

Lying face up on the back seat, bound and gagged, was Veronica, her face chafed raw from the cloth. Right cheek bruised and swollen.

"Veronica," she said.

The young woman nodded.

The driver's side rear door to the sedan was unlocked. Sara knelt on the back seat and raced to cut the rope around Veronica's feet with the Swiss army knife. Veronica's hands were secured with handcuffs, and she was expertly trussed up with the seat belts around her body. As Sara started to pull Veronica toward the door, her eyes widened, and she shook her head wildly. Muffled screams escaped through the gag. Sara glanced behind her as a man with slicked gray hair covered her mouth, forced her arms against her chest.

"Dr. Sullivan?"

She kicked and clawed at the man, gouging her nails into his hands. A second man appeared, holding a machine gun.

Senator Edward Marburg.

"Who the hell are you?" She kicked and flailed and tried to wrestle herself free from the older man squeezing her arms.

"Not a very lady like introduction. I prefer women with a few social graces so I can dress them up *and* take them out," said the man with the slicked-back hair.

She recognized the voice now.

Lindstrom.

She kicked harder behind her, but Lindstrom dodged her bullish kicks and placed his right leg across hers.

"I'm Wesley Lindstrom. I believe we spoke over the phone."

"Stay still, or I'll blow both you and your friend over the edge of this cliff, and take half this mountain with you." Edward Marburg aimed the Uzi submachine gun and stepped closer to her.

She relaxed, and she kept her eyes on the senator, fearful as the ground beneath him gave way, and a slurry of wet rock tumbled hundreds of feet off the mountainside to the cresting river below.

"Doctor, you're wanted for fleeing quarantine while under investigation, endangering the lives of millions of Americans while potentially infected with a level 4 biohazardous virus used as a weapon of mass destruction, and aiding in the destruction of a government-contracted research facility," said Marburg.

"I had nothing to do with the bombing," she said.

Lindstrom squeezed her arms tighter.

"If you cooperate, I can see to it that the charges are dropped. You'll be free to return to your usual routine," said Marburg.

"I don't want to return to my goddamn routine. That's how I got dragged into your mess. I want the cure for *Labrador*." She struggled against Lindstrom's grip, and he smiled, wide and shark-like, adjusted his glasses with his free hand.

"So do we," said Marburg. "To wrap up this ugly mess and get the cure and the vaccine out to the masses. It'll be best for everyone."

"You haven't got an alibi, Doctor," said Lindstrom. "We can have you charged for being in the lab."

"You both commissioned Phaedrex and NewfoundVax to make drugs for *Labrador* before it ever killed a single American. There was practically zero risk of it here in the states. And zero potential for drug sales, until you two opportunists played with fire," she said.

"It's an exciting story, isn't it?" said Lindstrom, holding her wrists.

Veronica clambered from the BMW, fell into the mud. Lindstrom smiled.

"It was supposed to be that—a story, a thriller. What kind of monster are you? Thousands of people are dying." She threw her head back at Lindstrom, just missing his forehead.

"You don't find this thrilling? I always say you can't make an omelet without—oh never mind," he said, laughing. "Sounds a little too clichéd, don't you think? Kitten, I really want to cut you a deal. Be *reasonable*. How would you feel if my lovely wife, Jane, acquired your novel and secured full movie rights? She knows all the right people. I can guarantee you instant success. She wanted to publish it, you know."

"Why didn't she?" she asked, through clenched teeth.

"I wanted it for myself, naturally."

She broke free and she spun around and she gripped Lindstrom's wrist. He grabbed his pistol and fired it with his left hand, sending a covey of white bobtail quail flying across the field with a raucous clatter of whistles and beating wings. He maintained a firm grip on the weapon. Lindstrom pressed his knee into her back, forcing her into the ground, next to Veronica.

"I thought aristocrats were better at quail hunting. That was a pathetic shot," she said.

"Shut up, both of you," said Marburg. With his Uzi trained on Veronica, he recited: "The writer serves a movement of history as its mouthpiece, but doesn't create it." His face was smug.

"Karl Marx." She twisted at her wrists, trying to break free. "Is that your election platform, Senator?"

Lindstrom held her arms and forced her up against a tree stump with his knee. "So, you're not just a pretty face. You're much smarter than I gave you credit for, which is unfortunate, because now you know too much. The story isn't supposed to play out like this. We need to work on the ending a bit, sweetheart. See, it was supposed to be a quick deal. Drug companies work on supply and demand. Without the demand, there's no need for supply. A little epidemic and *voila!*"

She kicked her right leg backward into Lindstrom's groin. Lindstrom winced, pulled at her arms, gripping them tightly. As he forced her up by her hair, two rifle shots startled them, hitting the BMW and setting off another flurry of whistles and wings from the forest path. The white Tahoe tore up the gravel, skirting the perilous cliff, blocking the path of the sedan. A man and woman got out of the truck and slammed the doors and loaded their guns again. The woman yelled something to the man in what sounded like French, aimed her handgun at Lindstrom, who was cowering behind a boulder. A swirl of dust kicked up as the bullet glanced off the rocks with a loud ping, missing him by inches.

She squatted on the opposite side of the car where Veronica grappled at the door. "Give me your hands," she whispered. She set them on the tree stump behind her and removed Marty's pistol from her back. "Don't move." She shot at the handcuffs, breaking them, and shattering the locking mechanism.

The man from the Tahoe aimed and shot at Sara, then at Veronica, missing them both. He looked back at his accomplice, who had a better shot with her handgun. Sara quickly grabbed Veronica's hand, raced around to the driver's side of the Tahoe.

"That's a lovely little .38 special you've got there," said Lindstrom, to the woman.

"There's nothing special about it. It's small, like your dick."

"Jessie," the man screamed, but before the woman could react, a dozen bullets from Marburg's Uzi found her chest. Her blood splattered the Tahoe. The man stood frozen, his feet planted in the mud, his face drained of color.

Then, Marburg shot and killed him, too.

She quickly got in the truck and gassed the Tahoe into reverse as Marburg dove out of the way, sending rocks tumbling off the steep edge of the cliff. They sped off in a cloud of gravel and dust. With Veronica at her side, she drove around the back of the corn labyrinth and parked the car a considerable distance from the cult gathering.

Hidden by the apple trees, they witnessed the multiple white-robed members of the society congregating around the entrance of the maze. There was a great fire roaring now, the KKK members encircling it. The blaze roared, crackled, spitting embers at the corn. With Bourdain's society assembled at the entrance of the labyrinth, the women entered the front of his cabin, searching desperately for Kayla Reeves.

Just past the screen door, lying on the pine floor in a pool of bloody vomit, they found Kayla's hairclip and her cell phone.

-27-

Sara Sullivan

Sara took a deep breath and she stepped over the wooden threshold and into the living room of the hunting cabin. Flies whizzed about the garbage receptacle. She approached the tattered mattress where Kayla lay, barely breathing.

"Kayla, open your eyes." Veronica shook her shoulder gently, but the girl's breathing was shallow.

She was unconscious.

"Let me help," Sara said, quietly. "You watch the back."

She'd seen trauma victims' chests cracked open in the ER, and she'd been elbow deep in their blood. Gangrenous limbs crusted to a blackish-purple by infection and diabetes. She'd been coughed on, sneezed on, even wet on by the occasional pediatric patient. Medicine certainly wasn't the glamorous profession everyone thought it was. Critically ill patients like Kayla didn't make her squeamish. But Bourdain's racist compound made her nauseous to the pit of her soul, the place where she held her final remaining shreds of hope in the good of humanity.

She'd read plenty about psychotic behavior and schizophrenic breaks, but according to Veronica, Jorge had never indicated a desire to harm anyone. Veronica had said he was reserved, reclusive, and good at video games and mathematics. Everything he'd done so far seemed carefully calculated, premeditated, and she loathed him for it.

The scent of deer meat and animal urine, used to lure animals to the kill, filled the room and permeated their clothing. In the kitchen, the smell of truck-stop diner grease was even stronger. Out the back window, the Klan members continued their ritual, moving in sinewy shadows of evil. There was chanting, dancing. Passages read aloud from an oversized book. The smell of patchouli incense and apples wafted in, masked the animal odors.

"Come on, Kayla. Open your eyes." She checked the girl's pulse—weak and rapid. Extremities cool and mottled pink and white.

She removed the supplies from the backpack she'd lifted from the hospital now. She slapped the veins in Kayla's hand a few times, trying to make them protrude, but they hid deep under her parched skin. She prayed as she placed the IV against her flat veins and pierced the girl's hand. To her relief, the IV threaded in.

But there was no antibiotic that would save her from the virus.

Kayla's only hope was the vial of experimental antibody that Veronica had saved from the explosion.

But was it enough to save her life?

Using her only syringe, she drew up the medication from the vial. Then she administered it into the collapsed vessel, pushing half of it in first, careful not to spill a drop. Normally, it would've been given over several hours, but Kayla's vital signs were deteriorating faster than that.

She turned to Veronica, said, "We've got to get Kayla and LeTorneau to a hospital. Marburg and Lindstrom will be back."

"Are they working with Jorge?"

She said, "I don't think so, but I believe Marburg and Lindstrom were involved in the initial cases somehow. LeTorneau said the numbers spiraled out of control when Jorge discovered the evolutionary propensity the virus showed for people of color. He said that Jorge altered the virus synthetically, making it one thousand times more virulent—said he plans to release it all over the country."

"So how are those two involved? And how did they find you, Sara?"

She raised her eyebrows. "What motivates politicians?"

"Money?" asked Veronica.

"Right. Filoviruses have never been seen in North America. I noticed an uncanny similarity to the novel I sent Wes Lindstrom's wife, Jane. Wrote it with the dream of seeing it come to life on the big screen as a movie—not for it to become a reality in my own life. The outbreak fleshed itself out exactly like I wrote it—so I investigated. This nightmare was all a pet project of that creep Lindstrom to make an easy ten million dollars or so. When my daughter got sick, there was no turning back. I'd do anything now to know she'd be alright."

"You think the virus was originally released here?"

"No, that would be too obvious, and the mistake would be bad for politics—and it would make Lindstrom and Marburg look bad." She felt Kayla's pulse again, pressed the back of her hand to the girl's flushed forehead—her fever was climbing. "In

Africa, one of the burial practices is to kiss the body of the dead. It's also one of the ways filovirus outbreaks like *Ebola* and *Lassa fever* have wiped out entire villages."

"What does that have to do with *Labrador?*"

"I spoke with some of the patient's families. One of the victims traveled to Africa as a Make-A-Wish gift. Took a safari—a dying wish granted by the Make-A-Wish Foundation. Her parents thought she died of complications related to her cancer, but that wasn't the case. I believe she was the index case that spread the virus to the United States."

"She died of *Labrador?*" asked Veronica.

She nodded. "Not only that—her body was sent to Finnegan Funeral Home. The director who handled the body also became infected. She may have infected dozens of others before she died."

"It only takes a few to light the fire," said Veronica.

"And that was before Jorge altered the structure of the virus. Every last ember has to be stomped out to bring the outbreak to an end."

Veronica looked somber, and Sara knew it meant that she thought the worst. The window was closing on the chance to rid the world of *Labrador* infection forever. The exponential numbers were almost mathematically impossible to grasp.

"The virus couldn't have come from our lab initially, Sara. LeTorneau would never have been a party to something so horrible. And the initial cases infected *all* races. Where was the safari that the index case traveled to?"

"Uganda. A small village high in the mountains. The village is isolated. It may not have spread beyond the mountains there, but the District is a different animal."

"There had to be other cases there, too," Veronica pointed out. "I don't believe those two greedy scumbags would have made a deal with Jorge if they'd known he was mentally unstable, plotting to infect millions, destroying government buildings and creating a disaster area out of the nation's capital. They're ruthless, but not stupid."

"There wasn't much publicity surrounding the outbreak initially. I found an article about a mysterious illness wiping out an entire African village. The area is so remote and secluded and nearly impossible to reach, that it's likely that *Labrador* quickly killed the entire village and eliminated any further spread beyond the township—until the Make-A-Wish safari happened to come through there after they'd released the virus. It could've spread through contact with any infected animal."

After hearing this, Veronica stood up and she snapped her fingers and she put her hand on her forehead, like she had just figured out something crucial.

"Claus," said Veronica. "I didn't even think of Claus. And Jorge wouldn't take on the virus alone like this, unless he knew he was protected from it."

"What do you mean? Who's Claus?"

"Claus Recart," Veronica said. "His lab worked on the vaccine in Labrador, Canada. He discovered the virus and named it for the province. Claus and LeTorneau were once friends, but they were in close competition to be the first to market for many drugs and vaccines."

"Keep your friends close, and your enemies closer?"

"Exactly. When Claus discovered the virus in Uganda, naturally he set to work on the vaccine immediately. But he knew as well as Marburg and Lindstrom, that there's only money in it for him if there's a need for it."

"Supply and demand." She nodded. "Veronica, we've got to get LeTorneau to safety, and get out of here fast. I need his help to save my daughter. If she dies, I'll have failed as a mother, a wife and a doctor. I can live without my career, but I can't go on without my family." She looked down at Kayla. "And time is running out for your friend."

They lifted Kayla's body toward the door. She was fading, and her breathing was agonal, and Sara knew that the girl's only chance at survival was to get her to a hospital, despite the roadblocks and risks in their way. They'd have to explain themselves, and pray that they were heard.

With LeTorneau alive, they had a chance.

"So, Doc. You're into the arts, too? I'm impressed," said Veronica.

She shrugged. "I try. Writing has always been a passion of mine, but I never dreamed that my imagination could create this evil. I haven't slept since I started looking into this. I'm terrified that things will never be as they were before *Labrador*."

"It's a very impressive resume, Doctor. I've been looking forward to meeting you." Jorge Bourdain stood in the cabin doorway now. The marmalade cat was butting its orange head against his legs. Bourdain held a rifle, and he pulled down the hood of his white robe. "I didn't think you'd be settin' pretty for me right here in my living room like a tied hog, though. Shoot.

You're cute as a coon hound, and you're right—things will never be as they were." Bourdain winked. "They'll be better."

Bourdain approached. The hair on the back of her neck stood on end. She wanted more than anything to shoot him, pumping all of the lead in Marty's pistol through his inhuman heart.

"Jorge," said Veronica. "I—we've—come to help Kayla. She's dying, Jorge, but Dr. Sullivan's given her half a dose of antibody that I rescued from the lab—the last dose. She's going to help her. I know how much you care for her, Big Jorgey. I know you'd never let anything happen to Kayla."

Bourdain's gaze fell, and he lowered the rifle and he responded as she knew Veronica had hoped. His hardened features relaxed, and he reached out to Kayla. Sara turned her back to hide the pistol, and every muscle in her body tensed as Bourdain grew closer. His white robe brushed against her skin.

"Are you fond of white men, Doctor?"

Her brain snapshotted the images before her of the man burned to death outside the labyrinth. She tried to reject the violent image from her mind, but as Bourdain touched the fading student, she envisioned herself as his prisoner, tied to one of the wooden crosses and surrounded by his fellow Klansmen. Veronica rested Kayla's head against the worn sofa. At once, Bourdain's eyes narrowed.

"Get back. Both of you. Against the wall." Bourdain pushed the butt of the rifle against Veronica's shoulder, as they backed toward the corner.

Kayla's breathing came in shallow rasps as Sara watched him stroke the girl's hair. She cringed, trying to find the right moment to draw the pistol. Would she be able to hit him before he fired the rifle?

She trembled.

Her own breathing was labored in the humidity, in the stench of the cabin.

She reached slowly around her back.

Veronica backed away from Bourdain, looking toward the door.

If they ran, he'd shoot them both at once.

Kayla's color changed from a mottled pink to an ashen grey, and then to a bluish pallor, in a matter of seconds. Bourdain's eyes fell as he released Kayla's limp hand.

"She's cold," Bourdain said, his face emotionless. He shook her gently, brushed the tendrils of blonde hair away from her face. He opened the lids of Kayla's eyes as his cat licked at her cheek, but the girl's pupils were fixed and dilated, and without any reaction to light.

She swallowed, looked toward Veronica, who nodded.

"She's gone, Jorge," said Veronica.

He walked toward the front window. The massive muscles in his neck and shoulders rose, his breathing deepened. It was obvious he was processing the girl's death, and she could feel a tangible sense of rage intensifying in the room. Was Bourdain truly distraught over the loss of Kayla Reeves, or over the failure of the altered virus to exclusively take the lives of African-Americans? Kayla's fair skin and her light eyes demonstrated her Anglo-Saxon lineage, yet she'd quickly succumbed to the genetically modified virus.

The research was flawed.

Bourdain cracked his knuckles.

He clenched his fist, smashed the window before him.

Veronica screamed, covered her face.

Blood covered Bourdain's knuckles.

"No," Bourdain screamed, punched the window again.

Glass shattered outwards onto the porch. He smashed another window and tore open the door to his left, revealing what looked like an old computer with blinking blue and red and yellow lights. Bourdain began to type, as fast as he could with his meaty fingers, and a code appeared on the screen above the lights and switches that she suspected was his connection to the previous explosions. Bourdain input another code into the old keyboard as Veronica reached for the rifle, propped beside him.

As Veronica wrapped her tiny fingers around it, an ear-splitting alarm blared, and the black and white screen displayed the digits: *9:59:59*. The device began counting down as Bourdain spun, ripped the gun from Veronica's hands. He swung it like a baseball bat with his weak arm and hit her across the temple, knocking her to the ground. Veronica screamed and lay with her hand across her right eye, forehead gashed and bleeding badly, kicking at Bourdain's large feet.

Sara drew the pistol. It was an instinctive mistake. Hearing her move, Bourdain spun around with the speed and precision of a Navy SEAL, and aimed the barrel at her. He laughed, a contemptuous and patronizing laugh filled with the hatred of two-hundred years of civil discord and racial tension, encompassing all of the unhealed wounds of the South.

"Don't move," she shouted. "I'll kill you. I swear I will."

Bourdain laughed. "What were you doing in my lab?"

"Why did you destroy it?"

"I'll ask the questions." Bourdain grunted, pushed her back with the barrel of the rifle.

"You racist monster," she said, her eyes emblazoned with the deepest anger she'd ever known, but also fear, and she couldn't wrap her mind around anything that could've incited Bourdain's horrific intentions. Mental illness couldn't justify the calculated, premeditated evil.

"I had everything I needed from the lab. My work was done there. Now throw down the gun, Doctor, and I'll spare Ms. Laughlin."

"Kill him," Veronica pulled herself up, ran toward Bourdain, sinking her fingernails into his biceps, but with the palm of his left hand, he tossed her to the floor and pushed the sole of his work boot firmly against her chest.

"Go ahead. Kill me." He smiled, revealing his missing front teeth.

She found it difficult to maintain her gaze at this beast, his leviathan arms poised to take her life without hesitation, his tree-trunk leg pinning Veronica effortlessly.

Bourdain laughed.

She kept the Glock steadily trained on the ogre, her eyes boring into his. They regarded her with disdain, with sadistic satisfaction. Bourdain looked pleased with her appearance, licking his lips, and his suggestive stare infuriated her. She wanted badly to pump a bullet into his chest, or his brain, making him unable to breathe a whisper, but before she could act, she spotted Marburg and Lindstrom, pulling up the gravel road to the top of the orchard.

Instead, she looked at him and said what she had just realized herself.

"You have no control over me."

The weapon didn't feel as heavy as it usually did when she fired it in target practice. She gripped it as secure and confidently as she ever had now, didn't remove her eyes from Bourdain. His dark eyes were close together, hiding some impish wounds of his past that she didn't care to examine.

He wouldn't kill her right then, she realized.

He hadn't succeeded until he'd filled her with all of the fear that he was trying to build among blacks, by manipulating *Labrador* to pit race against race.

She refused to succumb to it—it was everything Jorge Bourdain wanted, and she saw the intoxicating fury fester in his eyes as she refused him. She could feel his torment, his desire to inflict terror within her, but she showed no outward signs of her horror. Jorge Bourdain wanted her trembling, begging for mercy, terrified of his presence—it was the mission of the Klan as far back as it existed in history. She stood rocklike and unwavering. Defensive. Protective. But not the aggressor.

She couldn't deny her desire to see him suffer. A single shot with the Glock would be too humane of a death for this monster.

She longed to hobble him with a bullet to the leg, fire another into his testicles, and stand over him while he pleaded for mercy, as she emptied the chamber point blank between his eyes. She wished she had the vengeance now to end his existence—but her purpose remained directed, focused on saving Elyse's life. She couldn't do anything that would interfere with her clearing her name, returning to her family, whole and sane.

Marburg and Lindstrom would lock her up for murder.

Something was festering inside him. She could see it, trying to come out.

Bourdain was breathing faster.

His veins bulged from his temple, grew bright blue, glistening with his sweat.

They were face to face.

Bourdain pointed the rifle at Sara, and then down at Veronica. "You killed Kayla. Both of you."

Veronica screamed, and backed herself against the wall. Bourdain tore back the wooden door, typed into the computer. "Jorge, we tried to save her."

"I've armed the bomb to annihilate the White House. I'll release *Labrador* in five American cities at midnight. The bulk of my work is done. We'll see what kind of control I have over your race when no one can access your pathetic hospitals, your clinics, your doctors."

"I want him alive, Wes," said Marburg. He and Lindstrom stepped across the threshold of the front door.

Jorge Bourdain turned around.

"Good afternoon," said Lindstrom.

"Well aren't you slick as owl shit." Jorge Bourdain looked Lindstrom up and down.

"He knows how to cure the fucking virus, Wes. I'll look even better when we bring him in and we bring the outbreak to an end." Marburg clutched the submachine gun.

"You'll be a national hero. A presidential hopeful." Lindstrom's teeth gleamed.

"That's right," said Marburg. "A presidential hopeful."

"How long have you lived in Washington, kitten?" Lindstrom asked Sara. He took several casual steps toward her.

"My whole life." She kept the Glock, and her eyes, trained on Bourdain. "I know all about you. Every contribution your company has made in the last ten years. And they've all gone into his pocket." She jerked her head toward Marburg.

"Then you should know how things are done. People like the senator and I make the laws. Some would say we are the law."

"You didn't think anyone would notice that you made a real-life national disaster out of my story?"

"That wasn't the initial plan, until the scientist here got carried away," said Marburg. "We had a deal with Dr. Recart, but he seems to be indisposed at the moment. Maybe Mr. Bourdain can help us locate him."

"That's why we're all gathered here today," said Lindstrom. "To clean up this mess and go the fuck home. I've probably got supper waiting for me as we speak. We'll go back to the law-making sandbox and you—"

"We've got to get the cure out fast. We're all losing time. We've already lost Hans, Kayla and the lab." Veronica was getting up from the corner.

Lindstrom fired a shot at the floor, narrowly missing her leg. "The senator and I don't like to be interrupted, young lady."

"You'll never find Claus." Bourdain laughed. "He took your money and ran. If I know Recart, he's living in a hole in the wall somewhere in Tijuana."

Veronica tried to get up from the creaky floor again. "There are only a handful of us who know how to cure *Labrador*, but we can end it. Be logical about this."

Veronica was still protesting when Lindstrom aimed a Colt and shot her in the chest as though he was swatting a fly.

Sara flinched, nearly dropped the Glock.

Lindstrom looked up, frowning, shrugged. "Now there's one less. Not bad for my first shot. What do you think, Mr. Bourdain? Care to negotiate with us now about ending the outbreak? We can work out a solution that's lucrative to both parties."

"I'm not in this for money, you imbeciles." Through clenched teeth, paranoid eyes, Bourdain explained, "We're going live in a matter of minutes. My father and the *world* will see the man that I've become, and the leader that I'm capable of being—a man who has pulled himself up from...*nothing*."

There was no reasoning his perspective.

No justification for his actions.

She gripped the gun tighter, until the muscles in her hand cramped. Jorge Bourdain could be a wild shot, a loose cannon.

She couldn't move her aim from him. The senator and Wes Lindstrom wanted him alive. But they'd want her dead—even her family.

She knew too much.

Shoot to kill.

Don't shoot to wound, she heard Marty saying now.

Shoot to kill.

But she couldn't afford to kill either of them and expect to walk free. Not with the current state of suspicion and unrest and corruption compromising national security. And she couldn't kill both of them with one shot. If she died, Bourdain would find LeTorneau and kill him. Thousands, maybe millions, would die of infection.

Elyse.

Sweat dripped from her brow.

She was paralyzed.

She wasn't trained for this.

With his broken leg, LeTorneau was too weak to escape without her help. If he was dead, she had no protection from Marburg, Lindstrom. They'd put her away, if they didn't kill her first. LeTorneau was her alibi, even though she was surrounded by the real criminals. She had to get them both out alive.

"Drop the gun, princess," said Lindstrom.

She didn't budge.

Marburg aimed his Uzi with one arm at Jorge Bourdain. He drew back the door with the other, revealing the alcove where the glowing red and yellow lights, and the timer, were concealed. "Is this another one of your fucking science projects?"

Bourdain laughed.

"It's a bomb." Sara glanced at Marburg for an instant, then back at Jorge Bourdain.

"Let's go, big boy," said Marburg.

Bourdain turned, walked out of the cabin, into the backyard, with his hands up, still laughing.

"Stay on him," shouted Lindstrom.

"Wes, we need backup," said Marburg. "Look at the coordinates on the bomb."

"Mr. Bourdain doesn't offer equal opportunities," she said. "Not even to the president and First Lady. His employees are out back." She swallowed and stared to the left, as Lindstrom pressed his Colt to her temple. Her sweat dripped against the cold metal.

"Get me backup, Wes," Marburg repeated. "This motherfucker is behind every one of the explosions, including Arlington National Cemetery. We're bringing him in alive. We're going to keep him until he shares the cure with us. Then we'll go after Claus."

"It's too risky to call in a favor now. Not until we take care of things here. We'll both go down." Lindstrom cocked his pistol, still calm. To Sara, he said, "Drop it. I'll ask you nicely for the last time."

"Only a matter of hours before this thing detonates the goddamn White House, Wes."

"Plenty of time to evacuate, Senator."

Lindstrom's overconfidence was almost convincing.

She shifted her aim toward Marburg, who'd watched Bourdain disappear out the back door of the cabin. Lindstrom pressed the Colt further into the skin of her temple. If he were going to shoot now, he would've done it. He needed something from her.

LeTorneau.

Was he still alive?

She conceded, tossed Marty's pistol to the wooden floor, stepped back with her hands in the air. Marburg followed after Jorge Bourdain, holding his semiautomatic now with both hands. Lindstrom put his pistol in his holster and twisted her arms behind her back. He tied her wrists with the rope Bourdain used for dragging animal kills. Then he secured them around the heaviest piece of furniture in the room, an eight-foot armoire, pushing her to her knees.

"Are you crazy? Don't worry about her. She'll be dead by the time they get here. Just get me the fucking FBI, Wes," Marburg called, exited the back door of the cabin. "This is going to go down quick."

"Here's what's going to happen," said Lindstrom, to Sara. His grin grew wider as he explained. "We're going to get the recipe these bat shit crazy scientists cooked up to cure this virus. And you're going to tell us where the professor is, so we can get the capital back to its usual state of health. Then the senator and I are going to erase every money, cell phone and paper trail between us and them. You're going to go back to writing stories and prescribing antibiotics for the common cold, and we're both going to pretend we never met, *Capiche*?"

"No Capiche." She spit in his face. "Most colds are caused by viruses, and not cured by antibiotics."

Lindstrom pulled the cord tighter around the leg of the armoire, making it nearly impossible for her to move. She groaned. "Usually women scream a little louder when I tie them up, but at my age, I'll take what I can get."

She struggled against the weight of the armoire. She kicked fruitlessly at Lindstrom's ankles without effect. She tried to loosen the restraints. "You're going to kill me. I'm not telling you where LeTorneau is until I get the cure to save my daughter."

"That a girl. You should've stayed home with her and been a good mommy, instead of sticking your nose in government business where it doesn't belong." He bound her wrists with a sailor's knot. She winced as he pulled the rope taut. "I guess you know a lobbyist like me is lying when my lips are moving. I shouldn't pretend to deny that—it's bad for my character." He rose to his feet, examined his finger nails, and smoothed his suit coat.

"You're disgusting."

Lindstrom frowned and examined his reflection in the dusty wall mirror. "Listen, you're right—I can't promise anything for you, Dr. Sullivan, or even your husband. You *both* know too much, but your daughter, we can talk about. Everyone loves a baby. Now there's a deal I might be able to keep my word on. A man has nothing if not for his word." He winked. Then he picked up the Glock, walked out onto the back porch.

Outside the cabin, the *bratatat* sound from Marburg's Uzi rang out. She loosened the cord bound around her as much as she could, and she stood, restrained and hunched over, peering out the back window. With cold-blooded precision, Marburg mowed down the neo-Confederates assembled around the pulpit. They twitched, shook, their spines crumpled, as bullets ripped through their robes, fell to the ground like burlap sacks of Idaho potatoes.

Marburg loaded another magazine.

Bourdain snatched a small gas lamp on the stacked hay bales, raced into the labyrinth. Marburg chased after him, holding his fire.

Lindstrom followed.

From what she could see, they split in different directions when they entered the maze.

By then, it was dark. The dew on the grass silenced the crunch of footsteps on the stalks. She saw only shadows as they ran into the corn. Now a faint smell of burning leaves reached her nose. It was not unpleasant, much like a campfire. But she craned her neck and saw the stalks igniting into larger flames, spreading quickly into the west end of the orchard, burning and crackling, smoking where the corn was wet and throwing embers onto the grass and into the westward wind.

Jorge Bourdain had set fire to the maze.

It was obvious he'd wanted Marburg and Lindstrom to follow. Was he leading them to something important—the cure? Maybe he'd reason with them. They had power, influence, money, and connections.

She had none of those things.

Bourdain knew the way out, but if she went in after them, would she be able to solve the maze and get LeTorneau away alive? Was the professor still alright, waiting for her rescue in the back of the John Deere? It had been some time since she'd left him to search for Kayla. Even worse, finding a way to detonate the bomb and to prevent Jorge Bourdain from releasing more of the *Labrador* virus seemed the most impossible task of all. As her thoughts raced, another pungent smell reached her senses, mixed with the smoky air.

Gasoline.

She had only a few minutes before the entire labyrinth and cabin went up into another explosive inferno. From her back pocket, Marty's cell phone rang.

The voice prompt on the phone announced an incoming call, followed by a series of numbers that she recognized as a hospital number.

It had to be Marty.

She shook the phone from her back pocket and it fell to the floor. Why hadn't she asked for his help sooner? She'd hear it from him for sure, but she wasn't entirely ready to let him know that she'd forgiven him for setting her up in his attempt to protect her. With the heel of her boot, she answered the call, tapped the speaker button.

"Hi, honey."

"Sara, are you alright? Where are you?"

"I'm a little tied up at the moment. How's my baby doing?"

"I'm fine, Sara. Where are you?"

"I meant Elyse."

"Sara, Elyse's test results came back negative for *Labrador*. She has some other bacterial infection whose name I can't pronounce. But thanks to the intravenous line you started, she's hydrated and improving on antibiotics. They're moving her out of the *Labrador* isolation unit."

"That's great, Marty." She exhaled, looked around at her current dilemma. "Stay with her. Please. Don't leave her side."

"She's improving. And she doesn't have the virus. You can come home now."

"I'm kind of in trouble," she said. "Can you send help?"

"Sara, *where are you?*" His voice was loud and gruff now, more like the Marty she knew, and she knew this meant that Elyse really was improving. The connection was full of static, and she was worried about losing the call.

"Somewhere between Fredericksburg and Charlottesville — where you go hunting, Marty."

"Never mind. I'll get the coordinates from the 'Find My Phone' app online. Just don't turn it off again," said Marty. "Sara, why don't you ever know when to ask for help?"

"I know. I'm working on that," she said. "I think I've got this, but if you could send some backup, that would be great. There's another explosion set to detonate in a few hours."

"Where?"

"Fifteen-hundred Pennsylvania Avenue."

"*The White House?* I'm coming to get you."

She knew she should've involved him sooner, but she had to stay focused to get out of Jorge Bourdain's racist playground alive, with Professor LeTorneau.

"No. Stay with Elyse. I'll be okay. Just find help. Please. I have to go." She disconnected the call, still searching around the room for a way out of the restraints.

The screen flickered on above the stone pulpit where the dead Klansmen lay. Jorge Bourdain's face consumed the monitor, an attempt to advance his cult of personality. Behind him, a black man was tied tightly to the largest of three burning crosses inside the maze.

She squinted to see.

It was LeTorneau.

Bourdain's deep voice had the confidence of a dictator already in power. *Hitler. Stalin. Mussolini.* A reprise of all the depravity of the last two centuries was personified in him, a timeless evil, repeated in this loathsome man.

His brown hair clung in greasy chunks against his sloping forehead. She had no doubt that he harbored fears, childhood wounds. She dismissed any excuses, and she swallowed, and she rubbed the cord binding her wrists against the armoire. She strained her back muscles pulling at the furniture, dragging it across the room to where a knife lay on the table. Then she pulled even harder.

It was no use to her without the use of her hands.

Jorge Bourdain had been educated.

He'd attended college, Veronica had said.

He was a graduate student, a PhD candidate.

He could've rejected his fears, defeated the wrongs of his upbringing, but he'd chosen not to rise above that weakness. He wasn't the first man to be poisoned by the past. It angered her so much that the adrenaline ripping through her bloodstream gave her the strength to drag the heavy wooden armoire across the room.

With her shoulder, she bumped the table, knocked over a kerosene lamp on the wooden table.

It smashed to the floor.

The flames licked the spilled liquid on the throw rug.

She held her bound wrists over the fire, felt the heat scorching her skin.

Now she felt her own flesh burn.

With a scream, she ripped the frayed rope apart.

She stamped out the remaining flames, and then she stood and she tore off the rest of the rope. She ran to the back, facing the orchard. LeTorneau was still pinned to the white cross, rising from the center. The fire threatened his life from all sides.

Bourdain had a huge advantage: he knew every twist and turn in the network of passages he'd created. Lindstrom and Marburg were her other obstacle.

She had no gun now.

She grabbed the serrated knife on the table beside her.

Outside, the keys were still in the John Deere tractor-truck. She got behind the wheel and she drove it full speed through the east end of the orchard, through cottonwood trees, thorny bushes, tearing through the stalks to LeTorneau's rescue.

Overhead, a helicopter circled.

She honked the tractor's horn, waved it down, but it passed again. On its third sweep over the orchard, it hovered closer to her, and she waved to it again and she screamed with her head out of the cab of the John Deere. The flames expanded, engulfing the apple trees. She swerved, changed direction. The helicopter circled back, lowering near a row of blackberry bushes.

They'd spotted the fire.

The blades chopped at the wind, creating a downdraft. Although it was a relief from the heat, it fueled the flames. They grew higher inside the stone walls of the maze now, and she turned her face from the intense heat.

She spotted LeTorneau—he was tied to a cross in a clearing of pear trees, just as she'd seen on Bourdain's broadcast, screaming for help. Two other victims were tied to smaller crosses on either side of him, also screaming wildly. Flames engulfed the area from three sides now, with the blaze expanding rapidly. She parked the John Deere and she rushed out and she loosened the ropes. She pulled LeTorneau down and she hoisted him into the back of the tractor-truck bed. Then she untied the two others, a middle-aged black woman and an elderly black man. She helped them into the back of the tailgate. They clutched the sides as she tore out of the clearing.

If the flames grew any closer to the truck, she'd risk an explosion. There was no way she could get them out safely on foot.

She couldn't see over the concrete and the stone walls to the other side.

She prayed.

The chopper lowered its rotors over the center of the maze.

LeTorneau wasn't strong enough to walk on foot.

His fractured bone was pushing through the skin. Bleeding marrow protruding inches from the integument, bulging further when he attempted to move. Despite the heat, he was shivering. She knew it was from the blood loss, and that he'd need a blood transfusion in order to survive. He was going into shock, and she'd have to help get him into the chopper, but she had to steer the John Deere away from the expanding inferno first. She looked back at him. LeTorneau held pressure on his own wound as she made sharp turns through the cornfield.

The others screamed as she smashed through walls and tore down rows of corn, hoping to avoid the ditches Bourdain had dug as traps, but as the John Deere blew through a dead end, the front wheel of the vehicle sunk beneath her, into a pit filled with leaves and mud. Behind her, the flames were crackling, intensifying with the southwesterly wind, and blowing dangerously close to the vehicle.

"Shit." She gunned the tractor in reverse.

The vehicle was stuck.

She gassed it forward again and then in reverse, rocking the front end loose, and barreling backward out of the depression. Then she floored the pedal and veered over the side of the pit, careening over it and barely clearing the back end with her tires.

"Get me out of here," screamed the middle-aged African-American woman. "Don't you let me burn in here!"

"Look out," The elderly man, whose name was Darius Carding, dodged one of the rectangular beams covering the archways, as it fell on the front end of the vehicle, ablaze and glowing hot.

It hit the hood with a loud thud, smashed the windshield, and flew back over the top of the speeding vehicle. Darius Carding grabbed the hysterical woman and pulled her down into the bed of the tractor-truck, as the beam flew over the back end of the vehicle.

"Don't you let me burn." The woman would not stop screaming. She seemed to be hallucinating as well, batting at objects that weren't there, a traumatic stress reaction perhaps. "You drive us out of here or we're all going to burn alive."

"What's your name?" asked Sara.

"Jennie Thomas," the woman said. "Don't you let me burn."

"Jennie, I need you to be quiet. I'm trying. I'm trying to save you," she said. "Please sit down." The screams pierced her ears, as the woman leaned over into the cab of the John Deere. She tried to focus on obstacles ahead, getting the attention of the helicopter and avoiding the flames, but every time she tore through a dead end, the fire seemed to spread, swallowing them from all directions.

"There he is," Jennie Thomas screamed.

"Jennie, please. I'm trying," she begged. At first, she was certain the woman was hallucinating, but Jorge Bourdain had in fact, appeared before them. She made a sharp left, following him, said, with determination, "He knows the way out."

The helicopter hovered down.

They were confined by fire with nowhere to go.

Even Bourdain was trapped.

She could see the search and rescue crew above her, ebbing away and then drawing near, trying to get within reach, while keeping a safe distance from the flames.

The rescue team called out to her.

It was difficult to hear with the chopper blades and the engine gusting in the wind. The team lowered a crane. It swung back and forth until she was able to grab the hoist. She pulled her body up onto the door of the pickup. With the tractor-truck in park, Jorge Bourdain ran toward them among the burning stalks.

She fastened the harness around LeTorneau, clipped him to the cable.

The crew lifted him up.

LeTorneau winced as the cable brushed his leg. It dangled, motionless, and his weak body was pulled up into the interior of the helicopter.

A second chopper lowered a cable with a sling. She could've fit herself, Jennie Thomas and Darius Carding in the hoist—it was the kind of crane lift capable of hauling heavy equipment, but Jorge Bourdain was climbing up the hood.

She couldn't let him get control of the vehicle.

She had securely fastened the others into the sling when Jorge Bourdain threw the vehicle out of park, knocking her off her balance, as she stood up in the back of the truck. The vehicle began to move, slowly at first, away from the rescuers, with Jennie Thomas and Darius Carding dangling from the rescue cable.

She kicked open the back window, smashing the glass. She tried to wrestle Jorge Bourdain from the wheel.

"Jump," screamed Jennie Thomas. "Get in now."

Fire was burning against the right side window of the vehicle. She felt the heat off the smoldering glass.

"I can't," yelled Sara. "It's too far."

She signaled to the driver to hoist the others. She'd have to hope they could make another pass, or she'd have to find another way out of the maze, now almost completely encircled in flames. The first chopper that had rescued LeTorneau was lowering its harness, but the John Deere was moving now.

Jorge Bourdain was behind the wheel.

She grabbed the pocket knife, put it to his throat.

"Get us out of here," she screamed.

"I'm getting out of here, but not with you," Bourdain said.

Behind her, the first chopper drew closer. It had a smaller hoist, and she wasn't sure she could reach it. Its lights were visible, but it was difficult to see the cable against the night sky, even with the fire illuminating the dark. Bourdain grabbed at her wrist, and she stabbed at his weak arm with the deer knife, causing him to veer from his path. The truck hit a stone wall, blowing right through it, and sending debris over the top of the tractor-truck in all directions.

She glanced over her shoulder.

The rescue cable was dangling again, swaying from the helicopter in a pendulous arc.

She grabbed the steering wheel and with all her strength, she pulled it to the right, and closer to the cable.

Jorge Bourdain's weak arm was not able to stop her, and the vehicle blew through the corn maze and barreled into the cabin, now completely ablaze. A burning beam crashed onto the roof of the tractor-truck just as she jumped off, at the last instant, catching the cable with her arms. The metal was almost too hot to touch, but she clung to it with all the strength she had in her shoulders and trunk, as it pulled up and away from the explosive wreck of the John Deere. Bourdain screamed as it smashed into the cabin, bursting into a ball of fire that rose above the flames in the house, swallowing him in heat, with no one to extricate him from the crash.

LeTorneau was being medically stabilized in the chopper. The team pulled Sara into the helicopter. She looked back in horror as Bourdain, his body a human torch, burst from the cab of the tractor, and staggered blindly, pitifully, for several paces, before falling in a heap in the dirt, where his prone form continued to burn.

-28-

Sara Sullivan

Sara looked down from the cockpit of the chopper. Below them, police and fire trucks raced up to the burning orchard. Marburg and Lindstrom stood on the center stone, awaiting rescue, where Bourdain had built the wooden crosses. It was the highest point of the orchard, overlooking the Blue Ridge Mountains for miles. She was relieved to be alive, but the bomb in the White House and the biological weapons armed with the *Labrador* virus were set to detonate in a matter of hours.

With Jorge Bourdain and his secret society of neo-Confederates dead, who else knew how to stop it?

The helicopters landed in the back of the orchard. A third chopper hoisted Marburg and Lindstrom. The fire trucks extinguished the portion of the blaze surrounding them, and with most of the cornfield burned away, she could see the large shrine on a decayed concrete platform that Jorge Bourdain had constructed in the center of his twisted path. At its pinnacle was a white stone tomb, reminiscent of the old cemeteries of New Orleans. It was much like the graveyard on Legion Drive where she'd discovered the neo-Confederate cult. An iron gate surrounded the shrine with spiral pickets, where stone gargoyles guarded the entrance.

The FBI quickly accessed the structure, which remained protected from the heat of the blaze. Cars from the Albemarle County Sheriff's and those of Marty's precinct pulled up alongside rows of apple trees. She covered her mouth and coughed on the smoky air, gasping for breath, as a paramedic wrapped her bare shoulders in a blanket.

She figured it would take hours to completely extinguish the massive fire.

"We'll need to get you medical treatment. You may have a smoke inhalation injury. I see a few singed nasal hairs, and I hear crackles in your lungs." The medic hung his stethoscope around his neck. "We have to be careful administering oxygen near the fire, but if you're alright, we can observe you here until we can transport you safely to the hospital."

"I'm fine." She rose to her feet, starting toward the federal agents. Then she coughed again, gasped, tried to get a larger breath of air. "On second thought, I'll take it easy. Thank you."

She smiled at the medic, and he patted her on the back.

Inside the ceremonial tomb, the Feds exhumed the remains of a single man from the recess, filled with relics and memorials of New Orleans. Faux golden crosses and crystal charms and ornate candelabras decorated iron baker's shelves inside the underground coffin. Symbols and masks of voodoo worship covered the walls. Inscribed on the tomb and across the sanctified altar was the name of the man laid to rest, Henri Bourdain, Jorge's father.

Whether Jorge had taken his father's life was uncertain, but the more significant discovery was the stone basement and remains of the foundation surrounding the shrine. A hidden network of tunnels went far beneath the exterior structure. Bourdain had filled it with many of the same French Quarter religious and voodoo relics, adorned it in *Milagros* charms.

She wondered: How long had this diabolical hate group been operating under the benevolent guise of the Louisiana Conservation Group? Despite the heat from the dwindling blaze, the enormity of Bourdain and his followers' depravity gave her chills. She wanted answers—to examine the cult's history and sick philosophy and to piece the whole sordid story together, but she could only digest a little at a time. According to the agents, the people the Klan members had killed were likely men and women with no family, possibly homeless, whose disappearances were unlikely to be reported. Their bodies, too, were exhumed from the remains. The pattern suggested that Bourdain had chosen his victims carefully.

Inside the network of tunnels, Bourdain had placed stolen equipment from LeTorneau's lab: his laptop, numerous USB drives and files regarding the *Labrador* antibody production.

What still confused her was how Lindstrom and Marburg had struck a deal to somehow release the virus. Their motive was obvious—driven by money and power, but they were as shocked as she was to uncover Bourdain's neo-Confederate network. If LeTorneau hadn't been involved with them as Veronica had insisted, where had they gotten access to the virus, and to someone mad enough to release it just to drive up the stock for the pharmaceutical cure?

Veronica had mentioned another scientist—Claus Recart.

Dr. LeTorneau was giving a preliminary statement to an FBI special agent from the Richmond, Virginia office, as the medics placed an intravenous line in his arm. They quickly splinted and immobilized his fractured leg. A sheriff's deputy and a detective from Marty's precinct were also present during the interview.

She listened carefully.

"There are few accidents, Doctor Sullivan," explained Dr. LeTorneau. "I'm afraid there are far more premeditated crises than we appreciate."

"I don't follow, Professor LeTorneau." She was grappling with the sequence of the events, the index cases that had started in a remote village in Africa, and she was still worried that Senator Marburg and his lobbyist from Phaedrex could use their influence to indict her in the catastrophe. *Labrador* was spreading, and even with Bourdain dead, the cure was not accessible to those who needed it. "I'm still trying to wrap my mind around this."

"Dr. Claus Recart worked on the vaccine for the virus in his lab in Canada. He isolated it there, named it after the province of Labrador. It's not the kind of big government facility like the one that allowed me to discover the antibody—Claus is a recluse. His lab is hidden away in a remote fishing village where not even the locals know what goes on inside, but that should fool no one. He had plenty of funding, sponsorship—public and private. There's always stiff competition to be first to market. His company, NewfoundVax, had the vaccine ready for manufacture." LeTorneau pointed to Marburg and Lindstrom, who were being escorted out of the helicopter by federal agents. "Those two struck a deal with him for the vaccine. They never imagined what *Labrador* would do. How quickly it would spread. They expected it to work for them: money, power, more money. *Labrador* doesn't operate like Washington."

"How did Bourdain know?"

"I don't believe he knew anything of their plan. He was a good fit in Recart's lab. Spoke French well enough, and for the most part he did whatever Claus told him to do. He sent Jorge as a mole to work in my lab, but he never really fit in. I suspected it right away. He looked at me strangely. Avoided me. And life in D.C. was different than anything he'd known. When I discovered evidence of him keeping stockpiles of the vaccine that only Claus had worked on—I confronted him. It was only a day before the Society of Evolutionary Biology meeting. I'd been getting racist threats, but I wanted to keep it quiet—figure out what was going on. I had no idea about any of this."

"How much of the vaccine did he steal?"

"Only enough to vaccinate himself and a few of his allies. I believe he became involved with this resurgent faction of the Ku Klux Klan on the Internet, and started concocting his own radical ideas. Altered the virus. There is no denying he was scientifically gifted. These people bought into it."

"I feel sick," she said. "I regret ever sending my story to Lindstrom's wife."

"It would've been worse if not for your bravery. You may have stopped a biological Armageddon, and I thank you for saving my life."

She offered a humble nod. She was still terrified about Elyse, the bomb, the plan to release the virus. The capital was still under a state of martial law, and the citizens had limited access to healthcare.

"What about Dr. Recart? He must have the knowledge, maybe enough of the vaccine to stop *Labrador* from spreading?"

Her face was dirty and her eyes were heavy. She wanted more than anything to be home with Marty and Elyse, to say she was sorry for abandoning them, for being an absent wife and mother, but the epidemic wasn't over.

She couldn't rest.

Not yet.

"I have no doubt he does. But finding him may be another obstacle. He wanted to cut another deal with those two." LeTorneau motioned toward Marburg and Lindstrom, who were being examined near an ambulance at the far end of the field. "He got greedy. Tried to involve me. Promised me instant wealth beyond my wildest dreams."

"What did you tell them?" asked the FBI special agent.

"I told him to go to hell, never trusted him." LeTorneau grimaced, as the medics elevated his leg. "Then before the society meeting, I started receiving the racist threats. I was kidnapped the night before my speech."

LeTorneau was growing too weak to speak. He closed his eyes and she covered him with the blanket. Then, to the lawmen, she explained, "Marburg and Wes Lindstrom commissioned Claus to develop the vaccine before the virus ever touched our soil, and they staged a release to make it look like tourists brought it back from Africa. Maybe they did, but they were fully responsible. Dr. LeTorneau's right. They knew a few cases would demand a vaccine, and with them invested in it, that meant millions in payoff."

"They got in over their heads with their idea," said the FBI agent. The deputy and the detective nodded in agreement.

They stood on guard, as the politician and his lobbyist drew near. "How did you get involved, miss?"

She glared at him.

"Doctor, I mean. Sorry."

She gave a single nod. "You might say Lindstrom plagiarized my scenario about a catastrophic healthcare crisis and turned it into reality. It was a story—I wrote and sent it to his wife, a publishing house editor. It was never supposed to come to fruition. I started looking into things. The events were just too similar to my story to be a coincidence, but I never expected anyone to be so reckless for what—a few million dollars?"

"A few million? Doctor, this is Washington," said the detective. "They'll swindle you for a sandwich here."

"I know I wasn't the one who started this, but I feel responsible—I thought I was going to lose my daughter, Elyse, to it. I still might." She knew she could be home now, smelling the scent of her daughter's baby skin, rubbing Desitin on her bottom, and taking in her sweet breath. She was at Bourdain's nightmarish compound by choice, now captive to the events.

The FBI agent said, "It's very likely that if it weren't for Jorge Bourdain, their plan would've succeeded and stopped at a few cases. No one could've predicted this kind of chaos."

Graham LeTorneau's eyes fluttered open, and he cleared his throat. "When Recart knew I wasn't far behind him with the antibody to cure the virus, he sent Bourdain in as a mole, but Jorge had his own motives. Jorge told me about his abusive upbringing many times. I believe he spent hours online and self-radicalized there first. His mind was filled with such hatred, such unrest." The medic offered LeTorneau some water, and he swallowed it in large gulps. "He always wanted to please his father, and became unglued trying to do so. The old man was a Cajun—his family emigrated from Newfoundland a few generations back, but he was stuck in the ways of the antebellum South. I saw that in Jorge. His mind was a prison to his fears, to the scars of his past, but this…I never imagined he was capable of such evil." LeTorneau's voice was barely audible.

The medic offered more water, took LeTorneau's pulse.

"Racism is still an ugly, ongoing part of our history. There's no excuse for it. There's some level of mental illness here, but this was all premeditated," the special agent remarked.

"He was slipping deeper into his psychosis. We can tell by the way he got sloppy—forgetting to cover his tracks, leaving evidence in plain sight. Not exactly a careful killer," said the detective. "I just radioed two men at his apartment. SWAT team just raided the place, said he left information about the explosions pinned to the wall. He was proud of his work. And of this unholy place." The detective shook his head.

Another contingent of FBI agents appeared from the smoldering wreckage, with Marburg and Lindstrom in tow. The conspirators' faces were covered in soot. Their hair was singed, disheveled. Marburg's suit had gotten soaked, and he looked rather like a drowned rat.

"Officer, I want this woman arrested," Marburg shouted over the police and fire sirens. He pointed an accusatory finger at her.

"Senator, *you're* under arrest," said the FBI special agent. He jerked his head at Lindstrom, added, "And your sleazy wingman, too. Deputy, place these men in handcuffs and read them Miranda rights.

"You have nothing on us," said Lindstrom. "You can't place a United States senator in handcuffs like a common criminal."

"Don't we?" said the FBI special agent. "We've had orders signed by a judge to investigate you. We've discovered email and money trails on both of you from a bank in Newfoundland and Labrador that ran through Lindstrom's laptop. You were both in Miami when the funds were transferred, and Marburg's tracks through Uganda have you caught like fat kids in a Cape May candy store."

"The Senator attempted to bring in the conspirator alive. He risked his own life," Lindstrom objected. "We're one move away from getting the cure and the vaccine to the American public."

"The American public can't even get to a doctor's office under your management of this crisis," said the deputy.

"You're officially relieved of your position as chief of the *Labrador* response, and relieved of your duties as a sitting United States senator. You are being indicted on charges of fraud, conspiracy, endangering the lives of Americans with a biological weapon of mass destruction. Shall I continue?" the FBI special agent said.

"I'm not saying a thing. I'm an attorney. I know my rights," said Marburg.

He looked at her and even though he was restrained now, he looked sinister in the firelight, and she feared him. Marburg had connections, contacts in Washington that could get him out of trouble and destroy the prosecution's attempt to convict him—and ruin her.

"Officer, this woman is responsible for inciting fear and mass hysteria, and I have her publication to prove it." Lindstrom raged, as an officer shoved him into a police car.

Marburg was loaded into a separate vehicle.

"What about the bomb?" she asked. She coughed again as the wind blew the smoke towards them.

Another FBI agent spoke up. "Every government building in the District's been evacuated, ma'am. From the looks of the evidence from the other explosions, it doesn't look like Bourdain's knowledge of explosives was too advanced. We've got a team on site—a guy who worked under Dwight Eisenhower on diffusing bombs left behind from the Second World War—and a full disposal team with him. He's older than dirt, but he was a trained Ammunition Technical Officer, and he has more knowledge than anyone I've ever seen. He's willing to die going in there. He's been doing this for decades and never failed yet."

"We have full confidence that he'll be able to detonate the explosive ordinance device and live to tell about it," said his partner.

"The White House depends on it," she said. "What about the biological weapons Bourdain planned to release? He altered the virus to specifically target blacks, and it's mutating fast."

"We're not certain how many people exist in Bourdain's network," the first FBI special agent replied. "It's been on the NSA watch list for a while. Their Internet activity has been flagged, but we've had no hard evidence to bring them in until now. We believe it's a small, close-knit group confined to an area in D.C. and the Appalachians, but there could be outliers."

"How many are dead here?"

"Fourteen, including Bourdain," said the Albemarle County Sheriff. "Another six from the restaurant on Legion Drive have been taken into questioning."

"Our only hope is to make the cure available—get people vaccinated in the areas of potential exposure," LeTorneau advised. "It will take at least a few weeks, maybe months, with a very large scale response and a new lab, but it can be done. *Labrador* can be stopped."

"But how are you going to find this Claus guy if he's produced a vaccine as you claim?" asked the Sheriff. He looked concerned.

Sara stood up. "I know where to find him."

-29-

Mount Morungole, Uganda
Sara Sullivan

Sara had been tapped for her medical expertise to assist the special agents in extraditing Dr. Claus Recart on the ground in Uganda. She was fit enough to make the thousand-foot climb to the top of Mount Morungole, and she could've raced to the top on her adrenaline alone, and turned the village upside down, if there were anything left of it, but the United States Central Intelligence Agency had provided transportation and security personnel for the pursuit and capture of Dr. Recart with cooperation from the Ugandan government.

And Marty had pulled a few strings to get her a place on the mission—to make up for his mistake.

Back home on U.S. soil, the CDC had commissioned a second lab for the exigent manufacture of *Labrador* antibody in Washington. The chemical process was time-consuming and labor-intensive on its own, but Sara and Dr. LeTorneau presented the late students' findings, that convinced the administration to circumvent the bureaucratic delays and FDA red tape.

The government estimated that it would take three-hundred-million dollars to create enough doses to treat newly-infected patients, and to vaccinate in all of the areas of potential exposure in order to stamp out the virus. Legislators agreed that the quarantines and limited access to care were worsening the situation, and they appointed a physician at the CDC to head the response. The education and proper screening and prevention measures that were botched by Senator Marburg's team were assigned to a new official. These measures were expected to reduce the number of new cases to zero within four months—provided that they could also produce enough vaccine for the circulating strains. Every day the cure was delayed meant new cases, and an increased risk that the pernicious virus would be an inextirpable part of American life.

The window to eradicate *Labrador* was closing, the embers of its fire still kindling.

Interpol had put out several red notices on Dr. Recart. The FBI had been given information about his possible location by Ugandan officials, as well as permission to extradite him on the ground. Now, as the expedition team went after the vaccine, and Recart, the plane broke through the gray blanket of mist, landed in a field, blowing the whispering thorns and elephant grass, as it made a rough landing that jarred Sara's neck. She'd had trouble sleeping for weeks, and even the magnificent scenery failed to brighten her eyes.

She drove the jeep to the top of the mountain through the humid jungle, unafraid of the hairpin turns. When the group reached the summit where the Make-A-Wish safari had traveled earlier that year, they found it deserted, with the exception of a few women and children. She surveyed the primitive scene: empty thatch huts and bare pits, devoid of livestock, the smell of acrid flesh and smoke.

The Ik people had been known to eat their young in times of starvation. A single male elder stood in the center of the village, swathed in yellow and purple cloth, attempting to start a fire. The women scattered into their huts as the jeep bounced closer up the hillside. A young girl, carrying a baby on her back, stopped, stared at her and the two FBI agents.

The tribal elder shunned the group, but the young girl held her hands out, and Sara extended half of her bologna and cheese sandwich with mayonnaise on wheat. The girl scrunched her eyes shyly, but smiled, and took the offering. The elder man immediately confiscated it, and stashed it among his belongings in a cloth sack, scolded the young child. The girl shouted in protest and he kicked at the ground at her feet, brushing her away like the arid dirt. The child's muscles were atrophied, and her breath smelled of famine where Sara knelt beside her, but her eyes were bright, innocent. The girl crinkled the corner of her mouth in a smile, perhaps another desperate plea for food, and it made Sara smile, reflexively. The girl's frayed hair was wrapped tightly in yellow cloth. She tucked it in further and pointed to a clearing, surrounded by acacia trees, and shaded from the sun.

"She knows," special agent Thomas McConnell muttered.

The girl and the baby made a shy procession with the expedition toward a huge canvas platform tent. As Sara pulled back the tarp, the girl scampered back to the village.

Sara surveyed the interior of the primitive clinic: laboratory equipment, a bin filled with clean needles and syringes, intravenous fluids and glass beakers full of liquid, cots in the corner covered with threadbare cloth, a basin of water.

"Do you always get your way, Doctor?" asked special agent Jeffery Berg.

"Only when I'm right," she whispered. She pointed her finger toward the underbrush. "Please wait there. This is between me and Dr. Recart."

"Alright, but be careful," Berg said. "We'll be monitoring the situation."

She nodded. She was wired so that the federal agents could hear her, and provide backup if she needed help.

Peering through the tent flap, she observed the tall man's work. He used a knife to slaughter a fruit bat against the stone counter. Six other bats lay in a pulverized mess on the stone mortar in front of him.

A hard suitcase and a silver briefcase rested on the floor.

Keys on the counter.

Knives of various serrations, sizes.

A large container displayed a biohazard logo, and a medical apparatus for rudimentary blood collection and centrifugation. Her foot snapped a twig as she stepped inside, setting off a large flurry of whistles from the red-breasted birds in the trees.

The man turned abruptly, faced her.

His yellowed linen shirt was covered in the blood of the animals.

"You'd make a lousy hunter," the man said. He set down the knife. "How did you find me?"

"I didn't know it was you I was looking for." She barely got the words out. "Until now. Dr. Recart?"

She held a pistol by her side, knowing special agents Berg and McConnell were ready to rush in if the situation became unstable or posed any threat, biohazardous or otherwise.

"Yes, Claus Recart," the man said. His unnerved look faded, but she regarded him with caution. "Are you here to kill me?"

"No, she said. "I want the vaccine. Stopping *Labrador* depends on it. So does the fate of the United States."

"You were sent by Lindstrom?" Recart rinsed the slaughtered fruit bat in the basin, turning the water into a blood bath. Then he withdrew a clean syringe and drew back a straw colored liquid from a glass vial and injected it into the winged mammal.

"Lindstrom's indisposed. He'll be behind bars for quite a while—and they promised him it wouldn't be a comfy federal prison with a nice room and a view. He and the ex-Senator Marburg will be doing real time."

"If you've come to take me, I'm afraid I'll not join you—or them." Recart's French accent was pretentious. He continued his work. "But you may come in. I've been taking care of what's left of the people of this village, and doing what I can with this experiment. It's not the high-tech equipment I'm used to working with."

"How could you harm these innocent people?"

"We came here to test the vaccine I developed in my lab in the province of Labrador, Canada. Marburg and Lindstrom gave me a private grant, and a few million-dollar stipend in 2010. I thought it seemed outrageous when we'd never seen a single case of *Labrador* on North American soil, but I couldn't refuse. I made a deal with those two corrupt investors. They were sure they could fast track my vaccine through FDA. When it had been tested and proven effective here in Uganda, they approached me with a larger deal—to release it, start a few cases on U.S. soil, then bring the outbreak to an end quickly, once the vaccine stock skyrocketed."

"I'm quite familiar with the plot."

"And how is that, mademoiselle?"

"I wrote the story. Wesley Lindstrom took the novel I sent to his wife and used his connections with the drug companies to turn it into a near global pandemic, a for-profit health threat on a case-for-cash basis."

"I understand now. It's usually a chain of events that results in large scale catastrophes like this—not a single mishap," Recart said.

"I'm aware of that."

She detected a trace of humility in his arrogant manner now. Recart continued.

"When I saw what *Labrador* could do, I took their money and ran. I never released it in Washington as I promised. The cases stemmed from the few infections here. It's highly virulent."

"That's an understatement."

"Practices such as kissing the bodies of the dead before burial, and eating bush meat, spread it through the village. It quickly wiped out this entire village—except for the few villagers we vaccinated."

She nodded. "That confirms my suspicions. The virus came back on the Make-A-Wish Foundation safari, and it spread to the funeral director who handled the patient zero's body."

"I can assure you, I just want to see the epidemic end as much as you do."

"Is this a typical day on the job for you—conducting research on nonconsenting human beings—to spread biohazardous disease, and then cure it in a get-rich-quick scheme?"

"The cases in D.C. were never supposed to happen. There is another force at work here."

"Was. There *was* another force at work. Jorge Bourdain is dead now."

"I see." Recart swallowed. "I don't deny that I got greedy—tried to spin off another deal with those investors by getting the trade secrets that Dr. LeTorneau developed—the cure, if you will. I'd initially sent Jorge as a mole."

"He had his own plans."

"I feared that. When Bourdain contacted me about vaccinating a group of his associates, I suspected something more sinister. I immediately set out to right the situation—tried to collaborate with LeTorneau cautiously, without bringing myself down, and getting caught. We've always had a healthy competition."

"You tried to bribe him."

"My dear," Recart said. His face was weary, and he set down the winged creature he was holding. The stone slab was covered in its blood. "I'm afraid the way man destroys society outstrips any of nature's attempts to save it."

"I've heard that, though it doesn't help me. You made the vaccine. Where is it? How is it manufactured? LeTorneau can do it." She shifted her weight, pointed the pistol at him.

"Yes. He'll get all the credit, and I suppose he deserves it. I have myself to blame."

"We'll throw a pity party for you later. And the formula?"

Recart washed his hands off, pouring water from a pitcher into the basin. "I've enough stockpiled in my lab to end the outbreak. Thousands of vials. Save it before *Labrador* mutates further."

She pointed to his laptop. "Is the recipe for it there—the formula to manufacture it?"

"Yes. Take it." Recart held his hands in the air. "But I'll never get another penny to fund my research. I've run out on my grant funding, and I'm afraid I cannot live with what I've done." He reached below the table and into his bag for something—a revolver.

She drew the safety on the pistol.

"Freeze," she cried. "Put your arms up and drop the gun."

"Arm yourselves with the knowledge contained in my lab. Use it wisely."

"Freeze," she repeated.

The FBI agents entered the rear of the tent and echoed her order, standing behind Recart with their guns aimed at the scientist. All three had a clear shot.

Recart placed the revolver to his head.

"Don't you da—"

He pulled the trigger.

The shot sounded, and she screamed, "You coward!"

She put her head in her hands, sank to the ground.

He was gone, and she knew exactly how he felt.

Like the inventor of dynamite, Alfred Nobel, whose fortune was used posthumously to award Nobel Prizes. Despite his belief in pacifism, he'd been known as a merchant of death. At that moment, she wanted to burn her manuscript about the biologic weapon, and never speak of it again.

-30-

Washington, D.C.
Five months later
Sara Sullivan

As Sara held Elyse at the presidential award ceremony to recognize her extraordinary valor and resourcefulness in helping to end the *Labrador* epidemic, she smiled at Dr. Graham LeTorneau, who was recovering well, but still walking on crutches. He'd been awarded the Nobel Prize in Science in October for his discovery. As the President of the United States placed the medal around her neck, the crowd cheered. She shook the president's hand, and squeezed Marty's, and then returned her gaze to Elyse. The capital felt renewed, a sharp contrast to the protesting and violent brutality she'd seen during the epidemic. American flags proudly decorated the homes in the District. The guarded looks and skepticism were gone from the faces of the people, replaced by a palpable camaraderie. Taking the place of the infectious disease was a contagious fervor to put aside racial differences and move forward.

A renewed feeling of exceptionalism as a country, finally united.

"I can't change you, Sara. I know that, and I'm sorry," said Marty, as they stepped down from the podium at the Washington Memorial. "Your bravery amazes me."

"Oh stop. You'll give me a head as big as a pumpkin at a county fair." She handed Elyse to her mother, who kissed Sara on the cheek.

"Dr. Sullivan?"

She turned around. A young man in a suit extended his hand to her.

"Russel Gaviotta, BrightLight Film and Television. Your fascinating story is unparalleled — it's an inspiration to millions." Gaviotta shook her hand.

"Thank you," she said. "You're very kind."

"I'd like to speak with you about acquiring the rights to it. We're looking at a biographical movie, perhaps even a mini-series." Gaviotta shoved his business card into her hand. "Call me when you're ready to talk business. Nice meeting you all," he said, and disappeared into the crowd.

Her smile grew into the biggest childhood grin, one that rivaled the one she'd sported in her mother's pictures of her on Santa's lap.

"What did you say about getting big-headed?" Marty asked.

"Don't even think about standing in the way of this, Marty."

Marty looked hurt, said, "As I was saying, I never want to change you. I'm proud of all you've done."

She touched his nose. "I was thinking, too. About how you've been hoping for a second child before we're too old." She smiled.

"Really?"

"We have so much fun trying not to go for it."

"Sara that's great." Marty's smile was beaming now.

"And it wouldn't be all bad for you to make *some* of our decisions. I think I can handle that." She pointed her finger up at him with a coy smile, as they stood facing each other. "And maybe a gentle spanking if I can't," she whispered in his ear.

Marty wasn't too old to blush.

His face turned a crimson red.

She was teasing him relentlessly, of course, mocking him, even, but he was enjoying every moment of it.

She kissed him quickly and the baby giggled and the cameras flashed, snapping pictures of her and her family, leaving the mall.

The End

Melissa Franckowiak is an MFA student and practicing anesthesiologist in Buffalo, NY. Her short fiction piece, *The Very Pertinent News of Gabriel Vincent DeVil*, recently placed in the 86th Annual *Writer's Digest* Literary Fiction Awards, and her work has appeared in *Nanny Magazine*, *Traffic East*, Parent Co., MothersAlwaysWrite.com, *Blood Puddles*, and the anthology *Children of Zeus,* among other journals. She writes as Melissa Crickard. Melissa attended Georgia Institute of Technology and the University of Buffalo, and after being awarded two Bachelor's degrees in Physical Therapy and Chemistry, she advanced toward her M.D. degree from the State University of New York at Buffalo. Melissa is the mother of two children, the owner of a chatty Panama Amazon parrot and a lover of all things outdoors.

www.ingramcontent.com/pod-product-compliance
Lightning Source LLC
Chambersburg PA
CBHW051555100726
47898CB00001B/106